IF SHE KNEW

IF SHE SAW

IF SHE RAN

(a kate wise mystery—books 1, 2 and 3)

IF SHE KNEW

(a kate wise mystery—book 1)

BLAKE PIERCE

BLAKE PIERCE

B lake Pierce is author of the bestselling RILEY PAGE mystery series, which includes thirteen books (and counting). Blake Pierce is also the author of the MACKENZIE WHITE mystery series, comprising nine books (and counting); of the AVERY BLACK mystery series, comprising six books; of the KERI LOCKE mystery series, comprising five books; of the MAKING OF RILEY PAIGE mystery series, comprising three books (and counting); of the KATE WISE mystery series, comprising two books (and counting); of the CHLOE FINE psychological suspense mystery, comprising two books (and counting); and of the JESSE HUNT psychological suspense thriller series, comprising three books (and counting).

An avid reader and lifelong fan of the mystery and thriller genres, Blake loves to hear from you, so please feel free to visit www.blakepierce-author.com to learn more and stay in touch.

ONCE COLD (Book #8)
ONCE STALKED (Book #9)
ONCE LOST (Book #10)
ONCE BURIED (Book #11)
ONCE BOUND (Book #12)
ONCE TRAPPED (Book #13)
ONCE DORMANT (book #14)

MACKENZIE WHITE MYSTERY SERIES
BEFORE HE KILLS (Book #1)
BEFORE HE SEES (Book #2)
BEFORE HE COVETS (Book #3)
BEFORE HE TAKES (Book #4)
BEFORE HE NEEDS (Book #5)
BEFORE HE FEELS (Book #6)
BEFORE HE SINS (Book #7)
BEFORE HE HUNTS (Book #8)
BEFORE HE PREYS (Book #9)
BEFORE HE LONGS (Book #10)

AVERY BLACK MYSTERY SERIES
CAUSE TO KILL (Book #1)
CAUSE TO RUN (Book #2)
CAUSE TO HIDE (Book #3)
CAUSE TO FEAR (Book #4)
CAUSE TO SAVE (Book #5)
CAUSE TO DREAD (Book #6)

KERI LOCKE MYSTERY SERIES
A TRACE OF DEATH (Book #1)
A TRACE OF MUDER (Book #2)
A TRACE OF VICE (Book #3)
A TRACE OF CRIME (Book #4)
A TRACE OF HOPE (Book #5)

TABLE OF CONTENTS

PROLOGUE

He saw no one watching him as he crept down the quiet suburban street at night. It was one in the morning and it was the kind of neighborhood where people went to bed at respectable times, a rowdy weeknight consisting of one too many glasses of wine while watching *The Bachelor.*

It was the kind of place he despised.

They paid property association dues, they scooped up their dogs' shit into little plastic bags as to not offend their neighbors, and their kids surely played sports not just in high school leagues but in private county leagues. The world was their oyster. They felt safe. Sure, they locked their doors and set their alarms, but ultimately, they felt safe.

That was about to change.

He walked up a particular lawn. Surely she would be home now. Her husband was away on business in Dallas. He knew which window was her bedroom window. And he also knew that the security alarm at the back of the house was faulty when it rained.

He shifted and felt the reassurance of the knife, tucked away in the small of his back, between the elastic of his boxer shorts and his jeans. He stuck to the side of the house, opening the bottle of water he carried, and when he came to the back of the house, he stopped. There was the glowing green light of the small security box. He knew that if he tried to damage it, the alarm would go off. He knew if he tried to open a door or pry it open, the alarm would go off.

But he also knew it messed up in the rain. It was something about the moisture, even though this type of system was supposed to be one hundred percent waterproof. With this in mind, he raised his bottle of water and doused it.

He watched as the little green light flickered, grew weak.

With a smile, he walked into the small strip of backyard. He made his way up the stairs of the screened in back porch. Using the knife to pry the screen door open was easy; it made very little noise in the quiet of the night.

He crossed to the wicker chair in the corner, lifted the cushion, and found the key underneath. He picked it up in his gloved hand, went to the back door, slid the key in, turned the lock, and stepped inside.

A small lamp was on in the thin hallway that ran out of the kitchen. He followed this hall to a stairway, and he began to climb.

Anxiety swirled in his guts. He was getting excited—not in a sexual way but in the way he used to get excited when he rode a roller coaster, the anticipation thrilling him as he ascended, clacking up the biggest hill on the tracks.

He gripped the knife, still in his hand from having pried open the screen door. At the top of the stairs he took a moment to appreciate the thrill of it. He breathed in the cleanliness of the upper-class suburban home and it made him a little sick. It was too familiar, too detached.

He hated it.

Gripping the knife, he walked to the bedroom at the end of the hall. There she was, lying in the bed.

She was sleeping on her side, her knees slightly bent. She was wearing a T-shirt and a pair of running shorts, nothing too impressive being that her husband was gone.

He walked to the bed and watched her sleep for a while. He wondered about the nature of life. How fragile it was.

He then raised the knife and brought it down almost casually, as if he were simply painting or swatting a fly.

She screamed, but only for a moment—before he brought the knife down again.

And again.

CHAPTER ONE

Of the many life lessons her first full year of retirement had taught Kate Wise, the most important was this: without a solid plan, retirement could get boring very fast.

She'd heard stories of women who had retired and picked up different interests. Some opened up little Etsy shops online. Some dabbled in painting and crochet. Others tried their hand at writing a novel. Kate thought these were all fine ways to pass the time, but none of them appealed to her.

For someone who had spent more than thirty years of her life with a gun strapped to her side, finding ways to be happily preoccupied was difficult. Knitting was not going to replace the thrill of an on-foot pursuit of a killer. Gardening was not going to recreate the adrenaline high of storming into a residence, never knowing what waited on the other side of the door.

Because nothing she tried seemed to even come close to touching the joy she had felt as an FBI agent, she had stopped searching after a couple of months. The only thing that even came close were her trips to the gun range, which she made twice a week. She would have made more if she didn't fear that the younger members at the range might start to think of her as nothing more than a retired agent who was trying to recapture a moment in time when she had been great.

It was a reasonable fear. After all, she supposed that's exactly what she was doing.

It was a Tuesday, just after two in the afternoon, when this fact struck her like a bullet between the eyes. She had just come back from the range and was setting her M1911 pistol back in her bedside drawer when her heart seemed to break out of nowhere.

Thirty-one years. She'd spent thirty-one years with the bureau. She'd been a part of more than one hundred raids and had worked as part of a special enforcement unit for high-profile cases on twenty-six occasions. She'd been known for her speed, her quick and often razor-sharp thinking, and her overall don't-give-a-damn attitude.

She'd also been known for her looks, something that still bothered her a bit even at the age of fifty-five. When she'd become an agent at the age of twenty-three, it had not taken her long to get crude nicknames like Legs and Barbie—names that would likely get men fired these days but which, back when she had been younger, had sadly been commonplace for female agents.

Kate had broken noses at the bureau because male agents would grab her ass. She had thrown one across a moving elevator when he'd whispered something obscene in her ear while behind her.

While the nicknames had stayed with her until well into her forties, the advances and leering looks had not. After word had gotten around, her male peers had learned to respect her and to look beyond her body—a body which, she knew with some degree of muted pride, had always been well-maintained and what most men would consider a ten.

But now at fifty-five she found herself missing even the nicknames. She had not thought retirement would be this hard. The gun range was fine, but it was just a whispering ghost of what her past had been. She had tried to shove the yearning for her past away by reading. She had decided she would read up on weapons in particular; she'd read countless books about the history of weapons use, how they were manufactured, the preference for certain weapons by military generals, and the like. It was why she now used an M1911, because of its rich history with being involved in a multitude of American wars, an early model of it being used as far back as World War I.

She'd tried her hand at reading fiction but could not get into it—though she did enjoy a lot of the cybercrime–related books. While she *had* revisited books she'd adored in her younger years, she could find nothing interesting in the lives of fake characters. And because she had not wanted to become the sad recently retired lady who spent all of her time at the local library, she'd ordered all of the books she'd read in the last year off of Amazon. She had more than one hundred of them stacked in boxes in her basement. She figured one day she'd build a few bookcases and turn the space into a proper study.

It wasn't like she had much else to do.

Rocked by the idea that she had spent the last year of her life doing not much of anything, Kate Wise sat slowly down on her bed. She stayed there for several minutes without moving. She looked to the desk across the room and saw the photo albums there. There was only a single family picture there. In it, her late husband, Michael, had his arms around their daughter while Kate smiled at his side. A picture from the beach that was poorly taken but had always warmed her heart.

All of the other pictures in those albums, however, were from work: behind-the-scenes shots, pictures of inner-bureau birthday parties, her in her younger years swimming laps, at the gun range, running track, and so on.

She had lived the last year of her life the same way the small-town jock who never leaves his small town would. Always hanging around anyone who would pretend to listen about all of the touchdowns he'd scored thirty years ago playing high school football.

She was no better than that.

With a slight shudder, Kate got up and went to the photo albums on her desk. Slowly and almost methodically, she looked through all three of them. She saw pictures of her younger self, evolving through the years until every picture ever taken was on a phone. She saw herself and people she had known, people who had died right beside her on cases, and started to realize that while these moments had been instrumental in developing her, they had not defined her completely.

The articles she had clipped and saved in the back of the album further told the story. She was the featured story in all of them. SECOND-YEAR AGENT NABS KILLER ON THE LOOSE read one title; FEMALE AGENT LONE SURVIVOR IN SHOOTOUT THAT CLAIMED 11. And then the one that had really started spurring the legends on: AFTER 13 VICTIMS, MOONLIGHT KILLER FINALLY TAKEN DOWN BY AGENT KATE WISE.

By all reasonable health standards, she had at least twenty more years in her—forty if she could somehow manage to really buckle down and fight death away. Even if she averaged it out and said she had *thirty* years left, kicking the bucket at eighty-five … thirty years was a lot.

She could do a lot in thirty years, she supposed. For about ten of those years, she could maybe even have some very good years before old age really started to sneak in and start plucking away her good health.

The question, of course, was what she might find to do with those years.

And despite having a reputation as one of the sharpest agents to go through the bureau in the last decade, she had no idea where to start.

Aside from the gun range and her almost obsessive reading habits, Kate had also managed to make a weekly habit out of meeting with three other women for coffee. The four of them made fun of themselves, claiming they had formed the saddest club ever: four women early in retirement with no idea what to do with their newly freed up days.

The day following her revelation, Kate drove to their coffee house of choice. It was a little family-owned place where not only was the coffee better than the overpriced gruel at Starbucks, but the place wasn't over-run with millennials and soccer moms. She walked inside and before she went to the counter to place her order, she saw their usual table in the back. Two of the three other women were already there, waving to her.

Kate grabbed her hazelnut brew and joined her friends at the table. She sat down beside Jane Patterson, a fifty-seven-year-old who was seven months retired from springing back and forth between companies as a proposal specialist for a government telecommunications firm. Across from her was Clarissa James, a little over a year into retirement ever since working part-time as a criminology instructor with the bureau. The fourth member of their sad little club, a fifty-five-year-old recently retired woman named Debbie Meade, had not yet shown up.

Odd, Kate thought. *Deb is usually the first one here.*

The moment she took her seat, Jane and Clarissa seemed to go tense. This was particularly weird because it was not like Clarissa to be any-thing other than bubbly. Unlike Kate, Clarissa had quickly grown to love retirement. Kate supposed it helped that Clarissa was married to a man nearly ten years younger than her who competed in swimming competitions in his free time.

"What's with you guys?" Kate asked. "You know I come here to try to get motivated about retirement, right? You two look downright sad."

Jane and Clarissa shared a look that Kate had seen countless times before. During her times as an agent, she'd seen it in living rooms, interrogation rooms, and hospital waiting rooms. It was a look that translated one simple question without a spoken word: *Who's going to tell her?*

"What is it?" she asked.

She was suddenly very aware of Deb's absence.

"It's Deb," Jane said, confirming her fear.

"Well, not Deb exactly," Clarissa added. "It's her daughter, Julie. Did you ever meet her?"

"Once, I think," Kate said. "What happened?"

"She's dead," Clarissa said. "Murder. So far, they have no idea who did it."

"Oh my God," Kate said, genuinely saddened for her friend. She'd known Deb for about fifteen years, having met her at Quantico. Kate had been working as an assistant instructor for a new crop of field agents and Deb had been working with some of the tech rats on some sort of new security system. They'd struck it off right away and had become fast friends.

The fact that Deb had not called or texted her with the news before anyone else showed just how quickly friendships could shift over the years.

"When did it happen?" Kate asked.

"Sometime yesterday," Jane said. "She just texted me this morning about it."

"They have *no* suspects?" Kate asked.

Jane shrugged. "She just said they don't know who it is. No clues, no leads, nothing."

Kate instantly felt herself go into agent mode. She figured it was the same way a trained athlete must feel after being away from their arena of choice for too long. She may not have turf or an adoring crowd to remind her of what her glory days had been like, but she *did* have her finely tuned mind for solving crimes.

"Don't go there," Clarissa said, trying on her best smile.

"Go where?"

"Don't be Agent Wise right now," Clarissa said. "Right now, just be her friend. I can see those wheels turning in your head. Jeez, lady. Don't you have a pregnant daughter? Aren't you about to be a grandmother?"

"What a way to kick me when I'm down," Kate said with a smile. She let the comment go and then asked: "Deb's daughter ... did she have a boyfriend?"

"No idea," Jane said.

An awkward silence sat over the table. In the year or so their little group of recently retired friends had been meeting, the conversation had always been mostly light. This was the first heavy topic and it did not fit with their routine. Kate, of course, was accustomed to it. Her time in the academy had taught her how to handle these situations.

But Clarissa was right. In hearing the news, Kate had so easily slipped into agent mode. She knew she should have thought like a friend first—thinking of Deb's loss and emotional state. But the agent in her was too strong, the instincts still there at the forefront after having been on the shelf for a year.

"So what can we do to make her comfortable?" Jane asked.

"I was thinking a meal train," Clarissa said. "I know a few other ladies that might get on board. Just making sure she doesn't have to cook for her family in the next few weeks as she deals with all of this."

For the next ten minutes, the three women planned out the most effective way to get a meal train going for their grief-stricken friend.

But for Kate, the conversation remained on the surface. Her mind was headed elsewhere, trying to dig up hidden facts and tidbits on Deb and her family, trying to find a case where there might not even be one.

Or there might, Kate thought. *And I guess there's only one way to find out.*

CHAPTER TWO

After retirement, Kate had moved back to Richmond, Virginia. She'd grown up in the little town of Amelia, about forty minutes away from Richmond, but had gone to college right near the cusp of downtown. She'd spent her undergrad years at VCU, originally wanting to be an art major of all things. Three years in, she'd discovered that she'd had a heart for criminal justice through one of her elective courses in psychology. It had been a winding, crooked trail that had led her to Quantico and the thirty-year stretch of her illustrious career.

She now drove through some of those familiar Richmond streets. She'd been to Debbie Meade's house only once before but knew exactly where it was located. She knew where it was because she envied the location, one of those older-looking buildings on the streets off the center of downtown that were lined with trees rather than street lights and tall buildings.

Deb's street was currently awash in fallen leaves from the elms that overhung the street. She had to park three houses away because family and friends had already started to fill in the spaces in front of Deb's house.

She walked down the sidewalk, trying to convince herself that this was a bad idea. Yes, she planned to enter the house as only a friend—even though Jane and Clarissa had decided to hold off until later in the afternoon in order to give Deb some space. But there was something deeper there, too. She'd been looking for something to do these past few months, some better and more meaningful way to fill her time. She'd often dreamed about somehow picking up freelance work from the bureau, maybe even just basic research tasks.

Even the most minor of references to her work got her excited. For instance, she was due in court next week to testify at a parole hearing. She was not looking forward to facing the criminal again but just being able to delve back into her work for such a brief amount of time was welcome.

But that was next week—and right now that seemed like an eternity away.

She looked up at Debbie Meade's front porch. She knew why she was really there. She wanted to find some answers to questions that were storming in her head. It made her feel selfish, like she was using her friend's loss as an excuse to dip her toes back into waters that she had not felt in over a year. This situation involved a friend, which made it tricky. But the old agent in her was hoping it might evolve into something else. The friend in her, though, thought it might be risky. And all together, those parts of her wondered if maybe she should have stuck with simply fanaticizing about a return to work.

Maybe that's exactly what I'm doing, Kate thought as she walked up the stairs to the Meade residence. And honestly, she wasn't quite sure how to feel about that.

She knocked on the door softly and it was answered right away by an elderly lady Kate did not know.

"Are you with the family?" the woman asked.

"No," Kate answered. "Just a very close friend."

The woman scrutinized her for a moment before allowing her inside. Kate entered and walked down the hallway, passing by a living area that was filled with somber people sitting around one single person in a recliner. The person in the recliner was Debbie Meade. Kate recognized the man standing beside her and talking to another man as her husband, Jim.

She awkwardly entered the room and went directly to Deb. Without allowing Deb enough time to get out of the chair, Kate leaned down and hugged her.

"I'm so sorry, Deb," she said.

Deb was clearly drained from crying, managing to only nod into Kate's shoulder. "Thanks for coming," Deb whispered into her ear. "Do you think you could meet me in the kitchen in a few minutes?"

"Of course."

Kate broke the hug and gave little nods of acknowledgment to the few other faces in the room that she recognized. Feeling out of place, Kate made her way to the end of the hallway which emptied into the kitchen. There was no one there but there were empty plates and glasses from where people had been not too long ago. There were a few pies sitting on the counter along with ham rolls and other finger foods. Kate set to cleaning up, helping herself to the sink to start washing the dishes.

Several moments later, Jim Meade made his way into the kitchen. "You don't have to do that," he said.

Kate turned to him and saw that he looked tired and impossibly sad. "I know," she said. "I came by to show my support. It seemed like things were pretty heavy in the living room when I came in, so I'm supporting you guys by washing dishes."

He nodded, looking like he might nod off right then and there. "One of our friends said she saw a woman come in a few minutes ago. I'm rather glad it's you, Kate."

Kate saw another person coming toward the kitchen behind him, looking equally tired and heartbroken. Deb Meade's eyes were puffy and red from crying. Her hair was in disarray and when she looked at Kate to try on a smile, it seemed to fall right off of her face.

Kate put down the dish she was washing, quickly dried her hands on a hand towel by the sink, and went to her friend. Kate had never been much for physical touch but knew when a hug was needed. She expected Deb to start weeping in the midst of the hug but there was nothing, just her sagging weight.

She's probably all cried out for now, Kate thought.

"I only just heard this morning," Kate said. "I'm so sorry, Deb. Both of you," she said, casting her eyes to Jim.

Jim nodded his appreciation and then looked down the hall. When he saw that no one else was lurking there, the slight murmur of their company still in the living room, he stepped closer to Kate as Deb broke the hug.

"Kate, we need to ask you something," Jim said in a near-whisper.

"And please," Deb said, taking her hand. "Let us get it all out before you shoot us down." Kate felt a little tremble in Deb's grip and her heart broke a little.

"Sure," Kate said. Their pleading eyes and the overall weight of their sorrow hung over her head like an anvil that was sure to drop at any moment.

"The police have absolutely no idea who did it," Deb said. Suddenly, her exhaustion morphed into something that looked closer to anger. "Based on some things we said and some texts they found on Julie's phone, the police arrested her ex-boyfriend right away. But they held him for less than three hours and then let him go. Just like that. But Kate...I *know* he did it. It *has* to be him."

Kate had seen this approach multiple times before during her time as an agent. Grieving families wanted justice right away. They'd look past logic and a sound investigation to make sure some sort of vengeance was taken out as soon as possible. And if those results weren't speedy, the grieving family assumed incompetence on the part of the police or FBI.

"Deb...if they released him so quickly, there must have been some very strong evidence. After all...how long has it been since they dated?"

"Thirteen years. But he kept trying to connect with her for years, even after she was married. She had to get a restraining order at one time."

"Still...the police had to have a good alibi for him to have released him so quickly."

"Well, if there was, they aren't telling me about it," Deb said.

"Deb...look," Kate said, giving Deb's hand a comforting squeeze. "The loss is too recent. Give it a few days and you'll start to think rationally. I've seen it a hundred times."

Deb shook her head. "I'm certain of it, Kate. They dated for three years and not once did I trust him. We're pretty sure he hit her at least on two occasions but Julie never came out and said it. He had a temper. Even *he'd* tell you that."

"I'm sure the police are—"

"That's our favor," Deb interrupted. "I want *you* to look into it. I want you to get involved in the case."

"Deb, I'm retired. You know this."

"I do. And I also know how much you miss it. Kate...the man that killed my daughter got nothing more than a little scare and some time in an interrogation room. And now he's at home, sitting comfortably while I have to plan to put my daughter in the ground. It's not right, Kate. Please...will you look into it? I know you can't do it on an official basis but......anything you can do. I'd appreciate it."

There was so much heartache in Deb's eyes that Kate could feel it passing between them. Everything within her was telling her to stand firm—to not allow any false hope to enter into Deb's grief. But at the same time, Deb was right. She *had* missed her work. And even if what was being proposed was just a few basic phone calls to the Richmond PD or even to her former co-workers at the bureau, it would be *something*.

It would certainly be better than obsessively reflecting back on her career with lonely trips out to the gun range.

"Here's what I can do," Kate said. "When I retired, I lost all of my pull. Sure, I get calls for my opinion here and there, but I have no authority. More than that, this case would be completely outside of my jurisdiction even if I *were* still active. But I will make a few calls to my old contacts and make sure the evidence they found to free him was strong. Honestly, Deb, that's the best I can do."

The gratitude was evident in both Deb and Jim right away. Deb hugged her again and this time, she did weep. "Thank you."

"It's not a problem," Kate said. "But I really can't promise anything."

"We know," Jim said. "But at least now we know that someone competent is watching out for us."

Kate wasn't comfortable with the idea that they were looking to her as an inside force to assist them, nor did she like that they assumed the police didn't have their backs. Again, she knew it was all about their grief and how it was blinding them in their search for answers. So for now, she let it slide.

She thought about how tired she had been near the end of her career—not really physically tired but emotionally drained. She had always loved her job, but how often had she come to the end of a case and think to herself: *Man, am I tired of this shit*...

It had happened more and more often in the last few years.

But this moment was not about her.

She held her friend close, puzzling over how no matter how hard people tried to put their pasts behind them—whether it was relationships or careers—it somehow managed to always limp along not too far behind.

CHAPTER THREE

Kate wasted no time. She returned home and sat at the desk in her small study for a moment. She looked out of her study window, into her small backyard. Sunshine came in through the window, laying a rectangle of light on her wooden floors. The floors, like most of the rest of the house, showed the scars and scabs of its 1920s construction. Located in the Carytown area of Richmond, Kate often felt out of place. Carytown was a trendy little section of the city and she knew she'd end up moving elsewhere fairly soon. She had enough money to get a house just about anywhere she wanted but the very idea of moving exhausted her.

It was that sort of lack of motivation that had perhaps made retirement so hard for her. That and a refusal to let go of the memories of who she had been while with the bureau for those thirty years. When those two feelings collided, she often felt unmotivated and without any real direction.

But now there was Deb and Jim Meade's request. Yes, it was a misguided request but Kate saw nothing wrong with at least making a few calls. If it came to nothing, she could at least call Deb back to let her know that she had tried her best.

Her first call was to the Deputy Commissioner of the Virginia State Police, a man named Clarence Greene. She had worked closely with him on several cases over the last decade or so of her career and they shared a mutual respect for one another. She hoped the year that had passed had not totally obliterated that relationship. Knowing that Clarence was never in his office, she opted to skip his landline and called his cell phone.

Just when she thought the call was not going to be answered, she was greeted with a familiar voice. For a moment, Kate felt as if she had never left work at all.

"Agent Wise," Clarence said. "How the hell are you?"

"Good," she said. "You?"

"Same as always. I have to admit, though…I thought I was done with seeing your name pop up on my phone."

"Yeah, about that," Kate said. "I hate to come to you with something like this after more than a year of silence, but I have a friend who just lost her daughter. I gave her my word that I would look into the investigation."

"So what do you want from me?" Clarence asked.

"Well, the main suspect was the daughter's ex-boyfriend. It seems that he was arrested and then let go in about three hours. Naturally, the parents are wondering why."

"Oh," Clarence said. "Look…Wise, I can't really divulge that to you. And with all due respect, you should already know that."

"I'm not trying to interfere in the case," Kate said. "I was just wondering why no real reason has been given to the parents for letting the only suspect go. She's a grieving mom looking for answers and—"

"Again, let me stop you there," Clarence said. "As you well know, I deal with grieving moms and fathers and widows pretty regularly. Just because you happen to know one personally right now doesn't mean I can break protocol or look the other way."

"As closely as you've worked with me, you know I mean only the best."

"Oh, I'm sure you do. But the last thing I need is a retired FBI agent poking around in a current case, no matter how hands-off it may seem. You have to understand that, right?"

The hell of it was that she *did* understand it. Still, she had to try one last time. "I'd consider it a personal favor."

"I'm sure you would," Clarence said, a bit condescending. "But the answer is no, Agent Wise. Now if you'll excuse me, I'm about to head into court to speak to one of those grieving widows I just told you about. Sorry I couldn't help you."

He ended the call without a goodbye, leaving Kate to stare at that slowly shifting square of sunlight on the hardwood floor. She considered her next move, noting that Deputy Commissioner Greene had just revealed that he was about to head into court. She supposed the smart move would be to take his refusal to help her as a defeat. But his unwillingness to help only made her desire to keep digging that much stronger.

I was always told I had a stubborn streak as an agent, she thought as she stood up from her desk. *It's good to see that some things haven't changed.*

Half an hour later, Kate was parking her car in a parking garage adjacent to the Third Precinct Police Station. Based on where the murder of Julie Meade—married name Julie Hicks—had occurred, Kate knew it would be the best resource for information. The only problem was that aside from Deputy Commissioner Greene, she didn't really know anyone else within the department, much less the Third Precinct.

She entered the office with confidence. She knew there were certain things about her current situation that an observant officer would notice. First of all, she did not have her sidearm. She did have a concealed carry permit but given what she was up to, she figured it might cause more problems than it was worth if she was caught being even the slightest bit dishonest.

And dishonesty was really something she could not afford. Retired or not, her reputation was on the line—a reputation she had built with great care for over thirty years. She was going to have to walk a fine line in the next minutes, something she welcomed. She hadn't been this anxious in the entire year she had spent retired.

She approached the information desk, a brightly lit area separated from the central room by a pane of glass. A woman in uniform sat at the desk, stamping something in a ledger as Kate approached. She looked up at Kate with a face that looked as if a smile had not graced it in days.

"What can I do for you?" the receptionist asked.

"I'm a retired agent with the FBI, looking for some information about a recent murder. I was hoping to get the names of the officers in charge of the case."

"You got an ID?" the woman asked.

Kate got out her driver's license and slid it through the opening in the glass partition. The woman looked at it for a grand total of one second and then slid it right back. "I'm going to need your bureau ID."

"Well, like I said, I'm retired."

"And who sent you? I'll need their name and contact information and then they have to fill out a request to get you the information."

"I was really hoping to step over all of the legalities."

"I can't help you, then," the woman said.

Kate wondered how far she could push it. If she went too hard, someone would surely notify Clarence Greene and that could be bad. She racked her brain, trying to think of another course of action. She could only come up with one and it was much riskier than what she was currently attempting.

With a sigh, Kate gave a curt, "Well, thanks anyway."

She turned on her heel and walked back out of the office. She was a little embarrassed. What the hell had she been thinking? Even if she *did* still have her bureau ID, it would be unlawful for the Richmond PD to give her any information without approval from a supervisor in DC.

It was beyond humbling to walk back out to her car with such an absolute feeling—the feeling of being a basic civilian.

But a civilian who hates to take no for an answer.

She took out her phone and placed a call to Deb Meade. When Deb answered, she still sounded tired and far away.

"Sorry to bother you, Deb," she said. "But do you have a name and address for the ex-boyfriend?"

As it turned out, Deb had both.

CHAPTER FOUR

While Kate did not have her old bureau ID, she did still have the last badge she had ever owned. It was propped up on the mantel over her fireplace like some relic from another time, no better than a faded photograph. When she left the Third Precinct station, she headed back home and scooped it up. She thought long and hard about also taking her sidearm. She looked longingly toward the M1911 but left it where it was in her bedside drawer. Taking it with her for what she had planned would be asking for trouble.

She did decide to take the handcuffs she kept in a shoebox under the bed with a few other treasures from her career.

Just in case.

She left her house and headed for the address Deb had given her. It was a place in Shockoe Bottom, a twenty-minute drive from her home. She was not nervous as she made the drive but she did feel a sense of excitement. She knew she should not be doing this, but at the same time, it felt good to be out and on the hunt again—even if it was in secret.

Just as she reached the address of Julie Hicks's former boyfriend, a guy named Brian Neilbolt, Kate thought about her husband. He popped up in her head from time to time but sometimes he seemed to pop up and sort of settle in for a while. That happened as she turned onto the destination street. He could see him shaking his head in frustration.

Kate, you know you shouldn't be doing this, he seemed to say.

She grinned thinly. She missed her husband fiercely sometimes, a fitting contrast to the fact that she sometimes felt she had managed to move on from his death rather quickly.

She shook the cobwebs of those memories away as she parked her car in front of the address Deb had given her. It was a rather nice house, split into two different apartments with porches separating the properties. When she got out of the car she could tell right away that someone was home because she could hear someone speaking very loudly inside.

When she climbed the porch stairs, she felt as if she had taken a step back in time, about one year ago. She felt like an agent again, despite the lack of the firearm on her hip. Still, being that she was in all actuality a retired agent, she had no idea what she would say after she knocked on the door.

But she didn't let that stop her. She knocked on the door with the same authority she would have one year ago. As she heard the loud talking inside, she figured she'd stick with the truth. Lying in a situation that she was already not supposed to be a part of would only make things worse if she was caught.

The man who answered the door took Kate a little off guard. He was about six feet three inches and was absolutely jacked. His shoulders alone showed that he worked out. He could have easily passed for a professional wrestler. The only thing that betrayed that façade was the anger in his eyes.

"Yeah?" he asked. "Who are you?"

She then made a move that she had missed very much. She showed him her badge. She hoped the sight of it would carry some weight to counter her introduction. "My name is Kate Wise. I'm a retired FBI agent. I was hoping you could speak with me for a few moments."

"About what?" he asked, his words quick and snappy.

"Are you Brian Neilbolt?" she asked.

"I am."

"So your ex-girlfriend was Julie Hicks, correct? Formerly Julie Meade?"

"Ah shit, this again? Look, the fucking cops already hauled me in and interrogated me. Now the feds, too?"

"Rest assured, I'm not here to interrogate you. I just wanted to ask some questions."

"Sounds like an interrogation to me," he said. "Besides, you said you're retired. Pretty sure that means I don't have to do anything you ask."

She pretended to be hurt by this, looking away from him. In reality, though, she was looking over his massive shoulders and the space behind him. She saw a suitcase and two backpacks leaning against the wall. She also saw a sheet of paper sitting on top of the suitcase. The large logo identified it as a printout of an Orbitz receipt. Apparently, Brian Neilbolt was leaving town for a while.

Not the best scenario for when your ex-girlfriend had been murdered and you had been taken in and then immediately released by the police.

"Where are you headed?" Kate asked.

"None of your business."

"Who were you talking to so loudly on the phone before I knocked?"

"Again, none of your business. Now, if you'll excuse me..."

He went to close the door, but Kate persisted. She stepped forward and wedged her shoe between the door and the frame. "Mr. Neilbolt, I'm only asking for about five minutes of your time."

A wave of fury passed through his eyes but then seemed to subside. He hung his head and for a moment, she thought he looked sad. It was similar to the look she had seen on the faces of the Meades.

"You said you're a retired agent, right?" Neilbolt asked.

"That's right," she confirmed.

"Retired," he said. "Then get the fuck off of my porch."

She stood resolute, making it clear that she had no intention of going anywhere.

"I said *get the fuck off of my porch!*"

He nodded and then reached out to push her. She felt the force of his hands when they struck her shoulder and acted as quickly as she could. Right away, she was amazed at how quickly her reflexes and muscle memory kicked in.

As she went stumbling backward, she wrapped both of her arms around Neilbolt's right arm. At the same time, she dropped to a knee to stop her backward momentum. She then did her best to hip toss him but his bulk was too much to handle. When he realized what she was trying to do, he threw a hard elbow into her ribs.

The breath went barreling out of Kate's chest but because he had thrown the elbow, his leverage was thrown off. This time when she attempted the hip toss, it worked. And because she put everything she had into it, it worked a little too well.

Neilbolt went sailing off the porch. When he landed, he hit the bottom two stairs. He cried out in pain and tried to get back to his feet right away. He looked up at her in shock, trying to figure out what had happened. Fueled by rage and surprise, he hobbled up the stairs toward her, clearly dazed.

She faked him out with a right knee to the face as he neared the top step. When he went to dodge it, she caught the side of his head and again went to her knees. She forced his head hard into the porch while his arms and legs scrambled for purchase on the stairs. She then freed the handcuffs from the interior of her jacket and applied them with a quickness and ease that only thirty years of experience can provide.

She stepped away from Brian Neilbolt and looked down at him. He was not fighting against the cuffs; he looked rather dazed, in fact.

Kate reached for her phone with the intention of calling the cops and realized that her hand was trembling. She was pumped up, flooded with adrenaline. She realized that there was a smile on her face.

God, I've missed this.

Although the blow to her ribs did hurt like hell—a lot more than it would have hurt five or six years ago for sure. And had the joints in her knees always ached this way after a skirmish?

She allowed herself a moment to revel in what she had done and then managed to finally make a call to the cops. Meanwhile, Brian Neilbolt remained groggy at her feet, perhaps wondering how a woman at least twenty years older than him had managed to so thoroughly hand his ass to him.

CHAPTER FIVE

Honestly, Kate had expected a little bit of blowback about what she had done, but nothing to the degree of what she experienced when she reached the Third Precinct Station. She knew something was coming when she saw the glances from the police who passed by in the midst of their office errands. Some of the looks were of awe while others stank of a sort of leering ridicule.

Kate let it slide right off of her back. She was still too riled up from the confrontation on Neilbolt's porch to care.

After she'd waited several minutes in the lobby, a nervous-looking officer approached her. "You're Ms. Wise, right?" he asked.

"I am."

A flash of recognition showed in his eyes. It was a look she had once gotten all the time when officers or agents who had only ever heard about her record met her for the first time. She missed that look.

"Chief Budd would like to speak to you."

She was frankly quite surprised. She was hoping to speak to someone more along the lines of Deputy Commissioner Greene. While he might have been a hard ass on the phone, she knew he could be persuaded more effectively in face-to-face meetings. Chief Randall Budd, though, was a no-nonsense kind of man. She'd only ever met him on one occasion a few years ago. She barely remembered the occurrence but *did* remember Budd leaving an impression of someone strong-willed and strictly professional.

Still, Kate did not want to seem intimidated or at all worried. So she got up and followed the officer out of the waiting area and back through the bullpen. They passed by several desks where she got more uncertain glances before the officer led her down a hallway. In the center of the hall they came to Randall Budd's office. The door was open, as if he had been waiting for her for quite some time.

The officer had nothing to say; once he had delivered her to Budd's doorway, he turned on his heel and left. Kate looked into the office and saw Chief Budd waving her in.

"Come on in," he said. "I won't lie. I'm not happy with you, but I don't bite. Close the door behind you, would you?"

Kate stepped inside and did as she was asked. She then took one of the three chairs that sat on the opposite side of Budd's desk. The desk was occupied with more personal effects than work-related items: pictures of his family, an autographed baseball, a personalized coffee mug, and some kind of sentimental shell casing sitting in a plaque.

"Let me start off by saying that I am well aware of your track record," Budd said. "More than one hundred arrests in your career. Top of your class in the academy. Gold and silver placement in eight consecutive kickboxing tournaments *in addition to* standard bureau training where you also kicked ass. Your name got around while you were running things and most of the people here in the Virginia State PD respect the hell out of you."

"But?" Kate said. She didn't say it in an attempt to be funny. She was simply letting him know that she was more than capable of being reprimanded … although she honestly didn't think she deserved much of it.

"But despite all that, you have no right to go around assaulting people just because you think they might have been involved in the death of one of your friend's daughters."

"I didn't visit him with intent to assault," Kate said. "I visited him to ask some questions. When he got physical with me, I simply defended myself."

"He told my men that you pitched him down the porch stairs and banged his head against the floor of the porch."

"I can't be blamed for being stronger than him, now can I?" she asked.

Budd looked closely at her, scrutinizing her. "I can't tell if you're trying to be funny, taking this lightly, or if this is really your everyday attitude."

"Chief, I understand your position and how a retired fifty-five-year-old woman beating up someone that your men had questioned briefly and then released could cause you a headache. But please understand... I only visited Brian Neilbolt because my friend asked me to. And honestly, when I learned a bit more about him, I thought it might not be a bad idea."

"So you just assumed my men didn't do an adequate job?" Budd asked.

"I said no such thing."

Budd rolled his eyes and sighed. "Look, I'm not trying to argue about it. Honestly, I would love nothing more than for you to leave my office in a few minutes and once we are done talking about this matter, it's done. I need you to understand, though, that you crossed a line and if you happen to pull something like this again, I might just have to place you under arrest."

There were several things Kate wanted to say in response. But she figured if Budd was willing to press all arguments down, so could she. She knew that he was well within his power to really bring the hammer down on her if he wanted, so she decided to be as civil as possible.

"I understand," she replied.

Budd seemed to think about something for a moment before interlocking his hands together on the desk, as if trying to center himself. "And just so you know, we are certain that Brian Neilbolt did not kill Julie Hicks. We have him on security cameras outside of a bar on the night she was killed. He went in around ten and didn't leave until after midnight. We then have a text message trail between him and a current fling that went on between one and three in the morning. He checks out. He's not the guy."

"He had bags and suitcases packed," Kate pointed out. "Like he was trying to leave town in a hurry."

"In the text thread, he and this fling of his discussed visiting Atlantic City. They were supposed to be leaving this afternoon."

"I see." Kate nodded. She did not feel embarrassed per se, but she did start to regret acting so aggressively on Neilbolt's porch.

"There's one more thing," Budd said. "And again, you have to view things from my position on this. I had no choice but to contact your former supervisors at the FBI. It's protocol. Surely you know that."

She *did* know that but honestly had not thought about it. A slight yet gnawing irritation started to bloom in her guts.

"I know," she said.

"I spoke with Assistant Director Duran. He wasn't happy, and he wants to speak with you."

Kate rolled her eyes and nodded. "Fine. I'll give him a call and let him know it's from your instruction."

"No, you don't understand," Budd said. "They want to see you. In DC."

And with that, the irritation she was feeling quickly morphed into something she hadn't felt in a while: legitimate worry.

CHAPTER SIX

Following her meeting with Chief Budd, Kate made the appropriate calls to let her former supervisors know that she had received their request to visit them. She was not given any information over the phone and never actually spoke to anyone in power. That left her to leave a few rather rude messages with two unfortunate receptionists—an exercise that actually helped to relieve some of her stress.

She left Richmond the following morning at eight o'clock. She was curiously more excited than she was nervous. She figured it was kind of like a college graduate revisiting their campus after a brief time away. She'd missed the bureau terribly over the last year or so and was looking forward to being back in that environment... even if it was to be disciplined.

She distracted herself by listening to an obscure cinema-based podcast—a suggestion made by her daughter. Within five minutes of the podcast, the commentators had been drowned out and Kate was instead reflecting on the last few years of her life. For the most part, she was not a sentimental person but for some reason she had never understood, she tended to get nostalgic and reflective whenever she got on the road.

So instead of focusing on the podcast, she thought of her daughter— her pregnant daughter, due in about five weeks. The baby was to be a girl, named Michelle. The baby's father was a good enough man but, by Kate's estimation, had never quite been good enough for Melissa Wise. Melissa, called Lissa by Kate ever since she'd started to crawl, lived in Chesterfield, an area technically within Richmond but considered different by those who lived there. Kate had never told Melissa, but that was why she had moved back to Richmond. It had not been only because of her ties to the city due to her college experience, but because that was where her family was—where her first grandchild would live.

A grandchild, Kate often thought. *How did Melissa get that old? Hell, for that matter, how did I get that old?*

And when she thought of Melissa and the unborn Michelle, Kate typically turned her thoughts to her deceased husband. He'd been murdered six years ago, shot in the back of the head while walking their dog at night. His wallet and phone had been taken and she'd been called to ID the body less than two hours after he'd left the house with the dog.

The wound was still fresh most of the time but she hid it well. When she had retired from the bureau, she'd done so with about eight months left before official retirement age. But she had been unable to commit her full time, attention, and focus to her work after having finally scattered Michael's ashes over an old derelict baseball diamond near his home in Falls Church.

Perhaps that was why she had spent the last year so depressed about leaving her job. She had left months before she'd legally had to. What might those months have offered her? What else could she have done with her career?

She'd always wondered about these things, but had never fallen on the side of regret. Michael had deserved at least a few months of her undivided attention. He actually deserved much more than that but she knew that even in the afterlife, there's no way he would have expected her to ditch her work for too long. He would have known that it would have taken some work for her to properly grieve—and that work had meant literally working at the bureau for as long as she had been emotionally capable after his death.

She was relieved to find as she drew closer to DC that she was not feeling as if she was betraying Michael. She did personally believe that death was not the end; she didn't know if that meant Heaven was real or if reincarnation was possible and quite frankly she was okay with not knowing. But she did know that wherever Michael might be, he'd be happy that she was heading back to DC—even if it was to be severely reprimanded.

If anything, he was probably having a laugh at her expense.

This made Kate smile in spite of herself. She cut the podcast off and focused on the road, her own thoughts, and how even if she'd screwed up, life somehow always ended up seeming cyclical in nature.

She didn't get a rush of emotion when she stepped through the front doors and into the large lobby at the FBI headquarters. If anything, she was very aware that she felt she no longer belonged here—like a woman revisiting her old high school to find that the halls now made her feel sad rather than nostalgic.

The sense of familiarity helped, though. Despite feeling displaced, she also felt like she really hadn't been away that long after all. She walked through the lobby, checked in at the front, and headed for the elevators as if she had been here just last week. Even the enclosed space of the elevator was comforting as it carried her up to Assistant Director Duran's office.

When she stepped off the elevator and entered Duran's waiting area, she saw the same receptionist who had been behind the same desk a little over a year ago. They had never really been on a first-name basis, but the receptionist got up from her desk and rushed to hug her.

"Kate! It's so good to see you!"

Thankfully, the receptionist's name came back to her just the right moment. "You, too, Dana," Kate said.

"I didn't think you'd do well with retirement," Dana joked.

"Yeah, it's sort of a big snore."

"Well, go ahead and go on in," Dana said. "He's waiting for you."

Kate knocked on the closed office door. She found that even the somewhat gruff response she got from the other side made her feel at ease.

"It's open," the voice of Assistant Director Vince Duran said.

Kate opened the door and stepped inside. She had been fully prepared to see Duran and had readied herself for it. What she had not been expecting, however, was the face of her old partner. Logan Nash smiled at her right away, getting up from one of the chairs in front of Duran's desk.

Duran seemed to look aside for a moment to allow the reunion. Kate and Logan Nash met at the visitor's chairs in a friendly embrace. She had worked with Logan for the last eight years of her career. He was ten years younger than she was but had been well on his way to piecing together an illustrious career for himself when she had left.

"It's good to see you, Kate," he said lightly into her ear as they hugged.

"You, too," she said. Her heart swelled and slowly, almost teasingly, she realized that no matter how she tried to paint it, she *had* dearly missed this part of her life over the past year.

When the embrace broke, they both awkwardly took their seats in front of Duran. During their time together as partners, they had sat in this exact same place numerous times. But it had never been for matters of discipline.

Vince Duran took a very deep breath and sighed it out. Kate could not yet tell just how upset he was.

"So, let's not dance around it," Duran said. "Kate, you know why you're here. And I have assured Chief Budd that I would handle the situation in a very effective way. He seemed fine with that and I am fairly certain the entire ordeal with you tossing a suspect from his front porch will be swept under the rug. What I would like to know, though, is how you even came to be on that poor man's front porch."

She knew then that whatever harsh conversation she had been expecting was not going to happen. Duran was a monster of a man, roughly two hundred and forty pounds and the majority of that was nothing but muscle. He'd spent some time in Afghanistan in his early twenties and although she had never learned all he had done over there, the rumors were rampant. He had seen and done some harsh things and it often showed in the lines of his face. But today, he seemed to be in a good mood. She wondered if it was because he was no longer speaking to her as someone who worked under him. It almost felt more like catching up with an old friend.

That made it easy for her to tell him about the murder of Julie Hicks—the daughter of her good friend Deb Meade. She walked through speaking with them at a visitation at the Meade house and how certain the Meades had seemed. She then replayed the scene on Neilbolt's porch, explaining how she had started off by defending herself and then admittedly taking things perhaps a step too far.

On a few occasions, she got a soft chuckle from Logan. Duran, meanwhile, remained mostly expressionless. When she was done, she waited for his reaction and was confused when all she got out of him was a shrug.

"Look…as far as I'm concerned," he said, "it's a non-issue. While you *might* have been sticking your nose where it didn't belong, this guy had no business putting his hands on you—especially after you told him that you were former FBI. That was stupid on his part. The only thing I'd raise an eyebrow over is you slapping the cuffs on him."

"As I said…I admittedly went a little overboard."

"You?" Logan asked in mock surprise. "No!"

"What do you know about the case?" Duran asked.

"Just that she was killed in her home while her husband was away on business. The ex-boyfriend was the only real lead and the cops dismissed him in pretty quick fashion. I did find out later that his alibi was airtight, though."

"Nothing else?" Duran asked.

"Nothing that I've been told."

Duran nodded and then managed a cordial smile. "So aside from pitching grown men from their porches, how has retirement been treating you?"

"Like hell," she admitted. "It was great for the first few weeks but it got old fast. I miss my job. I've taken to reading an insane amount of true crime books. I'm watching far too many crime shows on the Biography Channel."

"You'd be surprised how often we hear that from agents in their first six to twelve months after retirement. Some of them call begging for some sort of work. Anything we have. Even paperwork of bullshit wiretaps."

Kate said nothing but nodded to indicate that she could identify.

"But yet you didn't call," Duran said. "If I'm being honest, I expected you to. I didn't think you could just drop it so easily. And this little incident proves me right."

"With all due respect," Kate said, "did you call me down here to slap me on the wrist over this or to rub my nose in how I can't outgrow my old job?"

"Neither," Duran said. "I was looking through your files yesterday after I got the call from Richmond. I noticed that you've been asked to testify at a parole hearing. Is that correct?"

"It is. It's for the Mueller case. Double homicide."

"Is it the first time you've been contacted about work since you retired?"

"No," she said, pretty sure he already knew the answer. "I had an assistant to an agent call me about two months after I retired to ask questions about a cold case I last worked on back in 2005. Some of the guys in records and research have reached out a few times about my methodology on some older cases, too."

Duran nodded and reclined back in his chair a bit. "You should also know that we have instructors at the academy using some of your earlier casework as examples for coursework. You left your mark here in the bureau, Agent Wise. And honestly, I was rather *hoping* you'd be one of those agents who started calling up to see what you could do to help even after you had retired."

"Are you saying you want me to start assisting with some cases, then?" Kate asked. She did her best to keep the hopeful tone out of her voice.

"Well, it's not that cut and dried. We were thinking of perhaps bringing an agent or two with an exceptional track record to work on cold cases. Nothing long term or full time, mind you. And when we have discussed it, your name was the only one that kept coming up in unison. Now, before you get too excited, please know that this is not an immediate thing. We still want you to relax. Take some time off. *Real* time off."

"I can do that," Kate said. "Thank you."

"Don't thank me yet," Duran said. "It could be a few months. And I'm afraid I'm going to have to revoke the offer if you go back home and start beating up men much younger than you on their porches."

"I think I can restrain myself," Kate said.

Again, Logan couldn't help but let out a little muffled laugh from beside her.

Duran seemed just as amused as he got to his feet.

"Now ... if you truly are going to assist, I'm afraid we have to revisit one of the less spectacular parts of the job."

Assuming he meant paperwork, Kate sighed. "Forms? Documents?"

"Oh no, nothing like that," Duran said. "I've scheduled a meeting to get this going. Figured it would be the best way to keep all channels up to date."

"Ah, I hate meetings."

"Oh, I know," Duran said. "I remember. But hey ... what better way to welcome you back?"

Logan chuckled beside her as they got to their feet and followed Duran out of the office. For Kate, it all seemed eerily familiar.

Really, it turned out not to be a bad meeting at all. There were only three other people waiting for them in the small conference room at the end of the hallway. Two of them were agents, one a male, the other female. As far as Kate could tell, she had met neither of them before. The third was a man who looked vaguely familiar; she was pretty sure his last name was Dunn. As Duran closed the door behind them, one of the agents got to his feet and instantly extended his hand.

"Agent Wise, I'm so pleased to meet you," he said.

She took his hand awkwardly and shook it. As she did, the agent seemed to realize that he had made a small spectacle of himself.

"Sorry," he said under his breath as he quickly returned to his seat.

"That's fine, Agent Rose," Duran said as he took a seat at the head of the table. "You aren't the first agent to be floored by the presence of near-legendary Agent Kate Wise." He said this with a bit of sarcasm and cut a thin smile Kate's way.

The man she thought was named Dunn stood out from the other two—both clearly younger agents. He was a supervisor of sorts; it was clear from his stoic expression to his finely pressed suit.

"Agent Wise," Duran said, "these two agents are Agent Rose and Agent DeMarco. They have been partners for about the last seven months, but only because myself and Assistant Director Dunn have had problems finding a place for them. They both come with their own set of unique strengths. And if you do end up taking the lead on this case in Richmond, one of them will likely be assigned to work with you."

Agent Rose still looked embarrassed but refused to break his concentration. Kate couldn't remember the last time someone had been so visibly shaken to meet her. It had been somewhere around the next-to-last year of her career when someone from Quantico had ended up working with her for a day in the labs. It was humbling but also a little off-putting.

"I should add," Assistant Director Dunn said, "that Deputy Director Duran and I are the ones that have pushed for this program to bring recently retired agents in. I don't know if he has told you yet, but your name was the first that came up."

"Yes," Duran agreed. "Needless to say, we'd really appreciate it if you kept it under wraps for now. And, of course, knock it out of the park."

"I'll try my best," Kate said. She was beginning to understand that there was now a bit of pressure being applied here. Not that she minded, really. She usually operated better under pressure.

"Great," Duran said. "For now, do you want to go over the details of this case as you understand them?"

Kate nodded and instantly fell back into her old role. It was as if she had never missed a day, much less a year. As she filled them in on what was going on in Richmond and how she had gotten involved, Agent Rose and Agent DeMarco held steady eye contact with her, perhaps studying her to see how they might work alongside her.

But she didn't let that distract her. As she went over the details of the case, she felt as if she had stepped back in time.

And it was far superior to the present she had been living.

CHAPTER SEVEN

Three hours later, Kate and Logan were sitting at an outdoor table beneath a canopy at a small Italian restaurant. Logan was eating a meat-packed sub while Kate was eating a pasta salad and enjoying a glass of white wine. She did not drink often and almost never before five in the afternoon, but this was a special occasion. Even the mere idea of a reality where she might once again become active within the bureau was cause for celebration as far as she was concerned.

"So what kind of cases are you working on right now?" Kate asked.

"All things that would bore you, I'm sure," he said. But she knew he'd tell her; he'd tell her because he loved the job just as much as she did.

"Trying to crack some scammers that have been tampering with ATMs for the most part. I'm sort of working in a partnership with a few other agents in what might be a small prostitution ring coming out of Georgetown, but that's about it."

"Yikes," Kate said.

"Told you. Boring."

"So a far cry from these cold cases Duran mentioned? What do you know about that anyway? How long has that little side project been cooking?"

"A while, I think. I was only brought in to the loop two weeks ago. Duran and some of the other behind-closed-door types were asking about some of the cases we had worked on that never got solved. Not looking for methodology or anything like that, just asking for details and old case files."

"And they didn't give you a reason?"

"No. And…wait, why do you sound suspicious? I thought you'd be jumping all over this opportunity."

"Oh, I plan to. But it makes me wonder if there is one particular cold case they are more interested in. *Something* had to have spurred on this sudden interest in cold cases. I seriously doubt it's just so Duran could find some way to bring me back."

"I don't know," Logan said. "You'd be surprised. You've been missed around here. Some of the newer agents still talk about you like you're some kind of mythological character."

She ignored the compliment, still stuck on her train of thought. "Also, why would he call me in only to send me back, telling me he wanted me to take some more time before starting? It makes me wonder if whatever the *real* reason behind it is might not quite be fleshed out just yet."

"Well, you know," Logan said. "Based on the way you're overthinking this whole thing, maybe he's right. Relax, Kate. Like he said…there are tons of retired agents who would die for this chance. So yeah, go back home. Relax. Do absolutely nothing."

"You know me well enough to know that's not how I am," she said. She took a sip from her wine, thinking that maybe he was right. Maybe she *should* just revel in the joy of coming back to work…sort of.

"Retirement didn't change that, huh?" Logan asked.

"No. If anything, it made it worse. I can't stand to sit still. I hate an idle brain. Cross word puzzles and knitting aren't going to cut it for me. Maybe deep down Duran knew that I'm too young to be put out to pasture."

Logan smiled and shook his head. "Yeah, but the grass in those pastures is pretty lush and green."

"Yeah, and there's cow shit everywhere."

Logan sighed as he took the final bite of his lunch. "Okay," he said. "Some of us need to get back to work."

"Cheap shot," she said, taking the last sip of her wine.

"So what are you going to do?" he asked. "Head back home?"

She honestly wasn't quite sure yet. Part of her wanted to stay in DC just for the hell of it. Maybe she'd get some shopping done or go out to her favorite spot at the National Mall and just sit to reflect. It was certainly a gorgeous day for it.

But then again, she wanted to be back home, too. While she had struck out in terms of Brian Neilbolt, the fact remained that *someone* had killed Julie Meade. And it seemed that the police were at a loss so far.

"I'm not sure," she said. "I may hang around town for a bit but I'll likely head back home before nightfall."

"If you change your mind, give me a call. It was really nice seeing you, Kate."

They paid their checks and left the table after a brief embrace. Even before Kate left, her mind seemed to have snagged on one particular thought, one that had come out of nowhere, it seemed.

Julie was killed in her home, while her husband was out of town. If there was a break-in of any kind, no one mentioned it to me. Not the police while I was being lectured, and not Debbie or Jim. If there had been a break-in, you'd think that would have been mentioned.

It made her wonder ... did the killer enter the house because he was invited? Or did they perhaps, at the very least, know where a spare key was hidden?

Those questions settled it. Once she'd given her glass of wine enough time to run its course, she was going to drive back to Richmond. She'd promised Assistant Director Duran that she would not beat anyone else up.

But she'd said nothing about not investigating.

Of course, the funeral was first. She'd pay her respects and do her very best to be there for Deb tomorrow. And after that, she'd step back into her role—perhaps with a bit more excitement than she cared to admit.

CHAPTER EIGHT

The next afternoon, Kate was standing in the back row of mourners as the Meade family and their closest friends assembled at the cemetery. She stood with her little breakfast crew—Clarissa and Jane dressed in black and looking genuinely heartbroken—who had managed to love on Debbie earlier in the morning. Debbie seemed to be doing much better than she had on the day she had asked Kate to look into the murder. She wept openly and let out a single anguished moan of sorrow, but she was still *present*. Jim, on the other hand, looked like a very broken man. A man who would go home and think long and hard about how sometimes, life just wasn't very fucking fair at all.

Kate couldn't help but think of her own daughter. She knew she'd have to call Melissa when the funeral was over. She hadn't known Julie Meade very well but based on conversations she'd had with Debbie, Kate assumed she had been around the same age as Melissa, give or take a few years.

She listened as the preacher went through the familiar Biblical passages. While her thoughts were very much with Debbie, they were also still slightly obsessing over how this could have happened. She had not come out and asked directly if there had been a break-in since she had gotten back from DC but she had kept her ears open. She had noticed that neither Jane nor Clarissa had ever mentioned a break-in, either. And that was odd because Clarissa somehow had a knack for knowing everything thanks to her nose for gossip.

She looked up at Debbie and Jim, noticing that there was a tall man standing by Jim. He was relatively young and dashing in a clean-cut sort of way. She lightly nudged Jane beside her and asked: "The tall guy next to Jim. Is that Julie's husband?"

"Yeah. Tyler is his name. They hadn't been married long. Less than a year, I think."

It occurred to Kate that maybe her little breakfast clique really didn't know one another very well after all. Sure, they knew all about their former jobs, favorite caffeinated beverages, and wishes and dreams for retirement. But they had never really gone much deeper. It had been sort of a mutual silent understanding. They had rarely talked about their families, keeping conversation surface level, fun, and entertaining.

There was nothing wrong with that, of course, but it left Kate knowing very little about the Meade family. All she knew was that Julie had been their only child... in the same way that Melissa was *her* only child. And while she and Melissa were not as intimately close as they had once been, it still hurt to even think about losing her.

Once the service was over and the crowd started to disperse in a tangle of hugs and awkward handshakes, Kate and her little coffee group follow suit. Kate, however, hung back where a few people had kind of hidden themselves away for a cigarette. While Kate was not smoking (she thought it a disgusting habit), she wanted to stay out of sight for a while. She scanned the crowd and found the tall figure of Tyler Hicks. He was speaking to an elderly couple, both of whom were openly weeping. Tyler, however, seemed to be doing his best to remain calm.

When the elderly couple left, Kate made her way toward him. Tyler was heading in the direction of a middle-aged woman and her two children, but Kate made a point to reach him first.

"Excuse me," she said, angling herself in front of him. "You're Tyler, right?"

"I am," he said. When he turned to face her, she could see the grief all over his face. He was drained, tired, and looked to be empty of just about everything. "Do I know you?"

"No, honestly," she said. "I'm a friend of Julie's mother, though. My name is Kate Wise."

A flicker of recognition sparkled in his eyes for a moment. It made his face look almost alive for a split second. "Yeah, I heard Debbie mention you. You're an FBI agent or something, right?"

"Well, recently retired. But yes, that's the gist of it."

"Sorry she sent you looking into what happened to Julie. I can imagine that made for an awkward situation."

"No need to apologize," Kate said. "I can't even imagine what she's been going through. But look … I'll make this quick. I won't want to take up too much of your time. I know that Debbie wanted me to look into the ex-boyfriend and while I haven't been able to speak with her about it yet, he *is* clean."

"Mrs. Wise, you don't have to do this for her."

"I know," she said. "But I was wondering if you could maybe answer a few really quick questions for me."

He looked insulted at first but then resigned himself. A curious and sad look crossed his face as he asked: "Do you think there are questions worth asking?"

"Perhaps."

"Then yes, I'll answer a few. Quickly, please."

"Of course. I was wondering if you had seen anything around the house once you returned home that might have seemed strange or out of place. Maybe something that didn't seem like that big of a deal considering what has just happened to Julie. Maybe something you thought you'd look into later, when things had calmed down a bit."

He shook his head slowly, looking back to the place where his wife would be lowered into the ground within the hour. "Not that I can think of."

"Not even any signs of a break-in?"

His attention went back to her and now he looked a little spooked. "You know, I've started to wonder about that myself," he said. "All of the doors were locked when I got home that next day. I rang the doorbell because my keys were in one of my bags and I didn't want to dig for them. But Julie never answered. I didn't even bother to think about that until yesterday, when I was trying to get to sleep. Someone came in easily, without breaking in. And then they locked the door behind them. So they *knew* how to get in. But that doesn't make sense."

"And why not?"

"Because there's a code for the security system that only Julie, myself, and our cleaning lady knows. We change it every two months."

"Any suspicion about the cleaning lady or her family?"

"Well, she's pushing sixty and we don't know her family. The police were looking into it but found nothing."

"Well, how about you?" Kate asked. "Is there anyone you can think of that would have even considered doing this?"

He shook his head without giving it much thought. "I've spent every waking moment since I came home and found her body trying to think of someone who would have any reason to kill her—to even be *angry* with her. And I keep coming up blank." He paused here and then looked at her skeptically. "You said you're retired. So why are you so interested in this case?"

She gave the only answer that would be acceptable. "I just wanted to do everything I could to ease Debbie's mind."

She knew that there was a deeper truth, though. And it was a selfish one.

Because being just a little involved in this case is the most purposeful I've felt since I retired a year ago.

"Well, I appreciate your help," Tyler said. "And if you need anything else from me, please let me know."

"I will," she said as she gave him a lame sympathetic clap on the back and left him to his sorrow. The truth was, though, that she doubted she'd ever speak to him again. She'd been an agent long enough to know an innocent and truly heartbroken man when she saw one. She'd bet everything she owned on the fact that Tyler Hicks had not killed his wife. She already felt terrible for hijacking him after his wife's funeral. She'd stay away from Tyler from this point on; if he could be of any further help, let the cops handle it.

She went to her car and pulled out into the slumbering line of traffic that was leaving the graveyard. She drove back toward her house in silence, her thoughts continually drifting to Melissa and her forthcoming granddaughter.

Her phone rang, obliterating the train of thought. There was a number, not a name, on the display screen. She answered it suspiciously, still shaken over the funeral and how the experience was making her think long and hard about her own daughter.

"Kate Wise?" a man on the other end asked.

"Yes, this is Kate," she said.

"This is Randall Budd. How are you?"

"Somber," she answered honestly, a little pissed that she was having to speak to Chief Budd in that particular moment.

"You go to the funeral today?" he asked.

She was rather surprised that he even knew Julie had been buried today. Maybe she should cut the guy some slack after all. "Yeah," she answered. "Just left about fifteen minutes ago."

"Well, look. I wanted to call to let you know that at about eight o'clock this morning, we got an anonymous tip. An arrest was made in the death of Julie Hicks. We've still got the guy here in interrogation. Some guy that came out to fix their Internet a few weeks back. He's got some intimate knowledge of the family *and* he has a previous arrest record for—get this—sexual misconduct. We're looking into his story and accounts and it all looks solid."

"Who is it?"

Budd sighed, a sound that was like static electricity through the phone. "Ms. Wise, you know I can't tell you that."

"Of course you can. I'll do nothing with the information other than try to help you."

"Yes, but with all due respect, I have not asked for your help."

"Can you at least tell me if the suspect knew the victim personally?"

The other end of the line was quiet for about three seconds, finally broken by a thick sigh and Budd's voice saying: "No."

She almost pushed harder but left it at that. If she really wanted to know, all she'd have to do was place a call to Logan. It would be a cheap thing to do but at least the option was there.

"And it's looking like he's the guy?"

"It's certainly a possibility," Budd said. "Once we have enough to book him for it, we're going to notify Debbie and Jim Meade. So please keep it to yourself for now. I just thought I'd do you the courtesy of knowing … in the hopes that you don't go all vigilante on us again."

"Thanks for that," she said. "Have a good day, Chief."

She hung up with a sense of relief. Case closed. That was a good thing. Now Debbie and Jim could maybe begin to start looking at what grieving was like with closure involved.

But then she thought about what Tyler Hicks had said about the security code. And even the things he had not said. About how someone would have to know how to get in unseen. How someone would have to know the family well enough to get inside the house after dark, past the security measures and locked doors.

By the time she got back to her house in Carytown, that relief was gone. If anything, it had morphed into an entirely new kind of certainty.

A certainty that told her that whoever killed Julie Hicks was still at large.

CHAPTER NINE

If there had been one aspect of being an agent that Kate had hated, it was the few times she'd had to appear in court to give her testimony or to testify against a prisoner's parole. However, doing it now, a year removed from her job with the prospect of returning in a minor role in the future, she found it exciting.

She was set to testify against a man named Patrick Ellis. She knew the history like the back of her hand but still hung on every word as the judge recounted the case for those in attendance.

"It has been proven beyond reasonable doubt that Mr. Ellis killed a married couple while they were hiking on the Blue Ridge Mountain trails in 1993. The married couple, the Muellers, had been discovered three days following their fateful hike. Both of their heads had been smashed in, the wife had been raped and sodomized, they'd been stripped naked, and disemboweled. During the initial case, the defense pushed hard for a ruling of insanity, given the gratuitous nature of Ellis's crimes.

"In the end, Ellis had been found to be of sound mind, having given far too much thought into the killings not to have planned it beforehand. Further evidence had shown that the Muellers had not been random; they lived just three streets away from him. He'd even mowed their grass for them one time when the Muellers were vacationing in Florida."

He paused and looked out to the courtroom, making sure it sank in. As he went over the minutes and notes from previous dates, Kate relived the case in her head. It had been twenty-five years ago but the case, like most of the ones that had taken her into a courtroom, seemed just as fresh as one that had occurred last week. Even Patrick Ellis looked pretty much the same with the exception of a ratty beard and a few gray hairs.

He recognized her even before she was called up to testify. He gave her a smile that was just as sharp as a knife.

A knife I'm sure he'd be happy to plunge directly into my throat, she thought as she stepped up onto the stand.

"Before we begin," the judge said once he was done with catching everyone up, "I should make it clear to those in attendance that Ms. Kate Wise retired from the bureau a little over a year ago. Still, I have it on good authority that everyone she worked with, including her superiors, gives her their full trust and confidence. That being said ... Ms. Wise, I assume you know all of the reasons that are being given for the parole of Mr. Patrick Ellis, correct?"

"I do."

"Can you state those reasons for the court?"

"Of course, Your Honor. I know that during his first year in prison, Ellis was involved in three fights, one of which nearly killed him. I also know that during his third year, he began to attempt to get permission to reach out to friends and family members of the Muellers under the reasoning that he wanted to apologize. When he could not get that permission, he attempted to commit suicide by hanging himself. Lastly, I know he has regularly been attending chapel and Bible studies, and that he has apparently given his life to Christ. For the past four years, he's apparently been a model inmate and, in the words of several guards, is the very definition of a changed man."

"That's exactly right," the judge said. "Based on those details, what is your opinion of the possibility of parole?"

"Well, Ellis was originally sentenced to life in prison. And while the option of parole was tacked on to that sentence, I vehemently fought it at the time. And I will continue to fight it now. I can't say if Ellis is a changed man now or not. But I *can* tell you that the things I saw at the crime scene when the bodies were discovered was the work of a man that enjoyed what he had done. I can also tell you some of the deranged things he said to my partner and I when he was under interrogation. I know there are members of the Muellers' family in attendance today, so I'd rather not go over the things Ellis said in private. But I will if I have to in order to make sure that he never sees another day of freedom."

She snuck a glance toward Ellis and saw that his grin was gone. He now looked like a man who was being haunted by some nameless ghost.

"Do you not consider his good behavior and changed ways a sign of turning himself around?"

"I don't think it matters," Kate said. "Parole would make him a free man. Yes, he'd have tests and restrictions galore, but he'd still be free. He'd have some semblance of a life back. The married couple I found disemboweled in the side of a mountain twenty-five years ago don't get that option. So no ... I don't find Mr. Ellis's change of personality any reason to grant parole."

She saw the grim expression on the judge and the shocked silence that fell through the audience like a series of boulders from the sky. Yes, in the past she had hated this part of the job. But it had come back quite naturally and as much as she hated to admit it, she felt incredible even under the evil glare of Patrick Ellis.

She was on her way out of the courthouse twenty minutes later, directly after it had been decided not to grant parole to Patrick Ellis. The discussions in the courtroom had brought back very vivid images of the murders. It was hard to understand that those kinds of scenes had made up her life at one point. Granted, the Muellers had been among the worst mutilated and abused bodies she'd seen in her career, but the number of bodies had kept piling up and somehow defining what she did.

It had taken her until retirement to understand that. For each case she broke or folded, there had usually been at least one dead body. She didn't dare ponder just how many she had seen or been around in her career. It was those kinds of details and numbers that, she thought, could dive a retired agent to the brink of insanity.

Kate did not have time to consider the thought much farther. She heard someone calling for her from behind as she made her way down the courthouse steps. She smiled when she realized how they were referring to her. Not as Ms. Wise.

"Agent Wise!"

She stopped and turned to see who would still refer to her as *agent*. She saw three people coming down the stairs to catch up with her. One of them looked vaguely familiar. Maybe one of the family members related to one of the Muellers.

"Can I help you?" she asked. "I'm Paul Mueller," the face she recognized said. "I'm Clark's dad. Clark was…"

"Yes, I remember," Kate said. And she did. Though when she thought of Clark Mueller, she saw the top of a head caved in with a rock and a small intestine hanging from a gash in his stomach.

"This is his best friend from college and his sister," Paul Mueller said, gesturing to the other two.

A brief round of introductions were made. It was all rather surreal to Kate. It was the kind of situation she'd tried her best to avoid when she'd been an active agent. But now she felt she owed some of her attention to these people—people who had lost loved ones a very long time ago and had found some peace and solace because she had managed to find the person who had taken away a large part of their lives.

"We just wanted to thank you for staying involved in all of this when you didn't have to," Paul Mueller said. "If that monster had gotten parole… I don't know what I would have done."

"It's my pleasure," she said. "Retired agents do this sort of thing all of the time."

"I'm sure they do," Paul said. "But you were always the one person involved in the mess that seemed to genuinely care. You wanted to catch Ellis, sure. But you had a good heart. I remember one night where you humored my wife when she fought through tears for close to an hour to tell you a meaningless story about Clark falling out of a tree when he was seven years old. You entertained her while every other policeman and agent in the house avoided her like the plague. That has always meant the world to me."

Kate, never the best at taking compliments, had no idea what to do with that. She decided to simply give him a warm smile. "As long as I'm alive, Patrick Ellis won't get parole," she said. "You have my word on that."

Paul gave her a hug, as did the college friend and sister. They split off and everyone went their separate ways. Kate headed to her car, trying to shake the memories of the Mueller case out of her head. As she did, she realized there was something that had been said during the hearing that had stuck in her head like a splinter. Something about how it had turned out that Patrick Ellis had not randomly selected the Muellers ... that he had *known* them.

She thought of Julie Hicks and couldn't help but wonder.

The thought was still with her when she got into her car and headed home.

CHAPTER TEN

The last serious relationship Kate had ever been in had lasted three weeks. It had gone no farther than a single awkward kiss and a few dinners. After Michael had died, she had told herself she would never even date another man. But life had gotten lonely and she'd tried her best. She'd tried with four different men and each had failed. She'd been too hard on them, almost *looking* for some reason for it to fail. And if she could not find a reason, she made sure to drive them away.

It would be easier if she could tell herself she'd been pushing these men away subconsciously, but that had not been the case at all. No, she'd done it on purpose each and every time.

Because of that, Kate had gotten quite adept at eating alone. She didn't mind it at all, not even the pitying stares of the younger couples who sometimes looked to her as a warning of their future. There was something almost liberating about eating alone and besides that, it was a great way to sort her thoughts. She'd often gone to coffee shops or martini bars when she'd been an agent when she needed time to think. She'd never liked the silence of an office, and trying to work quietly at home was unnerving. But in the midst of the noise of everyday people coming and going in restaurants, it was easier for Kate to gather up all of her thoughts. It always had been. It was one of the curious little quirks that Michael had enjoyed about her—or so he had always said.

Currently, she was eating fish tacos and cilantro-lime rice. A bottle of Dos Equis sat by the plate, half empty. She was sitting at a small table near the back of the restaurant as the dinner rush started to fill the place on this busy Thursday night. She was eating her tacos and thinking about the Meade/Hicks case. She wondered how possible it would be for her to get inside the house. She was pretty sure Tyler Hicks would entertain the idea but she also knew that such a request would be in bad taste right now. She figured she'd need to wait a few weeks. And if she had any hope of figuring out if the killer was still at large, she didn't have that kind of time ... especially when the cops thought they had their man.

And maybe they did. Who knew?

Her thoughts then turned to Michael. Ever since his murder, her thoughts had usually turned in his direction whenever she had trouble solving a case. Michael's murderer had never been caught, despite her own best efforts and innumerable man hours put in by a handful of other agents. As far as Kate could tell—and as far as she knew even to this very day—Michael's murder had been a random one. Maybe a mugging gone wrong or just some fucked up junkie wanting to feel the thrill of murder. There had simply not been enough evidence to suggest otherwise.

So his unsolvable murder usually popped into her head when it seemed that a case might be out of her grasp. This time, though—with Julie Hicks and her worried parents—Kate wasn't sure if it *was* out of her grasp. She couldn't help but wonder if she would have already cracked the case if she had the FBI's resources at her disposal.

Or, she thought as she took a drink from her beer, *maybe the cops are right. Maybe the guy Budd told me they got is the killer.*

She doubted it, though. She'd heard nothing from Debbie or Chief Budd. Budd might not extend another courtesy to tell her that they were now one hundred percent sure and had officially booked the suspect, but she was certain Debbie would have. And since she had not heard any-thing now, ten hours after Budd's call, she assumed that meant that their current suspect was not the slam dunk Budd had made him out to be.

She finished off her tacos and her beer. As she settled her check, she ran over a quick checklist of sorts in her head.

When can I see the crime scene for myself?

Where was Tyler visiting while on the road and why?

Did the cleaning lady even have reason to give the security code to someone else?

How reliable is the security system the Hicks had installed?

If she were still an active agent, these were the kinds of questions she would consider to be busy work. But as it was, it was all she had to go on for now. Until then, she could only wait for either Budd or Debbie to call her to confirm that they had indeed found Julie's killer.

But with every minute that passed, Kate expected less and less that she was going to get such a call.

Kate walked back to her house, just six blocks away from the place where had enjoyed her beer and fish tacos. Night had just fully fallen and the temperature was perfect. Not too hot but not too chilly as summer did its best to hang in there while fall came in to bully it away. She figured maybe she'd wrap up the night with a glass or two of wine out on the porch, listening to the traffic and the faraway crickets that seemed to think there might still be some forest left around the edges of Richmond.

Yet when she reached her house, she saw that there was already someone on the porch. The agent in her grew alarmed right away but within a full second, she knew she had no need to worry. The man sitting in the rocking chair on her porch was a friend of hers. More than a friend, she supposed. Of the men she'd attempted to date since Michael had died, the one currently in her rocking chair had been the only one she had kissed ... the only one who had spent the night at her home.

His name was Allen Goldman and as far as men went, he was a decent one. He was no Michael Wise, but no one was. Allen was one year older than Kate and also on the brink of retiring from a job in advertising. But he had his own little side business, doing niche advertising for independent publishing houses. He was always good to talk to, had entertaining stories, and Kate was pretty sure he'd treat her nice if she let him. Allen had gone through a divorce about twelve years ago and rarely spoke of his wife or the time he spent with her—which made Kate a little uneasy.

He got up from the rocking chair when Kate came up the stairs. He looked a little embarrassed but also glad to see her.

"Sit back down," she said, waving him away. "How long have you been there?"

Allen looked at his watch and shrugged. "Maybe twenty minutes."

"How long would you have stayed?"

"I figured half an hour. A full hour at most."

She pulled over the empty decorative flower pot on the other side of the front door. She turned it upside down next to the rocking chair. Perching herself upon it, she sighed and took Allen's hand. He seemed to appreciate the gesture.

"So what's up, Allen?" she asked, a bit skeptical.

He had a thing for just dropping by. He did it because she had told them on their first date that she enjoyed the element of surprise in a man. The last time he had done it—about two months ago—he had ended up spending the night. They'd slept together and discussed why it was a bad idea the next morning. They'd had dinner a few times since then but nothing had ever really felt the same.

"I thought I'd come by to see how you were doing," he said. "We hadn't talked in about a week or so."

"I'm good," she said. "Just... it's been a weird day. A weird week, actually."

"You want to talk about it?"

She thought about it for a moment and found that she *did* want to talk about it. She surprised herself when she started telling him all about the funeral. More than that, she shared with him that Debbie Meade had asked her to do some digging. She ended her account with her trip to DC and the potential offer to start working on cold cases.

"You really miss it, don't you?" he asked.

"Most of the time," she said. "How did you know? Is it that obvious?"

He smiled and said, "It's in the questions you ask. The way you talk to people. It spooked me on our first date but I quickly came to enjoy it."

"Yeah, I was impressed it didn't scare you off."

"Speaking of dates," he said, "I was hoping to take you on another one sometime."

She almost made a joke about how he likely wanted more than just a date if he was showing up on her doorstep. Given what had happened the last time he'd showed up unannounced, it was easy to assume he was hoping to replicate those results.

"Maybe some other time," she said. "This whole thing with Debbie's daughter ... and then the thought of maybe picking up some of my old work again ..."

"Things are getting busy, huh?"

"Hopefully. There are lots of things about my past coming up these last few days. I even had to testify against this real creep in court. A guy I put away in the nineties. Seeing his face and reliving the case ... it was like stepping through a doorway into the past. It was weird. But ... I sort of liked it."

"You know," Allen said, "I don't think I'd mind taking the back seat to your work."

"That's the problem," she said, kissing him softly on the cheek. "You're too good for that. You don't deserve the back seat."

He frowned and got up from the rocker again. This time, Kate did not tell him to sit back down. "So is that a no for now, or a no for the foreseeable future?"

"I don't know," she answered honestly. "Let's just say it's *for now* and see what happens later?"

"That's fair," he said, headed for the stairs.

"And Allen ... call next time?"

He gave her a smile and a wave, and then walked down onto the sidewalk.

Kate watched him disappear from sight, down the hill until he disappeared behind the curb and in the darkness of the night.

He's a good guy, she thought. And she had no idea if she was speaking to herself or trying to convince Michael, wherever he might be.

Honestly, though, Michael would want her to date again. He'd want her to enjoy life to the fullest in his absence. So maybe it was just her. Maybe it was her once again trying to fill a hole in her life with work rather than the company of someone who cared about her.

It was another one of those things from that past that seemed as if it would just not go away.

CHAPTER ELEVEN

He was watching her when she picked her twelve-year-old daughter up from cheerleading practice. A month ago, it would have been swim practice. But summer was on its way out, so the pool was old news. Now football was on the horizon, as were cheer pyramids and pompoms. Kids these days ... had to be involved in something. And the idiot parents were more than happy to keep them appeased.

He was parked on the far end of the football field. He watched her, squinting his eyes, able to make out the bob in her ponytail as she got out of the car and spoke to one of the other moms as their daughters chattered by the backs of the cars. After a while they parted ways and she started the car again,

When she pointed the car back out to the road, he did the same. He was on the other end of the parking lot, nearly fifty yards away. He watched her get onto the road, allowed two other cars in front of him, and then he pulled out as well.

It wasn't pursuit, not really. All the cars in the world could get between them and he'd know where she was going. It was Thursday. She and her daughter would stop by Subway on the way home. He wasn't sure what sub she got but the wrappers he'd seen in her trash had some sort of red sauce on them. Maybe a meatball sub.

When he passed by the plaza with the Subway ten minutes later, he pulled into the other end of the plaza. He parked in an empty spot in front of an Aldi's and watched the Subway until they came back out. The daughter was cute, but he wasn't into kiddy stuff. He guessed maybe he *could* be but he figured he had enough issues as it was. The fact that he had been following her for the better part of three months was proof of that. He'd followed her and studied her and these were the things he knew about her.

Her name was Lacy Thurmond. She was thirty-five years old. She was married to a man who claimed he had to work late on Monday and Thursday nights. But he had followed the husband, too. The work the husband was doing was in a motel room twenty miles away from the house, having sex with a girl who might be early twenties at most. Lacy Thurmond had an obnoxious laugh, a pet cat, a twelve-year-old daughter, and she liked to read. She worked from home, doing some sort of editing jobs for a telecommunications firm. She had at least two glasses of white wine or a couple shots of tequila every night. She and her husband had sex twice a week (though he had it four times, twice with the younger girl in the motel) and one of those days was always Sunday. The sex was usually rough and she rarely climaxed. When she did, she was very quiet and had to be on top.

He knew this because he had watched them on several occasions. They did not have a security system and because their only bedroom window faced the backyard, he could snoop and spy as much as he liked. It also helped that there was a kink in the blinds in the bedroom that allowed him to see in just fine.

He thought about those blinds as he watched them leave the Subway and get back on the road. He thought about something as mundane as a set of blinds, how married couples at some point had to agree on them and install them. It was both sad and comforting to him at the same time.

He allowed five cars between them between the Subway and their home—a distance of three and a half miles. He was driving by their house when she pushed the garage opener in their car and the door started sneaking its way open. He saw the empty space in the garage, the space her husband's truck would fill sometime around ten o'clock. One time he had gotten in as early at nine forty-five but it was usually ten or a little after.

He checked his watch. That meant he had a little more than three hours. If he had to, he'd kill the husband, too. But that wasn't what he wanted. He only wanted her.

But yeah, he'd kill the husband if there was no other choice.

But he really didn't want to hurt the girl.

Even *he* had to draw the line somewhere.

Lacy rushed through helping Olivia with her homework. There were some nights where she allowed herself to be a half-assed mom. Tonight, she was more worried about getting to that first shot of tequila than she was her daughter's homework. She'd had a miserable day at work and with the passing of each hour, she knew what the night was going to be like, making her feel stuck ... making her feel like she couldn't care less if the day ended or not.

Olivia finished her homework as Lacy did her best to straighten up the house. She did a load of laundry and paid a few bills online while Olivia sulked on the couch with her iPhone, playing around on Snapchat.

As the clock wound down to 8:30, the night went as it usually did. Olivia said a half-hearted *goodnight* and retired to her room. Lacy knew she wouldn't go to sleep until around eleven, spending the rest of her time alone either drawing or reading. She was fine with this; she knew girls around the age of twelve or so started to distance themselves, spending lots of alone time in their rooms. Besides ... Lacy counted herself lucky. She knew Olivia was a bookworm. She could be up there investigating porn or sexting some guy on her phone.

With Olivia in her room, Lacy allowed herself a few shots of tequila. It had never been her drink of choice but it *was* the drink that got her drunk the fastest. She'd been going to it a lot as of late, especially on Monday and Thursday nights. It helped her get through putting on a fake smile for her husband.

She knew what he did on Mondays and Thursdays. But she didn't know with *whom*. The dumb ass had used a credit card to pay for the room one time and he did a poor job of hiding the smell of perfume and sex. He *tried*, dousing himself in Axe body spray as if that in and of itself wasn't a clue as to why he came home late on Mondays and Thursdays.

So the tequila helped with that. She was usually pretty sloshed by the time he got home, making the conversation easier and making it simpler to slide into bed next to him when the lights went out, pretending that everything was just fine.

She sat at the kitchen table, taking several shots as she scrolled through his Facebook profile. She looked for any messages or comments from women she didn't know, anything that might be taken as flirting. But there was nothing incriminating.

It was nine thirty when she realized that if she didn't stop drinking now, she was going to get sick. She capped the tequila and placed it back in the cabinet. As she did, a very light knock came at the door. She found this odd and had she been of a sober mind, she might have been a little more scared rather than just curious.

She walked to the door, half of her heart expecting her husband to be there—maybe with flowers and champagne. Maybe he was going to tell her everything, to come clean and beg for her forgiveness.

She went to the door, trying to be as quiet as she possibly could as to not alert Olivia. Even as Lacy walked to the door, she could hear the light murmuring of whatever pop music garbage her daughter was listening to these days. It came from upstairs like a bored person whispering to themselves.

The knock came again just as she reached the door. She turned on the porch light and looked out through the trio of small square windows at the top of the door. The face she saw was not her husband's but it was a familiar one. Confused as to why she had a visitor so late, she opened the door. She wasn't afraid; she knew her visitor quite well. While he wasn't the nicest guy and, quite frankly, creeped her out at times, she thought he was mostly harmless. Also, being here at this hour, maybe something was wrong...

She opened the door and he stepped forward.

She did not even see the knife. All she saw was him making a hard slashing motion and then her neck felt like it had popped open. She tried to speak, to ask the question *What are you doing?*

But all that came out was blood. So much blood.

She stumbled back, falling to a knee, and then he was on her. And then the knife came down again and again.

Unable to draw breath and feeling the actual rush of blood from her body, Lacy turned her head toward the stairs.

Please God, let him stop with me. Please God ...

And that plea to a God she had never really even believed in was the last coherent thought that raced through her mind as the knife came down again and her blood started to collect in a pool around her on her nicely polished hardwood floor.

CHAPTER TWELVE

One of the things Kate had not shared with her coffee community was the fact that she hadn't slept worth a damn since she had retired from the bureau. She'd originally had issues sleeping after Michael died but that had been more from getting used to having one side of the bed empty than anything else.

But after the bureau, the lack of sleep had come from a series of dreams and nightmares that had nearly made her afraid to sleep. Her doctor had prescribed some natural remedies that had worked for a while but had eventually tapered off. For a while, she'd relied on heavy-duty allergy medicine to knock her out cold, allowing her a peaceful night's rest here and there.

The thing about those sleepless nights, though, was that she could usually tell when they were coming. She'd feel something like a weight on her shoulders as the sun went down, followed by an anxiousness she could nearly touch and taste and feel.

She felt all of those things the night after the court hearing for parole concerning the Mueller case. She'd tried just ignoring it at first because it had been nearly two months since she'd had one of those nightmare-plagued nights. But when she settled down to bed, she knew what was going to happen; she knew what was coming. She could feel it almost like another presence in the room.

She thought about going to the medicine cabinet for a few shots of allergy medicine but decided against it. As stressful as the idea of the oncoming nightmares was, she also knew that they could, on occasion, help her to later analyze and structure her life. Also, as morbid as it may seem, they were usually an excuse to get a glimpse of Michael in something other than the few pictures and videos she had of him.

So she went to sleep, her thoughts chaotic as they were spread across thoughts of Michael, of Julie Hicks, of the Mueller case, of having recently met with Logan and Assistant Director Duran. Despite the knowledge that she would almost certainly be plagued with nightmares before the sun towed in a new day, Kate was able to find sleep almost right away.

And as it turned out, her hunch was dead on.

The dream started in a way it had not before. In it, she saw herself twenty-five years younger, scaling down the side of a small drop-off along the Blue Ridge Mountains. It was nearing noon and it was a gorgeous day. She knew the moment at once, knew that she was going to find the bodies of the newly married Muellers mutilated and gory at the bottom.

Only after Kate's feet descended the last few feet, holding tight to the nylon rope that was anchored about sixty feet above her head, the sun went dark and it was suddenly night. She found herself standing at the bottom of the drop-off. She looked up ahead and did not see the rest of the mountain. What she *did* see, though, was another person scaling down the side of the cliff face.

It was a man, dripping blood as he came. It splattered against the rocks directly beside Kate's foot. When the man got to the bottom, she saw that it was Michael. His face was distorted and bloody, over half of it covered by a black mass. And despite the gory state of him—the condition he had been in when his body had been found in the park—Kate found that she wanted to kiss him.

"It's all a wheel," Michael said. "It goes around and around. You either cling helplessly to it or you fall off and get crushed. A wheel…"

He crumbled to the ground and became dust, billowing out in all directions. And suddenly, Kate's subconscious mind understood that what she was experiencing was much worse than the typical nightmares she'd had in the past. This was something darker, something *deeper*…

She turned around in the direction of where she knew she would find the Muellers. When she had first been on the case, she'd been here with three other agents, a series of police, and a forensics team. But now there was just her, in the dark, knowing there were gruesome bodies somewhere along the dark rocky terrain.

"Hello?" she called into the darkness, not sure who she wanted to answer.

"Kate!"

A familiar voice very much like music came from the darkness ahead. There were looming shapes up there, the jagged edges of trees. Only, it appeared that some of them were moving.

"Who's there?" she asked.

Another figure stepped out of the darkness. A smiling man, waving at her in a way that reminded her of old footage from silent film, a disjointed and almost broken sort of motion.

It was her father. When he smiled at her a wave of panic, terror, and disgust rode up her back. He took a step toward her, his eyes shining white in the darkness. Without hesitation, Kate reached for her sidearm only to find that it wasn't there. She took a step away from him, feeling her heart shrink inside of her chest as, in one dreaming moment, she resorted to her nine-year-old self. She was terrified at the sight of him, of the dark around him, of the—

A hand reached out and grabbed her shoulder from behind.

She wheeled around and there were both of the Muellers, freshly killed with their blood still glistening. The wife's head was bludgeoned, resulting in a crooked and fragmented smile. Her very recent wedding band shone in the moonlight, the last sign of light Kate saw as the darkness closed in on her and swallowed her whole.

She woke up the next morning to start her daily routine. But rather than sliding out of bed right away like she usually did, she lay there for a few minutes, shaking off the cobwebs of last night's nightmare. She had not dreamed of her father in a very long time. Having him show up in her dreams so suddenly felt strangely like an invasion of privacy.

She took a moment as she sat up, looking at the three pictures hanging on her wall. One was of her during her second week as an agent, fresh off of her first arrest. It had been a drug bust, netting nearly one million dollars in cocaine. Her very first partner, a guy named Jimmy Parker, stood in the background with a smile.

That was back before shit got complicated and my career started to form a little history—almost like an urban legend.

She supposed that was why she was so drawn to it—why she wanted to go back so badly. If people were going to view her as a legend of sorts, she had something to live up to. Legends didn't just call it quits and live their days for chats over coffee or reading books on the back porch.

She looked sadly away from the picture of her and Jimmy Parker, fully aware that dwelling on the past could only make things worse.

She usually started her day off with a run through Carytown, or, if her ankles were giving her hell, she'd opt for the small treadmill in the basement. But she didn't feel up to it this morning, every ounce of her drained from the nightmare. When she finally did drag herself out of bed and started banging around in the kitchen for breakfast, she started to wonder why last night's nightmare had been so powerful. Was it perhaps the stress of being asked by a friend to look into the death of her daughter? Was it revisiting a courtroom and having to come face to face with Patrick Ellis again?

She supposed it could be all of those things, all coming to a head and raising up her nightmares again.

But why my father? Kate wondered. *I let that part of my past go a long time ago.*

Just thinking about him as she fried up a few eggs made her feel immature and small. It made her feel that what Michael had said in the nightmare last night had been true. Life is like a wheel that you either cling to or fall from and get crushed. And one way or the other, it just keeps rolling on and on in an infinite loop.

As she sat down at the table with her eggs and a cup of coffee, her cell phone rang. When she saw that it was Debbie Meade, she answered it right away.

"Hey, Debbie," she answered. "How are you doing?"

"As well as anyone could expect, I suppose," Debbie said. "It feels surreal knowing that I can no longer make a phone call and Julie will be there on the other end. I tell you, Kate...I don't know how parents get through this when it's a younger kid—a kid that lives in their home, under their roof..."

Debbie trailed off here, as if distracted. Kate could hear a series of shaky breaths on the other line and decided it would be best to let Debbie take her time to collect her thoughts. She didn't want to seem pushy, even though it was Debbie who had called her and not the other way around.

"Look, Kate, I apologize if this is out of line, but I felt you should know something."

"What is it?"

"There was another murder sometime last night. Another woman, a little older than Julie but pretty close to the same age."

"Do you know where?" Kate asked.

"I do. And that's why I'm calling you. Kate...it was in the same neighborhood. A woman Julie knew pretty well."

"How did you find out?"

"There were police cars everywhere this morning. Clarissa somehow found out first and called to see if I had heard anything. This is...well, it has to be related, right? Same age range, same neighborhood..."

"It would seem that way," Kate admitted.

"Do you think you can get in on it?" Debbie asked. "I know it sounds stupid but knowing that someone I know would actually be looking into it..."

"No, I understand that. It's just...there are protocols in place, you know? The local police aren't exactly eager to hand over information."

"I figured as much," Debbie said. "Well, nonetheless, there you go. You at least have the information now. Do with it what you will."

Debbie attempted to insert a chuckle after this comment but it came out flat. She still sounded infinitely sad and at a loss of how to carry on.

"Thanks, Debbie," she said. "And please...let me know if I can do anything for you."

"I will."

But as they ended the call, the weariness in Debbie's voice made Kate think that she'd do no such thing. For the foreseeable future, Debbie Meade would be wallowing, sitting in the loss and trying to come to terms with it on her own.

And feeling his, Kate felt that she had to at least *try* to see what she could do.

Without any hesitation at all, she picked up her cell phone and placed a call.

Chapter Thirteen

It took three different calls, but Kate eventually got Duran on the phone. She was bounced back and forth between Logan, Duran's receptionist, and then, after ten minutes of waiting, a return call from Duran. She'd expected him to sound a little flustered and maybe annoyed that she was pestering him so soon after his offer of coming in on a part-time basis.

Surprisingly, though, he seemed happy to hear from her. "Look, Wise... I know you miss the work and you loved seeing me the other day, but let's give it some time, okay?"

"Don't flatter yourself," Kate said. "Look, I have a favor to ask. And maybe one that's going to piss you off."

She heard a sigh on his end of the line before he responded. "You already heard about the second murder, I take it?"

"I have," she said. "The mother of the woman that was killed four days ago told me. The location of this new murder and the age range of the women killed can't be a coincidence."

"Right as always," Duran said. "I have a couple of agents working with the State Police on it right now. I expect to have a pair of agents assigned to it by the end of the day. I think it's clear we have a serial on our hands and would love it if we could stop things before anyone else has to die."

"Likewise," Kate said. "Which brings me to my favor. I want you to temporarily reinstate me. Let me in on this one."

"Wise, I can't do that. It would be impractical."

"No, it would be impractical to not at least consider it. I live in the area. And it's not like this is coming out of left field. Two days ago we talked about having me come on as a part-time agent."

"Yes, to spend most of your time riding a desk and working on cold case files. Not to be an active agent out in the field. No offense, Wise but you're fifty-five years old."

"And you're fifty-eight. What the hell does that have to do with anything?"

"We discussed bringing you on for cold cases. This is not a cold case. You aren't trying to get greedy with my offer, are you?"

"No. I'll be honest. This one is right here in my backyard and a friend of mine is involved. So yes, I want it for selfish reasons. There ... .that's my reasoning. Now what's yours for keeping me off of it?"

"You mean except for the fact that you've been out of practice for a year?" he asked.

"That's the best argument you have?" she asked.

She was glad she'd always had a mostly friendly relationship with Duran. She knew some directors who would practically behead their agents for speaking to them in such a way.

"Let me make some calls," Duran said. "I promise nothing, but I'll call you back in about an hour."

He didn't bother with a *goodbye*. He simply ended the call, leaving Kate to wait and wonder. Never one to just sit idly by, Kate finished up her breakfast and left the house. She got into her car and headed east, toward the subdivision of Amber Hills, where the two murders had taken place.

As she expected, there were police cars at all three entrances to the neighborhood. At the third entrance, she tried her luck at getting inside. As she pulled her car into the entrance, driving between two decorative pillars with the name AMBER HILLS emblazoned in gold trim on them, two officers stepped forward. Their cars were parked to the sides of the road, flashers twirling red and blue lights in the morning sun.

She gave the officers a little nod of salutation and entered the community. As she'd expected, there were a few looky-loos walking up and down the street. They were all looking to the south, down the same street Kate was driving down. She rounded a bend and saw several police cruisers parked in front of a two-story house that looked identical to most of the other houses on the street. An ambulance was also on the scene, but pulled to the side and not running; it was obvious that it would not be used for anything urgent.

She passed the scene and came to a T-intersection at the end of the street. She took a left, connecting back to the street that the Hickses lived on. She drove by their house, noticing that there were two cars in the driveway. One of them, she saw, was Debbie's. She wondered if she was currently in her daughter's house, collecting things to remember her by.

Kate made her way back out of Amber Hills and was five minutes back toward her house when her cell phone rang. Duran's name popped up on the display. She let it ring a few times before answering, not wanting to seem too anxious.

"Hello," she said, resisting the urge to answer with: *"This is Agent Wise."*

"Wise, here's the deal," Duran said. "I've had a conference call with the Section Chiefs and we came up with something that's a win-win for everyone involved."

"Sounds promising."

"We are going to grant you a temporary reinstatement," Duran said. "It will last for one month. In the course of that month, we expect you to crack the case down there in Richmond and to get your hands dirty in some of these cold cases I mentioned during your trip to DC. Based on your performance, that temporary reinstatement will be stretched out to a year. After that year, we'd keep you on staff as a consultant. Do you understand?"

"I do," Kate said, already excited about the prospects. She was, of course, hesitant. "How is that a win-win?" she asked. "What are you getting out of this?"

"Well, we'll be testing out something else during this initial month. We want you to work with a partner. This is a new partner, a young woman who quite frankly, has amazing potential. She reminds me of you in many ways."

"Sounds like a recipe for disaster, then," Kate quipped.

"Maybe," Duran said. "But she's not gelling with any partners. We think it might do her some good to work with you. Someone seasoned and with an amazing track record."

"I don't know," she said. "Why can't you just pair me with Logan?"

"Look, this is the stipulation. You either agree to the partner or I can't offer you the reinstatement. That's how it's going to have to go."

She was irritated but as far as Kate was concerned, it wasn't even a choice. If she had to serve as some ambitious young agent's mentor just to get in on this case, so be it. She figured she could have it wrapped in a day or two and then be done with the new agent.

"Agreed," Kate said. "Can you send me some information on this agent?"

"I can send you the basics via email," Duran said. "Do you still have your badge?"

"I do."

"Okay. I'll get your new ID and badge to you as soon as I can. In the meantime, use your old one. If anything arises, you can give local authorities my name and number but I'd really appreciate it if it didn't come to that. And one more thing, Wise."

"What's that?"

"I don't want you active on this case until your partner arrives. When you and I get off of this call, I'm making a call with a few other directors. Your partner will be on the way down to Richmond within a few hours. I know it's hard but I need you to hold off on being active on this until the end of the day. We have several other younger agents that could use this to cut their teeth on … and the last thing I want is to seem like I'm showing favoritism."

He was right. Knowing that she was in but had to wait several hours was like swallowing acid. But she also knew not to buck up against an opportunity like this. She had to be obedient, had to make sure she didn't cross any lines.

"I can do that. Which agent did you decide to go with? Rose or DeMarco?"

"Kristen DeMarco. I'll send you her details in a second. And Kate … I'm excited about this. I think everyone could come out a winner here. Play it right, would you?"

"I'm insulted that you'd assume otherwise."

Duran laughed on the other end of the line, a noise that Kate cut off by ending the call. But honestly, she wanted to laugh, too. Instead, she pushed the ball of excited nervousness she felt deep down into the pit of her stomach and headed back home with her hands itching to dig her old service weapon out of hiding.

Chapter Fourteen

As promised, Duran sent Kate an email less than five minutes after their phone conversation. Kate pored over it when she got back to her house and learned a great deal about her temporary partner. She did her best not to be too impressed but by the time she was done, Kate found that she was looking very forward to working with Kristen DeMarco.

She recalled briefly meeting DeMarco during her meeting with Duran and Nash back in DC. She'd seemed calm, collected and somewhat formal. But based on what she had read in DeMarco's dossier, Kate saw something else—something potentially special. So when the two women met at Amber Hills just after three o'clock that afternoon, Kate had high expectations.

As Kate got out of her car and walked across the street to the generic government sedan parked alongside the curb, she tried to remember DeMarco seeming so small. It would have been hard to judge as she had sat down at the conference room table, but DeMarco looked quite petite. Five foot five at most, and *maybe* one hundred and twenty pounds. Still, Kate knew it was not the appearance that mattered, but the drive and commitment to the job.

According to the records Duran had sent over, Kristen DeMarco had graduated at the top of her class from the University of Oxford, obtaining a Bachelor of Science in Psychology. She then went on to the FBI Training Academy in Quantico where she graduated with honors and absolutely rave reviews and comments from her instructors. She officially joined the FBI just over a year ago, coming in just as Kate had been on her way out. She'd spent most of that time in the Violent Crimes Unit until, without any real reason given, she requested to be released from that unit to work as a field agent not contained within one division.

All of that and DeMarco was only twenty-five. And despite that impressive background, the woman Kate saw stepping out of the bureau sedan looked like she was barely out of college. She was quite pretty, her blonde hair a bit beyond shoulder length. Her svelte shoulders sagged a bit, as if she were uncomfortable. She wore a dark navy blue top and a pair of pants that were somewhere between dress and casual. Her sidearm was not concealed at all, the holstered Glock clearly prominent on her little hip.

"Agent DeMarco," Kate said as the two women met. "Nice to see you again."

DeMarco shook her offered hand and gave her a quick smile. "Same here. It's a pleasure to be working with you. Any questions for me before we head inside?"

"What do you know about the scene?" Kate asked. "All I know is what the State Police offered and they were pretty miserable when they realized I had been given permission to work the case."

"Pretty cut and dried from what I understand," DeMarco said as they started walking toward the Thurmond residence. "The killer seems to have attacked right from the front door with a hard slash across the throat. Came inside and stabbed her at least six more times. Blood everywhere. Her daughter was upstairs the whole time but never knew a thing. The father came home around ten fifteen, screamed when he found the body, and alerted the daughter. That's all I know."

"Same here," Kate said as they walked up the lawn and toward the porch. "Let's see if we can find out some more."

As they made their way up the porch, two local policemen stood in the doorway to block their way. When Kate flashed her badge, the feeling was almost too good to be true. She felt slightly intoxicated for a moment but squashed it down, not wanting to allow it to go to her head. She watched as DeMarco did the same behind her and they then filed into the house.

They had to enter the house basically hugging the foyer wall. The entryway had been blocked off with crime scene tape, making sure no one stepped in the crimson mess that covered most of the foyer. The blood had dried but there was so much of it that it looked wet in some places. It was practically covering the floor. It had also sprayed up on the walls, one splatter reaching to about three feet high.

As Kate moved past the roped off area, another officer came walking out of the adjoining living room. It was Randall Budd. When the Chief saw Kate, he looked a little embarrassed. Rather than scolding her right away, though, he simply took a few more steps toward her with a flare of red in his cheeks.

I guess Duran already contacted him to let him know I'm on the case now, she thought. She was glad this was the case; it saved her an awkward conversation.

"Chief Budd," Kate said. "I'd like you to meet my partner, Kristen DeMarco."

Budd and DeMarco nodded politely to one another, their eyes both falling to the floor where the trail of blood tapered off just before it reached the carpeted area of the living room.

Budd looked back to Kate and gave her an apologetic kind of look. "I got a call from your director, so I know the deal," he said. "I won't get in your way if you can promise the same thing. I understand this is your case now but please extend us the courtesy of wrapping things up on our own terms as we transition it over to you."

"Of course," Kate said. "In the meantime, can you fill us in on what's already been done so we don't do any double work?"

"Well, we've dusted for prints and found nothing. Not on the body, not on the door, not the doorframe, nowhere within the foyer. We had a woman from the Department of Social Services come in to speak with the daughter and she's swearing that she saw nothing, and heard nothing. She had headphones on until she heard her dad screaming his head off when he found the body."

"And where's the father?" Kate asked.

"At the station. As of right now he's the only suspect. He was very confrontational when we started asking him questions. Half an hour in the interrogation room and he tells us that he was having an affair. He was coming home from meeting with the other woman last night. Got home and found his wife dead. The man is wrestling with some intense guilt."

"Does he know about Julie Hicks and how the two deaths might be related?" DeMarco asked.

"Not yet," Budd said. "I wish I had more to offer, but that's all we have. We've only had four officers working the scene, not wanting it to get too crowded. But we've got nothing so far. All we know is what the coroner's report is telling us. Lacy Thurmond was stabbed at least a dozen times, one of which was a particularly deep one straight across the throat. That seems to be the one that killed her. The others looked to be for the killer's pleasure more than anything else."

"Thanks, Chief," Kate said. "Let us know what we can do to help."

With that, Budd took his leave, slinking out of the door like a man who had just been dismissed from a case. Which, Kate figured, he sort of was. The two officers who had tried block the door from Kate and DeMarco filed out after him, leaving the two agents alone in the house.

They both looked down to the blood. Kate found herself also looking *up* at it, trying to judge just how far it had flown.

"Thoughts?" DeMarco asked. She asked in the vein of someone wanting to learn, not someone testing their superior. Not that Kate was her superior but regretfully the age difference made it feel that way to Kate.

"Several," Kate said. "I think the most important question is why Thurmond answered the door. To answer the door at that hour of the night, she would have likely known the killer."

"It could have been unlocked," DeMarco pointed out. "The killer could have simply walked right in."

"The fact that Thurmond was right here in the foyer, by the front door, indicates that she was answering the door. And I'd say all of the blood shows that the killer wasted no time. I doubt he was even invited in. The door opened and he attacked."

"Probably with the deep cut to the throat first," DeMarco pointed out. She then pointed to the walls. "Lying on her back, I don't care what artery you hit, blood isn't going to fly that high. Also, did you notice it was almost as if the killer *tried* to keep the mess in the foyer? There are only a few stray droplets on the living room carpet."

"Which means he's smart," Kate said. "He wanted to keep his chance of leaving any kind of clues or prints to a minimum. No prints on the door or the body also indicates that he was wearing gloves."

"Which means this murder was most likely premeditated."

Kate nodded, enjoying the back and forth. She was warming up to Kristen DeMarco rather quickly. "I'd also assume the husband is innocent. No reason for her husband to knock on the door. And if he admitted to an affair and he was with the mistress last night, it shouldn't be too hard to nail down an alibi."

They walked further into the house, finding it in immaculate order. The only mess to speak of was a pile of wadded up tissues on the coffee table and a little black book, opened up to the Ts. Kate saw the name of a few other Thurmonds and assumed the husband had made a few very difficult phone calls last night to inform family and friends of what had happened.

"Agent Wise, check this out," DeMarco said.

Kate had to admit … it was nice hearing those two words put together again. She walked into the kitchen where DeMarco was reaching into the sink. She pulled up a shot glass.

"It's the only dirty dish in the sink," DeMarco pointed out. She then sniffed it and wrinkled her nose. "Tequila."

"Maybe that's how the husband coped last night," Kate said.

"Or maybe it's how the wife was coping. Maybe she knew about the affair already. Men are typically pretty lazy about covering their tracks, especially if the affair has been an ongoing one."

They left the kitchen and looked around the remainder of the house. After twenty minutes of searching, they found nothing. Kate even checked the garbage just to be sure. In the trashcan in their pantry, she found nothing but discarded Subway litter and more dirty tissues.

"We need to speak to the husband," Kate said. "The daughter, too, if social services will allow it."

"I'll make the call," DeMarco said, already reaching for her phone.

Young, teachable, and super eager, Kate thought as they exited the Thurmond residence. *Yeah, I'm going to get along just fine with her.*

CHAPTER FIFTEEN

Kate was delighted to find that Chief Budd had meant what he said. The moment she and DeMarco got to the station, he stood aside and handed them the reins. There were just a few polite formalities and exchanges between the agents and the State Police before Kate and DeMarco were escorted to the interrogation room where Peter Thurmond was being held.

When they stepped inside, Thurmond looked up at them like a man coming right out of a dream. He looked half asleep and absolutely miserable. The sight of two women he hadn't yet seen since being brought into the station seemed to jar him a bit, though. That jarring became something more when Kate and DeMarco sat down across from him. Kate showed him her ID.

"I'm Agent Wise and this is Agent DeMarco, from the FBI," she said. "We've just come from your house and would like to ask you a few questions."

"Sure," Thurmond said, as if he really didn't care at all. "But I don't know if you can ask anything new that the cops haven't already asked."

"We want to get to the bottom of this as soon as possible, so we hope to be quick," Kate said. "First of all, was there anyone you or your wife knew who might have had any reason to come by your house so late at night?"

"No," Thurmond said. "I've been wondering that same thing myself."

"What about the woman you were seeing?" Kate asked. "Did she have a husband or boyfriend who might want to exact a skewed sort of revenge?"

"No. She's single."

"You're certain?" DeMarco asked skeptically.

"Positive," Thurmond said. "And by the way, I'm calling it off with her when this is all over. Lacy is dead because of the affair. If I would have been at home…"

"How about your daughter?" Kate asked. "Do you know if she had any young boys at school who were interested in her? I ask because the fact that someone murdered your wife but left your daughter untouched seems peculiar."

"None that I know of," Thurmond said. "You really think some teenage kid would be capable of something like this?"

"At this stage, we just have to make sure we're covering every possible base," DeMarco said. "Another thing to consider, Mr. Thurmond, is that the killer striking on that day, at that particular time, suggests that they *knew* you wouldn't be there. Was there anyone else who knew about the affair?"

"No one," Thurmond said. "If anyone, *maybe* the clerk at the motel. We used the same one every time and I think if he was really paying any attention, he might have figured it out."

"We understand that the police are currently holding you as the prime suspect," Kate said. "That's primarily because they can't find anyone else. So here's the deal: you've admitted to the affair. If you name the woman and allow us to contact her, you'll be cleared. All you need is that alibi."

Thurmond nodded, looking to the table between them. "Is there any way to do all of that without my daughter knowing? Without Lacy's parents knowing?"

"We can see to it," Kate said. "Of course, what the woman you've been seeing decides to do with this information is out of our hands."

There was a pen and a pad of paper on the table, presumably from where someone else had been in earlier, taking notes during the interrogations. Thurmond grabbed them both, scribbled down some information, and pushed it over to Kate. He pushed it away as if it were some disgusting, moldy meat. Kate looked it over and found the name of the mistress as well as her cell phone number.

"If the police are having problems with suspects, I think I know where you can start asking some questions," Thurmond said.

"Where might that be?" DeMarco asked.

"There's this tight-knit group of women in Amber Hills. Lacy was part of them. I'm pretty sure Julie Hicks was, too. At the risk of sounding insensitive, they're mostly made up of stay-at-home moms. A few of them aren't even moms ... they're housewives. Nothing wrong with that, of course. But I always thought that whole group felt sort of like a clique. And as ashamed as I am to admit it, I can almost guarantee that they know more about Lacy's personal life than I do."

"So you mean to tell me that Julie Hicks and your wife were friends?" Kate asked.

"I suppose. I mean, they weren't like best friends or anything like that. But they hung in that same circle."

"Do you know the names of any the other women in that group?" DeMarco asked.

Thurmond gave a shaky smile and reached back out for the pad he had just handed to Kate. He took it and wrote on it for several seconds. When he slid it back over to her, he had added four more names.

"There are plenty more, but those are the only ones I know for sure. I figure they might be in danger if this guy is focusing on that group for some reason. And, like I said, they should be able to give you more information on Lacy than I can."

"Thank you," Kate said, getting to her feet.

"Mr. Thurmond, we'll check your alibi," DeMarco said. "Assuming she's cooperative, I don't see why you shouldn't be out of here soon."

Thurmond gave a nod of appreciation but his eyes again went down toward the table. He was more than just beaten and sad. He was ashamed.

Kate gave him a sorrowful look and took up the pad with the information he had given them. Once they were back outside, DeMarco instantly made the call to Thurmond's mistress while Kate sought out Chief Budd to request records on local citizens hoping to get the addresses to line up with the names of the other women Thurmond had given them.

And just like that, Kate was on the hunt again after a year on the sidelines.

CHAPER SIXTEEN

The drive back over to Amber Hills took longer than usual, as Kate and DeMarco hit the grinding stream of five o'clock traffic. People were rushing home from work and ambitious students who participated in after-school activities packed buses that all seemed to stagger traffic.

DeMarco took advantage of the situation, not letting the extended drive time sidetrack them.

"I guess now is as good a time as any to let you know that I did a little schoolgirl somersaults when I was told I was coming down here to partner with you," she said. "And somersaults are not something I do."

"That's much better than running away in terror, I suppose," Kate said.

"No, I mean it. Even when I was still in the academy, I heard stories about you. And then when I started at the Violent Crimes Unit at the bureau, I looked through a lot of your old files for pointers on how to break down a scene. I mean...you were the only one to get *anywhere* on the Paulson murders in 2005. And let's face it...getting out of that hostage situation alive in '89...they should make a movie about that! How many men did you have to kill to get away?"

"Agent DeMarco, that's not a very professional question," Kate said. But really, she didn't mind it. After a year in retirement, she needed the reminder of what she had once been.

What she still *was*.

"Sorry," DeMarco said. "I'm just honored to be working with you."

"That's flattering," Kate said. While she had received lots of praise throughout her career, this was different somehow. With DeMarco sitting right beside her in the car, it was more personal; she couldn't just brush the words of affirmation off with a shrug. "So it seems you already know quite a bit about me. What can you tell me about yourself?"

"Nothing worth noting. Grew up in a small town in Pennsylvania. Wanted out as soon as I could. When I was in tenth grade, one of my best friends was raped, killed, and placed on her front porch afterwards. No one ever found who did it. That made me quickly change my future plans of being a veterinarian, instead wanting to do something in law enforcement."

"Any reason you started out at the bureau with the Violent Crimes Unit?"

"No real reason on my part. It's apparently what I leaned towards in terms of abilities. It seemed like a good fit for a while."

"Do you mind me asking what happened?" Kate asked.

"I'm still not sure. This one case … it sort of just broke something in me. And it wasn't the blood or the gore—and there was a lot of it. It was a triple homicide and suicide. A father killed his wife, his ten-year-old daughter, and his six-year-old son before killing himself. Something at the scene just triggered something in me. You start to wonder just what the hell is wrong with people, you know? And sometimes you think on that for so long that you start to hate all humans. It makes you not want to be around anyone."

Kate did understand it. She'd felt it herself a few times earlier in her career. Sadly, there was no way to bear it other than to outgrow it. "So this case … are you going to be able to handle it?"

She cringed as the question came out. She noted DeMarco's slightly annoyed look, a look the younger agent tried to catch before it showed. But it came through, and Kate took note to choose her words more carefully from here on out.

"Yes," she said. "I don't think I would have been sent out here if that was even a question."

"Sorry," Kate said. "Bad choice of words."

DeMarco simply shrugged and looked out the window as they inched closer toward Amber Hills. Kate remained quiet after her little blunder. If the silence would be broken, she'd wait for DeMarco to do it again. She remembered what it was like to be a younger agent, tasked with working alongside someone more seasoned. You were always overthinking every-thing, even the words you said.

Kate felt for DeMarco, especially given that she had already opened up about such a personal part of her story. She wasn't sure she could have done it. It made her think about the nightmare she'd had last night, her father leering out of the darkness with a dark secret shackled to him, linking him to the darkness.

Kate quickly shook the thought away and focused on the traffic ahead that was, even then, just beginning to unclog.

Kate had arranged to meet with one woman from the circle of friends that Peter Thurmond had mentioned. Yet when they arrived at their destina-tion, she was pleasantly surprised that there were two of them there.

The woman she'd planned to meet was Wendy Hudson. She lived just five houses down the street from Julie Hicks in a stunning two-story house that was one of the newer ones in the neighborhood. When Kate and DeMarco arrived, she answered the door holding a large glass of red wine. She was a striking woman, somewhere in her early to mid-thirties. It was apparent that she spent a lot of time at the gym and the tanning salon.

She led Kate and DeMarco into her dining room, where another woman sat at a large oak table. She also held onto a glass of red wine. And from the way her eyes narrowed and she seemed to make a point of sitting up a little too straight, Kate guessed it was nowhere near her first of the afternoon.

Wendy Hudson sat down next to the other woman and said, "This is Taylor Woodward. She and Lacy were best friends."

"Ever since middle school," Taylor said.

Kate guessed that on any other day, Taylor Woodward was just as pretty as Wendy Hudson. But the loss of her friend had apparently wrecked her. She looked tired, heartbroken, and about one more glass of wine away from being shit-faced drunk.

Kate made her own introductions as she and DeMarco took seats at the table. Kate gave DeMarco a little nod, letting her take the lead.

"We were wondering if there's anyone who might have something against your group of friends," DeMarco said. "We've got a killer not only striking the same neighborhood, but apparently the same circle of friends, too."

"I don't think we have any enemies that would resort to *killing*," Wendy said. "Look...we know how it looks. We're housewives. And I know that a lot of people in the neighborhood look at us like those women that used to be on *Desperate Housewives*. We do all work, but it's either very few hours or just things we do from home. Lacy had her editing gigs. She made about two grand a month. But still...most of her time was free and we all spent it together."

"What sort of things did you do together?" DeMarco asked.

"Nothing exciting," Taylor slurred. "Shopping. Julie, Lacy, and myself sometimes go to the pool just to lounge around. And, even though I'm married, I honestly just like the attention from the few dads that end up having to take their kids."

Yeah, she's well on her way to being drunk, Kate thought.

"You mentioned some of you having jobs with minuscule hours," Kate said. "What other jobs besides Lacy's editing job are we talking about?"

"Well, Julie worked some part-time hours at this clean eating place," Wendy said. "Making smoothies and stuff. Maybe twelve hours a week."

"And did she work with anyone that she ever crossed?" DeMarco asked.

"Not that I know of," Wendy said.

"But you know," Taylor said, "Lacy used to work for a small marketing firm. She was one of the supervisors. One of the reasons she quit was because she said it was a toxic work environment."

"How long ago was this?" Kate asked.

"A year and a half, maybe," Taylor said. She followed this with a large gulp of her wine, her eyes wandering as if she was calculating the passage of time in her head.

"What was so toxic about it?" DeMarco asked.

Taylor shrugged, looking blankly into her glass of wine. Wendy frowned at her friend and then looked at the agents. "She never went into great detail about it, but there was a man there that apparently had issues with taking orders from a woman that was much younger than him. He called her names, started rumors about her, even one that claimed she had sex with him in the bathroom at work."

"And that's why she quit?"

"No, she quit because when she tried to fire him, the owner of the company sided with the man. When she left, she went to the media. No one really believed the story, though. The owner was a well-respected guy."

"Did she ever have contact with the man or the owner afterwards?" DeMarco asked.

"Not directly," Wendy said.

"But the asshole sent her dick pics a few times in the weeks after she left. Told her if he ever saw her again, he'd make the sex-in-the-bathroom thing much more than a rumor whether she liked it or not."

"And her husband never did anything about this?" DeMarco asked.

"No," Taylor said with a vicious laugh. "He was too busy fucking college girls on the side to care."

"Any chance you know the name of this man?" Kate asked.

"Daniel Seal," Taylor said, spitting the name out like venom.

"She's right," Wendy said, as if making sure the agents took the tip seriously despite the fact that Taylor was heavily inebriated. "He'd be a good one to check out. He actually used to go to the very same pool that Taylor mentioned earlier. Sort of a skeevy guy. Made no attempt to hide the fact that he was checking women out."

Kate glanced over toward DeMarco, every bit as pretty as the two younger women sitting at the table. If they were right about this guy, she couldn't wait to see how DeMarco handled him.

It made her think, however briefly, of tossing Brian Neilbolt off of his porch. With a thin smile, she looked at DeMarco and just like that, the tension that they'd felt in the car for a moment was obliterated and they were on the same page without speaking a single word between them.

CHAPTER SEVENTEEN

Kate had forgotten how spoiled the convenience of having the bureau's resources at her fingertips could make her feel. With just a single phone call, she was able to get the address and criminal record for Daniel Seal within ten minutes. He lived downtown, a trip that took about twenty minutes now that the afternoon rush had cleared off of the highways. Daniel Seal lived on a row of townhouses in a well-to-do neighborhood, everything standing at an equal height, and even the cars parked perfectly in front of the buildings.

As it turned out, they arrived just in time. As Kate and DeMarco were walking toward Seal's townhouse, he came out of the front door. He was dressed in a pair of gym shorts and a dry-fit T-shirt. He carried a small gym bag in his left hand, the handle of a racquetball racquet sticking out of the zipper.

"Excuse me," Kate said as they approached him. "Are you Daniel Seal?"

He looked both women up and down, saw the way they were dressed and the serious looks on their faces, and grew confused. "I am," he said. "Who's asking?"

"Agent Kate Wise, FBI," Kate said, flashing her ID and again relishing the familiar feel of the motion. "This is my partner, Agent DeMarco. We were hoping to ask you a few questions."

"Concerning what, exactly?" Daniel asked.

"About Lacy Thurmond," Kate said.

"Ah Jesus, this again? Is she going to ever let the past go? Look, I've talked to cops and lawyers and all sort of people about the little tiff we had at work a while back and—"

"Let me stop you right there before you put your foot in your mouth," Kate said. "We're here to ask you about your working relationship with her because she was killed last night. In her home, while her daughter was there."

The shock on his face was not of an emotional source, but of a stutter in his thoughts. He'd been so flustered about his past with her that the idea of her being murdered seemed to freeze his brain for a moment.

"She was killed?" he asked.

"Yes," DeMarco said. "And from what we've been able to gather, you had something of a toxic relationship with her."

"Yeah, like almost two years ago," Seal said. "You think because of all of that I killed her? You actually think I'm a suspect?"

"That's what we'd like to talk to you about," Kate said.

Daniel Seal vehemently shook his head. "No. Look, I'm sorry she was killed. Really, I am ... she was good enough at heart, I guess. A bit of a bitch when she wanted to throw her power around as a supervisor, but a good enough person. But no ... I'm not getting dragged into this. I'm not a killer. That's ridiculous."

He started to step away from them, heading in a diagonal direction across the parking lot. Kate went to step in front of him to block his way but DeMarco was already there. She moved quick, so fast yet casual that Kate barely even saw her do it.

"Where were you last night between nine and eleven?" DeMarco asked.

"At a concert," he said. "At the National. Jason Isbell was playing."

"You have proof of this?" Kate asked.

Seal was getting frustrated and doing very little to hide it. He dropped his gym bag on the sidewalk and pulled out his cell phone. He scrolled through some of his photos until he came to a video. He pressed Play and showed it to them. The video was a shaky hand-shot video of a concert. The audience was more audible than Jason Isbell, though.

"Still got the ticket stubs on my dresser if you need to see them," he said as he stopped the video and shoved his cell phone back into the bag.

"That won't be necessary," Kate said. She honestly hadn't expected Daniel Seal to be the killer anyway but to have it proven in such a concrete way so quickly was aggravating.

"We may call you later if her work history comes into question during the investigation," DeMarco added.

Furious, Seal picked up his bag and headed in the direction he had originally been walking. Kate watched him get into his car and slam the door. He hesitated for a while before cranking the car, perhaps letting the reality of what had just happened to him sink in.

"He seemed genuinely shocked," DeMarco said.

"Yeah, he did."

"That was enough for me to know it wasn't him. It's hard to fake that sort of shock. He's emotionally trying to hide the shock with being pissed at us."

Kate couldn't help but smirk. DeMarco knew her stuff, that was for sure. She probably also knew that a solid tell when speaking to a killer was that there was usually a split second of recognition and pride in a killer's face when confronted about their murders. Kate had seen not a single flicker of that from Daniel Seal.

"You a night owl, Agent DeMarco?" Kate asked.

"I happen to do my best thinking after the sun goes down."

"Same here," Kate said.

This was true, but it had been a while since she'd stayed up past eleven at night. On the few occasions she had in the last few months, it had been out of fear of having one of her nightmares.

"What are you thinking?" DeMarco asked.

"I'm thinking I'll buy the first round of coffee on the way to speak to the coroner."

"You think the police missed something?"

"Probably not," Kate said. "But I do know that even when dead, people can tell stories. Sometimes it's just harder to hear them talking. You have to really look hard to see what they're trying to tell you."

DeMarco smiled at the thought. Again, nothing verbal was exchanged between them as they headed back for their car with the night wide open ahead of them.

CHAPTER EIGHTEEN

Kate kept her word and paid for the first round of coffee just after seven thirty that evening. After visiting a drive-thru Starbucks, they headed for the morgue. This time it was Kate who made sure none of their time was passed in awkward silences. But instead of trying to pry more life details from DeMarco, she focused on the case at hand. She'd always relied on partners as a sounding board—a social way to think out loud and get real-time constructive feedback.

"After the coroner, I want to go back to the house. The killer was there at night. He knocked on the door when it was dark. I wonder if he just walked right up to the door."

"With the Julie Hicks case, there was evidence that the security panel outside had been tampered with. Someone poured water on it from what they could tell."

"I read that, too," Kate said. "So if it's the same killer, that fact shows that he knew the house well. It also meant he was in the yard. He was bold. It was like he knew the property well."

"Maybe he does," DeMarco offered. "Maybe he's even a local to the neighborhood. Maybe he lives in Amber Hills and just had enough of the stay-at-home mom clique. There was this case I worked my second year on the Violent Crimes Unit about this guy who raped three women that all belonged to the same pool. The guy had no connection to them; he worked for the snack company that filled the vending machines at the pool. When we busted him, he said he did it because he couldn't stand seeing them flaunt themselves around the pool. Said it drove him crazy and he just couldn't stop himself."

"It's a good direction to think down but seems like a bit of stretch at first glance," Kate said. "I'm leaning towards the train of thought that it's a killer who has chosen that particular neighborhood for some reason. *Maybe* for the same sort of reason your rapist did."

They spit-balled ideas back and forth for the next twenty minutes as Kate drove to the morgue. When they got there, Kate was not at all surprised to find that the effort put into Lacy Thurmond had been minimal. After all, the cut to the throat made the cause of death fairly clear.

Still, the coroner was more than willing to speak with them. He was a tall, lean man named Smith. The sort of gaunt figure you'd almost expect to work in a morgue or a funeral home. He took them to the body, laid out and prepared for the makeup artist to come in the following day to prep Lacy Thurmond for her funeral. The work to her throat was exceptional, though Kate imagined she'd need to be dressed in something with a high neck to truly cover it up.

"Any other findings at all?" Kate asked.

"Nothing," Smith said. "No bruising, not even any sign of a forceful shove. No sexual abuse, nothing."

"Any way to tell which stab wound came first?" Kate asked.

"I'm almost positive the cut to the neck came first," he answered. "It makes the most sense logistically."

Kate nodded, figuring that he was right. None of the other stab wounds would have incapacitated Lacy. One stab and she would have run. But one like that to the throat and you were basically done for right away.

"And do you recall the body of Julie Hicks from a few days ago?" Kate asked.

"Yes. Same thing there. A bunch of stab wounds, one directly to the heart. But no signs of an obvious struggle. There's a very good chance the same knife was used based on the shape and length of the entry points."

"Do you think we could see a copy of the report, including images of the wounds?"

"Absolutely," Smith said. "Physical or email?"

"Email is fine," Kate said. "We need to get going. But thank you for your time."

Smith nodded and covered Lacy Thurmond's body back up. Kate and DeMarco headed out of the examination room, walking down the hallway for the lobby.

"Tell me," Kate said. "How often have you made yourself wear the Violent Crimes hat ever since you left that department?"

"Once or twice," DeMarco answered.

"I'd like for you to dig it up and try to figure out why a man would kill two women of a similar age, similar body type, in the same neighborhood. No apparent sexual lure, no known history with the victims. Can you do that?"

"I've been trying ever since my drive from DC to Richmond," DeMarco said. "And that's just the thing ..."

"What?" Kate asked.

"It doesn't make any sense."

Kate parked in front of the Thurmond home half an hour later. She'd learned through updated reports that the husband was still at the precinct, cleared of his charges but unwilling to return home. And who could blame him, really?

As Kate and DeMarco approached the house, it had the feel of a haunted house. It was quiet, eerie, its windows like eyes leering at anyone who passed by. Before entering the house, though, Kate and DeMarco made a circuit around the outside perimeter. It was, Kate assumed, the very same way the killer had seen it before knocking on the door.

As she had suspected, there was no sign of forced entry. In fact, the yard was meticulously cared for, right down to the perfect shapes of the shrubs around the back patio. As they made their way back around to the front, she tried to see the house through the eyes of not just a killer but perhaps someone who could not afford to live in such a neighborhood. It was certainly an upper-class neighborhood, but not an exclusive one. Kate felt certain that if she were to check the property values, the average price of a home in Amber Hills would be around half a million.

This train of thought at least made *some* sense. Jealousy, after all, could drive men to do some pretty extreme things.

They entered the Thurmond house for the second time that day. The blood had not yet been cleaned, having set into the floor almost like paint. There'd be no cleaning it out now; it would simply have to be replaced.

"What kinds of things are we looking for this time around?" DeMarco asked.

It made Kate feel even more comfortable with her to know that not only was she open to learning, but she was humble enough to ask questions. Most new agents would avoid asking questions at all costs, just to make it appear as if they had everything together.

"Well, if we can't find motive among the victim or the crime itself, I'm hoping to find some clues within the house. The police have already ascertained that nothing was broken or stolen from what they could tell. The husband will come in later to confirm this. But at a scene as cut and dried as this one, I like to try to see the place through the eyes of someone who came here with the intent of killing."

"You thinking maybe the hot-wife suburban lifestyle might be the motive?" DeMarco asked.

Kate *had* been thinking this but did not feel it with any certainty just yet. Still, she couldn't help but think that if Lacy Thurmond had known the man well enough to answer the door for him at such a late hour, she'd apparently known him fairly well. And maybe that meant he had been inside their house before. Maybe he even had a look around when he was inside after killing her—bypassing the daughter's room.

Thinking of the daughter, Kate looked back to DeMarco as they headed up the stairs to the second floor. "Do you mind placing a call to the Department of Social Services to see where the daughter is? Might do some good to speak with her."

"Sure," DeMarco said. The expression on her face made it clear that she did not appreciate the busy work but she was as diligent as ever, pulling the phone out right away.

As she started making the information request on the phone, Kate checked the first room she came to on the second floor. It was obviously the daughter's bedroom; it was apparent by the clothes crumpled on the floor, the selection of girl-targeted paperbacks on the small bookshelf, and the set of cheering pompoms thrown up on the desk. It wasn't a messy room per se but it was disorganized enough to make it next to impossible to tell if there had been any kind of a struggle. There was no reason to assume this, though, as the daughter had not been pursued at all.

Kate zoomed in on a picture sitting on the desk among schoolbooks and craft stuff. It was a picture of Lacy Thurmond and a pre-teen girl Kate assumed to be the daughter. They were standing on a pier by a lake and looked genuinely happy. Kate started to wonder what kind of mother Lacy had been. If this picture was any indication, the two had been close.

DeMarco stepped into the room from behind. "Just spoke with DSS," she said. "They say the daughter is being transported to her grandparents' in Greensboro, North Carolina. They're asking for at least twenty-four hours before anyone speaks with her."

"That's understandable," Kate said. And honestly, she wasn't sure they even needed to speak with the daughter. She believed everything the husband was saying and part of his story was that their daughter had been in her room the entire time. According to the daughter, she'd seen and heard nothing.

The two agents scoured the house for another twenty minutes. Meeting up back in the foyer where the bloodstains remained, they both wore disappointed expressions. There had been nothing of note, not even something that could be considered a *possible* clue.

They left the Thurmond residence, Kate noting the presence of a patrol car parked across the street. It was good strategy, the local PD apparently hoping the killer might come walking by as a way to relive the moment. She wondered if there was another patrol car parked across from the Hicks residence.

"Want to meet for coffee in the morning?" DeMarco asked as they got into the car. "Maybe revisit everything with fresh minds and a good night's sleep?"

Kate honestly hated to call it a night. She had at least a few more good hours in her but she also knew that DeMarco was right. They had no leads and no matter how hard they looked, they likely wouldn't. It made Kate wonder if maybe they *should* speak to the daughter. Maybe she'd know of a family friend they had somehow overlooked. Or maybe she'd even know some sort of secret about her mother that she'd helped to keep hidden.

"Sounds like a plan," Kate said.

As they pulled away, she thought about Debbie Meade, wondering how she was coping with the loss of her daughter. As she thought of her, some kind of mental alarm went off in the back of her head, some indication that she may have missed something somewhere. She dug at the notion for a moment but nothing came to her. Maybe, like DeMarco said, a night's rest would help her uncover it in the morning.

Kate drove out of Amber Hills, the case gnawing at her. She took note of the patrol car parked out of plain sight behind the large stone sign reading AMBER HILLS. One thing was for sure: if the killer did choose to strike in Amber Hills again, he'd be trapped with so many cops around. And even if Kate wasn't there for the arrest, that was fine. Something about this case seemed more dangerous than usual. And although it was technically her first case since unofficially being asked back into the bureau, she'd be perfectly fine if someone else wrapped it up before she did.

CHAPTER NINETEEN

The moment she took her shoes off back at home, Kate realized just how tired she truly was. She'd been running full tilt today and most of yesterday as well. It had been a while since she'd asked that much energy of her body and now, as a result, she was beginning to crash. She went directly to the shower and spent most of her time under the water simply soaking in the heat. She'd prided herself with staying in shape for the last year but had apparently not done as good as she thought she had. She was sore, she was tired, and the case was beginning to taunt her.

As soon as she toweled off and slipped into a shirt and a pair of jogging pants, she sat down at the kitchen table. While she was certainly exhausted, she knew she would not be able to sleep with the case nagging at her like this. And now, more than ever, she felt that she had to get results. She had to knock this one out of the park if she wanted to have another few years at the bureau. If that was a flop, the men who had been working with Duran on this experimental project would likely pull the plug. She might even lose her chance to work on some cold case files as Duran had promised.

She looked over the case files as midnight approached. The only thing she knew for sure was that neither of the murders had been a result of love or passion. Even if there were affairs involved, killers in that situation usually made it known why they were doing the killing. But this guy was striking quickly and leaving right away. It was almost like he was playing some terrible mortal prank on the victims.

All in the same neighborhood, she thought. *All very pretty women. Victim Number One had no kids. Victim Number Two had one daughter, twelve years old.*

Both victims married. Victim Number One had a husband who traveled a lot for work. Number Two had a husband who was actively cheating on her.

That's when Kate's mind turned back to the little alarm that had been blaring at her while leaving the Thurmond residence. She had been thinking about Debbie Meade, wondering how she was getting along after Julie's funeral. There was something Debbie had said to her not too long ago, something she had shared with Kate and the other ladies during one of their little coffee get-togethers...

The ringing of her cell phone interrupted her. It actually made her jump a bit. Given the late hour, she was expecting the call to be from DeMarco or even Duran. She'd missed the days of randomly receiving calls about a case in the early morning hours and wondered if anyone every *really* got used to it.

But neither of their names was on her caller display. Instead, it was a name that made her heart feel like it had dropped into her stomach.

Melissa.

Oh God, she thought, thinking of that perfectly round baby-stomach her daughter had been sporting the last time they'd seen one another. She answered it quickly. Melissa was not due for another five weeks, making Kate think that this call was going to be of the bad news variety.

"Lissa?" she asked. "What's wr—"

"Mom, I'm on the way to the hospital."

Lissa's voice was thin and worried—the exact opposite of how she usually sounded. Kate had not heard her daughter this scared in a very long time. It broke her heart. It also sent a flare of panic through her.

"What's wrong?" Kate asked.

"My water broke. I'm having contractions and I feel sick to my stomach. There's...there's some blood, too."

"How far are you from the hospital?"

"Terry's driving...a little too fast for my taste," Melissa said, raising her voice at the end to maybe give her husband, Terry, a clue. "But we're about ten minutes away. Mom...I'm not due for another five weeks. Is this...am I going to be okay?"

"Five weeks isn't too terrible," Kate said, not absolutely sure if this was truthful or not. "It's not ideal but it should be fine."

"Will you come?" Melissa asked.

"Of course," she said, biting back her tears so Melissa wouldn't hear them and get even more worked up. "I'll be there as soon as I can. Can I bring you anything?"

"No," Melissa said, her voice sharp and hitched. It made Kate think she might be going through another contraction in that very moment. "Just you. Thanks, Mom."

Kate opened her mouth to tell Melissa to be as calm as she could but Melissa ended the call. Kate sat there for a few seconds, looking at the phone. Her heart resumed its position in her chest and she could not dent the absolute joy that flushed through her.

It was really happening. It was happening five weeks earlier than expected, but she was going to be a grandmother. Sure, there were a few jokes about age that passed through her mind, especially with the case files in front of her, but she didn't care.

All she could think about in that moment was her daughter and the new life she was about to bring into the world. Smiling from ear to ear, Kate swept up all of the case files into a single pile, leaving them on her bed, and then ran for her shoes by the front door.

After getting information from the front desk, Kate took the elevator up to the mother-baby section of the hospital. She went to the nurses' desk, hoping to find which room Melissa had been admitted to. Maybe she'd get to see her before things got underway. She had no illusions about being in the room for the birth; that was a duty Melissa would give Terry—a duty Kate would gladly forfeit.

Yet as she reached the nurses' station, she heard rapid footfalls coming from down the hallway behind her. She turned and saw Terry approaching. He looked frazzled, at his wits' end. It made him look haunted because Terry Andrews always looked so confident and well put-together.

"Terry ..."

"Mrs. Wise," he said, once again ignoring her order to call her Kate. "It's bad. They think it's bad. She's ..."

"Terry, slow down," she said, feeling her own spikes of fear starting to sting.

"Something's wrong," Terry said, tears brimming in his eyes. "They don't know what yet. But they just took her back for an emergency C-section. Her water broke at home but we didn't see until we got here ..."

"See what?" Kate asked.

"How much blood there was. She kept telling me something was wrong and I just didn't want to believe it."

Kate knew she'd have to be the strong one here. She had never seen Terry so shaken up. And God only knew what it would do to Melissa to see him in this state. So swallowing her own fears, Kate took Terry's hands and looked him in the eyes.

"You got her here safe and sound," she told him. "You did your job and you did it every well as far as I can tell. Now the rest is up to the doctors. Let's you and I go sit in the waiting room and let them work, okay?"

He nodded, still looking her in the eyes. And although he seemed calmer, he still would not budge until Kate pulled at his hands and led him into the waiting room. It wasn't until her face was turned away from him that Kate allowed a few of her own tears of fear and worry to spill down her face.

CHAPTER TWENTY

At 2:02 a.m., Michelle Elizabeth Andrews was born. She had a low birth weight and there was a scary moment of touch and go where the doctors thought they might lose her. But about half an hour after she had been removed from Melissa, she seemed to level out. And while she'd likely remain in the hospital for at least a week or so to make sure she was completely out of the woods, everything indicated that she was going to end up leaving the hospital as a healthy—albeit underweight—little baby girl.

Kate, Terry, and Terry's parents were all informed of this as they sat in a collected group within the waiting room at 2:55. The news did Kate's heart a world of good but her own thoughts instantly went to Melissa and her recovery.

"I'd like to see my daughter as soon as possible," Kate said.

"You can see her now if you like," the doctor said. "In fact, she's been asking for you. She's still a little woozy from the drugs, but you can see her if you like."

Kate wept the entire way down the hall. She'd spent the last two hours or so not knowing if there was something wrong with the baby, Melissa, or both. And now that she knew that both were fine *and* that she was a grandmother, she was overcome with a joy like she had only ever felt when Melissa was born. She tried to have her face wiped off and her emotions together when she stepped into Melissa's room but was pretty sure she'd done a terrible job.

Melissa was lying in bed, her head turning toward the door as it opened. She smiled at Kate and Kate returned it. Melissa looked beyond tired, incredibly frail, and almost unlike herself.

"Mom..."

Kate went to her, took her hand, and kissed her on the forehead. "You did so well," Kate said.

"Have you seen her yet?" Melissa asked.

"Not yet. The doctors say we need to wait a moment. It's driving Terry absolutely nuts. Speaking of which, I need to get out of here soon so he can see you. He's worried about you."

"I know. And I hope he understands, but I needed to see you first. I just kept thinking about Dad and how happy he'd be ... and Jesus, I miss him so much, Mom."

"I do, too. But he'd be so proud of you. For surviving this ordeal *and* for giving him a granddaughter."

Melissa smiled. "I bet he would," she said. "I love you, Mom."

"I love you, too. Now ... I can see by your eyes that you're fading ..."

"Sure am," Melissa said with a crooked little grin. It looked like she was drunk.

"So I'm going to tell Terry to come in now. But I won't go anywhere until you're of a completely sound mine. After all ... I'm going to need to hold that baby."

Melissa nodded and gave Kate's hand a squeeze. It was hard for Kate to let go but she knew she had to. She had always been good about stepping back to let her daughter live her life, never interfering in the marriage in any way. This was the hardest moment in that vein she'd ever lived through, but she made herself leave the room.

Terry was already at the door, stomping like a bull to get in. Kate nodded to him and he went in practically in a run.

Kate stood there for a moment, frozen in the hallway of a hospital at 3:05 in the morning, feeling her life change all around her.

I'm a grandmother, she thought with a smile. *A grandmother who just resumed a career with the FBI at fifty-five years of age.*

She had to bite her lip to keep the childlike laugh from bursting forth from her lips. Maybe if it wasn't three in the morning the thought would not have seemed so funny. But as it was, the thought pushed her back down the hallway in search of coffee, ready to face this new chapter in her life.

❧ ❧ ❧

Kate dozed uncomfortably in a chair in the waiting room for a while, the coffee not doing its job. The only reason she woke up was because her phone buzzed at her. When she jerked awake in the chair, she saw that it somehow came to be 4:15 in the morning. She also saw that the buzzing of her phone was a text from Logan.

She grinned sleepily, remembering how he'd always been a night owl. She wondered if he suspected her phone was always on silent after a certain time or if he was purposefully trying to keep her on her toes now that she was back.

Just checking in, the text read. *Hope all is going well. Let me know if you need anything.*

She rubbed at her eyes and stood up from the chair. She saw Terry's parents on the other side of the waiting room. His mother was hunched over asleep in her chair while his father was reading something on his Kindle. Terry, however, was nowhere to be seen.

She walked over to Terry's parents. Mr. Andrews looked up from his Kindle and smiled sleepily at her.

"I was going to wake you," he said, "but didn't want to be premature. The doctors came about ten minutes ago. They've given Terry the clear to see his baby. He's going to come out and let us know when—or *if*, I guess I should say—we can."

"Thanks," Kate said.

"Feel weird to be a grandparent yet?" he asked.

"I honestly don't really even know. Maybe when I hold her..."

"Same here," he said. "Terry's sister has been pregnant twice but miscarried both times. So this is a very bittersweet moment. I feel like we've technically already been grandparents."

"And how did it feel?" Kate asked.

"Pretty amazing," Mr. Andrews said.

Again, Kate felt alarms in the back of her mind. Something he'd said reminded her of Debbie Meade again ... and just like that, she knew she'd need to speak with Debbie as soon as she could.

She nearly headed for her chair, to get her phone and send a text to DeMarco. But just as she turned that way, she caught sight of Terry coming around the corner. He no longer looked tired and worried; he now looked proud and borderline euphoric.

"You guys want to see your granddaughter?"

Kate absolutely *did* want to see her granddaughter. She also wanted to get an update on Melissa.

So while the case was very much still front and center in her mind, the part of Kate that had retired gladly pushed her forward, her hands eager to hold her granddaughter for the first time.

CHAPTER TWENTY ONE

What the coffee had failed to do in terms of perking Kate up, holding her granddaughter for the first time had accomplished. Aside from her own child—Melissa, now twenty-six and very much her own woman—Kate had never been a "baby person." In fact, the idea of being around them scared her a bit.

But holding Michelle had seemed to open something within her while also closing a beautiful circle that had opened up when she'd given birth to Melissa twenty-six years ago. It was like seeing a ghost and welcoming it into her arms. She knew this was not Melissa in her arms but the feeling of it was the same. She had not expected such an emotional reaction from holding her first grandchild but in that moment, everything within Kate softened and gave itself over to the child.

She'd left the hospital at 7:15 with only two hours of sleep but with an energy like she'd never quite experienced before. The knowledge that she'd promised Melissa she'd be back that afternoon pushed her on. Melissa had fully understood, excited to hear that her mother had gotten involved in bureau work again despite her retirement.

She texted DeMarco, letting her know of everything that had happened the night before. She explained that it might be a very scattered day but she *did* have one idea to pursue.

After placing the text, she then placed a call to Debbie Meade. She hated to do it because, in her opinion, not enough time had passed since Julie's death for Debbie to get involved with the case in any way, but because Debbie kept coming to her mind, Kate thought it would be okay.

Debbie certainly seemed to be okay with the idea of meeting with her—not at a coffee shop like usual, though. She wasn't at all ready to go out in public as she was susceptible to sudden bouts of weeping that hit her out of nowhere. Instead, Debbie had invited her to her house for coffee. Kate agreed, volunteering to pick up donuts on the way.

When Debbie answered the door at eight o'clock, she looked awake and almost happy to see Kate. The house smelled of recently delivered flowers in the wake of Julie's death and freshly brewed coffee. Debbie led her into the kitchen, where they sat at the bar. Debbie poured them both generous cups of coffee and for a moment, it was almost like simply visiting a friend.

"Debbie, I wanted to speak with you outside of the group," she said. "A while back, you shared something with us. Something personal ... about an affair. I hate to ask you to go there so soon after everything that's happened but quite frankly, I don't know where else to go."

"You mean *my* affair?" Debbie asked, shame crossing her face.

"Yes. And if you don't feel it's appropriate ..."

"No, it's fine," Debbie said. "I've told Jim about it and we worked through it. And really, I don't even know that I'd call it an affair. It was two times and then I called it off."

"Does the guy live around here?" Kate asked.

Debbie shook her head, sipping from her coffee and looking to the bar; her embarrassment made it hard to look Kate in the eyes. "He was in town on business. I met him when he came to where I worked. He was selling some kind of new insurance for the employees. But Kate ... I don't see what this has to do with anything."

"Maybe nothing," Kate said. "But it has come out—and please keep this between you and me—that Lacy's husband was having an affair. He admitted to it. And ... well, I find it hard to see how a woman like Lacy, who spent most of her time at home, wouldn't be aware of it."

Debbie gave a guilty grin. "There were rumors that Lacy was having her own fun on the side," she said. "I assume you're asking me about my own affair to get into the mindset of someone that could have one?"

"More or less," Kate said. "Plus, you and Clarissa seem to have a better handle on the news that goes around smaller circles. I didn't know if maybe you'd heard something."

"Well, I can basically guarantee you that Lacy knew about Peter's affair. Everyone else did. He did a shitty job of hiding it. And if Lacy knew and kept it quiet... well, I for one assumed that meant the rumors I'd heard about her were true."

"That she was having an affair," Kate said thoughtfully. "Any idea who it might have been with?"

"No. And Kate, I see where this is headed. I know what your next question is going to be, so I can go ahead and cut you off right there. Julie was not having an affair. She loved Tyler very much. When he was away on business, she usually spent most of her time here with me or with that little circle of friends she had."

Maybe, Kate thought. *But you just said yourself that Lacy, a member of that group, was likely involved in an affair. And that she hid it relatively well.*

"You understand that I have to at least check, though, right?" Kate asked.

"Absolutely."

Kate took another sip from her coffee and stood up from the bar. "Thanks for your time, Debbie. And thanks for understanding when I had to ask the hard questions."

"Hey, I asked for your help," Debbie said. "I appreciate you sticking with it."

Debbie walked her to the front door and they hugged briefly. Kate had never really had any friends outside of the bureau so to know that she and Debbie were still developing a closeness between them was nice.

Walking back to her car, Kate pulled out her cell phone. While she believed Debbie that Julie had not been involved in an affair, she thought there might still be something to the thread of unfaithfulness, something that would drive someone to kill these two women in such an uncaring and almost casual way.

She pulled up DeMarco's name and sent a text. *The name Peter Thurmond gave us is next on the list. The mistress. Let's pay her a visit. Meet me in half an hour?*

She got a response before she was even in her car. She smiled and read the message, glad to have a partner who was as prompt and motivated as she was. Logan, while an amazing agent, had not been the best at returning calls and texts. Having someone so responsive by her side was a breath of fresh air.

Can do, the response read. *Meet me at my motel?*

DeMarco provided the address and Kate wasted no time. It was only 8:20 in the morning. If things continued to progress this quickly for the remainder of the day, she'd be back at the hospital with her granddaughter in her arms by lunchtime.

CHAPTER TWENTY TWO

The name that Peter Thurmond had scrawled on a sheet of notepad paper in the interrogation room the day before was Crystal Bryant. He'd also provided a number, which Kate didn't bother using. She knew if she gave the woman time to prepare, she could come up with lies and stories that could waste their time. She'd rather catch her off guard—a sneaky and almost dishonest tactic considering that Crystal Bryant was not involved in the case.

Ever diligent, DeMarco had already called in for Bryant's address and other pertinent information. Part of that information was discovering that she worked as a nurse at a physical rehabilitation facility from 8:30 to 5:00 Monday through Friday. This knowledge allowed them to skip a home visit and head directly to her place of business.

The office was located at one of the city's busiest hospitals and the waiting room was packed. Kate didn't see the point in singling Crystal Bryant out, so she stayed as nondescript as possible. When she and DeMarco approached the receptionist window, they kept their badges and IDs hidden. When she spoke to the receptionist, Kate kept her voice soft.

"I need to speak with one of your nurses," Kate said. "Crystal Bryant."

The receptionist looked a little confused, looking back and forth between Kate and DeMarco. "Okay ... do you have an appointment?"

"We don't," Kate said. "It's a private matter and rather urgent."

"Okay. Can I ask who's looking for her?"

"No. Again ... it's private."

Clearly unhappy with that response, the receptionist got up anyway. She walked away from the desk and disappeared down a hallway on the other side of the glass. Kate and DeMarco stood there for a few moments until one of the doors in the waiting room opened up. A pretty blonde woman of perhaps twenty-five years of age came walking toward them. She was dressed in nearly pressed nurse scrubs and looked very confused.

"Are you the women looking for me?" she asked.

"Yes," Kate said quietly. "I'm Agent Wise and this is my partner, Agent DeMarco, with the FBI. We'd like to ask you some questions about the Thurmonds."

Crystal Bryant looked as if someone had slapped her across the face. She looked all around, even back into the waiting room, as if to see if anyone had overheard Kate.

"It won't take long," Kate said. "And if you cooperate by answering just a few questions, it can be done without anyone knowing who we are or why we're here. So can we speak with you for a few moments?"

"Sure," Crystal said, obviously taken off guard.

They found three chairs in the far corner of the waiting room and settled down. Before Kate could even start asking questions, Crystal was talking.

"I guess Lacy's death made Peter come clean, huh?" she asked.

"Yes," Kate said. "Have you spoken with him since Lacy's death?"

"No. He texted and told me what had happened. He told me in the same text that he was done…that he couldn't see me anymore. Look, please…is there any way to keep this quiet? I don't want this getting out and hurting his reputation, especially after what happened with Lacy."

"We won't be telling anyone. We need to speak with you solely to get a better understanding of what you knew about Lacy. Do you think there was any chance she knew about the affair and was maybe having her own on the side?"

Crystal considered this for a moment. "I never thought about that," she said. "But I don't think so. She really didn't strike me as the vengeful type."

"So you knew her?" DeMarco asked.

"Not well. We had a few mutual friends but Lacy and I never actually hung out or anything."

"So you don't know anything about her personal life?" Kate asked.

"Just the few things Peter would tell me."

"Like what?"

Crystal shrugged and it was clear that she was getting uncomfortable. It even looked like she might be on the verge of tears. "He'd complain about her. About how she never wanted to have sex anymore. About how all she cared about was their daughter. He said he felt like he was always second. But...I don't know. I never really believed it. I'm not stupid. I'm ten years younger than he is and was...aggressive, I guess. He was just telling me things to keep me going back to him."

"So you can't think of anyone who might have anything against either Peter or Lacy?"

"No. I didn't know either of them that well."

Kate sighed, frustrated. She had secretly suspected this would happen, though. She'd been forced to look into multiple affairs in the many cases she'd worked on during her career. And in nearly every single one of them, the members of the affair were mostly distant. Aside from sexual preferences and their schedules, they typically knew very little about one another—much less the other's spouse.

"Well, thanks for your time," Kate said.

"Sure. How is he? Peter, I mean. Have you spoken with him?"

"He's grieving," DeMarco said. "And if he's asked you to please respect his wishes to no longer see one another, please do so."

Crystal seemed a little surprised to hear such a direct line of advice, but she nodded as she stood up and headed back to work. Kate and DeMarco also took their leave and as they walked back outside into a morning that looked to be thinking about rain, Kate's mind started to filter backward. This whole business with affairs was pinging some memory in the back of her head, one that she could almost pluck out and bring forward. But her head was too burdened with this new case, leaving her grasping at straws.

Some other case, she thought. *Something almost similar to this.*

"Hey, would you mind driving?" Kate said. "I need to make a call."

"Sure," DeMarco said as Kate tossed the keys her way. "Where are we headed?" "I don't know just yet. Let's start with the closest Starbucks. I forgot how taxing these long days can be."

She cringed when she realized how old that comment made her sound. She got into the car and as DeMarco started the engine, Kate took out her phone and placed a call. When the warm and familiar voice on the other end answered, it was like being thrown backward in time.

"Wise, is it really you?" Logan asked with an edge of sarcasm.

"Yes, it's me. Thanks for your text, checking in on me. It was sweet... but unnecessary."

"Well, I was raised properly. I was taught to take care of my elders."

"Go to hell."

"With you, anytime. What's up, Wise?"

She couldn't help but smile. God, she had missed the back and forth she and Logan had established over their years of working together.

"I'm trying to recall a case," she said. "I'm thinking it's no older than ten years. There were two or three people killed because of some sort of swingers' party. An affair that came out of it and caused a lot of trouble."

"Yeah, I remember that one. What do you need? I can pull the files and send you whatever you need to know. You seeing similarities in the one you're working on?"

"I don't know just yet. I'm hoping it might help me get on the right track, though. I'm trying to remember the killer... what his MO was, the sort of things he said in interrogation and at trial. That sort of thing."

"Give me a few hours and I'll send them to you. Anything else? You want me to come out there and go ahead and wrap this case for you? Seems to be a struggle for you."

"Nope, I'm good. Enjoy your nice comfortable office. And thanks for the assist."

She ended the call and saw that DeMarco was giving her an awed sort of smile. "How do you do that?" she asked.

"Do what?" Kate asked.

"Keep track of all of your old cases like that."

"I've got a pretty good memory. Not good enough, though. I should be able to remember the killer's name."

"From ten years ago? Really?"

"Yeah. Sometimes the harsher cases stick with you."

"Oh, don't I know it. Violent Crimes taught me that lesson pretty quickly. And another thing I've noticed about these cases ... something I also learned from earlier in Violent Crimes. Nothing about these murders seems personal, nothing passionate. I heard you asking on the phone just now about a swingers' party and an affair. But in my experience, most murders that spring from passion or lust or even love tend to be grisly. The killer seems to make a point to let everyone know *why* he's done it."

"I'm thinking the same thing," Kate said. "But I also can't help but wonder if it might be something oriented around secrets. Affairs being kept secret ... maybe the killer is reflecting that in his murders. Maybe he wants to show that he can be just as good at keeping a secret."

"Forgive me for asking," DeMarco said, "but is there any particular reason you feel so certain there's an affair at the core of this?"

"I don't ... not necessarily. But the fact that both women were married to absentee husbands has to be scrutinized. And the fact that one of those husbands was admittedly part of an affair makes it seem likely."

"Good point," DeMarco said, nodding as she pulled into a Starbucks parking lot. "The absentee husband thing is good. I mean, the Hicks husband was absent by necessity. Part of his job, with all of the travel. But being absent because of an affair ..."

"Yeah, it's both ends of the spectrum."

"So I guess we just need to figure out if either of those ends is going to yield any answers," DeMarco said.

Kate nodded her agreement, thinking of the empty shot glass in Lacy Thurmond's sink.

What was she drinking to numb? Kate wondered. *The knowledge of her husband's affair or something she was hiding herself?*

CHAPTER TWENTY THREE

Logan had told Kate it would take him a few hours to get results, but her phone was ringing less than an hour later. She and DeMarco were sitting in the records room of Chief Budd's station, scrutinizing the records from both the Hicks and the Thurmond cases. In both cases, new information was still coming in but none of it was helpful in establishing a trail to a killer.

"Hey, Logan," Kate said as she flipped through a copy of Julie Hicks's coroner report. "That was quick. Sure you didn't half ass it?"

"I'm positive," he said. "So here's some pretty great news for you. Not only do I have a transcript from the killer's interrogation sitting right here in front of me, but he's also currently in prison in Chesterfield. Which, I believe, is less than an hour away from you."

"Why'd they move him?" she asked. "Wasn't he placed in Lorton Correctional Complex in Fairfax?"

"He was indeed. But population problems and his apparent exceptional behavior had him moved to a less strict prison."

"Exceptional behavior?" Kate asked.

"I don't have those details here," Logan said. "But yeah, that's what I have. Anyway, you still need me to send you over the files I have on it? We have them digital so I can just email them."

"That'll be great," Kate said. "It'll give me something to read on the way to Chesterfield."

"Keep me posted on this," Logan said. "All jokes aside, Kate, I'm rooting for you on this. There are a lot of us back in here in Washington that are rooting for you, actually."

"That means a lot, Logan. Thanks."

With the call over and a clear next destination in mind, Kate started tidying up the piles of papers and files she had been looking through.

"Chesterfield, huh?" DeMarco asked.

"Yeah. No lead, but the killer from an old case that is sort of similar to this one is currently serving time there."

"Oh," DeMarco said. She seemed stalled, though, as if she was trying to understand the relevance of it. "By speaking to him and maybe understanding why he did the things he did, I hope to be able to maybe apply that mindset to our as-of-now faceless killer."

DeMarco smiled as she started gathering up her files, too. "Can you fill me in on that case on the way?"

"Of course," Kate said. She was again impressed with DeMarco's willingness to learn. She suddenly understood just how much sense it had made for Duran to send DeMarco down here to work with her. It was more than just training; it was testing DeMarco on a variety of things.

As far as Kate was concerned, she was passing every single test with flying colors. And Kate was very happy to be her guide along the way.

Kate spent the majority of the drive down to Chesterfield filling DeMarco in on the case. Because she did not fully remember every detail, she had DeMarco scroll through the information Logan had sent as she shared what she knew. It was yet another example of how well they worked together—Kate recounting the case while DeMarco filled in the gaps.

The case was ten years old and, as Kate had correctly remembered, had involved a swingers' party gone wrong. There were four couples involved, meeting once a month. These parties went on for seven months before a husband from one couple and a wife from another decided that they would rather be together with one another than with their respective spouses. The two jilted spouses pretended not to care and, oddly enough, the parties carried on for two more months. But that ninth party was the last one. The rejected husband, named Tate O'Brien, killed three of the members of the group, including his wife and her lover. O'Brien sat in the home they held the party in until the cops arrived, gladly admitted to the killings, and claimed he wished he'd "had the balls to kill everyone else in the house, too."

But he hadn't just killed the three people. He'd butchered them. He'd also apparently had sex with his wife after he'd killed her. And while the reports differed, it had appeared that O'Brien had broken his wife's lover's right leg with a hammer and made him watch as he killed her and then proceeded to have intercourse with her while she bled out.

"Jesus," DeMarco said. "I don't know that I'd say that was a crime of passion, but it was surely motivated by some strong feelings."

"True," Kate said. "And so far, it does not appear that our killer is acting on emotion. Or, if he is, he is hiding it well. But what interests me is the fact that in speaking about the murders, O'Brien was so casual about it. *Yeah, so what, I did it. And?* That sort of mentality. It's very similar to the approach our killer is taking."

"Yeah, sort of casual. Of course, he's not sitting around and just waiting for us to pluck him up, though."

Kate nodded, wondering if maybe she was grabbing at straws by going to visit O'Brien ten years after his crimes. But damn it, she had to check every avenue possible, especially when leads seemed nearly impossible to come by.

As they neared Chesterfield, Kate's mind went back to the court hearing just a few days ago. She pictured Patrick Ellis, aged but very much the same man. It had been like a ghost from her past had popped up to haunt her and without her permission to do so. She wondered if it would be the same when she came face to face with Tate O'Brien. She'd only been in his presence twice, as the case had been very simple. But she remembered the almost vacant look in his eyes, the ho-hum expression of a man who literally did not care about what he had done.

Logan said the reports indicated that O'Brien had changed. But Kate wondered. Deep down, could a man capable of that sort of malice ever really change at all?

There were no movie-like settings where Kate spoke to O'Brien through a glass partition. Instead, she and DeMarco were led through a side hallway at the front of the prison, which snaked around to the rear of the building. There, their guide left them in the company of an armed guard who stood by a large metal door. The guard opened the door for them and stood his ground by the doorway.

"Nice to see you back at work," the guard said.

It was an odd comment because Kate did not recall this guard's face. It was another of those moments when she had to remember that, like it or not, she had made quite a name for herself while working as an active agent.

"I'm here if you need me," the guard said without much expression.

Kate and DeMarco entered the room. There were only a few things inside the concrete and brick room: a battered and scarred metal table, four chairs, and Tate O'Brien. O'Brien sat on the opposite side of the table from where they stood. His left arm was cuffed to a small metal handle that had been bolted into the table. Other than that, he looked quite happy to have visitors.

Kate studied him as she made her way to the table. He had aged considerably, the ten years that had passed morphing him into a man who looked to have aged at least fifteen or twenty. She assumed this meant that the few years he'd spent in Fairfax lock-up before being moved here had been rough on him. He had grown his hair out; it was down past his shoulders, curled and rather oily looking. He'd also grown a very large beard that looked in very bad need of a trim.

"Do you happen to remember me?" Kate asked as she and DeMarco took the two seats closest to them.

O'Brien shook his head as he looked back and forth between the two agents. "Should I?" he asked.

"I was one of the agents that processed you," Kate said.

"Ah," O'Brien said with a chuckle. "That was quite a bit of time ago. I try to not look back into the past."

"Well, I'm afraid that's why I'm here," Kate said. "I was hoping to speak with you about what you did."

"And what for?" O'Brien asked. "That case is closed. I did it. No question. I admit it. At the time, I believe I *happily* admitted it."

"So you no longer admit it happily?" Kate asked.

"No," O'Brien said, shaking his head bitterly. "I've changed quite a bit over these last few years. I don't really even know the man who committed those murders anymore."

"I don't understand," DeMarco said. "Do you mean you've grown past that? That you've somehow distanced yourself from the acts?"

"You could say that," he said. "See, right before I was moved down here to Chesterfield, there was this man coming to Fairfax. He did this prison ministry thing, reading the Bible, teaching us about sin and salvation. I fought it like crazy but after about six months, Jesus got me. I gave my life to the Lord about three years ago. Been on the straight and narrow ever since. I've repented of my sins and Jesus has redeemed me. So yes . . . I no longer identify with the man that killed those people. I did it, yes. I can't escape that. But I'm free of my sin now and believe I've been redeemed."

Kate couldn't believe her luck. If O'Brien had legitimately changed to such an extent, he could be more helpful than she'd originally hoped. That was, if she played her cards right.

"I'm glad to hear that," Kate said. "We're currently working a case that we can't nail down any solid leads on. You came to my mind because the killings are sort of similar. Not a crime of lust or passion by any means, but it could be in that arena."

"And how can I help with that?" he asked. "I told you . . . that's not me anymore."

"All the better," Kate said. "If you have truly distanced yourself from the murder and no longer identify with the man you used to be, you should be able to clearly describe how you were thinking back then. Think of it as another person. Describe him to me. Describe what he was thinking when he killed those people."

For the first time since they'd entered the room, O'Brien looked unhappy. He took a deep sigh and nodded slowly. "It hurts to go back there. I do sometimes, just to remind myself that even though I'm forgiven, I still did those terrible things. It's not like watching a man. It's like watching a demon—a monster. But I can remember what I was thinking. It's really clear when I let myself go back."

"I know it's hard," Kate said, doing her best to seem sympathetic. "But it really could help us. Anything you can remember."

He would not look at them as she spoke. He looked to his right, to the blank wall along the other side of the room. He was ashamed. It made Kate think that O'Brien genuinely had experienced an awakening of some sort. Kate, while a believer in God, wasn't sure about the whole *giving my life to Jesus* thing. But O'Brien apparently believed it and it had changed him for the better.

"I remember thinking that if I killed them, it wouldn't be a big deal," he said. "She'd cheated on me but I'd allowed it. I mean, in those parties, I'd cheated on her, too. But to tell me she *loved* another man, it was painful. It hurt in a way thoughts of her having sex with him didn't. And something in me … something in me just went dark. I remember thinking if I killed her because I loved her, it wouldn't be as bad. But if I killed her because of the rage I felt, it would be this terrible, horrible act. And so that's what I told myself. I told myself I was killing her because I loved her—because we, together, had ruined our marriage but *she* had to be the one to die because she had let it affect her heart. At the time, I thought the sex and swinging was okay. It was fun and innocent because we both consented to it. But when there was emotion involved … well, it made it easier for me to kill them."

"So it was casual for you," Kate said. "You managed to convince yourself that killing her because it was an act of love—no matter how skewed—made it okay?"

"Yes."

"Is that why you were so casual about admitting to it? I remember speaking not only to you but to the police that were first on the scene. They said you admitted to it right away, almost as if you didn't see what the big deal was."

"That's right. And at the time, I honestly didn't."

"Had you ever thought about killing before?" DeMarco asked.

"I'd thought about it *plenty*. From an early age, I'd always thought about killing my stepmother. And the neighbor's dog. I actually almost went through with that when I was about sixteen."

"So you did it for love?" DeMarco asked. "All three people?"

"No. It was just my wife for love. It was out of rage for her lover. And that third one ... if I'm being honest, I just got carried away. It was almost ... *fun* by that point."

It looked like he was on the verge of tears and Kate wasn't sure how much more he'd be able to take. It was just as well, really. She was pretty sure she'd gotten everything she was going to get from him. And while it really didn't amount to much, it at least shone a light on the mindset of someone who had no problem with casual killing.

"You said you almost killed that dog when you were younger," DeMarco said. "Why the *almost*?"

Kate was pleasantly surprised. She had thought about asking the very same question but figured it might not even matter; it was a subject that could easily take them off topic. But for a rookie agent, it was a great tidbit to have picked up on.

"See, that was a *rage* one. That dog would always chase our cat. When our cat had kittens, the dog got to the litter. Ate all but one of them. I had this twenty-two rifle I used to hunt with and I went out on the back porch one day when it came around. I aimed at it, almost squeezed the trigger."

"Even then, did you realize it was a decision based on rage, not love?" DeMarco asked.

"You know, I never thought of it. But yes, that makes sense."

"Have you talked to other men here about it?" Kate asked.

"About the dog? Sure. And even about the difference between what I thought of killing out of love and rage. Because once I was washed of my sins, you realize that there is no such thing as killing for love. Not even if you were to kill an intruder that was threatening your family. Even in that case, *love* for your family isn't why you kill. It's self-preservation."

"So then how do you apply that to killing your wife and the rest of the spree?" Kate asked.

O'Brien gave this some thought and nodded, as if understanding for the first time. "I suppose that was self-preservation, too. This other man had caught my wife. I had to defend my honor, or my love for her."

"So are you of the opinion that any murder, particularly those with lust attached to it, could not be done out of what the killer sees as love? Do you think all killers try to place the blame there rather than on the rage?"

"Oh yes. I see that clearly now. No murder is ever out of an act of love—no matter how much the killer tells himself it is."

Kate thought of the little circle of friends and lovers around Amber Hills and tried to apply this principle. It was surprisingly easy. And even if O'Brien was spouting some religious nonsense, it was a principle she had never quite latched on to over the course of her career.

And it made a scary sort of sense, given the current case.

Whoever was doing the killing was in some way *attached* to the victims but likely held no truly deep affection.

"Mr. O'Brien, I do thank you for your time," Kate said as she got to her feet. "And I'm very glad to see that you've changed."

"I wish I could help you more," he said. "But honestly … it's like watching a different person when I pull up those memories. I can tell you this, though. Someone killing in such a way, without any care or passion to it … he doesn't care about sending a message. He's not trying to prove anything, I bet. And that would make him more dangerous, right?"

It was a good point, but Kate wasn't sure how accurate it was. True, it didn't seem like the killer was trying to send any sort of message, but the proximity of the murders and the fact that the women were part of the same circle of friends made Kate think he *was* trying to prove something.

But what?

Self-preservation, like O'Brien had indicated. Was the killer trying to protect himself? And if so, who was he afraid might hurt him?

CHAPTER TWENTY FOUR

"You buy all that Jesus stuff he was talking about?" DeMarco asked. The question caught Kate off guard. It was very direct and was easily the most personal question that had been shared between the two of them so far. It was also a question that was not easy for Kate to answer.

"I don't know," she said, trying her best. "I don't mind telling you that I believe in God. But when you get into the Holy Spirit and a resurrected Jesus, I start to have some serious doubts. Why do you ask?"

DeMarco shrugged. "Because I don't. I never have. I have no doubt that people can truly change—even people like Tate O'Brien—but I don't think it's because they symbolically give their lives over to the spirit of some man that may have never even lived."

"But you agree that a killer can have some sort of a change of heart?" Kate asked.

"Absolutely."

"They say Jeffrey Dahmer became a born again Christian in prison," Kate said. "So I guess that's some pretty substantial proof."

"Yeah, and he was killed by inmates later. So it appears that the Jesus he gave his life to cared nothing for him."

Kate couldn't help but smirk. She could tell that DeMarco was not broaching the topic out of the need for an argument. She was genuinely feeling Kate out, trying to get her thoughts on what they had just heard from O'Brien and how it might relate to their killer.

"You know, I can't help but wonder," Kate said. "We've been trying to get information out of the remaining friends in their little clique. But if there were secrets about their lives—things like affairs, for instance—then there's no guarantee they'd come clean. But there have to be others in Amber Hills who know those women ... and maybe don't like them. But just in a normal way ... the way some neighbors just don't like the people that live next to them."

"So you think we need to speak to neighbors as impartial parties?" DeMarco asked.

"Well, as neighbors, they'd hardly be impartial. But yes. If we're going to get the truth about that circle of friends, we have to go elsewhere. The truth we get might be stretched a bit but it's better than secrets."

"So we're assuming that Taylor Woodward and Wendy Hudson were being dishonest?"

"Not at all. That's a dangerous assumption to make about anyone. But I do think there's a chance they'd want to protect the reputation of their friends if there was anything dirty on them."

"Worth a shot, I guess," DeMarco said.

"Don't tell me you're one of those people that assumes the best about everyone," Kate joked.

"I do when there is grief involved."

Kate nodded. She usually felt the same way. But in a small gated community where she knew for certain there had been one affair and perhaps at least one additional one, she felt that no one could really be trusted. Because grief was one thing ... but shame was a totally different beast. It was much stronger and could, at times, make people behave irrationally.

Before revisiting Amber Hills, Kate dropped DeMarco off at her motel. She then kept her promise to Melissa, going back by the hospital. With both the mother and the baby cleared as healthy, she was allowed to go directly to the room. The scene was totally different than it had been in the morning. When she got to the room, Melissa was beaming, holding Michelle in a swaddle of blankets.

She was alone in the room, which surprised Kate. She had expected Terry to be with her, never leaving her side. He was a good man and Kate was very thankful that her daughter had ended up with him.

"How's it going?" Kate asked, walking proudly to the side of the bed.

"Good," Melissa said. "My abdomen is numb from the surgery but my nerves are so jittery that I don't even care."

"Nerves?"

"Adrenaline, I guess. And the suffocating worry that I'm going to be a terrible mother."

"Nonsense," Kate said. "How many books did you read about birth and parenting in the last nine months?"

"Pretty much all of them. Still … now that she's actually here, it's like nothing I read really even matters."

"It comes naturally," Kate said. "Trust me. Hey, where's Terry?"

"He went down to the cafeteria to see what they had. He's been nervous, too. He hasn't eaten since my water broke. He's still nervous about little Michelle, too. They're coming back to get her soon. She has to stay in the NICU for a few days. But they said I needed to see her. That she needs the time to bond."

"Sweetie, I'm sorry I had to leave earlier. This thing with the bureau … I wasn't expecting it and the case is just going absolutely nowhere."

"So retirement is treating you well, huh?"

"No. It treated me like crap. That's why I was so happy to go back. But the timing, with Michelle and everything, it's all off."

"Mom, I'm used to you having that jacked up schedule. I've been living with it all my life. It was a good model, you know?"

Kate shook her head and sat down on the edge of the bed. "Let's not go there, Lissa."

"Mom, it's going to happen. I didn't waste that time and those credits in college for nothing."

"Didn't I tell you enough horror stories to keep you away from the bureau?"

"You told plenty of stories. But I think your plan backfired."

Kate said nothing. Ever since Melissa had first expressed interest in following her mother's footsteps into the FBI at the age of fifteen, Kate had been terrified. Even after her father had been killed, she had not swerved. In fact, Kate was pretty sure the death of her father had pushed her even harder. It was why she had made the dean's list at Marquette University and why she had followed her mother's career so closely.

Kate had foolishly hoped that after having a child, Melissa might change her mind.

But why should it? It hadn't changed Kate's mind after giving birth to Melissa.

"We're not going to talk about that right now," Kate said. "Instead, why don't you tell me what that nursery is looking like?"

"Oh, friggin' adorable," Melissa said.

And just like that, the subject was changed. They both knew there was an unspoken sorrow between them, the fact that the grandfather would never meet this little bundle of joy. Kate had never come out and asked but she had always wondered if the name *Michelle* was a feminine approach to Michael, naming the baby after her late husband and Melissa's late father.

"I do want to say something to you, Mom," Melissa said. "I want to let you know that it's pretty bad ass that you're back at work. It suits you. You could be doing this when you're seventy and it would seem right, you know?"

"Thanks … I think."

"I look forward to the day when you can give me some tips of the trade," Melissa said with a sly smile.

"I told you, we aren't—"

"Lighten up, Mom. I couldn't resist."

Kate rolled her eyes, leaned forward, and kissed her daughter on the head. It was the first time she realized that there were three generations in the same room, huddled on the same bed. Something about it was incredibly moving but, as a mother and now a grandmother, a little intimidating, too.

Maybe because she knew that when she left here, she'd be back on the trail of a man who was killing women—women not much older than Melissa.

With a chill riding down her spine, Kate looked to her granddaughter and then to her daughter. And suddenly, her work seemed to take on a whole new meaning. She wouldn't be able to do this forever. And as much as they joked about it, one of these days Melissa would likely end up with a badge and a gun.

And what about little Michelle? Who was to say what the future held for her?

Kate knew she should get going; the case and DeMarco were waiting on her. But with those new thoughts bogging like dead weight in her head, she stayed just a little bit longer, enjoying the presence of family and a moment of peace.

CHAPTER TWENTY FIVE

It was 3:30 in the afternoon when Kate and DeMarco drove back into Amber Hills. The police cars were still parked at the front gates while a few others were parked at seemingly random spots all around the neighborhood. Their search for additional information from the neighbors of the victims was shortened when they discovered that the neighbor to the right of the Thurmonds was not home and the house on the left of their residence was for sale.

However, when they ventured over to Helmsdale Street, where the Hickses lived, they found the neighbor to the right at home. When DeMarco knocked on the door it was answered by a woman of about sixty or so. A tiny little dog yipped at their feet, a breed that Kate couldn't determine. Something small and fluffy and white.

"Can I help you?" the lady said, her tone wavering between pleasant cheer and suspicion.

Kate showed her badge, the motion like a second sense now. "I'm Agent Wise and this is Agent DeMarco. We're investigating the death of your neighbor, Julie Hicks. Would you happen to have a little bit of time to answer a few questions for me?"

The old woman's face lit up for a moment but she managed to rein it back. "Of course," she said. "Come in, come in."

Kate and DeMarco followed the woman through her foyer and into a nicely decorated living room. Right away, she introduced herself as Caroline Manners and asked if the agents would like some coffee or tea. When both declined, they took their seats—Kate and DeMarco on the plush couch while Caroline sat in a reading chair.

"As I'm sure you know," Kate said, "Julie Hicks was not the only one to lose her life recently."

"Yes, it's terrible," Caroline said. Her little dog had leaped up beside her, curling itself into her lap. "I heard about Lacy Thurmond. It's tragic, given the state of her life. I assume you knew about her husband's affair?"

"We discovered it, yes," Kate said. "But how did you know about it?"

"Good Lord," Caroline said with a boisterous laugh. "Just about everyone in the neighborhood knew about it. I don't know if she ever admitted to knowing about it, but there's no way Lacy *didn't* know."

"Did you know who her husband was having the affair with?" DeMarco asked.

"There were rumors it was with his ex-wife. Another rumor said it was with a nurse at the hospital."

A pretty accurate grapevine apparently runs through Amber Hills, Kate thought.

"Would you happen to have any other rumors you think might have a great deal of truth to them?" Kate asked. "Please understand, we're not looking for gossip. We're simply trying to get the entire story as we try to find the person responsible for these murders."

"Well, Lacy Thurmond was a sweetheart of a woman. I knew her pretty well but not enough to call her a friend. She was very involved in her church and was a good mother from what I understand. It's a shame her husband was such a miserable excuse for a man."

"Did you know him well?" Kate asked.

"No. Once I found out he was cheating on his wife, I didn't care to know anything at all about him."

"Well, how about Julie, your neighbor? We've spoken to some of her friends and they claim to know nothing the least bit negative about the Hicks family. Of course, it's hard to gauge the honesty of a group of friends. Would you say you could be an impartial party?"

"I suppose. Certainly a better source than those friends she kept. No woman should be *that* concerned about looking ten years younger than you actually are. Now, Julie and I would speak from time to time if we happened to be outdoors at the same time. She had me over for dinner once or twice last year after my husband passed away. But I wasn't close with her … not like those idiot friends of hers."

"Do you know if there was anyone in her life who was close to her that was *not* in her usual circle of friends?"

"Well, sure. I tell you, the sanctity of marriage means nothing to people anymore, now does it? Julie's husband was always on the road, traveling. No way to treat a marriage if you ask me. I started seeing this car in front of the Hicks house late at night about four months ago. I thought nothing of it until I saw a man get into it after coming out of the house early in the morning."

Kate dared to hope this would turn out to be a lead. But it was evident that Caroline Manners was a gossipy old lady with nothing better to do than to pry into the lives of others. She served as a great resource for information but there was no telling how much of that information might be accurate.

"You're certain of this?" Kate asked.

"Positive. I've been getting up with this weak bladder of mine at least three times a night for about two years now. Bladder infection from several years ago just never let them get back to their proper state. So I'm up at all hours. Sometimes when I get up for that four o'clock trip to the toilet, I just stay awake." She frowned and shook her head. "Sorry. That bordered on the entirely-too-personal, didn't it?"

"That's quite all right," Kate said. "But you say you actually saw this man leaving her home?"

"Yes. I saw him once but I saw the car three different times."

"Was it anyone you know?" DeMarco asked. "Anyone you've seen before?"

"No," Caroline said. "And I almost thought about taking down the number on the plates. But I didn't; I figured it's really none of my business."

Kate had to bite back a smile at that comment. "Do you recall the kind of car it was?" she asked.

"A newer one. Pretty sure it was a Honda. Gray or silver. Oh, and there *is* one more thing. Hell, I damn near forgot all about this little detail. When he was coming out, he had a jacket or hooded sweatshirt or something in his hand. He put it on as he was about halfway down the sidewalk. There was a logo and business name on the back of it. Pritchard Auto Glass."

"Did you get a good look at his face?" DeMarco asked.

"Just the side and just for a second," Caroline answered. "A clean-shaven man from what I could see. Looked a little young ... early twenties, maybe?"

"And how long ago was it when you actually saw him leaving Julie's house?" Kate asked.

"I'm not sure. No more than a month ago."

"And what about some of the other friends in her group?" Kate asked. "Can you tell us anything else about them?"

"I'm afraid not. I know that Wendy Hudson has a father in prison and that Taylor Woodward has a drinking problem. She was pulled over for a DUI a few weeks ago ... for the second time, the way I hear it."

Kate nodded and got to her feet. She had managed to pluck one promising bit of information out of the gossipy old lady. She was starting to get the feeling that the entire conversation might slip into pure gossip if they stayed much longer, though.

"Ms. Manners, we certainly appreciate your time," she said, already taking a step toward the door. DeMarco followed, also seemingly glad to be getting away from what looked to be devolving into a gossip-fest.

"Of course," Caroline said. The abrupt nature of her tone made it clear that she was disappointed her company was leaving so soon.

The agents made their exit as politely as they could. Caroline stood at the door and watched them get into the car, perhaps already twisting the story for entertaining her own circle of friends later.

"Sweet old lady," Kate said ironically.

"Or nosy old bitch," DeMarco countered.

"Either way, it looks like we got a lead," Kate said. What she didn't add was that it was, at most, a weak lead. She kept it quiet though because when a case was offering no clues or leads, even the smallest of breakthroughs could often serve as the motivation needed to get the case moving along.

With that hope pushing her, Kate got behind the wheel and headed out of Amber Hills while DeMarco pulled up the address for Pritchard Auto Glass.

Chapter Twenty Six

B road Street was beginning to thicken up with afternoon rush hour traffic when Kate turned the car into the parking lot of Pritchard Auto Glass. The lot was mostly empty, indicating that this was the slower time of the day for the business. It was set up like an actual auto garage, with bay doors to let vehicles inside the garage where some of the work was done. There was also an open space to the side of the building where a few vehicles were parked, one of which was in the midst of getting its rear window replaced.

Kate and DeMarco walked inside and approached the front counter. One man was inputting a customer's information into a computer while another smiled widely at them. "Can I help you?" he asked.

Neither of these men were the young man Caroline Manners had mentioned; they were both easily forty or older.

"Yes," Kate said, getting so close to the counter that she was nearly pressed against it. She set her ID on the counter long enough for the man to see it and then pocketed it. "We're looking for a young man that likely works here. Maybe in his early twenties or so. We don't have a name or a clear description, so we were hoping to maybe walk around the place to see if anyone stands out to us."

"Well, the manager has already left, so I don't know if I can grant that sort of permission."

"If you need us to, one of us can call him," DeMarco said. "But I know it's getting close to quitting time and I really can't afford to wait much longer. But if you want to hang around after closing time …"

Well played, Kate thought, again finding herself impressed at the way DeMarco approached things.

"Fine, okay," the man said. "Besides the two of us, there are only two other guys here anyway, Roger and Billy. We've got Diane who is out on vacation and then Wyatt, the manager, who already left."

"Where would we find Roger and Billy?" DeMarco asked.

"Out in the side lot, putting a back glass in."

"Thanks," Kate said, the word leaving her lips as she turned toward the door.

She and DeMarco walked back out and headed for the repair lot on the side of the building. They approached slowly as Kate took a moment to study the two men who were currently replacing a window on a red Ford Explorer. One was an African-American man who looked to be no older than thirty. The other was a skinny-looking man who did indeed look rather young. He had just enough hair on his face to be called a five o'clock shadow.

Given that Caroline Manners had not expressly said that Julie Hicks's late night visitor had been African-American, Kate assumed that the skinny man was the one they were looking for. But she also knew that even *that* was a stretch. The sweatshirt Caroline Manners had seen the man put on could have been a promotional item or had once belonged to someone else—a brother or father, perhaps. There was no guarantee that the man with the sweatshirt leaving Julie's home had been an actual employee of Pritchard Auto Glass.

Kate gave DeMarco a little nod, giving her the go-ahead to kick things off. DeMarco stepped forward gladly. Kate noticed the way she slightly pushed the front of her open jacket to the side. This revealed her holstered sidearm, making it apparent that she was here with a law enforcement agency. It removed the need for her to pull out her ID, a tactic that was useful in not overly alarming people. Kate smiled, recognizing once again that DeMarco was damned good at what she did.

"Excuse me," DeMarco said. "I'm Agent DeMarco with the FBI and I need to speak with you for a moment, please."

Both men stared at her, looking equally confused.

"Which one?" the African-American asked.

"Whichever one of you knew Julie Hicks," DeMarco said.

Genius, Kate thought. The mention of Julie's name struck an immediate chord with the skinny man. And once it struck, he didn't even try to hide it. He looked scared and a little sad.

"I knew her," he said, raising his hand in an unsure manner. When he realized what he was doing, he lowered it. "What's going on?"

"Can we talk in private?" DeMarco asked.

"The break room, I guess," the man said. "Is ... what is it? Did you guys find who killed her?"

"We can talk about all of that in a second," Kate said. "For now, why not just lead us to the break room."

The young man did exactly that. Kate could tell from the way he walked that he was trembling. It certainly wasn't a show of guilt but was more than enough to tell Kate that he was nervous—whether about sleeping with a married woman or something deeper, though, was anyone's guess.

The break room was a small little corner in the back of the shop. There was a Keurig coffee machine and two empty boxes that had once held donuts. Other than that and a mini-fridge, Pritchard Auto Glass offered very little in the way of a break room. The young man had introduced himself as Billy Cosgrove as he took a seat at the break room table. He asked for their names and then asked to see ID.

Kate and DeMarco entertained him, showing their badges and IDs. There was one other chair at the break room table but neither of them took it. Kate leaned against the small counter while DeMarco stood her ground on the other side of the table.

"Rumor has it," DeMarco said, "that you were sleeping with Julie Hicks. Is that true?"

"Shit," Billy said. "Did her husband find out?"

"No," DeMarco said. "But her neighbor did. You're apparently not the best at keeping a good cover when you're out and about at night."

"So he doesn't know?"

"No," Kate said. "And there's no reason to tell him. But we were hoping you could maybe shed some light on Julie—that you could reveal some things about her that we might not have picked up from her husband or her friends."

"For starters, how did you two get involved?" DeMarco asked.

"Well, she brought her car in a few weeks back—maybe five or six weeks ago. The front window on the driver's side got busted by some kid throwing a baseball in their neighborhood. We fixed it and when she was here, she sort of seemed flirty with me. Nothing serious, and nothing I really even thought much of, you know? But she came back a few days later saying that the window wouldn't go down. So we checked it and found some fragments of glass from the first window in it. We had to order a new window and she seemed sort of pissed about it, saying she had a busy schedule and all. So we volunteered to come out to her house to do it. So they sent me out because it's a pretty easy job. Just me. She came out and talked to me a bit. When I knocked on her door to tell her the job was done, she invited me in. And I said yes. She was really flirty and dressed in this tight shirt and …"

He stopped here, realizing that he was speaking to two women. He blushed a bit, looked away from them, and then carried on.

"We started messing around. I saw pictures of her and her husband on the fridge in the kitchen. I asked her where he was and she said he was out of town—that he was always out of town because of his work. One thing led to another and we ended up having sex in her kitchen."

"So she was the aggressor?" Kate asked.

"Absolutely." "And who initiated seeing one another again?"

"Her. But she made it clear to me that she wanted no relationship. She would not leave her husband. She just wanted something fun to do while he was away. She came out and told me she was just living out a wild side she'd never lived out in college."

"So this was an ongoing thing for how long?"

"About four or five weeks. The last time I saw her was two days before she died."

"Did you sleep with her then?"

"We had sex every time we saw one another. She was trying out all these things with me that she'd never done before. She was using me and, quite frankly, that was perfectly okay with me."

"So in this time with her, did she ever reveal anything about her personal life to you?" Kate asked. "Any people you heard of that might be upset with her?"

"No. Again...not trying to brag or be a smart ass, but there was never really any talking. I did ask her one time why she chose me and she said it was because I was different. She never explained it, but I knew what she meant."

"And what did she mean, exactly?" DeMarco asked.

"I was like hired help almost. Not someone from her neighborhood with its picket fences and expensive houses. She wanted a guy from the other side of town, you know? She wanted to feel like she was doing something *really* wrong."

"And you were okay with that?" Kate asked.

Billy looked at her with an incredulous expression on his face. "At the risk of sounding crude, yes. I was having regular sex—regular *rough* sex—with a hot older woman at least twice a week and there were no strings attached. Yes. I was okay with it."

"You never stopped to think about her husband and what it could do to their marriage?"

"No. I figure if he cared that much for her, he wouldn't stay on the road so much."

"Did she ever talk about any of her friends?"

He grinned nervously and nodded. "Yeah. Said she had a group of friends that all lived in the neighborhood. Most of them were stay-at-home moms or women that worked from home. Boring husbands with boring jobs. She told me she was going to arrange for a threesome with us and one of her friends but it never happened."

"What sort of people did she say her friends were?" Kate asked.

"She never went into detail about it but I got the gist that they were just like her. They slept around from time to time. Sort of adventurous, trying to live wild exciting lives before they got too old."

Kate knew she'd reached the end of the conversation. Billy was starting to sound like he was bragging and she was getting frustrated. She was all but certain he had no hand in the murders; there was no way he'd so openly admit to a sexual relationship with Julie Hicks if he was guilty.

"The night she was killed...where were you?" Kate asked.

"At home. Sleeping. Had a few too many beers with some friends and ended up passing out early."

"Any proof of this?" DeMarco asked.

"I think I have the receipt from the bar. I took a cab home, too. Paid with my debit card, so I can get that receipt if you need it."

Kate sighed and got to her feet. "Don't bother. Also, have you told anyone about your little excursions?"

"I told Roger, the guy I was working with when you got here. But I never told him a name."

"For the respect of the deceased and her family, please keep it quiet," Kate said.

"I absolutely will."

Kate and DeMarco left the break room, leaving a very shaken Billy Cosgrove behind them with a reflective yet sad look on his face.

"Now what?" DeMarco asked.

Kate wasn't accustomed to feeling defeated but she could feel it sinking into her bones, into her heart. She wasn't quite discouraged just yet but it was hard to stay upbeat.

"Now I want to go see my granddaughter again," Kate said. "And while I'm doing that, you think about what we'll have for dinner. It's going to be a long night of poring over case files, I'm afraid."

DeMarco nodded, although there was a disappointed look on her face. Apparently, this was not the high-octane experience she had been hoping to experience while partnered with the quasi-famous Agent Kate Wise.

And Kate understood it perfectly. So far, it wasn't panning out the way she had expected, either.

Chapter Twenty Seven

He'd been planning this one for a very long time. In a way, the first two had been practice. This was the one he had always had in mind when he'd started. And those first two women had proven to him that he had no real problem with killing. It seemed natural and almost therapeutic. It made him envy the jobs that men back in the Middle Ages had enjoyed—jobs like executioner or the general in charge of whatever group oversaw the torture and dismemberment of their enemies.

This woman was different. He knew her much better than he had known the others. He'd seen her naked, had watched her strip in front of a mirror in appreciation of herself—or, perhaps, in fear that her thirty-something body would maybe not be perfect much longer.

This time, he felt a sense of urgency. He'd allowed himself to enjoy the planning and anticipation of the other two. But now he knew the cops were on to him. They were crawling around Amber Hills like ants, looking for whatever honey had been spilled. Of course, when he had started it all, he knew the authorities would eventually become a problem. And while he certainly didn't want to go to prison, it was an outcome that he was ready for.

He'd been very quick and efficient with the first two. He'd planned it all out but had not overthought it. Each act had taken no more than five seconds. But this next one ... he thought he might stretch it out.

One thing was different this time, though. Something that made it perhaps a bit riskier, but he knew her schedule, knew it had to be different. He had to strike during the day. And with all of the fucking cop cars around the neighborhood, it might be tricky.

So he chose to blend in. He drove into the neighborhood like he belonged there. He even gave a little cursory wave to the cop who was stationed at the entrance. The cop nodded to him, bored and featureless.

He drove down the main stretch of Amber Hills, a wider road called Amber Drive. He took a left and within seconds was passing the Thurmond residence. There were no police cars there anymore but he still made every attempt not to look in the direction of the house. He passed by it like a motorist trying to avoid looking at a particularly bad car accident.

Then he saw the house. He saw the perfectly manicured landscaping and the lush green yard. He saw the porch swing, the large plants bordering the front door. And, keeping with his appearance of normalcy, he went so far as to even pull into the driveway, right behind the car that was already parked there.

Her car.

He took a moment to collect his thoughts, to collect his nerve. The dashboard clock read 6:15. He knew her schedule well. She would have just come back home from the gym about twenty minutes ago. She was either in the shower or lying on the back deck to catch some sun. But seeing how the day was overcast, he was thinking she'd be in the shower.

Upstairs. In the bedroom. By herself.

He smiled. As he walked to the porch, he wasn't sure what he was the most excited about: catching her naked in the shower or plunging the knife between her breasts.

Taylor Woodward knew she was attractive. She was thirty-one and could still catch the eyes of the younger men in the gym. But the thing of it was that she had worked her ass off to stay so hot. She dieted, she ate right, and she exercised regularly. Her mother had let herself go around the age of forty and when she'd died two years ago, she'd been almost three hundred pounds. Seeing her mother's chubby face in that open casket had driven Taylor to continue her healthy lifestyle. And although she knew she often carried it too far, she didn't care. She liked having her abs, her perfectly toned ass, her still-perky breasts.

And more than that, she liked the looks she got at the gym and the pool. And she loved the way her husband sometimes looked at her—in the same way boys had looked at her when she was a teenager, a way that made her think she was all he was thinking about.

As she came to the end of her shower, she wished her husband was there with her. Unlike most of her friends, she had never had an affair. She knew she had all the options in the world if she decided to have one—from the eighteen-year-olds at the gym to the wealthy forty – and fifty-year-olds in the neighborhood.

But she loved her husband. And as the water cascaded off of her body, she wished he was there, under the water with her. Sex had gotten a little formulaic as of late. She couldn't remember the last time he'd taken her by surprise, out of nowhere, a little rough and—

She smiled when she heard the bathroom door open behind her. She knew it was a little after six and that his work often brought him home as early as seven or as late as nine. But sometimes, every now and then, he'd manage to come home early. And if he was coming into the bathroom knowing she was in there, maybe he had the same thing on his mind—a little afternoon delight in the shower.

"I'm almost done," she said flirtatiously. "But I can take another one if I happen to get dirty again."

He said nothing but she could see him moving through the fog and haze of the steam and the misted over glass of the shower door. She smiled; it was good to see just how eager he still made her.

She turned to face the back of the shower, as that's where he'd come in. The door opened but he did not come inside. Instead, it was just an arm. It grabbed her by the shoulder and pulled her forward. She lost her footing on the wet shower floor. As she fell, he caught her by the hair and pulled her out of the open door.

Electric pain raced around her skull as she was pulled by the hair. She screamed, not fully sure what the hell was happening. But then she was thrown to the floor and he was on her.

She saw the face then and realized who it was.

You ...

She opened her mouth to scream again and this time a clubbing right hand came sailing at her mouth. She felt a tooth come out as her mouth filled with blood. She was afraid she'd choke on it but then that fear was replaced by an intense pain, a pain so blinding it was unreal.

It was then that she realized she could not breathe, that something had happened to her chest.

And then she saw the knife as he pulled it out of her.

She saw it one more time as it came sailing down toward her and although she felt it enter her again, she barely registered it.

She looked upward, to the ceiling, to the gathering steam of the shower, and prayed for it to end quickly as the shape of the man above her blurred into blackness until there was nothing left.

CHAPTER TWENTY EIGHT

Kate could not get over how the simple act of holding her newborn granddaughter was able to recharge her, but it did. It was both a mental and physical jolt to the system. And while it didn't have quite the same powerful effect as holding Melissa for the first time when she had been born, it was very similar. She assumed it had something to do with the instinctual human need to carry on a bloodline, to revel in the fact that she was holding a third generation in her hands.

She was marveling over this as she sat with DeMarco in her dining room over dinner. DeMarco had chosen Chinese for their dinner, which was absolutely fine with Kate. She usually tried to eat healthy but given the way the last two days had gone, she figured she could allow herself a cheat meal.

"You know something I'd like to find out from the police?" DeMarco said as she studied a file and swirled a lo mein noodle onto her fork. "I'd like to know what the police at the Amber Hills gates are looking for. There are no neighborhood decals or stickers of any kind on the cars for that neighborhood."

"That's a good point," Kate said. "And from what I can see, they aren't stopping people that come in or go out."

"And really, none of that would make a difference if the killer is actually an Amber Hills resident," DeMarco pointed out.

Kate nodded. These were all good points, ones that she had considered before. But until they found something relevant and tangible to go on, they could only guess. In her own head, she had started to compile a list of pros and cons. It was a list that might be made by a killer that would use Amber Hills as a killing field of sorts. For a killer to choose such a place to strike two times in a small window of time seemed both risky and, quite frankly, genius.

The biggest pro, of course, was that the victims were easy pickings. And based on the women he had selected—very attractive women who tended to stay at home, in their late twenties or early thirties—Amber Hills provided a promising group of victims. By staying in one centralized location, it was easier to pick your targets and to get a proper lay of the land. If the killer lived elsewhere in town, it also kept the investigation centralized in one place while he was very likely hiding somewhere else.

But then there were the cons. In a small area, the likelihood of someone seeing him would be much greater. It also meant that escaping through smaller side streets within the neighborhood would make a fast getaway virtually impossible. Someone would notice a speeding car and, in such a neighborhood, would likely report it out of fear of kids getting hurt.

If we had even just a hint *of motive, it would help wonders,* Kate thought as she closed one of the several files she had accumulated.

Her phone rang as she reached for another file. The name and number were familiar and for a moment, she almost didn't answer it. But she figured maybe stepping away and shifting her mind to something else for even just a few moments could be a massive help.

Reading Allen Goldman's name, she grabbed up her phone and stepped away from the table. "This will just take a moment," she told DeMarco as she hurried into the living room.

"Hey, Allen," she said, taking the call.

"Hey," he said. "I was honestly expecting to have to leave a message."

"Then why not just text?"

"I was hoping for the off chance you would actually answer. Also, the other night on the porch you told me to call next time. So here I am ... calling."

"I appreciate that," she said. "What can I do for you?"

"For one, wrap up this case you're on by Friday. I want to take you out to dinner."

"Well, I've got more than this case right now," she said. "Melissa had her baby."

"What? She wasn't due for like another what ... five or six weeks?"

"Yeah. Little Michelle came early. She and Melissa are doing fine, though. I've already been able to hold her twice."

"That's great, Kate. So you're officially a grandmother now. How's it feel?"

"Better than I thought. It's sort of amazing, actually."

"Good. Well, for you, anyway. Sounds like your life is absolutely nuts right now. My timing ... it's just wretched, huh?"

"It is. But that's okay. We can—"

She was interrupted by a beep on her phone—an incoming call. She quickly checked the display and saw that it was Chief Budd calling.

"Speaking of bad timing," she said, "I have to get this. It's about the case."

"Okay," he said, trying to hide the sigh in his voice but failing.

"But Allen ... thanks for calling. And maybe do it again soon, okay?"

"Absolutely. G'night, Kate."

Kate switched over to the incoming call, hoping Budd calling meant that there was finally some sort of break. Maybe from the coroner or someone on his investigative team.

"This is Wise," she answered.

"Agent Wise, this is Randall Budd. Are you still in Richmond or have you gone back to DC?"

"Still in Richmond. Why? What's up?"

"We've got another body. This one is very fresh."

"Amber Hills?" Kate asked.

"Yes."

"What's the address? We can be there in twenty minutes."

Budd gave her the address and she was not at all surprised to find that it was on the same street Lacy Thurmond had lived on. She ended the call and headed into the kitchen where DeMarco was eating an egg roll and looking through the coroner's reports.

"Study session is over," Kate said. "Budd just called. There's been another murder."

"Holy shit," DeMarco said. "How long ago?"

"He says it's fresh. No details yet. Let's just get over there as soon as we can."

Yet even before the comment was out of Kate's mouth, DeMarco was shoveling the remainder of the egg roll into her mouth and getting up from the table. Kate was starting to appreciate DeMarco more and more. Her go-get-'em attitude and teachability made her miss Logan a little less. Though, to be honest, she did miss the sarcastic back and forth they had shared most of the time.

But maybe such a thing took time to develop between partners. While she had not quite reached that point with her first partner, it had come naturally for her and Logan. And now, with DeMarco as her partner, she was beginning to understand that all partnerships evolved in their own different way. And as she and DeMarco raced out of her house, she looked forward to seeing where this new partnership would go.

Hopefully, she thought, *it will lead to closing this case.*

As she got into the car and slammed it into Drive, she thought of that first partner from twenty-seven years ago. She'd partnered with him for nearly ten years and they had never gotten close emotionally. But he had been one hell of a mentor and during her time away from the bureau, she'd thought of him often.

And he was there again, at the edge of her mind, as she sped toward Amber Hills. She wondered what his take on this case would be. His wisdom and experience may see the case from a different perspective. She mulled over this, wondering if he'd even take her calls anymore.

It was something to consider. If this next crime scene offered nothing of substance, maybe she'd reach out

But she couldn't go there yet. Instead, she chose to hope that the next crime scene would offer something—perhaps some clue, no matter how small or seemingly insignificant.

Besides, even at fifty-five years of age, her life was still evolving. She was a grandmother now. She had a man who was very interested in her. And she was back on the job, on a case that was proving to be among her toughest. To dredge the past back up seemed to make no sense.

So with the present and the future in mind, they closed in on Amber Hills as night slowly started to fall around Richmond.

CHAPTER TWENTY NINE

The house was just like any of the others along most stretches of Amber Hills. The only thing that made it stand out was the blue and red flashing lights from the police sirens, strobing against the dusk. When Kate pulled her car in behind one of the six police cars on the scene, she noticed that there were other police cars parked all along the sides of the streets. It seemed that the police were doing everything they could to keep prying eyes from getting a good glimpse at what was going on.

As she walked up the sidewalk, she saw Chief Budd on the porch, speaking to a pair of officers. Kate hurried toward him and when he noticed her approaching, he instantly stopped the conversation with the other officers.

"That was quick," Budd said.

"You said this one was fresh. I wanted to keep it like that. Where's the body?"

"Come with me," he said. "I've already told everyone that when you got here, it's your show. CSI is even going to wait until you're done. Unless you want them."

"Just keep them close," Kate said. "I'm not trying to slow this down for anyone."

"Well, that shouldn't be a problem. So far, it seems as cut and dried as all the rest. Only ... well, I guess dried is the wrong word."

"What?" DeMarco asked, confused.

"You'll see," Budd said as he led them inside.

He led them down the main hall to where a flight of stairs led to the second floor. He marched down the upstairs hallway, into the master bedroom. Kate saw that the bathroom door was open and as they neared it, she could actually smell the blood.

As she headed for the door, an agonizing wail filled the house. It was a male's voice, coming from downstairs.

"That's the husband," Budd said. "He came home and found his wife exactly like you're about to see her. He called nine-one-one and the first officer on the scene found him passed out in his own puke right over there," he said, pointing to the far side of the king-sized bed.

Kate carefully stepped into the bathroom. It was muggy and moist, but that was not nearly the worst of it. A woman lay on the bathroom floor, staring up at the ceiling. She was completely naked, making the stab wounds to her chest, abdomen, and pelvic area easy to see.

While the stab wounds were grisly indeed, it was the woman's face that shook Kate. She knew this woman. She had seen her in the last few days.

Behind her, DeMarco gave voice to what was on Kate's lips. "That's Taylor Woodward."

"You know her?" Budd asked.

"Not personally," Kate said. "We questioned her with another woman yesterday. They were both friends of Julie Hicks and Lacy Thurmond. The other woman present was Wendy Hudson. And please send a car to her house right now. Three out of four friends is *not* a coincidence. Wendy Hudson needs to be placed in protective custody as far as I'm concerned."

"I'll get on that right now," Budd said. When he quickly turned away from the bathroom door, he seemed glad to do so.

DeMarco stepped up beside Kate, both women now standing in the bathroom. There was a pool of standing water at the back of the shower, puddled up on the floor. Some of the copious amounts of blood that had spilled from Taylor's body had mingled with it, turning it into an almost pretty kind of fractal pattern.

"This isn't exactly the same as the others," Kate said.

"I noticed that, too," DeMarco said. "There's a stab wound just above the vagina. More than a stab; he stabbed and then sliced up and down.

It's intentional. If you're aiming for the heart and the stomach, you don't miss by *that* much."

"And that's a pretty blatant spot to aim for," Kate said, doing her best not to grimace at the sight. "Like you said … this was intentional. It's the first sign from this killer that this was more than just murder. I think this might be the first sign of a murder of emotion. Sexual in nature, I'd safely assume."

"So why her and not the others?" DeMarco asked.

"I guess we need to find that out."

The tortured wailing of the husband filled the house again. There was rage in his screams as well as sorrow. He wanted vengeance. The lacing of obscenities that followed his mournful cries was further proof of this.

Kate stepped further into the bathroom, careful to watch for any other stray water. She hunkered down and looked for any stray streaks or marks on the white tiled floor. While she saw nothing of the sort, she did see a small white fragment of something, all the way over by the edge of the shower.

She inched a little closer, careful not to disturb the body. With a few more steps, she realized what she was looking at. It was a portion of a tooth.

"She was hit," Kate said. "See this piece of tooth?"

DeMarco nodded and then got closer to the body. She leaned down and looked at Taylor Woodward's face. "Very slight bruising just above her upper lip on the left side. If she was struck, it'll be more than enough to get a print."

"This guy's smart," she said. "Not a single print yet—not on a body, on a doorknob, nothing. I'm suspecting he wears gloves."

"Any theories on how this played out?" DeMarco asked.

"All the water on the floor makes me think he just grabbed her right out of the shower," Kate said. "But the lack of any real sign of a struggle makes me think it was another case of Taylor knowing the killer, or at least expecting someone she knew. He got in easily enough. I'd even venture that he knew she was showering."

"You think this is another affair-related thing, too? That sort of knowledge about someone's schedule ..."

"Well, but the husband had to have come home very soon after she was killed. If the killer was a lover or something, you'd think they'd be more careful with their time tables." She looked around the bathroom one more time and shook her head. "Something just doesn't add up here."

"We need to speak with the husband," DeMarco said.

"For sure. But from the sound of it, he's not in the best state. In the meantime, I think we should have a look around the rest of the house. Maybe even outside."

They both slowly left the bathroom, Kate giving the body one last look. As grisly as it seemed, her eyes kept going back to that stab wound below the waist. It showed intention, maybe even the kind of malice and spite that had been absent from the other two scenes.

He's either starting to enjoy the act of killing more or there was something different about Taylor Woodward, Kate thought. *If it's the latter, that could point to motive or a solid lead.*

She also thought about something Tate O'Brien had said when she'd spoken with him.

DeMarco had asked him: *"So you did it for love?"*

His response had been: *No. It was just my wife for love. It was out of rage for her lover. And that third one ... if I'm being honest, I just got carried away. It was almost ... fun by that point."*

She wondered if this killer was going through a similar evolution.

They headed back downstairs to the sounds of an anguished husband. She'd heard similar cries at murder scenes before but it was something she had never gotten used to. Even when she and DeMarco circled the property for any signs of breaking and entering, the husband's wails followed her, sending little chills into her heart.

CHAPTER THIRTY

Some of Budd's men managed to talk the husband down from his heart-broken state. At some point, his mother had showed up to console him. Kate assumed the mother had done more good than the policemen. Kate and DeMarco were back in the bedroom, looking around for any signs that the killer might have been looking for something in particular, when Budd came for them.

"He's still obviously in a wrecked state, but he wants to speak with you. He understands that the sooner he does, the better chance we have of finding the killer. He's currently across the street with his neighbors. His mother had to drag him out of this house kicking and screaming."

On the way back downstairs, Budd filled them in on what he had picked up on while around the husband. His name was Daryl Woodward. He worked as an insurance salesman in town. His office was less than twenty minutes away from home but it sometimes took him as much as forty-five minutes to get home from work if he got caught in traffic at the wrong time. When his mother had gotten there, she'd taken him out of the house, not wanting him to grieve knowing that his dead wife was in the bathroom over his head.

Kate and DeMarco walked across the street to the neighbor's house. A few cops were on the porch, speaking with the neighbors. They acknowl-edged the agents as they passed but said nothing. The entire porch and house beyond was veiled in an overwhelming silence.

When they entered the living room, they found Daryl Woodward and his mother sitting on the couch. They were huddled together in a sad embrace. Kate hated to break their silence but she took a moment to introduced DeMarco and herself. She noted how Daryl Woodward nodded and followed her with his eyes like he was in some sort of dreaming state. The mother, who introduced herself as Miranda Thomas, held her son close as if he were a fragile kid who had scraped his knee on the playground. There was nothing creepy or overprotective about it as far as Kate was concerned. She was simply a mother, heartbroken for her suddenly distraught son.

"Mr. Woodward, I can't imagine how you must be feeling right now," Kate said. "So I'm going to only ask basic questions to make this as quick as possible."

He nodded his understanding, His bottom lip was trembling and his eyes were both wide and tired-looking at the same time. It was a rather creepy-looking expression.

"Do you know what Taylor had been doing before you arrived home?" Kate asked.

"Yeah. She had just gotten back from the gym. Her gym bag was at the foot of the bed. I don't think she'd even cleaned it out yet."

"How often does she go to the gym?"

"Three or four times a week. She prefers to go later in the afternoon because the crowd isn't as bad."

"How was she holding up as of late with the deaths of her two friends, Julie Hicks and Lacy Thurmond?"

"It hurt her. She cried hardest for Julie. They were pretty close, I think."

"Mr. Woodward, I know it's a hard question, but can you think of anyone who might have wanted to do this to Taylor?"

He shook his head and started wailing instantly. It was a deep groaning that came out of him in something akin to a grunt. Kate watched him valiantly try to fight it off so he could answer their questions. It was the first time in a while that Kate felt like a terrible person. She was interrupting his grieving, stopping him from properly mourning his wife. But, as Budd had said, certainly Daryl knew that the sooner he spoke, the better the chance of finding the killer.

"Mr. Woodward, I have to ask you some very hard questions now. Questions you're going to hate me for asking. And you may not want your mother here."

"It's okay," Daryl said. "I'm expecting them. After what happened with Julie and Lacy ... I know what you're going to ask. And no. I can guarantee you that she was not having an affair."

"But you acknowledge that her friends were?" DeMarco asked.

"Julie was. She told Taylor all about it. But if Lacy was having an affair, it was being kept very quiet. Pretty sure her husband was messing around behind Lacy's back though."

Miranda Thomas seemed appalled at all of this information but said nothing.

"What about social situations?" Kate asked. "Was there anything you know of that Julie, Lacy, and Taylor were all involved in?"

"No. I mean, nothing like clubs or anything like that. We all have memberships at the same pool, but that's about it. It was just the women, mind you. There were never dates with all of us as couples. Hell, I've never even met Julie's husband."

"You told Chief Budd that you work close to your home," DeMarco said. "What time do you usually get home?"

"Some nights it's as early as seven. But there are nights when it's as late as eight o'clock. I try to sneak home as early as five on the days where I've busted my ass but the damned traffic makes it hard, you know?"

He was sobbing as he spoke, making some of the words very difficult to understand. Kate couldn't help but wonder if, as he spoke, he was beginning to understand that for the next few years, it might not matter much *when* he got home from work.

"One last question," Kate said. "When you were on your way in—that is, once you made it into Amber Hills coming from work—did you pass any cars that you noticed were speeding or maybe even driving recklessly?"

"No, I didn't notice anything like that," he said.

Kate knew that Daryl Woodward was doing his absolute best. But she also knew that he'd be much more effective in terms of useful information in the coming days. Given that, she took out one of her old business cards, another of the relics she had held onto in the year between retirement and being brought back in to the bureau several days ago. She nearly handed it to him but then realized that the number on it was to the old bureau phone she'd had back then.

Got to get news ones, she thought, a little embarrassed. In the context of what Daryl Woodward was going through, though, it felt stupid.

"Mr. Woodward, would you mind giving me your phone number? I'm going to text you my number. And in the coming days, I want you to call me if you think of anything else. I'm very interested in anything Taylor and her friends might have been involved in together. Or maybe the names of people you heard Taylor talking about that only came up on occasion. That sort of thing. Can you do that?"

"Sure," he said. "I wish I could help. I wish there was something…"

An explosion of grief came out of him in that moment. Daryl sank into his mother's shoulder and cried. He screamed so hard that Kate feared he might pass out. He had, after all, vomited from the sight of his wife less than an hour and a half ago. She couldn't imagine the trauma he was going through.

Only, she *could.* She remembered what it had been like seeing Michael after he'd been shot. She remembered that empty feeling, the sensation of being detached from the world.

Miranda looked at them with her own tears in her eyes. "Please … go," she said. "I don't mean that in a disrespectful way, but you can clearly see that he's in no shape…"

"Of course," Kate said. She'd wanted to exchange numbers with him, but she could manage that some other way. "Thank you for your time," she added as she stepped away.

DeMarco followed along, clearly not on the same page. Still, the younger agent said nothing until they were back outside, headed across the street back to the Woodward residence.

"That's it?" she asked. "That's all the questions we had for him?"

"For now," she said. "He needs to clear his head. I can't push him to answer questions that his grief is going to manipulate or make foggy."

"He did seem sincere, huh?" DeMarco asked.

"He did. But there's something else in his moaning and crying. There's rage there, I think. If he thinks of something, he'll call."

"Poor guy," DeMarco said. "You think I even need to look into him? Maybe I should call some of his co-workers to make sure he was there this afternoon?"

"Can't hurt," Kate said. But really, that would just be checking off a box. Based on what she had seen, there was no way in hell Daryl Woodward was a suspect.

While DeMarco did some digging, trying to get the phone numbers of Daryl's co-workers, Kate went back into the house and looked for Budd. He was standing in the kitchen, comparing notes with a few other officers.

"He's still in no shape to talk right now," Kate told Budd. "He did his best but we're going to step away for a bit. When he's stable, I'd like for you to give him my number if you don't mind."

"I can do that," he said. He turned his back to the officer he had been speaking to and looked Kate in her eyes. When he spoke, his voice was much quieter than it had been three seconds ago. "Did you see *anything* that might help?" he asked, looking up toward the ceiling.

"A few things of note, but we don't know for sure yet," she said. "I'll keep you posted. I want to keep you and your force on this alongside us. The more, the merrier—and the better chance to wrap this damn thing up."

Budd sighed and rubbed at his temples. "I appreciate that. And I'll make sure Daryl Woodward gets your number."

Kate left, noting the defeated look on Budd's face. He was angry, sure, but he also looked beaten. It was the look of a man who had no idea what to do.

Honestly, she felt for him. She knew that they were doing their very best. There were policemen at every single Amber Hills entrance and, as of about ten minutes ago, there were two police cars parked in front of Wendy Hudson's home. She figured the next step would be to canvas the neighborhood, to send police officers door to door looking for even the most minuscule bit of information.

But she knew that such measures were usually kept as last resorts—a desperate grasp for *something*.

And if that's where they currently were on this case, there might be nothing more than disappointment ahead.

Chapter Thirty One

Even after spending another half an hour at the crime scene and looking around the body, Kate and DeMarco were unable to find anything that was instantly beneficial. Kate, however, was more convinced than ever that Taylor Woodward would be the key to finding the killer. The focus on the genitals spoke volumes. Upon first glance, Kate had been pretty sure there had been no sexual activity involved in the murder, but of course, the coroner would have to be the one to confirm that.

There was also the punch to the face to be considered. It was not the killer's style based on what they'd seen at the other two scenes. Something about Taylor Woodward had apparently bothered him much more than Julie Hicks or Lacy Thurmond.

Due to the late hour, the door-to-door approach was nixed fairly quickly, though a few officers were sent out to neighboring houses of people who had known the Hicks, Thurmonds, and Woodwards relatively well. While Budd sent a few men out to tackle that assignment, Demarco had managed to find one of Daryl Woodward's co-workers who was able to meet with them on short notice.

Kate was driving to the address of the co-worker when her phone rang. There were so many loose ends on this case that she honestly had no idea who to expect on the other end. The voice she heard was, admittedly, not one she had expected to hear. It was Assistant Director Duran.

"Agent Wise, what is your current location?" he asked.

"There's been another murder," she said, feeling rather guilty for not notifying him sooner. "DeMarco and I are on the way to visit with a co-worker of the husband to make sure his story checks out."

"I know there's been another murder," he said. "When I gave you authority to work the case, I asked Chief Budd to keep me posted on any new developments. The victim is Taylor Woodward, right? Thirty-one years old, killed by multiple stab wounds to the chest and abdomen."

"That's right."

"Look, Wise … I won't lie about this: some of the other directors are thinking we made a mistake. There's grumbling about jumping the gun on this, on letting you take this case. So as your acting director, I'm officially pulling you."

"Are you serious?"

"Yes. While we certainly don't blame you, this third victim makes this case much more of a priority. We'd like to task another agent to it. Maybe a few more. And before you argue, you need to think it through. As of right now, plans are still in place to have you come in and assist with cold cases. But if you remain on this and results aren't found quickly, I'm afraid a decision will be made to scrap that effort as well."

"You gave me three days," she said. "Less than three days, actually. And in those three days, my daughter went into labor five weeks early and I became a grandmother. I've been a little rushed."

"You're only proving my point further," Duran said. "You have a life outside of the bureau now. You should live it."

This is *my life,* she nearly said. But even the thought alone sounded sad and pathetic.

"So what was the point of all of this? Do you think I can't wrap this case?"

"I didn't say that. But the decision has been made. I'm sorry, Kate."

She didn't want to grovel (not that she ever would) and she didn't want to seem desperate or needy in front of DeMarco. So she was essentially stuck.

"Is the cold case option still open if I let this go?"

"I'm fairly certain of it. And like I said … there has been no official decision to pull you from those above me. But it's coming. If I can report to them that I've already done it, it makes things much smoother for the cold case option."

"Fine. Do it, then," she said.

It was an odd feeling. She was angry to have been given the opportunity only to have it yanked away from her a few days later. But at the same time, she was grateful; she knew that it was extremely rare for retired agents to get such an opportunity.

"I appreciate your understanding, Wise," Duran said. "DeMarco will remain on the case. I'll have assistance out there to accompany her by eight o'clock tomorrow morning."

"I'll let her know," Kate said. And while it may have been a bit unprofessional, Kate ended the call without a proper goodbye.

"That didn't sound good," DeMarco said.

"It wasn't. Because of the lack of results and a third victim, I've been pulled from the case."

"What the hell?"

Kate shrugged. "It makes sense. They were already taking a risk by letting me on it. The case got out of my hands and they can't afford the bad PR. It also potentially salvages one other opportunity for me. You're still on, though. He's sending people to assist you tomorrow."

"Still ... this sucks."

Kate shrugged. "It does. But it is what it is."

"I'll keep you informed if you want me to."

Kate considered it for a moment and then shook her head. "Best not to. I need to remove myself from it completely. But I'm going to put in an excellent word for you. And who knows ... maybe you and I can work together again in the future."

DeMarco said nothing. She just looked out the window and watched the night pass by.

"I'm going to take you back to the motel," Kate said. "You should still go meet with Daryl Woodward's co-worker."

"Sounds good," DeMarco said.

But DeMarco now looked just as defeated as Chief Budd had while standing in the Woodwards' kitchen. Kate tried to think of something to say, something inspiring and motivating, but nothing came to mind.

They continued the drive back to the motel in silence as a sense of failure filled the car like the stench of a dead animal on the side of the road.

For the second time that day, Kate found herself thinking about the first partner she'd had while working as an agent. His name was Jimmy Parker and he'd quickly become something of a mentor to Kate. She'd worked with him for eight years before he had been promoted to the position of assistant director of a field office in Atlanta. He'd eventually come back to DC to fill in for another director who had lost his job very suddenly. Jimmy had filled out the rest of his years in that position and retired a few years later. Kate had been thirty-eight when he'd retired.

She thought back to those years, startled to find that nearly twenty years had passed since she'd been thirty-eight. She knew that Jimmy was still alive and well, having gotten a brief phone call the week she'd retired last year. Jimmy was nearing eighty years of age and although he'd said nothing about it during that phone call one year ago, there had been a rumor circulating that he was fighting some form of cancer and wasn't looking too well.

When Kate returned home from dropping DeMarco off at the motel, her thoughts instantly went to Jimmy Parker. Perhaps it was her ability to finally sympathize with him—the retired mentor who had always made a point to call the bureau heads at least once a month to check on things— not because he felt he could really contribute any further but because he had simply never learned to let go of that life.

With no one to talk to and well aware of the dangers of internalizing things like failure and confusion when it came to bureau work, Kate found herself pulling up Jimmy's number on her cell phone. She stared at it for a moment, unsure. Would he appreciate this call or feel almost obligated to her?

Before she could overthink it, Kate pressed CALL. When the phone started ringing, she realized that it was closing in on ten o'clock at night. Was that too late to call a man who was slowly creeping up on eighty years of age?

Apparently not. He answered on the second ring and when he did, it was in a bright and cheerful voice.

"Kate Wise," he said as if he were announcing her presence to a large room. "How in the hell are you?"

"Still here," she said, not wanting to dump her issues on him right away.

"Is retirement suiting you?"

"No. it never really did. Maybe that's why I somehow ended up working another case this week."

"On official grounds?" Jimmy asked.

"More or less. It was short-lived, though."

"You'll have to teach me how you talked your way into that," Jimmy said. "I pestered them for years about maybe coming back on for part-time work."

"I doubt they saw it as pestering," Kate said. "How are you, Jimmy? A real answer, if you please."

"I'm getting old," he said with a creaky laugh. "Seventy-eight is a bitch. I have arthritis in my right hand. I had a knee replacement last year. My bladder is weaker than thin toilet paper and I'm having to go to the doctor at least once a month to keep a check on my heart and prostate."

"How are you spending your days?" she asked, realizing just how thin of a question it was the moment it was out of her mouth.

"Sitting around. I watch TV. I read. I'm part of a chess club but I'm the oldest member and these young kids are beating me pretty bad. So if you have tales of somehow getting back into work after retirement, I'd love to hear them."

"It's really not very exciting," Kate said.

Nevertheless, she found herself telling him the series of events that had occupied the last week or so of her life. From Debbie Meade asking her to look into the death of her daughter all the way up to Duran relieving her of her temporary bureau duties. She even went into scant details of the case, noting the way Jimmy gave a series of *wows* and *you don't says* in all the right places.

When she came to the end of it, she realized that she really *had* been privileged to get the opportunity. She just hoped her inability to wrap the case would not reflect poorly on DeMarco.

"So, this case," Jimmy said. "You believe this last victim stands out among the other two because of some of the details of the killing, yes?"

"Seems that way," Kate said.

"So that would suggest that the killer perhaps had some sort of grudge against her. And that would lead me to believe that there was some sort of personal beef between the two—either directly or indirectly."

"That's the assumption I'm running with, yes. But it doesn't matter. I'm not on the case anymore. And the agent who has it is highly competent. She's going to be amazing in a few years."

"You can let a case go just like that?"

"I have to," she said. "I became a grandmother the other night. I'm toying with the idea of dating again. My life is sort of evolving all around me. And maybe going back to work in such a capacity was a step back. Maybe I need to let go of the past."

"That's the worst-smelling bullshit I've ever heard," Jimmy said.

"The grumpy old man persona really fits you," Kate said.

"Oh, I know. And I wear it with pride. It lets me call out people when they're talking foolishness. Like you are. Take it from me: if you have the chance to get one or two more cases in—even if it's working mundane tasks on cold cases—take it. If not, you'll always wonder if you wasted one last shot."

She let this sink in, knowing that even the possibility of staying in the game on those cold case files would be a great opportunity. It was either that or resigning herself to the fact that the retired life was all she had waiting. And while there was a new granddaughter in the picture, she knew she also had to live her own life. Fifty-five, after all, was not the end of the world.

"So tell me about this granddaughter," Jimmy said.

And just like that, the man she had learned most of the bureau basics from had turned her away from painful self-reflection and toward joy. *Some things never change,* she thought as she told him all about Michelle, Melissa, and her growing family.

It was good to talk about those things … refreshing in a way. It made her wonder what it might be like to give Allen Goldman a chance. Even if there wasn't perfect chemistry between them, she'd at least have someone who was interested in her, who would be there to listen to her brag about her beautiful baby granddaughter and the things she hoped to do with her life now that she was retired.

She stayed on the phone for another half an hour with Jimmy Parker. It was good to reconnect with someone who had played such a pivotal role early in her career. It made her think of DeMarco again and how these last few days would not harm her future in any way.

She got off the phone with Jimmy feeling lighter, not so bogged down with the knowledge that Duran had benched her. She found peace in it and was able to refocus her mind on her future. She thought of Melissa and the baby, of maybe giving Allen a call tomorrow and taking him up on dinner on Friday.

Still, when she closed her eyes in search of sleep, there was something sinister at the core of all of those things. She could not help but see the floor of the master bathroom in the Woodwards' house and all of that blood mingling with the water, as if the world itself was trying to wash any evidence away.

CHAPTER THIRTY TWO

Kate woke up to the ringing of her cell phone. She had not set an alarm, deciding to let herself sleep as late as she could. But when she grabbed at the phone, she saw that the blue digital letters on her alarm clock read 8:05.

Eight hours of sleep, she thought to herself. *When was the last time that happened?*

She saw DeMarco's name on the display and got excited. Maybe something big had occurred last night, some big break in the case perhaps. Despite the calming talk with Jimmy last night, her heart could not help but leap at the prospect of some exciting news involving the events that had been taking place in Amber Hills.

"Hey, DeMarco," she answered. "Miss me already?"

"The way this morning is going, yeah... I miss you tons. Duran called me at seven to let me know that two agents are on their way down to work this with me. One is straight out of the academy."

"You'll manage it," Kate said. "Something has to turn up eventually."

"Well, we do have a few updates. First of all, the medical exam came back early this morning. There were absolutely no signs of sexual intercourse. So I guess the cut to the genitals was symbolic."

"Or just the killer having some morbid fun," Kate pointed out.

"We also picked up what looks to be a print. It was right along the edge of the shower door. But it was so wet, we don't think it's going to amount to much. Some hair was also pulled from the drain but we're expecting it all to belong to the Woodwards."

"Thanks for the updates," Kate said. "But you don't have to do that. I'm off of it. You don't owe me updates."

"I know. But I know it has to piss you off to be put on something like this after a year away only to be pulled off of it. It's honestly not fair to you. I wonder if maybe I'm more pissed about it than you are."

"You might be," Kate said, already thinking of visiting the hospital to see Melissa and Michelle sometime after breakfast.

"You want me to stop calling you?" DeMarco asked.

"No, of course not. I appreciate it. I just don't want you to feel that you owe it to me."

"Look, if we aren't going to be partners, I'd like to consider you a friend," DeMarco said. "And that's hard for me to say. So yes ... as a common courtesy, I'm going to keep you updated."

"In that case, I look forward to your call. Best of luck out there, Agent DeMarco."

Kate ended the call and made herself the day's first cup of coffee. She sipped at it while watching the news, wondering if she'd make breakfast herself or grab some on the way to the hospital. *These are the kinds of important decisions I have to make while retired,* she thought grimly.

It was wild to think of just how fast-paced yesterday had been. Compared to the humdrum state of this morning, it was almost surreal.

When her phone rang again, she was expecting it to be DeMarco. Maybe she had finally met the new agents and wanted to complain about them. Or maybe the print from the shower door had come back and—

But there was no name on the display of her phone, just a number she did not recognize. She answered it hesitantly. She'd never trusted calls from numbers that weren't programmed into her phone—a lesson she'd learned in her life inside *and* outside of the bureau.

"Hello?" she asked.

"Is this Agent Wise?" a man's voice asked.

She nearly corrected the man to inform him that the "agent" in front of her name was no longer accurate. But she said nothing, curious to see what the call was about.

"Yes, this is Agent Wise," she said, not minding the minor lie.

"This is Daryl Woodward," he said. "Chief Budd gave me your number last night and I remember you told me to call you if I thought of anything else."

The safe and wise thing to do would have been to stop him right there and redirect him to DeMarco. But then there was the steadfast agent still residing over her, a part of her that not only did not want to extend the process any longer for Daryl Woodward, but also wanted to see if she could do anything at all to help with the case that wouldn't get her scolded later down the line.

"Did you come up with something?" she asked.

"Maybe. You asked if they were all involved in anything together, like a club or group or something. I'm pretty sure they were all part of this class at the gym. To be sure, I checked Taylor's planner. She had the class every Monday, Wednesday, and Friday at four in the afternoon. She would have been coming back from it last night. I ... well, a while back I found some text messages on her phone between her and her friends. Group texts, you know? They were talking about the class. Julie and Wendy got a little raunchy about the instructor."

"By raunchy, do you mean sexually suggestive?"

"As in Julie mentioned licking the sweat off of his chest. But some-where in there, Wendy also mentioned how the guy was sort of a douche-bag. There was a lot of suggestive talk and I think Lacy might even have slept with him. I don't know. I'm not proud of it, but I took pictures of the conversations, just in case Taylor ever deleted them. I wanted them as proof that her friends were nothing but trouble. I can send you the conversation if you'd like."

"That would be great. And do you happen to know the name of the class and the instructor?"

"It's all in the thread," Daryl said. "I'll send the pictures over to you as soon as we get off of here. The class was at New You Fitness. You know where it is?"

"I do," Kate said. "Thanks for this. This could potentially bring up a lead."

Daryl sounded hopeful when he ended the call. Kate wasn't sure if it would bring up a lead or not, but if the messages were as suggestive as he was letting on, then it could be very helpful indeed.

True to his word, Daryl sent the text thread over within a few min-utes. He sent it as a series of screenshots which Kate read while drinking her coffee. She read it all, noting some of the more surprising comments. Line by line, she became more and more certain that she did indeed have a lead at her fingertips. The messages were from two weeks ago, making it seem as if she were reading the final thoughts of ghosts.

Anyone else have dirty dreams of Julio last night? Julie had asked the group.

My God, Lacy said. *I didn't even wait to sleep. I went to the bed-side drawer and utilized some hardware while Peter was asleep. Good dreams?*

Yeah. I was licking the sweat off of his chest, Julie said. *Tasted like wine.*

Weirdo, Wendy said.

That man IS fine, Taylor replied. *I'd keep going to cycling class until my joints got old and busted if he'd keep teaching.*

Speaking of joints, how'd he treat your knees, Lacy? Wendy asked.

They still sting, but GOD it was worth it. He texted me later and said he's keeping my panties in his gym bag as a reminder. Says it turns him on. He's good at pretending it didn't happen, but the way he was looking at me yesterday ...

Stop it, Julie said. *Or I'm going to get MY hardware.*

That big one? Wendy asked. *I can hear that fucking thing all the way over here at my house.*

The messages went on from there, but that was the section that Kate honed in on. It did seem to suggest that Lacy had, at some point, slept with the instructor of their cycling class.

Looks like Lacy was seeing someone on the side while her husband did his own thing after all, Kate thought.

And just like that, she had a lead.

The only question that remained was whether or not she could pass it off to DeMarco and remain uninvolved.

The answer, of course, was no. She smiled as she called up DeMarco. The younger agent answered right away. "I thought I was supposed to be calling you," DeMarco said.

"Well, I got something. How long before those other agents show up?"

"About an hour, I guess."

"Okay. Meet me at your motel in twenty minutes. I might have something."

"Like what?"

Already headed out the door, Kate relayed her conversation with Daryl Woodward and the text thread he had sent her. With a sudden change to the morning's schedule, it looked like she'd be picking up breakfast on her way out after all.

CHAPTER THIRTY THREE

The early morning crowd was thin at New You Fitness. A few people were using the treadmills and only a handful of others were scattered around the various stations. Kate could see all of this from the front desk, as the gym area was visible through clear Plexiglas to the left of the desk. The place was a little too small to be considered an actual gym but it was also much cleaner than a typical gym.

With DeMarco at her side, Kate approached the desk. A young woman who was likely a part-timer with college classes in between looked up at them with a smile. "How can I help you ladies this morning?"

"We're looking for a man named Julio Almas," DeMarco said. "Your website says he's the instructor for cycling classes and Keto workouts."

"Oh, sure," the young woman said. "He should be back in Room Six. He's got a Keto class starting in about twenty minutes."

The agents nodded their thanks and headed around the desk where a thin corridor housed several private rooms. On the drive to the fitness center, they had discussed the best approach to take. It was agreed that DeMarco would take the lead just in case things got out of hand. The fewer chances Kate had to reveal that she was not an active agent—or to lie about it, for that matter—the better.

They came to Room 6 and found only one man inside. He was laying out several mats on the floor, getting ready for his next class apparently. DeMarco knocked on the door and walked inside, not waiting for the man to respond.

He turned to face them and Kate saw right away why Julio might be the subject of needy women's fantasies. He was of average height but was built like a Greek statue. His pecs and abs were just about visible through the tight tank top he wore. His long black hair was slicked back in what kids were now calling a "man-bun." He had dark eyes that were instantly captivating and every feature on his face seemed to complement everything else. To say the man was handsome was an understatement. Kate couldn't help but wonder if he had been hired to get more women to sign up for private classes.

She also wondered whether, if Lacy *had* been sleeping with him—even just the one time—if she was the only one.

"Need some help?" Julio asked.

"Yes, in fact," DeMarco said, keeping her cool. "We'd like to speak with you about a few recent participants in one of your cycling classes." She showed her ID and introduced herself. Kate watched him closely and saw a flicker of fear in his eyes. It was the first time since walking into the crime scene at Julie Hicks's house that she thought they might have something here.

"You mean Mrs. Hicks and Mrs. Thurmond, right?"

"And you know that how, exactly?" DeMarco asked.

"Word gets around. It's terrible. They were both murdered, is that right?"

"That's exactly right," Kate said. "Another of your members was killed last night as well. Taylor Woodward."

He seemed legitimately shocked, but there still seemed to be something off about him.

"We're here because your cycling class seems to be the one thing that linked them together aside from the occasional wine drinking session and hanging out at the pool. Do you know if they had any relationships established with your other students?"

"I can't say for sure. I don't know. I really didn't know them that well. Just enough to say hello when they came into class."

"You sure about that?" Kate asked. "You didn't know Lacy Thurmond any better than your other students?"

The question rocked him and if he tried at all to hide it, he failed miserably. "I ... I don't understand why you're here," he said. He was looking around the room like a caged animal seeking a way out.

"Did you have any sort of physical relationship with Lacy, Taylor, or Julie?"

He nodded his head nervously. "Yes. I did. I slept with Lacy. But it was just one time. We were planning on a second but then I heard about what happened and ..."

"Was the sex mutual?" DeMarco asked.

"Yes."

"How did it happen?" DeMarco asked.

"I'm not comfortable with this line of questioning," Julio said.

"Okay then," DeMarco asked. "Was it in her home?"

"No. It was here, actually. In the changing room after one of my shifts."

"And did you keep a souvenir?" Kate asked.

It was clear that Julio was truly shocked now. He shook his head violently as his bottom lip started to tremble.

"Please just tell the truth," Kate said. "You are in no trouble for hooking up with a married woman. We just need a better idea of how she spent her last few days before she was murdered."

"I ... I have the underwear she was wearing. They're in my gym bag."

"Is that all?" Kate asked.

"Yes. You have my word."

"Where is that gym bag?" DeMarco said. "Let us have a look inside and we might be able to get out of your hair before your next class starts."

"No, no ... you need a warrant, right?"

"If you choose to go that route, yes," Kate said. "But then we can go get it and make sure to come visit you again with that warrant right in the middle of one of your classes. So really, it's your choice."

Julio looked angry now but he started walking toward the door, waving him on behind him. He led them to the end of the hallway, to a room with a decorative sign that read STAFF ONLY. The room was a small one, boasting only a single table, several chairs, and an entire back wall of small lockers. He went to the one with his name marked on a piece of masking tape and popped it open.

"Here," he said, throwing a well-worn gym bag onto the table. He was clearly pissed off but was more driven by his need to get them out of there before his next class.

Kate stopped herself from stepping forward, reminding herself that DeMarco had to take the lead today. She could only imagine the look on Duran's face if he knew she was taking part in this. She nodded to DeMarco and the younger agent unzipped the bag. She rummaged around for a few moments and then, seemingly for no reason, yanked her hand back.

Kate, DeMarco, and Julio stood in a tight group, in silence. Kate locked eyes with DeMarco, trying to figure out what was wrong—what had happened to cause DeMarco to pull her hand away so quickly.

And then she saw the blood on the side of DeMarco's hand.

"What the hell?" Julio said, taking a cautious step forward.

DeMarco's hand went to her sidearm as she wheeled around on him. "Don't move," she said. "Stay right there. One more step forward and I *will* draw my gun."

Kate stepped forward, closer to the bag. She peered inside as, undaunted, DeMarco reached back inside. This time when DeMarco's hand came out, she brought a pair of white lace panties with her. The white of the material made the dark red of the blood stand out.

The blood was not brand new, but it was fresh enough to stick to DeMarco's skin. DeMarco looked inside and then back to Kate. "Have a look," she said.

Kate looked into the bag. She saw Julio's gym shorts, his wallet, and a pair of black gloves. The gloves had more blood on them, as did the nylon bottom of the bag. Like the blood on the panties and DeMarco's hand, it was still relatively new.

"Against the wall," DeMarco said, facing back toward Julio.

"I don't understand," he said. "What the hell is going on?"

"You're under arrest," DeMarco said. "If these are indeed Lacy Thurmond's underwear, you've got a ton of explaining to do. And this blood is fresh…not Lacy's but maybe from someone else you've seen recently?"

"The panties are Lacy's, yes. But I have no idea where the blood came from!"

"You can recite all of that in an interrogation room," DeMarco said as she took out her set of cuffs and applied them to Julio's wrists.

"What the *fuck*?" Julio yelled.

Kate looked back into the bag. The blood wasn't exactly pooled up, but there was enough of it to be glistening. She looked for any sign of a weapon, but there was none.

Seems almost too perfect, she thought. *Of course, if this last murder was based on passion and he maybe felt a sense of finality or accomplishment, maybe he got lazy in his clean-up.*

With Julio still facing the lockers and his arms cuffed behind his back, DeMarco looked back to Kate. "What now?" she asked. It seemed like a loaded question but Kate knew what she meant. If she wasn't supposed to be on the case, how should they proceed?

But there was the blood and the panties … an admitted affair to top it all off. Kate was pretty sure she could make the call and be in the clear.

"I'll start by calling Budd," she said. "And then I'll call Duran."

"You sure?" DeMarco asked.

The truth was, she *wasn't* sure. But she went ahead and placed the first call to Budd before she could lose her nerve.

CHAPTER THIRTY FOUR

An hour and fifteen minutes later, Kate was waiting outside of the interrogation room in Chief Budd's precinct. The last hour had been a particularly active one. First of all, there had been the small swarm of policemen who had come to New You Fitness to apprehend Julio. At about the same time, the two agents had arrived from DC to assist DeMarco. They were understandably pissed off to find that the case seemed to already be wrapped up. They waited outside of the interrogation room, too.

It was killing Kate not to partake in the questioning. But when she had called Duran to update him, he had been irate. Kate had expected him to be a little upset, but not as angry as he appeared to be through the phone. As a form of punishment, he'd ordered her to let DeMarco handle the interrogation and that she, Kate, was not to even watch through any sort of surveillance or monitors within the interrogation room.

He had, however, ended the call with a word of thanks for apprehending the man who seemed to be the killer. Even after being scolded, Kate couldn't help but smile. It had been a rocky start, but her first case after coming back had finally wrapped up.

Or had it?

She continued to feel that finding the panties and the blood had seemed too easy. Julio had even admitted to having the panties in his gym bag—but the blood had seemed to throw him off. If she was in the interrogation room, she thought she might be able to read his expressions. She hadn't been sure if the look on his face was a fear borne of guilt or of genuine shock at seeing the blood.

As she waited outside the room, Chief Budd came walking toward her from the front of the building. The two new agents from DC were walking in the other direction, looking to interview some of Julio's co-workers. As for Budd, Kate was pretty sure he'd been with his PR people, drumming up a draft of a press release. It seemed that they were already pretty sure they had their guy. And while even Kate had to admit that it certainly *looked* that way, something was nagging at her.

It's just too damned easy, she thought.

Budd approached her with a grin and extended his hand for a shake. "I understand you're in some hot water with your supervisor," he said. "That's none of my business and quite frankly, I don't care. I just wanted to thank you for cracking this thing. One more murder in that neighborhood and this place would have turned into a madhouse."

She was about to respond to him when the door to the interrogation room opened. DeMarco came out, looking mostly satisfied but a little troubled. Kate looked at her watch and saw that DeMarco had been in there for twenty minutes.

"What's your initial reaction?" Kate asked.

"Everything points to it being him," she said. "The time lines up. There's the sexual relationship to be considered. The blood in his bag..."

"And the gloves," Kate said. "It would explain why we weren't able to find any prints at the crime scenes. Does he have an alibi for between six and seven yesterday afternoon?"

"No. He says he left work, stopped at a WaWa for gas and to grab a snack. Says traffic was pretty bad so it took him a while."

"So you think it's him?" Kate asked.

"Like I said... it *seems* like it. Just the way he responded to me when I described the crime scene... he looked disgusted."

"You have to get that blood tested as soon as possible," Kate said. "And see if you can get some DNA off of the gloves. We should know with certainty if he's the killer within twelve hours."

"Seems like a lot of work to me," Budd said. "As far as I'm concerned, this case is closed. Damned good work, ladies." And with that, he gave them a little bow of appreciation and headed back the way he came.

"Duran feels the same way," DeMarco told Kate when Budd was gone. "He texted while I was in there. He wants me back in DC tonight. The two new agents are to stay here and run clean-up."

"How do you feel about that?" Kate asked.

"Weird. I don't know ... it feels too ... too ..."

"Easy?"

"Exactly," DeMarco said.

They both looked back at the closed interrogation room door and didn't say a word. Their tense silence, though, spoke volumes.

CHAPTER THIRTY FIVE

Kate knew better than to go against Duran's wishes again. But at the same time, she could not just let the case rest if she felt it was still active—especially while local law enforcement was practically celebrating that it was seemingly closed.

So she met in the middle. She returned to her house after DeMarco started filling out the necessary paperwork at the police precinct. But she took her case files with her. She was wondering if she could find something that linked to Julio now that they at least had a profile to work from.

She threw a sandwich together and ate it at the kitchen table with the notes out in front of her. But no matter where she looked, she could find nothing that tied in to the personality Julio exhibited. She supposed it might come down to forensics—the slashing motions of the wounds in relation to Julio's strength, hand preference, and so on. That, or the blood in his bag would indeed turn out to belong to Taylor Woodward and then that would be that. It would take a miracle for him to not be convicted of murder.

Kate pored over the same files she'd already scrutinized several times and found nothing new. She even pulled out the small stack of medical records that Budd's men had pulled in the aftermath of the Thurmond case. Before being taken to her grandparents', the daughter had spent a little time with the Department of Social Services. From what Kate could tell, they had requested the medical records—a standard practice if they weren't immediately sure how long a child would be in their care.

Kate scanned these documents, sure that nothing would be there. She saw where Peter Thurmond had gone to the doctor two years ago for prostatitis. The daughter, Olivia, had gone a few months ago for what turned out to be strep throat. And it was there that Kate saw something she had missed before. It was small and insignificant but was still *something.*

Let it go, she told herself. *Duran doesn't want you on this anymore. He thinks you've already caught the killer. Stop grasping at straws.*

Of course, Kate rarely took her own advice. She looked to the very small detail both she and DeMarco had overlooked. Underneath "Emergency Contacts" on Olivia's form, there were two names and titles. One was *Peter Thurmond – father.* The other read *Pamela Duncan – part-time nanny.*

Well, that's new, Kate thought. She looked at the number beside Pamela Duncan's name and wasted no time. Before fully thinking things through, she called it.

Are you trying *to get yourself in trouble?* she asked herself.

She had no time to come up with an answer. The phone was answered just after the first ring. "Hello?"

"Hi, is this Pamela Duncan?"

"It is."

"Hi, my name is Kate Wise. I'm a consultant with the FBI." A lie, sure ... but not as bad as stating that she was still an active agent. "I saw in some of our background information that you are listed on Olivia Thurmond's medical records as an emergency contact. Were you a nanny for the Thurmond family?"

"Every now and then, yes. Have you found who killed Lacy yet?"

"There is currently a suspect in custody but nothing is definitive yet. Ms. Duncan, I was wondering if you might be able to shed some light on what Lacy's life was like. Maybe even the lives of some of her friends, too."

"Have you talked to them yet? Lacy's friends?"

"Yes. Her closest friends, anyway."

Pamela hesitated for a moment before asking: "Where are you calling from, Ms. Wise?"

"I'm in Richmond. Your phone number indicates that you are, too."

"Can you meet me in about an hour?" Pamela asked.

Kate found the request a little strange but she wasn't about to turn down the opportunity. That old agent instinct was raising its head and sniffing the air. It seemed like there might be something there.

"Just tell me the place," Kate said.

Pamela did, and Kate was back out the door fifteen minutes later.

CHAPTER THIRTY SIX

They met at one of Kate's favorite little spots in Carytown, a place called the Galaxy Diner. It was the kind of trendy place that served fried pickles as well as gluten-free options. When Pamela Duncan took the seat across the table from Kate, she did not look nervous and reserved, as Kate had been expecting. Instead, she looked almost pleased to be there. She even smiled warmly at Kate as she sat down.

After a brief round of introductions, Kate wasted no time in getting to the center of the matter.

"How long did you work for the Thurmonds?" she asked.

"About eight months," Pamela said.

"And what sort of work did you do? I ask only because I find it odd that a mother and wife that stayed at home most of the time would need a nanny."

"Well, about a year or so ago, from what I understand, Lacy had strongly considered going back to college. Some online courses, maybe a few classes at the community college. She'd had everything ready to go when I was hired. I was brought on to mainly just pick Olivia up from school, tidy up the house, prepare dinner. That sort of thing. I only worked about fifteen hours a week—twenty on busy weeks. And even when the college thing didn't pan out, they kept me on for a few weeks. When they let me go, it was amicable. But they did ask if they could keep me in their contacts to call on me every now and then, and I agreed."

"How long ago since they let you go?"

"About five months ago."

"And did they ever call on your services afterwards?"

"A few times. Lacy never actually came out and said as much, but I got the feeling that she and her husband were having some rough patches. They planned these weekend getaways to try to work on their marriage. But as far as I could tell, Peter was cheating on her. He wasn't very good at hiding it, either."

"They apparently trusted you, right?" Kate asked. "You were put down on the medical records as Olivia's emergency contact. Given that, why did you feel the need to speak with me in person?"

"Because Lacy's really close friends ... they were trouble, you know? They seemed like such sweet, beautiful women when I first met them. I'd see them here and there, coming to the house. I was there one day when all of them were sitting around the dining room, drinking wine. I don't remember all of their names but there was one that openly admitted to cheating on her husband. And the others seemed to encourage it. It didn't seem right, you know?

"But there's something else ... something that never sat right with me. And it's sitting heavy on me now because of the murders."

"What is it?" Kate asked. "Ms. Duncan, if you have something that you think might seem like a stretch, it could help. We do have a suspect currently in custody but nothing is set in stone yet."

"The woman that died yesterday ... last name was Woodward, right?"

"That's correct."

"Well, there was this one time that the husband—Daryl, I think his name is—came by the Thurmond home. He was looking for his wife, Taylor. He was really worried about her. Given that group of friends, I don't blame him. He said he knew she was in some kind of trouble."

"Did Lacy ever tell her husband about the incident?"

"No. I think she was scared to. Whatever trouble the Woodward woman was in, I think all of the women might have been wrapped up in it. Her husband was worried sick about her."

"How long ago was this?" Kate asked.

"Maybe two months. Lacy had called me to pick Olivia up from school and take her to cheerleading practice. It's fortunate that I even stopped by the house. I wanted to check in to see how things were going with Lacy."

Kate thought back to the previous night, of how Daryl had been drowning in his grief. Usually spouses behaved that way when they felt they hadn't done enough to stop the murder. Daryl must have suspected all along that Julio was the killer. And now he was too ashamed to say, as he didn't act on his instincts and prevent it in time.

"Daryl was so worried about her, like to the point of almost crying in front of me. And then, two months later, she's dead," she added.

Kate finally felt certain: Julio was the killer, indeed. And now all she needed was for Daryl to confirm it, to tell her the entire story of exactly the type of man that Julio was.

Throughout the course of her career, Kate had come to firmly believe in the old saying *"When it rains, it pours."* Her first little drizzle had come from the meeting with Pamela Duncan.

Her next drizzle came when her phone rang as she was headed back toward Amber Hills. She picked it up right away, not even bothering to check the caller display. "This is Wise," she said, careful not to use the agent moniker.

"Agent Wise, this is Robert Smith from the coroner's office. While we didn't find anything conclusive on the body of Taylor Woodward, there was one detail I thought you might find interesting."

"I'll take whatever I can get," Kate said.

She wondered why he was calling her but then assumed he had no way of knowing that she had been taken off the case.

"The punch to the face left a very small bruise, leading me to believe that it was more of a jab—almost a playful one—than a powerful punch meant to severely hurt the victim. From the punch alone, there are two things that I believe we can determine. First of all, given the placement and the angle, I think it's safe to say that the killer is left-handed. Of course, any number of elements could prove me wrong but it seems very likely."

"And the second thing?" Kate asked.

"There are no prints, indicating the killer wore gloves. However, there is a small indentation along the bruise. It's barely visible at all to the naked eye but under the right lighting and magnification, it's there: a shape that suggests the killer wears a ring on his left hand. Probably either the ring finger or pinky."

"And if he's throwing punches, the pinky wouldn't leave much of an imprint, would it?"

"Likely not."

"A ring on the left ring finger," Kate said. "So the killer was married?"

"I'd say that's a safe bet," Smith said.

Julio, she knew, wore a wedding ring. *And* a pinky ring.

"Thanks for this," Kate said. She got a warm fuzzy feeling in her gut and her heart started pumping a bit faster. She ended the call and immediately pulled up DeMarco's number.

She answered after three rings. DeMarco sounded irritated and a bit tired. "Hey, Wise," she said. "If you're calling for updates, there are none. Duran and the local PD are hanging on the assumption that Julio Almas is our guy."

"Well, I just got a call from the coroner with an early report on Taylor Woodward's body. So tell me something... is Julio right-handed or left-handed?"

"I'm actually not sure. I never bothered looking."

"You still at the PD?"

"Unfortunately."

"Find some bullshit form and take it in there for him to sign. Tell him he'll be released soon after. Pay attention to which hand he signs with."

"Okay ..." DeMarco said, a hint of intrigue in her voice. "Give me a second."

"I'll hold."

Kate listened to the sound of movement from DeMarco's end. She heard the faint voices of the policemen in the background, the place still in a bit of an uproar from the morning's excitement. She was ready to put to rest her doubts about Julio Almas.

Three minutes passed. She was ten minutes away from the gates an Amber Hills when DeMarco came back on the phone.

"He signed it," DeMarco said. "He's a lefty. Why? What have you got?"

Kate sighed.

"Nothing," she said. "Just bad instincts, I guess. Or worn-out ones. Maybe there is a wisdom in retiring at 55. You've got your man. It's Julio."

She hung up and sighed. Maybe she was getting too old for this.

It was time to put all this to bed, once and for all. To find out the entire truth about Julio. And Daryl, she suspected, held the key.

CHAPTER THIRTY SEVEN

Kate wondered if Daryl was able to bring himself to go back home after the murder of his wife. There was no real timetable for grief; some would wait weeks before returning to the home where a loved one was killed while others had no problem with returning right away.

When she pulled up in front of the house, she saw Daryl's mother sitting in a rocker on the front porch. She eyed Kate when she got out of the car and started up the sidewalk.

"Hello again," Kate said as pleasantly as she could. "Is Daryl home?"

"He is," the mother said. "But he's very tired and understandably upset."

"I understand," Kate said. She approached the porch and slowly climbed the stairs. She then spoke in a low conspiratorial voice, hoping to sway the old woman. "This is not public knowledge yet, but we have a potential suspect in custody," she said. "If I could speak with him in private for no more than ten minutes, it could help us ensure that we do indeed have the right man."

Daryl's mother seemed happy at the news, nodding her appreciation. "Okay," she said. "He'd like that, I think. He feels helpless right now. Maybe this will give him a sense of purpose. Would you please let him know I'm going to run to the pharmacy to pick up my prescription?"

"Yes ma'am."

Kate entered the house at the same time Daryl's mother walked to the car in the driveway. As the screen door closed behind Kate, she could hear Mrs. Woodward's car cranking to life.

"Excuse me?" Kate called out. "Mr. Woodward? It's Kate Wise again. Your mother said it was okay if I come inside."

"Of course," he called out from elsewhere in the house. "I'm back in the kitchen."

Kate followed the sound of his voice through the foyer and down the small hallway. The house had a mostly open floor plan so she was able to see the kitchen immediately. She saw Daryl arranging pastries and bagels on the counter. They were still in boxes, some of the pastries still steaming.

"Sorry to bother you again," she said. "But I wanted you to know that we checked up on the cycling instructor. We found enough evidence to take him in."

"It was him?" Daryl asked.

"We don't know for sure, but we're looking into it right now. Looks like it could be a strong possibility. I hope you understand that even as the husband of a recent victim, we can't give you the strict details until an official arrest has been made."

"I understand," he said.

"In the meantime, I was hoping you might be able to help me out. We were told you were very worried about your wife at one point. Why was that?"

He frowned. She watched as his shoulders slumped and he slowly withdrew.

He remained silent.

"Mr. Woodward," she pressed on, "I know this is difficult. I know you don't want to implicate your wife in anything that may have been … unseemly. But, however concerning or embarrassing it may be, I need to know. We have a man locked up right now who may or may not be the right suspect. And I suspect that you may know of some difficulty your wife was in, some difficulty that may help us know for certain if we have the killer."

He stared back at her, his eyes dull and vacant, and opened his mouth to speak several times.

But each time, he remained silent, as if he couldn't bring himself to say it.

But there was more to it than that.

As she observed him closely, she noticed, just for a fraction of an instant, a flicker in his eye. It was something that made no sense. It wasn't one of recognition.

It was one of rage.

It came, and then it left as soon as it did—so fast that she wasn't even sure whether she saw it or imagined it.

Suddenly, her heart started to pound wildly.

No, she thought. *It can't be him.*

But could it?

She thought suddenly of what Tate O'Brien had said about murders committed in the acts of both rage and love.

Several wives were killed. Not just his. If he had killed his wife, that meant...he would have killed all of them.

But why? Why kill all the wives if he only wanted his own dead?

It couldn't be, she thought. *Could it?*

Were all those murders just to cover up his trail? To make this seem like a serial killer? To deflect attention from the real wife he wanted dead? From himself as a suspect?

To create the perfect murder?

"Did you hear me, Agent Wise?"

Kate snapped out of it, back to the present. She found Daryl staring at her questioningly. Her mind spun, and she felt light-headed, wondering if she could be standing a few feet from the killer.

"I'm sorry," she said, her voice trembling, trying to keep it calm. "I wasn't listening."

"I asked you if there was anything else I could help you with?" he asked, his voice so calm that she wondered if she had imagined the whole thing.

His hand, she thought fast. *Get him to write something. See if he's a lefty.*

She cleared her throat and tried to keep her voice calm.

"Yes," she said. "There is just one more thing. Could you perhaps give me the names of a few friends that Taylor hung out with?"

"OK," he said with a frown. "Want me to text them to you?"

"I'm old-school," she said as gently as possible. "Could you just write them down?"

He eyed her suspiciously, seemed to hesitate.

Finally, he turned and walked to the left side of the kitchen and opened up a drawer. He took out a pen and a Post-It.

He started writing.

With his left hand.

As his wedding band shone dully from his ring finger.

Stay calm, she told herself. *This still doesn't prove anything. You have to goad him. It's now or never. You can't walk out without knowing for sure.*

"I spoke with your mother out front," Kate said. "She wanted me to tell you she was going to run to the pharmacy." She paused a beat and then added: "Are you close to your mother?"

There it was again. The flicker of rage in his eyes, this time recognizable, and stronger.

And that was when Kate knew for sure. Many killers she had dealt with had been oppressed by their mothers in some way or another; too many times that had been the trigger to vent their feelings.

Daryl just gritted his jaw and stared back, the hostility pouring through his face.

"What business is that of yours?" he asked.

He sneered at her slightly and then turned his head. He walked to the coffeemaker and started pouring himself a cup of coffee. His hand was visibly trembling.

She didn't wait for him. She knew it was now or never. She knew she should leave the house, call for backup.

But she just couldn't bring herself to.

Her entire career, she just couldn't bring herself to. She always had to push it, just a little too far. Always had to disregard that voice of caution.

"Mr. Woodward, the coroner is all but certain that your wife was punched by a lefty—a lefty wearing a ring on his left ring finger," she said. "Julio Almas is right-handed and has no rings," she lied. "Why do you think that is?"

Daryl Woodward stopped for a moment, in the midst of bringing his coffee cup to his mouth. His back was mostly to her but she could see from the posture in his shoulders that he was taking a defensive position.

"*You're* a lefty, aren't you?" she asked.

He tensed up, his back still to her.

"You're insane," he muttered, his voice growing darker.

Now, she told herself. *Stop now and call for backup.*

She knew she should. But she just couldn't. She had to finish this thing. On her own.

"You hated the other women but didn't really want to kill them, did you? You really truly only wanted Taylor dead. But how could you kill her and not have the cops suspect you? Easy. You kill a few other wives and make it look like a serial. That way, a lone husband wouldn't so clearly be a suspect.

"But you went a little too far with your wife, Daryl. That was a murder of passion. The only one."

He turned around and smiled at her, as if impressed.

Then he charged.

Kate threw her arms up to defend herself, fully prepared to catch his left arm—which he was leading with—and whip him over onto the floor.

But she did not expect the hot coffee thrown at her. It splashed against her face, getting into her eyes. It was very hot, but not freshly hot. Still, the sting of it was enough to take her off guard.

Daryl threw his full weight into her. Her back slammed against the kitchen island behind her and as she recoiled and fell to the floor with her back spasming, she felt the first punch fall, splitting open her lip.

Blood flowed, instantly filling Kate's mouth. Just as she tasted it, thick and coppery on her tongue, he planted a knee in her stomach. The wind went rushing out of her and for the first time since entering the FBI, she allowed herself to think:

This is it. This is how I'm going to die.

CHAPTER THIRTY EIGHT

Had the coffee been freshly brewed and piping hot, Kate would have been in much worse shape. As it was, she was more concerned with her back. She'd hit the edge of the island hard and something back there was going numb. Meanwhile, Daryl had her pinned to the floor, a knee in her stomach and both of his hands on her shoulders.

"I wish I had the knife I killed those bitches with," Daryl said. "I'd slit you open right here, right now. And it would be a shame because you're not like them. They deserved it, you know?"

Good, she thought. *This idiot is going to brag on himself. He's strong and easily overpowers me, but the longer he keeps me here, in this position, the better chance I have of escaping.*

"It wasn't a mistake that I started with Julie. She's a ... well, she *was* such a tease. We were sleeping with each other. Had been for months. Taylor didn't know, though. She was too hung up on her own little activities. And yes, I knew all about the cycling instructor. He's slept with half the fucking neighborhood. So yeah ... why not pin it on him?"

He smiled and a chuckle escaped from his lips. It was this one little cocky action that gave Kate the opening she needed. As his right hand relaxed with his laughter, she pushed forward, sitting up and using her right shoulder to force the weight of the movement. She then threw her elbow up and out, catching him in the chin. She heard the sharp *click* of his teeth smashing together.

He tottered back, shocked, and nearly fell off of her. Enraged, he threw another punch downward. She caught him by the wrist, twisted hard to the left, and his entire body followed suit. Had he not struck the side of the kitchen island, she would have been able to apply an arm bar, ripping his elbow out of its socket and ending the fight there.

But the island was in the way. As she scrambled to her feet, Daryl opened a nearby cabinet. Kate was so confused by the action that she didn't see the rolling pin until it was too late. She swayed backward but the end of it still clipped her on the side of the head. She spun around as little black stars swirled across her field of vision.

He came at her again, the rolling pin raised like a club.

No, Kate thought with a maniacal sort of panic. *Not like this. Hell no ...*

He swung the pin again, straight across this time. Kate managed to block it with her left forearm. A bolt of pain rocketed up her arm. She cried out, looking around for a weapon to use. So far, she'd been burned by coffee and struck with a rolling pin. She'd be damned if she'd be insulted any farther.

She backed up against the kitchen sink and found a fork sitting in the edge. It was positioned on a plate with what looked like the remnants of scrambled eggs. As Daryl surged forward one more time, she grabbed it and jabbed forward in a move that reminded her of her younger days. She moved with the speed of a seasoned boxer, and the prongs of the fork tore into Daryl's left cheek before she yanked it back out.

He screamed, dropping the rolling pin and barreling forward. "Bitch!" he yelled. "I'll kill you, too. Then Wendy Hudson, then I'll be done with all of them!" He let out a roar of rage as he collided with her. She jammed the fork into his right shoulder, the prongs completely buried. She left it there. He howled again but kept coming. He rammed her hard against the edge of the sink once, twice ... the numbness in her back was spreading. She was afraid it might make her collapse. And if she hit the ground again ...

"They all teased me, even Julie," he went on. "Even during the affair, she'd threaten to tell Taylor if I didn't do certain things. They're all controlling ... every single one of them. Flirting. Showing skin. Making me weak ... they—"

Kate took advantage of his moment of weakness. She drove her knee up into his stomach. He hunched over and when he did, Kate brought her right hand down in hard downward jab. She clipped his chin and sent him to the floor.

On the way down, he grabbed her shirt. Had it not been a to-the-death sort of fight, it might have seemed like he was trying to grab her breast. He yanked down and she fought against it, bringing her knee hard into his chest. They fell in a heap of legs and arms, fighting for control against the side of the sink.

"Freeze!"

The shout came out of nowhere. Both Kate and Daryl turned toward the direction of the voice. Through blurred vision, Kate saw DeMarco standing at the entrance to the kitchen.

"Get off of her," DeMarco said.

Daryl responded right away. He raised his hands and backed off. He took a stumbling step away and then slowly turned to face DeMarco. The fork was still in his shoulder, standing as rigid as a beam in the ground.

"On your knees, hands behind your back," DeMarco ordered.

"You don't understand," he said as he obeyed her orders. "They were evil. They were using me. Unfaithful. Deranged. They *loved* to have men look at them ... even at the pool, even those teenage kids ..."

"You okay, Wise?" DeMarco asked, ignoring him.

Kate only nodded. Her back was a knot of nothingness, the numbness no longer spreading but seeming to centralize. The black stars were still in her vision and she was pretty sure the side of her head that had caught the rolling pin was swelling. She leaned against the sink, watching DeMarco as she moved around behind Daryl.

She saw Daryl moving before DeMarco did, her attention on her wounded partner.

Kate yelled a warning and the next few seconds seemed to explode into motion.

Daryl moved with the energy and desperation of a trapped man. In a motion that was so morbid it was nearly comical, he yanked the fork out of his shoulder and plunged it into DeMarco's leg. When she buckled and let out a scream, Daryl instantly went for her right hand. He sank his teeth into her wrist and yanked her hard by the arm.

She dropped the gun in her surprise and the moment it hit the floor, he went for it.

Kate raced forward, hoping her numb back would simply remember what it was supposed to do. She noticed that DeMarco was now on her knees, clutching her wrist. She was losing a hell of a lot of blood.

But Kate had to look beyond that. Daryl's hand was on the gun. His fingers were closing around it...

Kate brought her right knee up, connecting squarely with his face. There was a crunch as his nose shattered. He reeled back, dazed. His eyes swam and blood came gushing out of his nose. Kate retrieved the gun and kept it pointed at him. Her arms were trembling and she did everything she could not to just pull the trigger.

"DeMarco... how are you?"

"Bloody."

Still, she got to her feet and came forward, still clutching her bitten wrist. She yanked a dish towel from the handle of the oven door and wrapped it around her wrist. She then expertly put handcuffs on a nearly comatose Daryl Woodward. When she had them secured, she let him go. He took a single stumbling step forward and then fell face down on the floor.

The two women looked at one another in stunned silence. Kate could not remember the last time she'd taken such a beating. But that concern was secondary to what she saw in DeMarco. The younger agent was stumbling, having to catch the kitchen counter for balance. The dish towel she had laced around her wrist was pretty much soaked through with blood. Daryl had apparently bitten deep, perhaps nicking an artery.

"Stay with me, okay?" she told DeMarco. She pulled out her phone and dialed 911.

"Yeah," DeMarco said with a sleepy smile. "Not going anywhere."

She even managed a nervous little laugh before her eyes closed and she fell to the floor right beside Daryl Woodward.

CHAPTER THIRTY NINE

Kate found herself sitting in Duran's office for the second time in a week. This time, things weren't quite as cordial, though. DeMarco was sitting next to her and it was apparent that she was not used to being scolded. It was also apparent that she was not used to being injured. She'd received two shots and twenty-six stitches due to Daryl Woodward's bite. She'd lost a lot of blood but had been stable the entire time, as soon as the ambulance had arrived.

As for Kate, she was sore. The fight with Woodward had taken it out of her. It was proof of just how unconditioned she was these days. And it was more than not working out like she once had. It was age—something she had no say about.

Duran had just read them the riot act for going into Daryl Woodward's house two days ago. He was more aggravated about their direct disobedience than the fact that they had both been injured and had ended up nearly killing a man.

Their saving grace came in a series of audio recordings on Daryl's phone. He'd kept a record of the comings and goings of Julie and Lacy. The recordings went back over the course of over two months. He'd call them degrading names while he narrated their schedules. One particular recording had gone into great detail about a recent tryst with Julie. The description of a tattoo on her inner thigh basically sealed the case for them.

"So here's my conundrum," Duran said. "I will admit to thinking the case was over when you nabbed Julio Almas—another part of the case you should have never been involved in, Wise. But you were intuitive enough to see through that. Yes, you damn near killed a man before you were absolutely certain if he was the killer, but in the end it seems you might have saved a life. One of those recordings of his made it clear that Wendy Hudson was next."

"I have to apologize again," Kate said. "I had the hunch but wanted to be sure before I informed you. But as you know, I never really got the chance."

Duran waved it away. "You caught a killer, Wise. I don't keep up with this sort of thing, but that makes more than fifty for your career, right?"

She shrugged. She had honestly never kept up with it, even when other agents had whispered about her numbers and accolades in awed reverence.

"This case proves one thing to me, Wise. The fact that you still managed to get results—even after everyone else around you was saying the case was closed—shows that, fifty-five or not, your mind is still as sharp as ever."

"Thanks ... I think."

"I've spoken with the other directors," Duran said. "We want you back. We can get around the rules, find a way to get you a waiver to come back for one year. See how you feel then. We know you're bored with retirement. And we need you. And clearly, you are as capable now as you were one year ago when you left. What do you say?"

Kate nodded. She wanted to jump at the offer right away. But in the back of her mind she thought of Melissa, of Michelle ... and even of Allen Goldman.

I'm going to call him when I get back home, she thought, the idea random and foreign in Duran's office. *I'm going to call him and take him up on dinner. And if he tries to kiss me, I'm going to let him.*

She wondered why the thought occurred to her. And then she realized: it was a yearning for life. For real, normal life. For the chasing killers to end.

And yet, as much as she yearned for it, she also yearned to be back in the action.

She felt torn.

A part of her was tired. But another part, the stronger part, needed the action.

"Can I think about it?" she asked.

"Yes. And if you take this, I'd like for you to partner up with DeMarco indefinitely. She needs you, too."

"Thank you, sir."

DeMarco looked over to Kate with a sleek kind of smile—a look that said: *The ball is in your court ...*

For a moment, Kate found herself thinking of Jimmy Parker and Logan Nash—the first partner she'd worked with and the last before her retirement. Jimmy had been her mentor and Logan had looked to her for guidance in some areas. Looking to DeMarco, Kate wondered if it might be time for her to close the circle—to be the mentor and teacher to DeMarco in the same way Jimmy had helped her through her first few years.

Not that DeMarco wasn't already a stellar agent. But being chained to Violent Crimes for so long and then being let loose in the field, she would be an exciting partner to work with.

She thought of Melissa one more time, her daughter who was seriously seeking a career in the FBI, a career Kate had modeled for Melissa's entire life. The thought made her maternal instinct kick in. But honestly, it also excited her quite a bit.

She took her leave and left through the small waiting area in front of Duran's office. Before she made it to the hallway, DeMarco caught up to her.

"You'll come back, right?" she asked.

Kate smiled.

"I just might be too stupid to let it go," she said.

DeMarco laughed. It was a sweet sound, coming from the throat of the woman who had saved her life two days ago. DeMarco had gotten away with just stitches to her forearm and Kate had managed to get away with nothing more than a severe bruise along her back. And here they were now, laughing about it.

If it was a sign of things to come, Kate thought her year of retirement might just become nothing more than a foolish decision that shrank further and further away in the rearview mirror of her life.

The future, all of a sudden, bloomed brightly ahead on the horizon.

IF SHE SAW

(a kate wise mystery—book 2)

BLAKE PIERCE

BLAKE PIERCE

Blake Pierce is author of the bestselling RILEY PAGE mystery series, which includes thirteen books (and counting). Blake Pierce is also the author of the MACKENZIE WHITE mystery series, comprising nine books (and counting); of the AVERY BLACK mystery series, comprising six books; of the KERI LOCKE mystery series, comprising five books; of the MAKING OF RILEY PAIGE mystery series, comprising three books (and counting); of the KATE WISE mystery series, comprising two books (and counting); of the CHLOE FINE psychological suspense mystery, comprising two books (and counting); and of the JESSE HUNT psychological suspense thriller series, comprising three books (and counting).

An avid reader and lifelong fan of the mystery and thriller genres, Blake loves to hear from you, so please feel free to visit www.blakepierce-author.com to learn more and stay in touch.

ONCE COLD (Book #8)
ONCE STALKED (Book #9)
ONCE LOST (Book #10)
ONCE BURIED (Book #11)
ONCE BOUND (Book #12)
ONCE TRAPPED (Book #13)
ONCE DORMANT (book #14)

MACKENZIE WHITE MYSTERY SERIES
BEFORE HE KILLS (Book #1)
BEFORE HE SEES (Book #2)
BEFORE HE COVETS (Book #3)
BEFORE HE TAKES (Book #4)
BEFORE HE NEEDS (Book #5)
BEFORE HE FEELS (Book #6)
BEFORE HE SINS (Book #7)
BEFORE HE HUNTS (Book #8)
BEFORE HE PREYS (Book #9)
BEFORE HE LONGS (Book #10)

AVERY BLACK MYSTERY SERIES
CAUSE TO KILL (Book #1)
CAUSE TO RUN (Book #2)
CAUSE TO HIDE (Book #3)
CAUSE TO FEAR (Book #4)
CAUSE TO SAVE (Book #5)
CAUSE TO DREAD (Book #6)

KERI LOCKE MYSTERY SERIES
A TRACE OF DEATH (Book #1)
A TRACE OF MUDER (Book #2)
A TRACE OF VICE (Book #3)
A TRACE OF CRIME (Book #4)
A TRACE OF HOPE (Book #5)

TABLE OF CONTENTS

PROLOGUE

Growing up, Olivia never thought she'd see a day when she was actually *glad* to be home. Like most teens, she'd spent her high school years dreaming of getting away from home, of going to college and starting a life on her own. She'd followed through on her plan, getting out of Whip Springs, Virginia, and attending the University of Virginia. She was in her junior year now, heading into a summer that would be ripe with job opportunities and, by the end of the summer, an apartment search. Olivia enjoyed living on campus, but as a senior she figured it was time to live elsewhere in the city.

For now, though, it was a full month back with her parents in Whip Springs. And she knew her high school self would never forgive her for the relief and surge of love she felt as she pulled into her parents' driveway. They lived just off of a secondary road in Whip Springs—a sleepy little central Virginia town with a population of less than five thousand that was surrounded by forest on all sides, plus a stretch of forest that ran through most of Whip Springs.

It was beginning to get dark when she pulled into the driveway. She had fully expected her mother to have turned the porch light on for her, but there was no glow lighting up the front door. Her mom knew she was arriving this afternoon; they'd discussed it on the phone two days ago and Olivia had even texted three hours ago to tell her she was on the way.

Sure, her mother had not texted back, which was unlike her. But Olivia figured she was probably working overtime to make Olivia's childhood bedroom presentable and forgot to return her text.

As Olivia got closer to the house, she noted that not only was the porch light not on, it seemed as if every single light in the house was turned off. She knew they were home, though. Both of their cars were parked in the driveway, her mother's car parked right behind her father's truck, just like they had been doing for as long as Olivia could remember.

If these cheeseballs are trying to throw me some sort of surprise welcome home party, I might just cry, Olivia thought as she parked beside her mother's car.

She popped the trunk and got her luggage out, just two suitcases but one of which seemed to weigh a ton. She hefted them up the sidewalk and toward the porch. It had been almost a year since she had been back here for a visit; she'd nearly forgotten how absolutely secluded the place felt. The closest neighbors were less than a quarter of a mile away, but the trees surrounding the property made it feel like the house was completely isolated ... especially when compared to the crowded dorm spaces back at school.

She wrestled the suitcases up the porch steps and then reached out to ring the doorbell. When she did, she noticed that the door was partially open.

Suddenly, the lack of light from inside seemed sinister—like an alarm of sorts. "Mom? Dad?" she called out as she slowly reached out and opened the door with her foot.

It swung open, revealing the foyer and small hallway that she knew so well. The house was indeed dark but as she stepped inside against the advisement of her growing fear, she was instantly put at ease. From elsewhere in the house, she heard the television—the familiar *dings* and applause of *Wheel of Fortune*, a staple in their home from as far back as Olivia could remember.

As she neared the end of the hallway and approached the living room, she saw the wheel on the TV, which was mounted above the fireplace, a very large screen indeed, making it seem as if Pat Sajak was right there in the living room.

"Hey, guys," Olivia said, looking around the darkened living room. "Thanks so much for helping me with my stuff. Leaving the door cracked open was a—"

It was meant as a joke but when the words hung in her throat, there was nothing funny about it.

Her mother was on the couch. She could have very well been asleep and nothing more than that if it weren't for all the blood. It was all over her chest and soaked into the couch. There was so much of it that Olivia's mind couldn't quite comprehend it at first. Seeing it to the sounds of the clacking of the *Wheel of Fortune* wheel made it somehow even harder to comprehend.

"Mom…"

Olivia felt as if her heart had stopped. She backed slowly away as the reality of what she was seeing sank in. She felt like a small part of her mind had come unhinged and was floating off into space somewhere.

Another word formed on her tongue—*Dad*—as she backed slowly away.

But that's when she saw him. He was right there, on the floor. He was lying just in front of the coffee table and he had just as much blood on him as her mother had. He was lying face down, motionless. But it looked like he was in a crawling position of sorts, as if he had tried to get away. As she took it all in, Olivia saw what looked to be at least six very visible stab wounds in his back.

She suddenly understood why her mother had not answered her text. Her mother was dead. Her father, too.

She felt a scream rising into her throat as she did her best to unlock her legs. She knew that whoever did this might still be here. That thought did it—it brought the scream out, it brought the tears on, and it unlocked her legs.

Olivia dashed out of the house and ran—and ran—and didn't stop running until her screams finally caught in her throat.

CHAPTER ONE

It was funny how quickly Kate Wise's attitude had changed. When she had spent a year in retirement, she'd done everything she could to avoid gardening. Gardening, knitting, bridge clubs—and even book clubs—she had avoided like the plague. They had all seemed like cliché things that retired women did.

But a few months back in the FBI saddle had done something to her. She was not so naïve to think that it had reinvented her. No, it had simply reinvigorated her. She had purpose again, a reason to look forward to the next day.

So maybe that's why she found it okay that she had *now* resorted to gardening as a pastime. It wasn't relaxing, as she had thought it would be. If anything, it made her anxious; why put the time and energy into planting something if you were working against the weather to make sure it stayed alive? Still, there was a joy in it—putting something into the ground and seeing the fruits of it over time.

She'd started with flowers—daisies and bougainvilleas at first—and then went on to planting a little veggie garden in the back right corner of her yard. That's where she was currently mounding dirt over a tomato plant and slowly coming to the realization that she had not had any interest in gardening until she had become a grandmother.

She wondered if it had something to do with the evolution of her nurturing nature. She'd had friends and books tell her that there was something different about being a grandmother—something that a woman never truly tapped into while serving as a mother.

Her daughter, Melissa, had assured her that she had been a good mother. It was an assurance that Kate needed from time to time, given the way she had spent her career. She had admittedly put career over family for far too long and she counted herself lucky that Melissa had not ever resented her for it—except for a period after she had lost her father.

Ah, the one downside to gardening, Kate thought as she got to her feet and dusted off her hands and knees. *Thoughts tend to wander. And when that happens, the past starts creeping in, uninvited.*

She left the garden, walking across the backyard of her Richmond, Virginia, home and to the back porch. She was careful to kick off her dirt-smeared Keds at the back door. She also dropped her gloves beside them, not wanting to get any dirt in the house. She'd spent the last two days getting the house clean. She was babysitting Michelle, her granddaughter, tonight and even though Melissa wasn't a neat freak, Kate wanted to have the place sparkling clean. It had been almost thirty years since she'd been in the company of a baby and she didn't want to take any chances.

She glanced at the clock and frowned. She was expecting company in fifteen minutes. That was yet another negative aspect of gardening: time easily slipped away from you.

She freshened up in the bathroom and then went to the kitchen to put a fresh pot of coffee on. It was about halfway through percolating when the doorbell rang. She answered right away, happy as always to see the two women she had been spending a few hours with at least twice a week over the last year and a half or so.

Jane Patterson stepped through the doorway first, carrying a plate of pastries. They were homemade Danishes and had won the Carytown Cooks contest for two years straight. Clarissa James came in behind her with a large bowl of freshly sliced fruit. They were both dressed in cute outfits that would work either at a brunch at a friend's house or casual shopping—which was something they both did quite a bit of.

"You've been gardening again, haven't you?" Clarissa asked as they set their food down in the kitchen island.

"How can you tell?" Kate asked.

Clarissa pointed to Kate's hair, just below the shoulders where it came to a tapered end. Kate reached back and found that she had missed a bit of stray dirt that had somehow ended up in her hair. Clarissa and Jane chuckled at this as Jane took the plastic wrap off of her Danishes.

"Laugh all you want," Kate said. "You won't be when those tomato vines are loaded down."

It was a Friday morning, which automatically made it a good one. The three women situated themselves around Kate's kitchen island, sitting on barstools and eating their brunch and drinking coffee. And while the company, the food, and the coffee were all good, it was still hard to overlook the missing piece.

Debbie Meade was no longer a part of the group. After her daughter had died, one of three victims of a killer Kate had taken down in the end, Debbie and her husband, Jim, had moved. They were living somewhere out near the beach in North Carolina. Debbie would send pictures of the coast from time to time, just to jokingly rub it in. They had been living there for two months now and seemed to be happy—to be moving on from the tragedy.

The conversation was mostly light and pleasant. Jane talked about how her husband was eyeing retirement next year and had already started planning to write a book. Clarissa shared news about both of her kids, now in their mid-twenties, and how they'd both recently received promotions.

"Speaking of kids," Clarissa said, "how is Melissa doing? She loving motherhood?"

"Oh yes," Kate said. "She's absolutely insane about her little baby girl. A little baby girl that I will be babysitting tonight, in fact."

"First time?" Jane asked.

"Yes. It's the first time Melissa and Terry are going somewhere without the baby. Like an actual overnight thing."

"Has Grandma Mode kicked in yet?" Clarissa asked.

"I don't know," Kate said with a smile. "I guess we'll find out tonight."

"You know," Jane said, "you could go back in time and babysit like I used to in high school. I'd bring my boyfriend over with me and as soon as the kids went to bed..."

"That's pretty disturbing," Kate said.

"Do you think Allen would be up for it, though?" Clarissa asked.

"I don't know," Kate answered, trying to imagine Allen with a baby. They had been dating seriously ever since Kate and her new partner, DeMarco, had wrapped the serial case right here in Richmond—the same case that had taken Debbie Meade's daughter. There had been no real talk of the future; they hadn't slept together yet and rarely got physical at all. She was enjoying her time with him, though, but the thought of bringing him into the grandmother part of her life made her uncomfortable.

"Things still going well with you two?" Clarissa asked.

"I think so. The whole dating thing still seems weird to me. I'm too old to date, you know?"

"Hell no," Jane said. "Don't get me wrong... I love my husband, my kids, and my life in general. But I'd give anything to be back on that dating scene for just a while, you know? I miss it. Meeting new people, sharing firsts..."

"Yeah, I guess that *is* pretty nice," Kate conceded. "Allen finds the idea of dating strange, too. We have fun together but it's... it gets sort of weird when things start leaning towards the romantic end of things."

"Blah blah," Clarissa said. "But do you think of him as your boyfriend?"

"Are we really having this conversation?" Kate asked, starting to feel herself blushing a bit.

"Yes," Clarissa said. "Us old married ladies need to live vicariously through you."

"And that also goes for your sort-of job," Jane said. "How's that going?"

"No calls for about two weeks, and the last one was just to help with some research. Sorry, girls... it's not as adventurous as you're hoping it is."

"So are you back to being retired?" Clarissa asked.

"Basically. It's complicated."

That comment ended the questioning as they delved back into local topics—upcoming movies, a music festival in town, construction on the interstate, and so on. But Kate's mind had gotten snagged on the topic of work. It was comforting to know that the bureau was still considering her as a resource but she had been hoping for a more active role after she had tied things up with the last case. But so far, she'd only heard from Deputy Director Duran a single time, and that was to get a performance review on DeMarco.

She knew how strange it seemed to her friends that she was still technically an active agent while also leaning into her role as a grandmother. Hell, it was strange to her as well. Throw in a slowly blossoming relationship with Allen and she supposed her life *was* quite interesting to them.

Honestly, she counted herself lucky. She'd be fifty-six years old at the end of the month and she knew that many women her age would be envious of the life she lived. She always told herself this when she felt the pressing need to be more active at work. And some days, it worked.

And as it just so happened, with her granddaughter coming to visit for the first time since her birth, today was one of those days.

One thing that made it difficult to balance her new role as grandmother with her desire to get her hands deep into another case was trying to think like a grandmother. That afternoon, she left her house and walked down to some of the thrifty little shops in the Carytown district of Richmond. She felt like she had to get Michelle a gift to celebrate her first overnight stay at Grandma's house.

It was hard to push sidearms and suspects aside to focus on stuffed animals and onesies instead. But as she checked out a few shops, it became somewhat easier. She found that she actually enjoyed shopping for her granddaughter, even though she wasn't even two months old yet and would, honestly, not care about any gift she got. She found it hard not to snatch up every cute thing she found and buy it. After all, wasn't it the responsibility of a grandmother to spoil her grandchildren?

As she paid for her purchases at the third shop she visited, she received a text. She wasted no time in checking it. Over the last few weeks, she'd had a small hope every time she got a call or a text, thinking it might Duran or someone else within the bureau. She mentally scolded herself when she was disappointed to find that it was not the bureau, but Allen. Once she got over the sting of not being called upon by the bureau again, she realized that she was happy to hear from him—was *always* happy to hear from him, in fact.

"Allen, you have to help me," she joked as she answered the phone. "I'm shopping for Michelle and everything I see, I want to buy for her. Is that normal?"

"I don't know," Allen said. "Neither of my sons have settled down and made me a grandpa yet."

"Take it from me. Start saving up."

Allen chuckled, a sound that Kate was growing to like quite a bit. "So tonight's the big night, huh?"

"It is. And I know I raised a kid already and I know what to expect, but I'm a little terrified."

"Ah, you'll be great. You want to talk terrified ... I'm going out with my boys for drinks tonight. And I haven't had more than two drinks in a single sitting in about five years."

"Have fun with that."

"I was wondering if you might want to get together tomorrow for dinner. We can share our survival stories of tonight."

"I'd like that. You want to come by my place at seven or so?"

"Sounds like a plan. You have fun tonight. Is little Michelle sleeping through the night yet?"

"I don't believe so."

"Ouch," Allen said, and ended the call.

Kate pocketed her phone, juggling her bags of purchases as she did. She smiled in spite of herself. She was standing in the sunshine in her favorite part of town, having just gone shopping for a two-month-old granddaughter, whom she was babysitting tonight. Given the way her day was going, did she *really* want the bureau to call at all?

She was walking back to her home—a three-block walk from where she had taken Allen's call—when she saw a little girl with a *My Little Pony* T-shirt. She was walking with her mother hand in hand, just a few feet ahead of her, traveling in their direction. She was five or six years old, her blonde hair up in a ponytail only a mother's care could create. She had blue eyes and a sharp end to her nose that looked rather pixie-like. And it was that feature that sent a spike of despair through Kate's heart.

An image flashed through her mind, a little girl who looked almost identical to this one. But in this image, the little girl had dirt and grime on her face, and she was crying. The lights of police cars flashed behind her.

The image was so strong that it caused Kate to stop walking for a moment. She tore her eyes away from the girl, not wanting to appear creepy or strange. She clung to that image in her head and did her best to find the memory associated with it. It came to her gradually and when it did, it unrolled itself slowly, as if she were reading the case report.

Five-year-old girl, found three days after reported missing. Stored in a fishing cabin in Arkansas with the dead bodies of her parents. The parents were the fifth and sixth victims of a serial killer that had terrorized Arkansas for the better part of four months ... a killer Kate had eventually taken down, but only after he had claimed a total of nine people.

Kate was aware that she was suddenly standing as still as a statue on the street but couldn't seem to move. That case had haunted her for a while. So many dead ends, so many false leads. She had been running around in circles, unable to find the killer while he continued to add to his body count. God only knew what he had planned for that little girl.

But you saved her, she told herself. *In the end, you saved her.*

Kate slowly started to walk again. It was not the first time a random image from her past work had slammed itself across her mind and caused her to zone out. Sometimes they came casually, albeit out of nowhere. But there were other times when they came on strong and fast, like a post-traumatic stress flashback.

The image of the girl from Arkansas was somewhere in between. And Kate was thankful for that. That particular case had nearly caused her to step down as an agent back in 2009. It had been soul-shattering, enough for Kate to request two weeks off from work. And all of a sudden, for just a split second while walking back home with gifts for her granddaughter in her hand, Kate felt like she had been pushed back in time.

Nearly ten years had passed since she had rescued that girl. Kate wondered where she was—wondered if she had outlived the trauma.

"Ma'am?"

Kate blinked, jumping a bit at the sound of an unfamiliar voice in front of her. There was a teenage boy standing in front her. He looked concerned, as if he wasn't sure if he should be standing there or running away.

"Are you okay?" he asked. "You look... I don't know. Sick. Like you're about to pass out or something."

"No," Kate said, shaking her head. "I'm good. Thanks."

The kid nodded and carried on his way. Kate started walking forward again, ripped out of some hole in the past that she assumed had not yet quite closed up. And as she drew closer and closer to home, she started to wonder just how many of those holes from her past had been left uncovered.

And if the ghosts of her past would continue to haunt her until she, too, became a ghost.

CHAPTER TWO

K ate spent the next hour or so tidying up the house, even though she had already done so before leaving to go shopping. It made her feel off to be so anxious to have Michelle coming to her house. Melissa had lived in this house during her high school years so when she came to visit (which wasn't often enough in Kate's opinion), Kate didn't feel the need for the place to be spotless. So why was she so concerned about how it looked for a two-month-old?

Maybe it's some odd kind of grandmother nesting, she thought while she scrubbed the sink in the powder room ... a room she was well aware that her granddaughter would not even see, much less actually use.

As she rinsed the sink out, her doorbell rang. She was flooded with an excitement that she had not quite been ready for. She was smiling from ear to ear when she answered the door. Melissa stood on the other side, carrying Michelle in her car seat. The baby was fast asleep, a thick blanket tucked around her legs.

"Hey, Mom," Melissa said as she stepped into the house. She took a quick look around and rolled her eyes. "How much did you clean today?"

"I plead the fifth," Kate said as she gave her daughter a hug.

Melissa set the car seat down carefully on the floor and slowly unbuckled Michelle. She picked her up and handed her softly to Kate. It had been almost a full week since Kate had visited Melissa and Terry, but when she took Michelle into her arms, it felt like much longer.

"What do you and Terry have planned for tonight?" Kate asked.

"Not much, really," Melissa said. "And that's the beauty of it. We're going to go out for dinner and drinks. Maybe some dancing. Also, we changed our minds about asking you to watch her overnight because we realized we're not quite ready for that. The unbroken sleep is much needed, but I just can't be away from her for that long."

"Oh, I think I can understand that," Kate said. "You guys go out and enjoy yourselves."

Melissa shrugged the diaper bag from her shoulder and set it by the car seat. "Everything you need is in here. She's going to want to eat again in about an hour and she'd going to fight sleep. Terry thinks it's cute but I think it's of the devil. If she gets gassy, there are gas drops in the back pocket and—"

"Lissa…we'll be fine. I *have* raised a child, you know. She turned out pretty good, too."

Melissa smiled and surprised Kate by giving her a quick kiss on the cheek. "Thanks, Mom. I'll pick her up around eleven or so. Is that too late?"

"Nope, that's perfect."

Melissa gave one final look to her baby, a look that made Kate's heart swell. She could remember being a mother and having that internal feeling of love fill her—a love than translated to the sheer will of doing anything and everything to ensure this human you'd created would be safe.

"If you need anything, call me," Melissa said, though she was still looking at Michelle and not Kate.

"I will. Now *go*. Have fun."

Melissa finally turned away and headed out the door. As she closed it, little Michelle stirred awake in Kate's arms. She gave her grandmother a sleepy little smile and let out a tiny yawn.

"So what do we do now?" Kate asked.

The question was playfully directed at Michelle but she felt a weight behind it that made her wonder if she was simply voicing a rhetorical question to herself. Her daughter was grown up now, with a daughter of her own. Now here she was, nearing fifty-six and with her first grandchild in her arms. So…*what do we do now?*

She thought about that pull to return to work in any capacity and, for perhaps the first time, it felt small.

Smaller even than the little girl she now held in her arms.

❧   ❧   ❧

By eight o'clock that night, Kate was wondering if Melissa and Terry had simply managed to create the most well-behaved baby in recorded history. Not once did Michelle cry or even get fussy. She was simply content to be held. After two hours in Kate's arms, Michelle nodded off to sleep. Kate carefully placed Michelle on the center of her queen-sized bed and then stood at the doorway for a moment to watch her granddaughter sleep.

She wasn't sure how long she had been standing there when her phone buzzed from the kitchen table behind her. She had to tear her eyes away from Michelle but managed to get to the phone within a few seconds. The single buzz meant that it was a text rather than a call and she was not at all surprised to see that it was Melissa.

How's she doing? Melissa asked.

Unable to resist, Kate smiled and responded: **I limited her to just three beers. She went out with some guy on a motorcycle about an hour ago. I told her to be back by 11.**

The response came quickly: **Oh, you're not funny at all.**

The back-and-forth banter made her nearly as happy as the sleeping baby in her bedroom. After her father died, Melissa had become withdrawn—especially toward Kate. She'd blamed Kate's work for her father's death and even though she had come to understand that was not the case later on in life, there were times when Kate felt that Melissa still resented the time she had spent in the bureau after his death. Oddly enough, though, Melissa had shown some interest in pursuing a career in the FBI herself... despite a less-than-positive attitude about the events of the last year concerning her mother's interrupted retirement.

Still smiling, Kate took her phone into the bedroom and snapped a quick picture of Michelle. She sent it to Melissa and then, after some thought, she also sent it to Allen, only his had the message: **Partied out!**

She found herself wishing he was there with her. She found herself feeling this quite often as of late. She was not naïve enough to think she loved him, but she could see herself falling *in* love with him if things kept going the way they were. She missed him when he wasn't around and whenever he kissed her, it made her feel about twenty years younger.

She found herself smiling yet again when Allen responded with a picture of his own. It was a selfie of him with two younger men who looked exactly like him—his sons, presumably.

As she studied the picture, her phone rang in her hands. The name that appeared on the screen sent a flurry of excitement through her that she was unable to stop.

Deputy Director Vince Duran was calling her. This would have caused a stir of excitement regardless, but the fact that it was after eight o'clock on a Friday night set off alarm bells in her head—alarm bells that she enjoyed the sound of.

She took a moment, still staring at little Michelle, and then answered. "This is Kate Wise," she said, keeping her excitement in check.

"Wise, it's Duran. Is this a bad time?"

"It's not the absolute best, but that's okay," she answered. "Is everything okay?"

"That depends. I'm calling to see if you'd be interested in taking on a case."

"Are we talking a cold case like we've been discussing?"

"No. This one ... well, it looks and feels like one you cracked rather quickly back in ninety-six. As it stands, we've got four bodies at two different sites in Whip Springs, Virginia. Looks like the murders occurred no more than two days apart. Right now, Virginia State Police are running the scene but I've spoken to them. If you want the case, it's yours. But you'd have to move now."

"I don't think I can," she said. "I've got a commitment I need to keep." Looking at Michelle, this was easy to say. But nearly every nerve in her body fought against her newly acquired grandmother instincts.

"Well, listen to the specs anyway, would you? The murders are married couples, one in their early fifties, the other in their early sixties. The most recent were the fifty-somethings. Their daughter discovered their bodies when she came home from college earlier today. The murders occurred within thirty miles of one another, one in Whip Springs and the other one just outside of Roanoke."

"Couples? Any link between them other than they were married?"

"Not yet. But all four bodies were cut up pretty badly. The killer is using a knife. Making it slow and methodical. As far as I'm concerned, it points to another couple going down within two days or so."

"Yeah, it sounds like a serial in the making," Kate said.

She thought back to the case in 1996 that Duran had mentioned. In the end, a crazed woman who had been working as a nanny had taken the lives of three couples within the span of just two days. It turned out that she had worked for all three of the couples within a ten-year period. Kate had apprehended the woman when she was on the way to kill a fourth couple and then, according to her testimony, herself.

Was she *really* going to say no to this? After the intense flashback she'd had today, could she truly pass up another opportunity at stopping a killer?

"How long do I have to think about it?" she asked.

"I'll give you an hour. No more than that. I need someone on this now. And I thought you and DeMarco could work well on it. One hour, Wise ... sooner if you can."

Before she could give an *OK* or a *thanks,* Duran ended the call. He was typically warm and friendly, but when he did not get his way he could be very irritable.

As quietly as she could, she went to the bed and sat down on the edge. She watched Michelle sleeping, the gentle rise and fall of her chest so slow and methodical. She could clearly remember Melissa being this small and had no idea where the time had gone. And that was where her problem sprung from: she felt that she had missed so much of her life as a mother and wife because of her job but she felt a strong duty to it nonetheless. Especially when she knew that she could be out there right now, doing her part to bring a killer to justice.

What kind of a person would she be if she turned the offer down, leaving Duran to choose another agent who might not have the same skillsets as she did?

But what kind of grandmother and mother was she being if she had to call Melissa, telling her to come pick up her daughter early and end her night out because the FBI had come calling again?

Kate stared at Michelle for about five minutes, even lying down next to her and placing her hand on the baby's chest just to feel her breathe. And seeing that little flicker of life, of a life that had not yet learned about the kinds of evil that existed in the world, made the decision much easier for Kate.

Frowning for the first time that day, Kate picked up the phone and called Melissa.

Once, when Melissa was sixteen, she'd snuck a boy into her room late at night when Kate and Michael were already asleep. Kate had stirred awake at some noise (which she later found out was likely someone's knee hitting the wall in Melissa's bedroom) and went up to investigate. When she opened her daughter's door and found her topless with a boy in her bed, she had thrown him off the bed and screamed at him to get out.

The fury in Melissa's eyes that night was dwarfed by what Kate saw in her daughter's stare as she buckled Michelle into the car seat at 9:30— just a little over an hour after Duran had called her about the case in Roanoke.

"This is messed up, Mom," she said.

"Lissa, I'm so sorry. But what the hell was I supposed to do?"

"Well, from what I understand, people actually *stay* retired once they've retired. Maybe try that!"

"It's not that easy," Kate argued.

"Oh, I know, Mom," Melissa said. "It never was with you."

"That's not fair..."

"And don't think I'm just pissed because you cut my *one night* to relax short. I don't care about that. I'm not *that* selfish. Unlike *some* people. I'm pissed because your job—which you were supposed to be done with over a year ago, mind you—continues to win over your family. Even after everything... after *Dad*..."

"Lissa, let's not do this."

Melissa picked up the car seat with a softness that was not present in her voice or her body's strained posture.

"I agree," Melissa spat. "Let's not."

And with that, she walked out of the front door, slamming it behind her.

Kate reached out for the doorknob but stopped. What was she going to do? Was she going to continue this argument outside, in the yard? Besides, she knew Melissa well. After a few days, she'd cool down and would actually listen to Kate's side of the story. She might even accept her mother's apology.

Kate felt like a traitor as she picked up her cell phone. After she'd called Duran, he informed her that he'd planned on her showing up for the case anyway. As it stood, he had someone from the Virginia State Police lined up to meet with her and DeMarco at 4:30 in the morning down in Whip Springs. As for DeMarco, she had left DC half an hour ago with an agency car. She'd be at Kate's house sometime around midnight. Kate realized she could have easily kept Michelle until the originally planned on eleven o'clock and avoided the confrontation with Melissa. But she couldn't dwell on that now.

The suddenness of it all had taken Kate slightly off guard. Even though the last case she had taken had seemed to come out of nowhere, it had at least had some sort of stable structure to it. But it had been quite a while since she had been assigned a case at such an hour. It was daunting but she was also very excited—excited enough to be able to momentarily push Melissa's anger toward her to the back of her mind.

Still, as she packed a bag while waiting for DeMarco to arrive, a stinging thought pierced her. *And it's that right there—your ability to push everything to the side for the sake of the job—that caused so much trouble between the two of you in the first place.*

But that thought too was easily pushed to the side.

CHAPTER THREE

O ne of the many things Kate had learned about DeMarco during their last case was that she was punctual. It was a trait she was reminded of when she heard a knock on her door at 12:10.

I don't remember the last time I had a visitor this late, she thought. *College, maybe?*

She walked to the door, carrying her single packed bag with her. Yet when she answered the door, she saw that DeMarco had no intention of just rushing out to drive to the crime scene.

"At the risk of seeming rude, I really need to use your bathroom," DeMarco said. "Chugging two Cokes to stay awake for the ride was a *bad* idea."

Kate smiled and stepped aside to let DeMarco in. Given the speed and urgency Duran had instilled in her during their phone calls, DeMarco's abruptness was the kind of unintentional comic relief she needed. It also made her feel comfortable to know that even after almost two months apart, she and DeMarco were picking back up on the same comfort level they had shared before parting ways after the last case.

DeMarco came out of the bathroom a few minutes later with an embarrassed smile on her face.

"And good morning to you," Kate said. Maybe it was because of the caffeine intake, but DeMarco did not seem any worse for the wear, apparently not fazed by the early hour.

DeMarco looked at her watch and nodded. "Yeah, I suppose it *is* morning."

"When did you get the call?" Kate asked.

"Around eight or nine, I guess. I would have left earlier, but Duran wanted to make one hundred percent sure you were on board."

"Sorry about that," Kate said. "I was babysitting my granddaughter for the first time."

"Oh no. Wise … that sucks. I'm sorry this is screwing with that."

Kate shrugged and waved it away. "It'll be fine. You ready to get going?"

"Yeah. I fielded a few calls on the way over while this was being managed by the guys back in DC. We're scheduled to meet with one of the guys from Virginia State PD at four thirty at the Nash residence."

"The Nash residence?" Kate asked.

"The most recent couple to be murdered."

They fell into step together back toward the front door. As they made their way out, Kate turned the living room light off and picked up her bag. She was excited about what might lie ahead, but she also felt like she was leaving her home rather irrationally. After all, just a few hours ago, her two-month-old granddaughter had been snoozing on her bed. And now here she was, about to drive straight to a murder scene.

She saw the standard bureau sedan parked in front of her house, right along the curb. It looked surreal, but also inviting.

"You want to drive?" DeMarco asked.

"Sure," Kate said, wondering if the younger agent was offering the role as a show of respect or because she simply wanted a break from driving.

Kate got behind the wheel while DeMarco pulled up directions to the location of the most recent murder. It was in the town of Whip Springs, Virginia, a little hole-in-the wall town situated at the base of the Blue Ridge Mountains just outside of Roanoke. They spent only a little time on small talk—Kate filling DeMarco in on how it felt to be a grandmother, while DeMarco remained mostly silent, mentioning only yet another failed relationship after her girlfriend left her. This came as a surprise, as Kate had not pegged DeMarco as being gay. If anything, it showed her that she really needed to spend some more time getting to know the woman who was more or less her partner. Punctuality, she had picked up on. Homosexuality, she had missed. What the hell did that say about her as a partner?

As the crime scene drew closer, DeMarco read over the reports that Duran had sent them pertaining to the case. As she read them, Kate kept looking for any traces of the sun breaking the horizon but saw none.

"Two older couples," DeMarco said. "Sorry...one in their late fifties...so no offense."

"None taken," Kate said, not sure if this was DeMarco's weird attempt at humor.

"At first glance, they appear to have nothing in common, other than location. The first scene was right in the heart of Roanoke and this most recent one was no more than thirty miles away, in Whip Springs. There appear to be no signs that the husband or the wife were the preliminary targets. Each murder was gruesome and a little overdone, indicating that the killer enjoys it."

"And that typically points to someone who feels that they have been wronged by the victims in some cases," Kate pointed out. "That or some twisted psychological craving for violence and bloodshed."

"The most recent victims, the Nashes, had been married for twenty-four years. They have two children, one who lives in San Diego and another who is currently attending UVA. She's the one who discovered the bodies when she came home yesterday."

"What about the other couple?" Kate asked. "They have any kids?"

"Not according to the reports."

Kate mulled all of this over and for reasons she could not grasp, found herself thinking of the little girl she had passed on the street earlier in the day. Or, rather, the flashback that little girl had spurred up in her mind.

When they arrived at the Nash residence, the horizon had finally started to catch some of the light from the rising but still absent sun. It peeked through the tree line that surrounded most of the Nashes' yard. In that light, they could see a single car parked in front of the house. A man stood propped against the hood, smoking a cigarette and holding a cup of coffee.

"You guys Wise and DeMarco?" the man asked.

"That's us," Kate said, stepping forward and showing her ID. "Who are you?"

"Palmetto, with Virginia State PD. Forensics. I got the call a few hours ago that you two would be taking the case. Figured I might as well be here to hand off what I have. Which, by the way, isn't much."

Palmetto took one final drag from his cigarette and tossed it to the ground, snuffing it out with his foot. "The bodies have obviously been moved and there was very little evidence found anywhere. But come on inside anyway. It's ... eye opening."

Palmetto spoke with the emotionless tone of a man who had been doing this for quite some time. He led them up the Nashes' sidewalk and onto the porch. When he opened the door and led them inside, Kate could smell it: the smell of a crime scene where a lot of blood had been spilled. There was something chemical to it, not just the coppery smell of blood, but of recent movement and people with rubber gloves looking over the scene recently.

Palmetto turned each light on they made their way into the house— through the foyer, down a hallway, and into the living room. In the bright glare of overhead lights, Kate saw the first splotch of blood on the hardwood floor. And then another and another.

Palmetto led them to the front of the couch, pointing to the bloodstains like a man simply confirming the fact that water is indeed wet.

"The bodies were here, one on the couch and one on the floor. It appeared that the mother was killed first, probably from the cut to her neck, although one did seem to land pretty close to her heart, but through the back. It's theorized that there was a struggle with the father. There was bruising on his forearms, some blood coming out of his mouth, and the coffee table had been knocked askew."

"Any early ideas on the time that passed between the murders and the daughter discovering them?" Kate asked.

"No more than a day," Palmetto answered. "And it was probably more like twelve or sixteen hours. I'm sure the coroner will have something a little more concrete at some point today."

"Anything else of note?" DeMarco asked.

"Yes, actually. It's a piece of evidence ... just one single piece." He reached into the inner pocket of his thin jacket and pulled out a small evidence baggie. "I kept this. Got permission, so don't get all spooked. I figured you'd want to take it and run. It's the only evidence we found, but it's pretty unnerving."

He offered the clear plastic baggie to Kate. She took it and eyed the contents inside. From what she could tell, it was a simple piece of cloth, about six-by-three inches. It was thick, blue in color, and had a fluffy texture to it. The entire right side of it was stained in blood.

"Where was this found?" Kate asked.

"Stuffed into the mother's mouth. It was pushed deep down there, almost down her throat."

Kate held it up to the light. "Any idea where it came from?" she asked.

"No idea. Looks to be just a random scrap."

But Kate wasn't so sure. In fact, her grandmother's intuition started storming to the front. This was not some random piece of fabric. No ... it was soft, it was light blue, and looked to be quite fluffy.

This was part of a blanket. Perhaps a child's security blanket.

"You holding any other surprise evidence for us?" DeMarco asked.

"No, that's it out of me," Palmetto said, already heading back for the door. "If you ladies need any help from this point on, feel free to give us a call at the State PD."

Kate and DeMarco shared an annoyed look behind his back. Without having to say anything, they each knew that the term *you ladies* had pissed the other off.

"Well, that was brief," DeMarco said as Palmetto gave them a non-committal wave from the front door.

"Just as well," Kate said. "This way we can start looking the case over with our own eyes, without the influence of what anyone else has found."

"You think we need to speak to the daughter next?"

"Probably. And then we'll look into the first crime scene and see if we can find anything there. Hopefully we'll find someone who's a bit more sociable than our friend Palmetto."

They headed back out of the house, turning off the lights as they went. As they headed back outside, the sun finally peeking out from the edge of the world, Kate carefully placed what she thought was a scrap of a child's blanket into her pocket and could not help but think of her granddaughter sleeping under a similar blanket.

Walking toward the sun did nothing to suppress the chill that crept through her.

CHAPTER FOUR

Breakfast consisted of a Panera Bread drive-thru in Roanoke. It was there, while waiting in the small early-morning line, that DeMarco placed several calls to set up a meeting with Olivia Nash, daughter of the recently slayed couple. She was currently staying with her aunt in Roanoke and was, by her aunt's own words, an absolute wreck.

After getting the address and approval from the aunt, they headed for the aunt's house just after seven o'clock. The early hour was not an issue because, according to the aunt, Olivia had refused to sleep ever since having discovered her parents.

When Kate and DeMarco arrived at the house, the aunt was sitting on the porch. Cami Nash stood when Kate got out of the car but made no move to come meet them. She had a cup of coffee in her hand and the tired look on her face made Kate think it was certainly not the first she had enjoyed this morning.

"Cami Nash?" Kate asked.

"Yeah, that's me," she said.

"First and foremost, please accept my sympathies for your loss," Kate said. "Were you and your brother close?"

"Pretty close, yeah. But right now, I have to look past that. I can't...*grieve* right now because Olivia needs someone. She's not the same person I spoke with on the phone last week. Something in her is broken. I can't even imagine...what it must have been like to find them like that and..."

She trailed off and sipped down some of her coffee very quickly, trying to distract herself from the onslaught of tears that seemed to be rapidly approaching.

"Is she going to be okay to speak with us?" DeMarco asked.

"Maybe for a while. I told her you were coming and she seemed to understand what I meant. That's why I'm meeting you out here before you go in. I feel like I need to tell you that she's a normal, well-rounded young woman. In the state she's in now, though, I didn't want you to think she had some sort of mental issues or something."

"Thanks for that," Kate said. She had seen people absolutely devastated by grief before and it was never a pretty sight. She couldn't help but wonder how much experience DeMarco had with it.

Cami led them into the house. It was as quiet as a tomb inside, the only sound coming from the hum of the air conditioner. Kate noticed that Cami walked slowly, making sure not to make too much noise. Kate followed suit, wondering if Cami was hoping the silence would help Olivia finally fall asleep or if she was simply trying not to alarm the already-fragile young woman in any way.

They entered the living room, where a young woman was half-sitting, half-lying on the couch. Her face was red, her eyes slightly swollen from recently weeping. She looked as if she hadn't slept in about a week rather than just a day or so. When she saw Kate and DeMarco enter, she sat up a bit.

"Hi, Ms. Nash," Kate said. "Thank you for agreeing to meet with us. We're so sorry for your loss."

"It's Olivia, please." Her voice was hoarse and tired—almost as worn out as her eyes seemed to be.

"We'll make this as quick as possible," Kate said. "I understand that you had just come in from college. Do you know if your parents had planned to have anyone else over that day?"

"If they did, I didn't know about it."

"Please forgive me for asking, but do you know if either of your parents had any long-standing grudges with anyone? People they might have considered enemies?"

Olivia shook her head firmly. "Dad was married once before ... before he met Mom. But even with his ex-wife, he was on good terms."

Olivia started crying noiselessly. A series of tears slipped from her eyes and she did not bother trying to wipe them away.

"I want to show you something," Kate said. "I don't know if it has any significance to you or not. If it does, it could be quite emotional. Would you be willing to take a look and let us know if it looks familiar to you?"

Olivia looked alarmed, maybe even a little scared. Kate really didn't blame here and almost didn't want to show her the scrap of fabric Palmetto had handed them—the scrap Kate felt certain was part of a blanket or quilt. A bit reluctantly, she pulled it out of her pocket.

She knew right away that Olivia didn't recognize it. There was an immediate sense of relief and confusion on the young woman's face as she looked at the plastic bag and what it held inside.

Olivia shook her head but kept her eyes locked on the clear plastic bag. "No. I don't recognize it. Why?"

"We can't reveal that right now," Kate said. Truthfully, there was nothing unlawful about revealing it to the next of kin ... but Kate didn't see the point in traumatizing Olivia Nash any further.

"Do you have any idea who did this?" Olivia asked. She looked lost, like she did not recognize where she was ... maybe not even herself. Kate couldn't recall the last time she had seen someone so clearly detached from everything around her.

"Not right now," she said. "But we will keep you posted. And please," she said, looking from Olivia and then to Cami, "contact us if you can think of *anything* that might help."

At that remark, DeMarco withdrew a business card from the inner pocket of her jacket and handed it to Cami.

Perhaps it was the years she had spent in retirement or feeling guilty for having to abandon her post as grandmother last night, but Kate felt awful when she left the room, leaving Olivia Nash to her intense grief. As she and DeMarco made their way out onto the porch, she could hear the young woman let out a low moan of distress.

Kate and DeMarco shared an uneasy glace as they headed to the car. From within her inner pocket, Kate could feel the presence of that scrap of fabric and it suddenly felt very heavy indeed.

CHAPTER FIVE

As Kate left the small town of Whip Springs and headed for Roanoke, DeMarco used her iPad to pull up the case files on the first set of murders. It was nearly an exact copy and paste of the Nash crime scene; a couple had been murdered in their home in a particularly gruesome fashion. Preliminary results turned up no likely suspects and there had been no witnesses.

"Does it say anything about anything left behind in the throats or mouths of either of the victims?" Kate asked.

DeMarco scanned the reports and shook her head. "Not from what I can see. I think it's maybe a—no, wait, here it is. In the coroner's report. The fabric wasn't discovered until yesterday—a day and a half after the bodies were discovered. But yes ... the report says that there was a small piece of fabric lodged in the mother's throat."

"Does it give a description?"

"No. I'll give the coroner a call and see if I can get a picture of it."

DeMarco wasted no time, making the call right away. While she was on the phone, Kate tried to think of anything that might be able to link two seemingly random couples, given what had been found in the throats of the females. While Kate had yet to see the piece of fabric that had been taken from the throat of the first female victim, she was fully expecting it to match the one that had been found in the throat of Mrs. Nash.

DeMarco's call was over three minutes later. Seconds after she ended the call, she received a text. She glanced at her phone and said: "We've got a match."

Approaching a stoplight as they inched their way further into the city of Roanoke, Kate looked over to the phone as DeMarco showed it to her.

As Kate expected, the fabric was soft and blue in color—an exact match for the one found in the throat of the Nash mother.

"We've got pretty extensive records on both couples, right?" Kate asked.

"Decent, I suppose," she said. "Based on the records and case files we have, there might be *some* stuff missing, but I think we've got quite a bit to go on." She paused here as the GPS app on the iPad dinged. "Turn left at this light," DeMarco said. "The house is half a mile down this next street."

Kate's mental wheels were turning quickly as they neared the first crime scene.

Two married couples, slaughtered in a brutal way. Remnants or scraps of some sort of old blanket found in the throats of the wives ...

There were many ways to go with the clues they had been given. But before Kate could focus on a single one and put it together, DeMarco was speaking up.

"Right there," she said, pointing to a small brick house on the right.

Kate pulled up alongside the curb. The house was located on a thin side street, the kind that connected two main roads. It was a quiet street with a few other small houses taking up the space. The street had an almost historic feel to it, the sidewalks faded and cracked, the houses in a similar state.

Faded white letters on the mailbox read LANGLEY. Kate also spotted a decorative L hanging on the front door, made of aged wood. It stood out against the bright yellow of the crime scene tape that hung from the porch railings.

As Kate and DeMarco headed for the front porch, DeMarco half read, half recited the information they had in the reports on the Langley family.

"Scott and Bethany Langley—Scott fifty-nine years of age, Bethany sixty-one. Scott was found dead in the kitchen and Bethany was in the laundry room. They were found by a fifteen-year-old boy who was taking private guitar lessons from Scott. It's estimated that they had only been killed a few hours before the bodies were discovered."

When they entered the Langley residence, Kate stood in the doorway for a moment, taking in the layout of the place. It was a smaller house, but well kept. The front door opened into a very small foyer which then became the living room. From there, a small bar top counter separated the kitchen from the living room. A hallway stood off to the right, leading to the rest of the house.

The layout of the house alone told Kate that the husband had likely been killed first. But from the front door, there was pretty much a clear view into the kitchen. Scott Langley would have had to have been quite busy not to notice someone walking through the front door.

Maybe the killer came in some other way, Kate thought.

They entered the kitchen, where bloodstains still stood out prominently on the laminate floor. A frying pan and a can of cooking spray were sitting by the edge of the stove.

He was about to cook something, Kate thought. *So maybe they were killed right around dinner time.*

DeMarco started for the hallway, and Kate followed her. There was a small room immediately to the left, the door opening to reveal a crowded laundry room. Here, the blood splatter had been much worse. There were bloodstains on the washer, the dryer, the walls, the floor, and on a load of neatly folded clean clothes sitting in a hamper.

With the bodies already removed, there seemed to be very little the Langley residence could offer them. But Kate had one more thing she wanted to check. She walked back out into the living room and looked at the pictures on the walls and atop the entertainment center. She saw the Langleys smiling and happy. In one picture, she saw an older couple with the Langleys posing by the end of a pier at the beach.

"Do we have a breakdown of the Langleys' family life?" Kate asked.

DeMarco, still holding the iPad in her right hand, scrolled through the information and started to read out the details they had. With each one, Kate found that the hunch she had been sitting on for a few minutes was likely true.

"They were married for twenty-five years. Bethany Langley had a sister that died in a car accident twelve years ago and neither of them have any surviving parents. Scott Langley's father passed away recently, just six months ago, from an aggressive form of prostate cancer."

"Any mention of kids?"

"Nope. No kids." DeMarco paused here and seemed to catch on to what Kate was speculating on. "You're thinking about the fabric, right? That it looks sort of like a kid's blanket."

"Yeah, that's what I was thinking. But if the Langleys didn't have kids I don't think there would be any obvious connection to be found."

"I don't know that I've ever seen an *obvious* connection to anything," DeMarco said with a shaky little laugh.

"That's true," Kate said, but she felt like there had to be one here. Even with the seemingly random victims, there were a few things they *did* have in common.

Both couples were both in their mid-to-late fifties, early sixties. Both were married. The wife of each couple had a piece of what appears to be a blanket shoved down her throat.

So yes … there were similarities, but they were leading to no real links. Not yet, anyway.

"Agent DeMarco, do you think you could make a call or two and make sure we can get some office space at the local police department?"

"Already done," she said. "I'm pretty sure Duran handled all of that before we even arrived here."

He thinks he knows me so well, Kate thought, a little irritated. But then, on the other hand, it appeared that he *did* know her pretty damned well.

Kate glanced around the house again, at the pictures, at the bloodstains. She was going to have to get deeper into the details of each couple if she wanted to get anywhere with this. And she was going to need to get some kind of forensic results on the fabric pieces. Given the similarities between the two scenes, she assumed some good old basic research more than anything would uncover some leads and clues.

They returned to the car, Kate again reminded that they had started this day ridiculously early. When she saw that it was just after ten in the morning, she was somewhat invigorated. They still had most of the day ahead of them. Maybe, if she was lucky and the case broke the way she felt it might, she'd be back in Richmond by the close of the weekend to see Michelle one more time—if, that was, Melissa would allow it.

See, some wiser part of her spoke up as she got back behind the wheel of the car. *Even in the midst of multiple bloody murders, you're thinking of your granddaughter—of your family. Doesn't that tell you something?*

She supposed it did. But even as she stepped foot into the later quarter or so of her life, it was still very hard to admit that there was something more to life than her work. It was especially hard when she was on the trail of a killer and knew that at any moment, he could be killing again.

CHAPTER SIX

A small conference room in the back of the City of Roanoke Police had been set aside for Kate and DeMarco. Once they arrived at the station, a small portly woman at the front desk led them through the building and to the room. As soon as they sat down and started to set up a makeshift workstation, there was a knock at the door.

"Come in," Kate said.

When the door opened, they saw a familiar face—Palmetto from the State PD, the somewhat curmudgeonly man who had met them in front of the Nash residence much earlier in the day.

"I saw you guys headed back this way while I was signing all of my paperwork," Palmetto said. "I'm on the way out, driving back to Chesterfield in a few hours. I thought I'd check in to see if there was anything else I could help with."

"Nothing big," Kate said. "Did you happen to know that there was also a scrap of that same fabric discovered in the throat of Bethany Langley?"

"I didn't until about half an hour ago. Apparently, one of you called the lab to ask them to send a picture."

"Yeah," DeMarco said. "And it seems to be a match with the one you gave us."

At the mention of the scrap of fabric, Kate set the plastic bag Palmetto had given her on the table. "As of right now, it's the only solid evidence we have that links the murders in any concrete way."

"And forensics found pretty much nothing on that one," Palmetto said. "Aside from Mrs. Nash's DNA."

"The forensic report I'm seeing from the scrap from the Langleys offers up nothing, either," DeMarco said.

"Still might be worth a trip to the forensics lab," Kate said.

"Good luck with that," Palmetto said. "When I spoke with them about the Nash scrap, they were clueless."

"Were you at all involved with the scene at the Langley home?" Kate asked.

"No. I came in right after it had happened. I saw the bodies and checked the place over, but there was nothing. When you talk to forensics, though, ask them about the stray hair found on the clean laundry. It didn't seem to belong to Mrs. Langley, so they're going to run some tests on it."

"Before you go," Kate said, "do you want to offer up any theories?"

"I don't have one," Palmetto said dryly. "From the digging I've done, there seems to be absolutely *no* link between the Nashes and the Langleys. The fabric in the throats, though … something that personal and explicit to the killer *has* to link them somehow, right?"

"That's my thought," Kate said.

Palmetto gave the door a playful slap and then Kate saw him smile for the first time. "I'm sure you'll figure it out. I've heard about you, you know? A lot of us on the State PD have."

"I'm sure," she said with a smirk.

"Mostly good things. And then you came out of retirement to bring someone down a few months ago, right?"

"You could say that."

Palmetto, seeing that Kate wasn't going to just sit there and soak in accolades, gave her a shrug. "Give the state boys a call if you need anything on this one, Agent Wise."

"I'll do that," Kate said as Palmetto took his leave.

When Palmetto had closed the door behind him, DeMarco playfully shook her head. "You ever get tired of hearing people sing your praises?"

"Yes, actually," Kate said, but not in a rude way. While it was uplifting to be reminded of all that she had done throughout her career, she knew deep down that she had always just been doing her job. Perhaps she done her job with a bit more passion than others had, but it had been just that—a job well done … a job she could not seem to leave behind her.

Within a few minutes and some help from the station's systems administrator, Kate and DeMarco had access to the station's database. They worked together, looking into the pasts of the Nashes and the Langleys. Neither family had records of any kind. In fact, both families had records that made it hard to imagine anyone having a grudge against them. As for the Langleys, they had served as foster parents for a few years of their lives, so they'd had to undergo rigorous background checks several times throughout the course of their lives. The Nashes were heavily involved in their church and had been on several mission trips in the past twenty tears, most notably to Nepal and Honduras.

Kate gave up after a while and started pacing the floor. She used the conference room's dry erase board to jot down notes, hoping that seeing everything written down in one place would help her to focus. But there was nothing. No link, no clues, no clear course of where to go.

"You, too, huh?" DeMarco said. "Nothing?"

"Not so far. I think maybe we just go with what we *do* have rather than trying to find something new. I think we need to reevaluate the fabrics. While the forensics tests came up with nothing, maybe the fabric itself can point us somewhere."

"I don't follow you," DeMarco said.

"That's fine," Kate said. "I'm not sure I do, either. But I'm hoping we'll know it when we see it."

Kate felt the first true pangs of fatigue as she and DeMarco drove from the police station to the forensics lab. It was a stark reminder that she had not slept in about twenty-seven hours and that her work day had started insanely early. Twenty years ago, this would not have bothered her. But with fifty-six staring her right in the face from a few weeks across the calendar, things were different now.

The drive to the lab was only five minutes, located in close proximity to a little network consisting of the PD, the courthouse, and a holding jail. After showing their IDs, they were escorted past the front desk of the forensic sciences lab and into the central laboratory area. They were asked to sit in a small lobby for a moment while the technician who had been in charge of the fabric swabs was paged.

"You think there's any chance the fabric is just some kind of calling card for the killer?" DeMarco asked.

"It could be. Might not have anything to do with the *why* of the case. It could just mean something to the killer. Either way, right now it seems that the fabric—from a blanket of some kind, I feel quite sure—is our only real connection to him."

It made Kate recall a gruesome case she'd once been a part of early in the nineties. A man had killed five people—all ex-girlfriends. Before killing them by choking them, he had forced each one to swallow a condom. In the end, he had no real reason for doing so other than his hatred for wearing condoms during sex. Kate could not help but wonder if these fabric fragments would turn out to be just as insignificant to the case.

Their wait was a short one; a tall older man came hurrying out of a door directly across from them. "You're with the FBI?" he asked.

"We are," Kate said, showing her ID. DeMarco did the same and the man studied each one quite carefully.

"Nice to meet you, Agents," he said. "I'm Will Reed, and I ran the tests on the fabric from the recent murders. I assume that's why you're here? Agent DeMarco, I believe you are the one I sent the picture to earlier?"

"That's right," DeMarco said. "We were hoping you could shed some more light on those scraps."

"Well, I'd be more than happy to assist with whatever you need, but if it's about those two scraps of fabric, I'm afraid there's nothing I can offer. It seems that the killer not only went through great lengths to shove the fabric into the mouths of the victims, but that he was also quite careful about not leaving any traces of himself behind."

"Yes, we understand that," Kate said. "But without any firm physical results to go on, I was wondering if there's anything you could tell me about the fabric itself."

"Oh," Reed said. "That, I *can* help with."

"I'm of the opinion that both scraps came from the same source material," Kate said. "Most likely a blanket."

"I think that's a safe bet to place," Reed said. "I wasn't too sure until I saw the second scrap. They fit together rather well—color, texture, and so forth."

"Is there any way to tell how old the blanket might be?" Kate asked.

"I'm afraid not. What I can tell you, though, is what the blanket is made up of. And it stuck with me because as far as I know, it's an odd fabric combination for a traditional blanket as you'd think of one. The vast majority of the blanket is made of wool, which, of course, is not uncommon at all. But the secondary material used in the fabric is bamboo cotton."

"Is that all that different from *regular* cotton?" Kate asked.

"I'm not positive," he said. "But we see a lot of clothes and fabric-related material come through here. And I can count on one hand the number of times I've come into contact with something with noticeable traces of bamboo cotton. It's not a very rare material but it's just not as widespread as your basic cotton."

"In other words," DeMarco said, "it wouldn't be too hard to locate companies that use it as a primary material?"

"That, I *don't* know," Reed said. "But you may be interested to know that bamboo cotton *is* present in lots of fluffier blankets. It's quite breathable from what I've seen. You're probably looking for something on the pricier side. As a matter of fact, there's a warehouse just outside of town that manufactures the very sort of thing I mean. Pricy blankets, throws, sheets, that sort of thing."

"Do you know the name of it?" DeMarco asked.

"Biltmore Threads. They're a smaller company that nearly went belly up when everyone started buying everything online."

"Anything else you can tell us?" Kate asked.

"Yes, but it's sort of grisly. With the Nash woman, I believe the fabric was shoved so far down that she nearly vomited, even that close to death. There was stomach acid on the fabric."

Kate thought about the amount of force and effort it would take for someone to do that … about how much of one's hand would go into the victim's mouth.

"Thank you for your time, Mr. Reed," Kate said.

"Certainly. Let's just hope I don't see a third piece to that blanket anytime soon."

CHAPTER SEVEN

Eerily enough, the drive to the Biltmore Threads warehouse took Kate and DeMarco down the same stretch of road they had taken into Whip Springs at four o'clock that morning. The factory and warehouse were located down a two-lane road that snaked off of the main highway. It was tucked away, along with the stretch of dying grass that served as its landscaping, in the very same woods that had hidden the Nash home from the main road.

From the looks of the parking lot, Biltmore Threads wasn't doing quite as badly as Will Reed had suggested. The place looked to employ at least fifty or so people, and that was based on just this time of day. With a factory like this, Kate assumed there was shift work involved, meaning another fifty or so would probably come in later on for the night shift.

They made their way inside, walking into a dingy lobby. A woman sitting behind a counter looked up at them with a peculiar expression. It was evident that they didn't get many visitors.

"Can I help you?" she asked.

DeMarco went through the round of introductions and after they showed their IDs, the woman at the counter buzzed them in through a door on the far end of the lobby. That same woman met them there and then led them down a small hallway. At the end of the hall, she opened a set of double doors that led onto the Biltmore Threads production floor. Several sets of looms and other equipment Kate had never seen were thrumming with life. On the far side of the large work floor, a compact forklift was carrying a pallet of stacked cloth elsewhere into the warehouse.

After leading them carefully around the edge of the floor, the woman stopped at another door and led them inside. Here, there was a thin hallway adorned with five rooms. The woman brought them to the first one and knocked.

"Yeah?" a man's voice boomed from inside.

"We've got visitors," the woman called before opening the door. "Two ladies from the FBI."

There was a few seconds' pause and then the door was opened from the other side. A dark-haired man wearing thick glasses greeted them. He looked them up and down, not out of nervousness but sheer curiosity.

"FBI?" he asked. "What can I do for you?"

"Can we have a minute of your time?" Kate asked.

"Sure," he said, standing aside and allowing them into his office.

There was only one seat in the office other than the one behind his desk. Neither Kate nor DeMarco took it. The dark-haired man did not take his seat either, electing to stand with them.

"I assume you're the supervisor?" Kate asked.

"I'm the regional manager and day shift supervisor, yes," he said. He extended his hand quickly, as if embarrassed he had forgotten to so earlier than this. "Ray Garraty."

Kate shook the offered hand and then showed her ID. She then reached into her pocket and withdrew the scrap of fabric from the Nash scene.

"This is a scrap of fabric from a recent crime scene," she said. "And we believe it could be key in catching a killer. The forensics lab found bamboo cotton in it, and I understand that Biltmore Threads uses bamboo cotton rather regularly."

"We do," Garraty said. He reached for the bag and then hesitated before asking: "Do you mind?"

Kate shook her head and handed it to him. Garraty looked it over closely and nodded. "Without actually tearing it further apart, I can't give you any guarantees, but yeah, it looks to have some in it. Do you know where the fabric came from?"

"I'm assuming a blanket," Kate said.

"Looks like it," Garraty said. "And while I'm not one hundred percent sure, I think it might have been designed and manufactured here."

"Right here at Biltmore Threads?" Kate asked.

"Perhaps."

Garraty handed the plastic bag back to Kate and then walked to an old beaten-up filing cabinet tucked away in the back corner of the small office. He opened the bottom drawer and after fishing through its contents for a while, pulled out two different books. They were both quite large and as he started leafing through one, Kate saw that they were both inventory catalogues.

"The color and the design you can sort of make out look familiar," Garraty explained as he went through the pages. "If it was made here, it will be in one of these books."

It was an exciting thought, but Kate wasn't quite sure what it would mean. If the blanket in question *was* made in Biltmore Threads, did it really even open up that many possibilities? There were many more questions to ask before coming to such a conclusion.

"Right here," Garraty said. He turned the book toward them and pointed to one of several different blankets listed on a page about three-quarters of the way through one of the books. "Does that look like a match to you?"

Kate and DeMarco both studied the page. Kate looked back and forth, making sure she wasn't *making* herself see some semblance of similarity. But after a few seconds, DeMarco answered for her.

"I mean, the fabric we have is faded, but it's the same. Even that little faded white checkered pattern."

"Well, it's faded because it's an older product," Garraty said. He pointed to a line from the item description. "Right here, it says it started being produced in 1991 and was eliminated from our production cycle in 2004."

"So you made this same blanket for thirteen years?" DeMarco asked.

"Yes. It was a very popular item, which is how I was able to recognize it so quickly."

"In other words, the last time you would have passed this blanket out of your warehouse was 2004," Kate said. "Meaning that this sample is somewhere between fifteen and thirty years old."

"That's correct."

Well, even if there could *be a link due to the blanket,* Kate thought, *that thirty-year window makes it* very *hard.*

"Mr. Garraty, how long have you been in your position here?"

"Going on twenty-six years," Garraty said. "I've got retirement coming up next year."

"While you've been here, has Biltmore Threads employed Scott or Bethany Langley, or Toni or Derrick Nash?"

Garraty thought about it for a moment and then shrugged. "The names don't ring any bells for me, but if we're looking over a span of more than ten years, I'd refer you to records. There are a lot of employees that come in and out of here."

"How soon can you find out for sure?" DeMarco asked.

"Within the hour."

"That would be appreciated," Kate said. "And if you don't mind, just one more question. Have you had any employees cause problems for you or the factory in the past month or so? Any troublemakers or just someone you and other management knew to keep an eye on?"

"Funny you should ask," Garraty said. "I had to fire a guy just two weeks ago. He was showing up to work stoned *and* we were pretty sure he was stealing material. When I confronted him about it, he got violent and I had to call security. And since we only have one security guard, the police got involved and he was eventually arrested. But he was out the next day."

"Stealing material?" DeMarco said, an edge of excitement to her voice.

"Yes ... but not that one," he said, pointing to the plastic bag. "If that's been discontinued, we haven't had that fabric in the warehouse for *years*. No, he came out and told us later, when he cooled down, that he had been stealing it for some projects his girlfriend was creating. She has an Etsy shop or something."

"Can we get a name?" Kate asked.

"Travis Rogers. He's about thirty years old. Has a record, I think. Some mild violent crimes. But we tend to give people a second chance at Biltmore Threads, you know?"

"Is he a local?" DeMarco asked.

"Yeah, over in Whip Springs. I can get you his address."

"Again, that would be appreciated," Kate said.

Garraty led them out of his office and back down the same path the receptionist had led them, only in reverse. When they were back in the lobby, Garraty spoke with the receptionist while Kate and DeMarco huddled by the lobby doors.

"The blanket being manufactured here," DeMarco said. "You think that's just a creepy coincidence?"

"It could be. I'm inclined to think so, given that the blanket hasn't been produced in so long. It *does* make me wonder, though..."

"Wonder what?"

"No matter where the blanket was from, we know that it's got to be old...at least fifteen years and as much as about thirty. And if that's the case, it makes me think someone held on to it. Why use something so old unless it has some sort of meaning or significance to you?"

She let the question linger as Garraty walked back over to them. He handed Kate a slip of paper with an address scrawled on it.

"I also went ahead and had her look to see if any of those names you gave me were in the system as former employees," Garraty said. "We got nothing."

"That's fine," Kate said. "It just needed to be checked. Thank you for your help."

"Glad to do it," Garraty said, still looking as if the entire visit had thrown him off.

Kate and DeMarco headed back outside. As they headed for the car, Kate looked past the dead lawn in front of the factory and warehouse. The expanse of trees made her nervous in a way she could not explain. Thick forests had always made her feel like that; they offered far too many places to hide. She gave the woods a skeptical look as she got back behind the wheel.

"GPS says this Travis Rogers lives less than half an hour away, on the other side of Roanoke."

"Then let's pay him a visit," Kate said.

Maybe it was because the day had started so early or maybe it was because she could feel herself getting more and more tired by the minute, but she was starting to get a good feeling about this case—a feeling that it might be over much sooner rather than later.

She pulled out of the parking lot of Biltmore Threads desperately hoping that she was right.

CHAPTER EIGHT

Travis Rogers lived in a townhouse not too far away from the thick traffic of a mall complex. Given that it was creeping up on lunchtime, the traffic was pretty bad as Kate neared the place. Passing a Starbucks and a Dunkin' Donuts also made her realize that, unprofessional or not, she was going to have to stop for coffee after they questioned Travis Rogers or she might very well fall asleep on the job.

She soldiered through and parked in front of the townhouse about forty minutes after leaving Biltmore Threads. She and DeMarco hustled up to the front door, neither of them having much hope that a man in his thirties would be at home in the middle of the day—especially not one who would likely be searching for a job.

So they were both surprised when the door was answered by a ruggedly handsome man. He looked a little scraggly around the edges but well-groomed. He *did* look a little tired, though, maybe like he had just rolled out of bed.

"Are you Travis Rogers?" DeMarco asked.

"I am. Who's asking?"

DeMarco took the lead this time, showing her badge and taking a step toward the door to let him know that they weren't going to be turned away.

"FBI? What the hell for?"

"Your name came up in passing in regards to a case we're working," Kate asked. "If you'd give us just five minutes of your time, we can be on our way."

Clearly confused and a little alarmed, Travis stepped to the side and opened the door. When he did, Kate saw that his right hand was in a cast from high on the wrist, all the way to the knuckles of his fingers.

It'd be pretty hard to kill someone the way the Nashes and Langleys were killed if you had a cast on your right hand, Kate told herself.

The front door opened into the living room, which was quite clean. A laptop sat on the coffee table. She saw a LinkedIn profile on the screen; apparently Travis was indeed doing some job hunting.

"I'm going to assume this is about what happened with the whole thing at Biltmore Threads, right?" Travis said as he sat down on the couch. "Although I don't know why the FBI would get involved in something that small."

"Can I ask why you got violent with Mr. Garraty?" Kate asked.

"It was just months and months of frustration, you know? I'd been asking for a raise for about half a year. I'd been there for almost five years and had only gotten two small pay bumps, so I thought I was due. Garraty basically told me that he could pass on my complaint but if I kept pestering them, it was going to look bad. We had some words and, quite frankly, I lost my shit. I threw his little name placard thing from his desk at him. I started to rush across the room at him but thought better of it."

"And what about your past offenses?"

"A bar fight when I was nineteen and then defending myself when some dipshit lost his cool in a fit of road rage when I accidentally clipped his car. Not to be a smart ass, but you're welcome to look all of that up. Look… this whole thing with Garraty and Biltmore Threads… it's embarrassing. So if there's anything you need from me, just let me know. I'd like to get it behind me as soon as I can."

"Well, what about the material you were stealing?" DeMarco asked.

"I only did it twice, and that was *after* I had started to get pissed off about not being paid fairly. I'm not proud of it. But I've been to court and I'm going to pay the fines."

"Garraty said you stole the materials for your girlfriend."

"Yeah. Jess runs this little Etsy shop. She makes these trendy little custom clutch purses and shoulder bags. She makes more than I did doing it… so yeah, I took some material for her."

Kate was all but certain that Travis was innocent. He'd made some dumb choices, sure, and he had unfortunate luck when it came to physical altercations, but he sure as hell wasn't a murderer.

"What happened to your hand?" DeMarco asked.

Travis rolled his eyes and looked at the floor. "Just another genius decision on my part. I was so pissed when the cops got called on me at Biltmore Threads that I punched the wall outside the building. It's a brick wall, and it hurt like a bitch. I broke three fingers and got a hairline fracture down the base of my hand."

"Do you have any proof of when you did this?" DeMarco asked.

"Yeah. Actually, the first bill for the x-ray came today." He got up and went to the edge of the counter in the attached kitchen. He retrieved a piece of mail from it and brought it back to them. Kate and DeMarco looked it over and saw that the initial consult for the x-ray had been three weeks ago—at least two full weeks before the Langleys had been murdered.

"At the risk of sounding nosy, can I ask what this is about?" Travis asked. Kate had just one more thing left to do. She almost decided against it because she was *that* certain that Travis Rogers was innocent. She took the evidence bag with the scrap of blanket inside of it and showed it to him.

"Does this look familiar to you?" she asked.

His initial reaction told her what she needed to know. There was no alarm, no guilt, no fear. He merely looked closely at it and shrugged. "I don't think so. Is it something from Biltmore Threads?"

"It is," Kate said, pocketing the bag again. "Thank you for your time, Mr. Rogers."

When they headed back out to the car, the feeling Kate had experienced coming out of Biltmore Threads started to unravel. The blanket fabric coming from Biltmore had seem like an omen of sorts, a sign that they were on the right track. But now, back to having no leads whatsoever, she felt a little lost.

"You think we should try speaking to the neighbors of the victims now?" DeMarco asked when they were back in the car.

"That's the best idea I can think of," Kate said. "Of course, the Nashes had no immediate neighbors—no one who would be able to see any coming and going from around their house."

"So the Langleys, then," DeMarco said.

"Right," Kate agreed. "But first...I have to get some coffee. This whole regular-sleep thing that comes with retirement has ruined me."

Coffee in hand, Kate stepped out of the car adjacent to the Langley residence. She looked to the house next to it and realized that they may have hit the jackpot. While she hated to give in to stereotypes—especially in her line of work—there was one that she had found *usually* proved itself true: the older the woman, the more prone they were to gossip. And there was just such a woman standing on the porch next door to the Langley home. She was carefully filling a bird feeder with some sort of liquid. A hummingbird feeder, if Kate was seeing it correctly.

Kate and DeMarco approached slowly, not wanting to seem threatening or in a hurry. The woman gave them an uncertain smile as she finished up with the bird feeder. It swung gently as she released it, the red liquid she had just put inside of it looking almost like Kool-Aid.

"Hummingbirds?" Kate asked.

"That's right," the old woman said. She was pushing seventy...maybe eighty. It was hard to tell due to the beaming smile on her face. "They come by and see me at least twice a day as long as I keep the feeder full. Now...can I help you ladies?"

"Yes, ma'am. I'm Agent Wise, and this is Agent DeMarco," Kate said, showing her ID. "We've been assigned to the case involving the Langleys and were hoping you could take some time to speak with us."

The woman looked over Kate's shoulder, toward the Langley house. The radiant smile on her face was gone now. There was no frown there, either...just a resigned look. A *what-has-the-world-come-to* look.

"Nice to meet you agents, I suppose," the woman said. She hunkered down in a lawn chair that sat against the porch rails and looked up at them. "I'm Callie Spencer, by the way. Been living here in this house for about twenty-five years now."

"So you've been here the entire time the Langleys lived there?"

"Yes indeed. Scott and Bethany moved in sometime in the early nineties, I'd say."

"Would you call them friendly?" DeMarco asked. "Social?"

"I guess so. I mean, they weren't rude or mean or anything like that. They were an okay couple, but a little private. Especially over the last few years."

"Any idea why?" Kate asked.

Callie frowned and nodded. "Bethany sort of got different after her sister died in that car accident. Ten years ago or so, I suppose."

"Can you expand on what you mean by *private*?" DeMarco asked.

"Well, you know ... *private* might not be the best word. If we crossed paths on the sidewalk, we'd chat it up for a while. But they never came over just to visit. Never really volunteered any information. Scott would catch me out trying to mow the lawn from time to time and insist on finishing. So, no, not private but not really outgoing, either."

"Do you know if they had any regular visitors?" Kate asked.

"None that I know of. I believe Scott had a friend or two from work come over every now and then during football season. And there was a period of time, you know, when Davey was living with them."

"Davey?" Kate asked.

"Yes. Well, I called him Davey. His real name is David. He's their nephew—the son of Bethany's sister. When she died, he came and stayed with them. He was only ten years old. He'd stay with the Langleys for a while and then would go away for months at a time. I found out later from Scott that during those times, he was staying with his uncle from his father's side down in Texas."

Kate and DeMarco shared a look. This wasn't necessarily a lead, but it was new information that could take them several different places. "Do you happen to know how long ago Davey was still living with them?"

"Oh, I think he moved out for good two or three years ago. About time, too. I felt sorry for him, you know? Passed back and forth between families. But the Langleys were good for him, I think. They were sweet people. They were foster parents. Did you know that?"

"Yes ma'am," Kate said, recalling the information they had found while digging around at the Roanoke Police Department.

"When was the last time they fostered someone?" DeMarco asked.

"Oh, I can't say with any certainty. At least a few years, I think. One time they kept this little girl for a few months. The sweetest thing. She'd come over here and we'd play checkers on the porch."

"And what about Davey?" Kate asked. "Did you have many interactions with him?"

"Not many. They were keeping Davey for the first go-round when my husband passed away. They all came over here—Davey, too—and gave their condolences. But, you know, being neighbors, it's pretty easy to sort of just *see* things about people, you know? And with Davey, he was always very quiet. He had this sort of brooding quality to him. I do know that as he got older, he became very hard to handle. Defiant, I guess."

"Do you know where he ended up after leaving the Langleys' care?" DeMarco asked.

"Oh, he's still around. He ended up going to community college but he ended up dropping out. I don't know why … grades, or just no commitment, maybe. I'm not sure where he's living but I *do* know where he works. He's been working at Gino's Pizza for at least several months now."

"You're certain of this?" Kate asked.

"I know he was working there oh, about six months ago, because he delivered a pizza to my door. I usually think it's stupid to have pizza delivered because then you have to give a tip, but I was sick, so …" She realized she was trailing off here. She smiled, rolled her eyes at herself, and continued. "Anyway, and then my friend Janell, whom I have tea with twice a week, said she saw him working down at Gino's not too long ago. Maybe about two or three weeks."

"Thank you," Kate said.

"Hold on, wait. You don't think Davey had anything to do with their murders, do you?"

"Most likely not," Kate said. "But he'd be a great source of information about the family. And right now, every bit of information is critical."

Callie seemed relieved at this, giving them a nod. As she did, a hummingbird floated into view at the feeder. The three women watched it for a moment, the smile returning to Callie's face.

"I do hope you can find who did this," Callie said. "Rumor has it that a family out in Whip Springs was killed, too. A husband and wife. Is that right?"

"We can't comment on that," Kate said, hating the sound of it. She knew that to someone like Callie Spencer, that noncommittal comment would sound like a big fat *yes*.

"Well, best of luck, Agents," Callie said as Kate and DeMarco started back down the stairs.

DeMarco got behind the wheel this time. As Kate opened the passenger door, she looked back to Callie Spencer on her porch. She was staring hard at the hummingbird—which had now been joined by two more. It was then that Kate realized that Callie wasn't so much interested in the birds, as she was intent on not looking in the direction of the Langleys' house. Finding something both sad and comforting about this, Kate got into the car and pulled up directions for Gino's Pizza.

CHAPTER NINE

They arrived at Gino's just as the lunch rush had apparently died down. Once inside, Kate's stomach responded right away to the delicious smell of pizza and calzones. She could barely remember grabbing breakfast that morning seeing as how much of the earlier part of the day seemed to be nothing more than a blur.

"Hungry?" DeMarco asked.

"You read my mind."

They approached the small booth adorned with a sign reading Please Wait to Be Seated. A teenaged girl greeted them with a smile. "Table for two?" she asked.

"And, if you don't mind, we'd like to speak to a young man that works here. Is Davey here today?"

"No, not today," the hostess said.

"How about the manager?" DeMarco asked. "Is he here?"

"Yes. Do you need to speak with him?"

"Yes, please," Kate said. She looked around the place and saw that it was practically dead. She wondered if this was a reflection of the food but her stomach was too hungry to really care. So she added: "While we eat, if you don't mind."

The hostess led them to a table at the back of the restaurant, took their drink orders, and headed back toward the kitchen area. After looking over the menu and deciding that they were both starving, Kate and DeMarco opted for a large pizza. They bickered over toppings for a moment—DeMarco was one of the oddballs who thought pineapple belonged on pizza—and it brought a smile to Kate's face. This was only the second case they had worked together and they had a natural chemistry that most partners took a long time to build.

I really need to get to know her better, Kate thought.

The hostess came back three minutes later with their drinks. A hefty middle-aged man was with her. His little nameplate pinned to the breast of his shirt read *Teddy*. The hostess took their order, leaving them with Teddy. He looked at both of them with a nervous look on his face, perhaps assuming they wanted to complain about the service or the employee they had mentioned by name to the hostess.

"I'm Teddy King," the man said in a soothing tone. It was the sort of tone someone who was used to making apologies tended to adapt to. "I was told you needed to speak with the manager?"

"Yes," Kate said. She again took a look around the place. If there had been more patrons (there were currently only three, all older people sitting together on the opposite side of the restaurant), she would not be speaking about the case at a table, out in the open. But this place was currently about as private and quiet as anyplace else. She took out her ID and plopped it on the table, not wanting to give those other three patrons the opportunity to see it if they happened to look over in this direction.

"I'm Agent Wise with the FBI, and this is my partner, Agent DeMarco. We're working a case that has led us to one of your employees, a young man named Davey."

"That would be Davey Armstrong," Teddy said. Kate thought she caught an edge of irritation in his voice.

"It sounds like you aren't too surprised that the authorities might be looking for him," Kate pointed out.

Teddy sat down at the chair at the edge of the table and shrugged. "Well, I mean I wouldn't paint him as a criminal or anything, but he's just the sort that always makes you feel on edge. He's a decent employee when he wants to be, I guess. A little lazy at times. I've nearly fired him on two different occasions, but ... I don't know. I'm a sucker for a sob story."

"What's the version of his sob story that you've heard?" Kate asked.

"Well, I knew his mother. Went to high school with her. And when he came in looking for a job about a year or so ago, I made the connection right away. I'd sort of kept up with him through word of mouth after his mom died. He was bounced around from family member to family member, never really having a home. I talked to him one time about his mother, just to let him know I had known her and thought she was an amazing woman. It made him sad but he seemed to enjoy hearing it. But even then, when trying to connect with him, I felt like it might have been a mistake to hire him."

"A mistake?" DeMarco asked. "Why is that?"

"Well, he's just not very responsible. He's twenty-six and just isn't motivated. And he's not very good with people. After I realized this, I made a point to put him on as a delivery driver—keeping him out of the shop and away from paying customers, you know? Plus, he just sometimes gets this look about him that—forgive me for saying so—creeps people right the hell out. I've had waitresses complain about it. And you know, he seems to prefer that … being out in the car, driving around and delivering food."

"If I were to give you a few small windows of time, would you be able to tell me if Davey was making deliveries during those times?"

"Yeah. Just let me go grab the schedule."

Teddy got up, leaving Kate and DeMarco to mull over what they had just heard. Kate tried to imagine a lackluster twenty-six-year-old who had been dealt a rough hand at life working in a place like this. Even driving deliveries around, she supposed she could see how someone like Davey Armstrong might seem to have a storm cloud on his heels at all times.

Teddy came back with the schedule and sat back down. He also brought their pizza with him. Kate was impressed. It had taken less than ten minutes to get it—which, in her experience, had to be a record of some kind. Maybe it was the FBI badge and ID. It came with certain perks, and apparently getting pizza quickly was one of them.

"The first date would be yesterday, sometime between lunch and six in the afternoon," Kate said. "The other isn't as certain, but would likely have been four or five days ago. So let's say Monday or Tuesday."

Teddy scanned the schedule and pointed to a column with Davey's name at the top. "Well, he was off Monday, but he worked the seven-hour stretch from two-to-nine on Tuesday night. And then yes, he was working yesterday from five in the afternoon until closing."

"Did you happen to notice anything off about him on either of those days?" Kate asked.

"Well, like I said ... he always seemed a little off. But no ... I didn't notice anything out of the ordinary. Although ..."

He stopped here, as if a thought had just sprung to the forefront of his mind.

"What is it?" Kate asked.

"He was late as hell getting back from one of those deliveries on Tuesday. I didn't lay into him too badly because we weren't all that busy. He claimed he knocked and knocked on this person's door but it took them forever to show up. Said that was why he was late."

"How late are we talking?" DeMarco asked.

"The run there and back should have only taken him about half an hour but he was gone for a little over an hour."

"Can we get the addresses he delivered to during that run?"

"Sure. I'll have to look back through the receipts and orders, though. Might take a few minutes."

"No hurry," Kate said. "When you do get the information, just give us a call." She slid a business card over to him and then added: "By any chance did you ever happen to hear him talk ill about the Langley family?"

"Not at all. He liked them quite a bit. Why ... is there something wrong?"

Kate did not want to tell this man the news of the Langleys. She was actually surprised he had not yet heard it. It made Kate wonder if Davey had learned of the fate of the family that had raised him for a while.

"I'm afraid Scott and Bethany were killed three days ago."

"Oh my God," Teddy said. "Well, I don't think Davey has any idea. Three days ago?"

"It appears that way," DeMarco said.

"And you think Davey had something to do with it?"

"It's far too early to make such a speculation," Kate said. "Do you happen to know where he lives?"

"I do, actually. I had to give him a few rides home when his car was on the mend. And I'm pretty sure you'd catch him there right now. He might not seem very committed to work, but he's sure as hell committed to Fortnite."

Kate had heard of Fortnite; she was pretty sure it was a recent online game that was insanely popular with teens. She didn't want to say anything, though, because she wasn't quite sure.

Ah, old age strikes again, she thought.

"Would you mind giving us the address?" Kate asked.

"I don't know the exact address, but I can give you the directions. You won't be able to miss it. He listens to his music so damned loud that his neighbors have called in noise complaints on him."

"That would be fine," Kate said.

And as Teddy gave them directions to Davey's apartment, Kate's mind wandered a bit. How could Davey not know about the deaths of the people who had helped raise him? It seemed peculiar to her. But even more peculiar than that was the idea that maybe he *did* know and had decided to keep it to himself, deciding not to tell Teddy or anyone he worked with.

And why would he do that? Kate could only think of one thing: because he was hiding a degree of guilt.

CHAPTER TEN

A simple call to the police was enough for Kate to discover that Davey Armstrong had *not* been informed of the Langleys' deaths. He was not listed as next of kin in any reports, the only link being a doctor's form from eight years ago where Bethany Langley had been listed as his emergency contact.

This made the impromptu visit all the more pivotal. Not only were they going to be questioning him about his whereabouts during the time of the murders and get a gauge on his mental state, but they were apparently going to be informing him of the deaths of his aunt and uncle.

Teddy's directions had been quite detailed, so they found the apartment complex with no problem. It was actually not so much a complex as it was a large house-looking structure with five separate living quarters. It was in a small complex with three other structures. As Kate and DeMarco got out of the car, they heard yet another of Teddy's details that turned out to be spot on: the booming sound of music turned up to an obnoxious volume. It was some sort of heavy metal from what Kate could tell, grinding guitars and a machine-gun-fire beat from double bass drums.

It was coming from apartment 3B, just as Teddy had said. The agents approached the door and Kate wasted no time trying to be polite. She pounded hard on the door, making sure she could be heard over the roar of the music. A demonic, throaty voice had joined in with the guitars and drums now.

After a few moments, the music came to a stop. Hurried footsteps could be heard coming toward the door. It opened quickly, but only enough for a hectic-looking man to peer through the doorway at them.

"Yeah?" he asked, clearly feeling that he was being horribly inconvenienced.

"Are you David Armstrong?" Kate asked.

"Yeah. And you are?"

Kate and DeMarco showed their IDs almost in perfect sync. Davey studied them with great interest, his expression going from awe to fright. He looked suspiciously at them but still showed an edge of irritation.

"I'm Agent Wise, and this is my partner Agent DeMarco. It has come to our attention that you are the nephew of Scott and Bethany Langley."

"I am," he said. He then peeked over his shoulder. Kate could see a computer behind him, the screen on some game menu screen. "Why is the FBI interested in me *or* the Langleys?"

"Can we come in?" Kate asked.

"Is that really necessary?" Davey asked.

"It would make things much easier and we'd be out of your hair faster," Kate said.

"Fine."

Davey stepped to the side and allowed them inside. As they passed through the doorway, DeMarco wasted little time. "When was the last time you spoke with them?" she asked.

"I don't know," Davey said. He sat down behind his computer desk and checked something on the screen. Kate assumed he was playing Fortnite, as Teddy had suggested. "Maybe a month or so. Aunt Bethany called to say hi. Just sort of checking in."

Kate looked to DeMarco and gave her a look that she hoped communicated to *"Don't worry, I've got this."*

"Mr. Armstrong, I'm sorry to be the one to tell you this, but Bethany and Scott are dead. They were killed in their home four or five days ago."

Something similar to shock washed over Davey's face but it didn't stay there for very long. He looked at the floor for a moment and it was then that Kate was certain he would break into tears. But he did nothing of the sort. He looked back up at the agents, looking back and forth between the two of them.

"Do you know who did it yet?" Davey asked. "Have you caught them?"

"No," DeMarco said. "That's why we're here. We were hoping you might be able to shed some light on why someone might want to kill them."

"Oh," he said, rather absently. He at least seemed to not care as much about the game behind him, but he also didn't seem quite as upset as Kate had expected. He looked detached—almost as if he was thinking about something else entirely. "Yeah, I don't know. They were good, you know? Good people. I can't think of anyone that would want to kill them..."

"Davey, are you okay?" Kate asked.

He looked up at her then and when he did, she saw the fear in his eyes. He was scared and clearly uneasy. Kate knew that the human mind went through a ton of stages as it tried to accept monumental loss, but this seemed out of place.

"And you're certain you hadn't spoken to them recently?" Kate asked.

"I told you, it's been weeks," he said, snapping at her. "Look...I just need to go. I need to get out of here and..."

He got up and headed for the door. He moved in such a way that for a split second, Kate thought he was going to attack—perhaps pulling a gun out. But he only made a beeline for the front door, doing everything he could not to look at them.

DeMarco surprised Kate by jumping to her feet and moving with catlike guile. She made it to the door before Davey, blocking his way.

"Davey, we know this is some miserable news to digest, but we really need you to stay here with us for a bit longer. Just a few more questions and we can—"

Davey let out a gut-churning scream that was half anger and half desperation. He threw a hard shoulder into DeMarco, sending her back hard against the doorframe. Just as her head rebounded from the frame, Davey bounded through the door. Kate noted that he had not fully closed it when they entered, indicating that he had planned to make a run for it from the start.

Kate leaped to her feet and chased after him. DeMarco looked a little woozy, bracing herself against the wall to make sure she didn't fall down. She took two huge strides after him as he slammed the door in her face from the outside. She blocked it with her forearm and pushed through it. She stepped out onto the porch just as Davey made it down the small flight of stairs.

Kate knew right away that she would not be able to match him in a footrace so she decided to take a chance to eliminate the race altogether. Rather than running after him, she took one big stride to the edge of the porch and launched herself forward. She knew right away that she had overestimated the distance; rather than take him in the back of the knees, she was going to end up slamming into his upper back.

She braced for the impact and felt a twinge of pain in her neck as they collided. Her full weight slammed into him from behind. He went down so quickly and so fast that as he fell, his legs nearly came up over his head in a half-flip. Kate managed to lock her right arm around his neck as they both fell, applying a rear-neck choke as they hit the ground, The air went out of her and the jarring pain that shot through her reminded her that she was well north of fifty years of age.

Still, the adrenaline was enough to help her roll on top of him, plant a knee in his back, and pull his arms behind him. She cuffed him with expert precision and was relieved when she heard DeMarco approaching from behind. With her help, they pulled Davey Armstrong to his feet. Kate hid a grimace when she saw that he had skinned up the side of his face in the fall. The fault was hers, though, as she could have been a bit gentler.

"Why'd you run?" DeMarco asked.

Davey said nothing. As they led him to the car, Kate hurried ahead. She popped open the trunk, hoping for a first-aid kit. She found one, plucked out the antibacterial wipes, and opened them. Before putting Davey in the back of the car, she wiped the blood away from the nasty scratch on his face. He winced at the sting but said nothing.

"Do you know why we're taking you with us, David?" DeMarco asked.

"Because they're dead," he said. "And I guess you think I did it."

As he scooted into the back seat, Kate and DeMarco shared an uneasy look over the roof of the car. "You okay?" DeMarco asked quietly.

Kate nodded, though it was hard to tell if she was hurt in any way. The adrenaline was still rushing through her. In that moment, she felt more than okay. She felt *great*.

"How about you?" Kate asked. "My head hurts. He gave me a good whack. But I'm okay."

"I should drive, then," Kate said.

"I'll call ahead to the station and let them know we're coming with a ... with a what? I guess he's a suspect?"

"Seems that way," Kate said as she got behind the wheel.

She recalled the fear she had seen in his eyes and the absolute berserker speed and fury in his escape and scream. It made no sense to her that he would be the killer but then again, why was he remaining silent? Why did he run?

With the last dregs of adrenaline coursing through her, Kate pondered these questions. In the back of the car, Davey Armstrong remained quiet, as if sitting on some dark secret.

CHAPTER ELEVEN

Kate was nursing another cup of coffee and waiting for her turn to speak with Davey Armstrong. She was sitting with DeMarco in the conference room that was serving as their temporary office, watching footage on a mounted television on the wall as the police chief sat down across the table from Davey in an adjacent holding cell. There was no formal interrogation room in the City of Roanoke Police Department, so Davey was currently in an informal holding cell.

From what Kate could tell, Davey was still not talking. She stared at his silent figure on the screen, trying to work it out in her head.

"You think it fits?" DeMarco asked.

"He has the history to suggest that there might be some sort of strain between him and the Langleys, but no. Those murders were grisly. If he killed them, I think he'd be more interested in talking. Letting us know why. Letting us know *how*."

"What if he's just staying quiet because he wants to see how much more we know?" DeMarco asked. "What if he's killed more people and wants to know if we've discovered the bodies yet? The Nashes, for instance."

It was a good thought and one worth running with. On the screen, the chief started to get to his feet, apparently tired of trying to get Davey to talk. As he started heading for the door and partially off of the screen, Kate's cell phone rang. It was an unfamiliar number, with a Roanoke area code.

"Hello?" she said.

There was a man's voice on the other end. He spoke to her for about thirty seconds before Kate said, "Okay. Thank you so much."

She ended the call and started for the conference room door right away. "Come on," she told DeMarco. "We got him. Davey Armstrong is our killer after all."

Kate sat across from Davey, on the same chair the Chief of Police had sat in moments ago. She looked at Davey through the bars of the holding cell. DeMarco sat beside her, deep in thought about the revelation that Kate had just told her.

"I'm going to give you one last chance to say something," Kate said. "I just got a phone call that doesn't tell the entire story, but it tells *enough* of the story. Enough to formally arrest you for murder. So you have five seconds to figure out something to say."

Kate gave him the five seconds. She noticed DeMarco silently keeping count on her fingers as the seconds passed.

"Fine," Kate said. "Earlier today, we spoke with Teddy King, your manager at Gino's. He told us that on Tuesday afternoon, you were very late coming back from one of your deliveries. He just called me a few moments ago with the names and addresses you visited on that run. One of them was the home of Scott and Bethany Langley. And that just happens to be within the window of time in which they were killed. So … *now* do you have anything to say?"

He looked up at them with all the integrity of a trapped animal. He'd been caught and he knew it. He gave a lazy shrug and, for the first time since being told that his aunt and uncle had died, shed a tear.

"I lied before. I actually hadn't spoken to them in months," he said. "Maybe as much as a year. They weren't exactly happy with me. They didn't kick me out of their house, but strongly urged me to leave. So I enrolled in college, got a job and a place of my own. They'd try to stay in touch but I sort of froze them out."

"Why did they ask you to leave?" DeMarco asked.

"This was almost ten years ago," Davey said. "I'd started doing drugs. Just a little coke here and there. I wasn't an addict. Not then …"

He trailed off here, sensing that he was either getting off the point or not ready to face a truth that was trying to surface.

"Was there an altercation of some kind when you stopped to deliver their pizzas?" Kate asked.

"No. I didn't even knock on the door. I left the pizzas on the porch, beeped the horn on the car, and took off."

Kate didn't believe him. Not one bit. He was talking too fast, like someone saying the first thing that popped into their heads.

"When you deliver pizzas, do they have to sign anything?" Kate asked.

"No. Not unless they pay with a check."

She could see the uncertainty in his eyes as he tried to calculate his next move. She could practically see the wheels turning in his head as he tried to anticipate every way out of this conversation—how to not get caught in a lie, how to answer each question in a way that wouldn't nail him down.

"How did the Langleys pay?" DeMarco asked. "If you just ditched the pizzas and ran, they had to have paid in advance, right?"

"Yeah. I guess they did. With Gino's, you can order online. We just started it a few months back. I guess they paid like that because the order didn't say anything about having to collect payment."

Kate considered all of this and made the decision to let it rest for now. Whether Davey realized it or not, he had just given them more than enough information. Based on everything he had just said, there would be *more* than enough to either catch him in a blatant lie or free him.

As for Kate, she was fully expecting a lie.

"Thanks, Mr. Armstrong," she said. "We do need to check on a few things but if you're telling the truth, you should be able to leave within a few hours."

"Check what?" he asked. "How the hell am I a suspect here?"

Kate smirked, unable to hide it. "Because I've been doing this long enough to know when I'm being lied to."

And with that, she left the room. She had expected Davey to voice some final truth as she left but he stayed silent. After a few seconds, DeMarco followed behind her, leaving Davey alone in the holding cell.

❧ ❧ ❧

"Did you see his forearms?"

DeMarco asked the question almost half-heartedly. She was looking directly at the wall, as if looking at a diagram that had all of the answers to the case.

"No," Kate said. "Should I have looked at them?"

DeMarco shrugged. "I almost missed it. But there were track marks. Faint, but there. If I didn't have some history with it—a relative, not me, so don't worry—I wouldn't have even seen it."

"Heroin?" Kate asked.

"Yeah, pretty sure," DeMarco said.

"So maybe he's in denial about it?" Kate suggested. "Maybe he was late from those deliveries because he was using. Maybe the thought of having to see the Langleys stressed him out."

"Could be. Some users are so ashamed of their habit that they'll keep it a secret at any cost. But still... I don't think that warrants attacking an FBI agent in an effort to escape."

"Agreed," Kate said, looking at the TV monitor on the wall. Davey still sat there, slightly hunched forward and looking at the floor.

Kate wanted another crack at him—wanted to ask him about the drug use and if there was any connection to his using and the Langleys. Based on what she knew of the Langleys, she doubted there was a connection at all. But any chance to get him to talk about his aunt and uncle would either dig him deeper into the pit or give them just cause to release him.

Before she could start to formulate a line of questioning, though, her cell phone rang. When she saw that it was Duran, she cringed. She knew the man was like a magician at getting details in a quick and timely manner. She wondered if he had somehow found out about her too-rough handling of Davey Armstrong.

"It's Duran," she told DeMarco. She then answered: "This is Wise."

"Where are we on the case?" Duran asked.

"We've got a man in custody right now," Kate said. "I just finished questioning him."

"You think it's the guy?"

258

"I don't know yet. He's guilty of *something*. Drug use, most likely. But I'm not certain there would be enough to pin the murders on him."

"Send me whatever notes you have, as well as the arrest report. I've got a research issue here in Washington that I could use your help on. One of your old cases that a few agents think might help put an end to a string of kidnappings and a suspected pedophile ring in the Baltimore area. You remember Frank Costello?"

"I do," she said with a chill.

Costello had abducted and killed seven children in 1998, taking them from an area that sprawled between Washington, DC, and Louisville, Kentucky. It was one of the cases that she looked back on as her crowning achievement but, at the same time, an ultimate failure. When Costello had been booked, he claimed to have abducted three more kids and that he had not worked alone. He had never given up the locations of the other three children or the person he claimed to have been working with. That information went with him to the grave, as he killed himself by gnawing open one of his wrists in his cell three days after being caught.

"I'd like you to come meet with this team. So much of what they've come up with mirrors Costello's movements and mannerisms. We can't help but wonder if this latest string of kidnappings is the work of the man Costello says he was working with."

"Yeah, I can be there."

"Good. I thought about just Skyping, but these guys could use you there face to face. A great learning opportunity. So … sorry, Wise. I feel like maybe I overbooked you. If there's more to that case there in Roanoke, do you think DeMarco could handle it on her own?"

"Yeah, I think so."

"Good. Have her send me that info over and get back into town. If you could be here tomorrow, that would be ideal. You good with that?"

Kate looked over at Davey Armstrong on the monitor. If he was the killer, she and DeMarco had wrapped the case much faster than she had expected. If he wasn't, Kate didn't think he'd do much in helping them locate the *actual* killer. But she also didn't think she was in any kind of position to tell Duran no. If she wanted this little deal that they had worked out between them and the bureau, she had to resist any urge to push back.

"That should be fine," she said. "I'll see you tomorrow."

With that, Duran ended the call. Kate pocketed her phone as a thought occurred to her. The story about leaving the pizzas on the porch just seemed too weak. There should be some way to easily find out if it was the truth or not. Maybe a call to Teddy King. Certainly a customer that found their pizzas on their porch would call to complain, right?

"Did you say *see you tomorrow*?" DeMarco asked.

"Yeah. He wants me back in DC. There are some agents who apparently found ties to one of my cold cases about a pedophile ring. I told him I thought you'd be good here."

"I appreciate that," she said, her expression signifying that she meant it.

"Agent DeMarco, would you mind gathering up the police report and making sure a copy is sent to Director Duran as soon as possible? But first maybe we should figure out your car and housing situation."

DeMarco nodded. She looked a little excited at the prospect of being left to run solo on this case but, at the same time, Kate thought she saw a smidge of disappointment.

"You okay?" Kate asked.

"Yeah. I ran cases by myself all the time when I was working violent crimes. And even if Davey Armstrong isn't our man, there's got to be a lead hiding on him or in one of his stories somewhere."

"Maybe," Kate said, but she really didn't think that was going to turn out to be the case at all.

CHAPTER TWELVE

"You know," Kate said as she drove DeMarco to the closest Holiday Inn, "you don't need me to crack this. You're capable of doing it on your own."

"I know," she said. "But if I'm being honest, I just don't like the way Director Duran thinks he can just yank and pull you around like he wants. You went what ... a month without him calling at all? And now he sends you out here to check out these murders and then expects you to shift gears and abandon the case at the drop of a hat?"

"Oh, I feel the frustration, too," Kate said. "But there's a really bizarre working arrangement with me coming back from retirement. Until something more concrete is established, I can't rock the boat too much."

"I imagine it's a little easier to be back in DC, though, right?" DeMarco asked. "I mean, with your granddaughter."

"Yeah," Kate said, feeling a sting in her heart when she was reminded of how she had ended her night yesterday.

Hard to think of it as yesterday when I still haven't slept, Kate thought.

"What about you?" Kate asked. "Any reason for you to not want to be around DC?"

"No, not really. I've always liked to travel, so the job suits me. My mom lives in Bethesda, but other than that there's no family around up there. No love interests, either."

"Yeah, you mentioned that on the way down here," Kate said. "And I have to admit ... I feel like I need to apologize. I haven't really done a good job in getting to know you. I had no idea you were gay."

DeMarco shrugged. "I'm not the type that lets it define me, you know? I don't have it on my business card or monogrammed on coats or

261

anything. You and I ... we just never had a conversation where it came up in a normal fashion."

"I know," Kate said. "And I think that might be because the conversations have always been about me and what it's been like to come out of retirement. Kind of selfish of me."

"No worries at all," DeMarco said. "I can't even imagine trying to stay on this job when you have grandkids. And you've done it *well* for so long."

Kate said nothing, though she wanted to explain to DeMarco that her dedication to her work had been a huge strain on her family. She also kept all thoughts of her husband, Michael, at bay, certainly not wanting to tell her that even after Michael had been killed, work had come first. It had simply been something she had never been able to unhinge herself from.

"You said your mom lives in Bethesda," Kate said. "Are you guys close?"

"I suppose. We've never been really tight or anything. But I'm all she's got, as sad as that sounds, so I suppose we're close enough."

DeMarco looked blankly out of the windshield as she briefly discussed her mother. She spoke quickly and in a flat tone as well. To Kate, it was a nonverbal and polite way of saying *I'd really rather not talk about it.*

As the Holiday Inn sign came into view, Kate felt a feeling of guilt for the first time. Was she abandoning DeMarco? Sure, she was only following Duran's orders but still ... they had come here together to attempt to solve these murders and here she was, barely over twelve hours later, about to head back without her.

"Please don't hesitate to call me with any new information. If this thing starts to escalate, I imagine Duran would send me back to assist."

"I'll keep that in mind, but I think I'll be okay," DeMarco said.

"Want me to call ahead to a car rental place?" Kate asked.

"Nah, I'll delegate that to the police. Maybe I'll get Palmetto to do it."

Kate chuckled as she pulled into the parking lot of the Holiday Inn. "I fully expect you to have this wrapped up by the time I return home," she said with a smile.

"We can't all knock cases out of the park like Kate Wise," DeMarco said. "But thanks for the vote of confidence."

Kate parked in front of the motel. She had been here before, stuck in limbo without knowing exactly where she was going to stay or how she was going to get from Point A to Point B. She remembered that part of her career fondly, particularly a case out in Utah where she had been stranded for two days because her rental car had broken down and there had been some miscommunication between the bureau and the airport. She did miss those days and she envied DeMarco a bit.

"Be careful and take care," Kate said.

"Says the fifty-five-year-old that threw a flying tackle on Davey Armstrong three hours ago," DeMarco said.

With a grin and a nod, DeMarco got out of the car. She gave one final wave as she headed in through the lobby doors and then disappeared inside.

Kate checked the time and saw that somehow, it was only 4:47 in the afternoon. She was no longer truly tired, having been reinvigorated by coffee and finding her second wind after chasing down Davey Armstrong. If she drove straight through without stopping, she figured she could be back home sometime around 8:30. She could sleep the night through and wake up around seven in the morning to call Duran to see how she could help with the research job.

While she hated to leave a case when it had not yet been officially closed, she also could not deny that it felt very good to feel wanted—to feel *needed* in a job that had once so strongly defined her.

Still, that promise of normal life shone bright. It was what caused her to pull out her phone and send a quick text to Melissa before pulling back out of the parking lot. She thought about what to say for several seconds and, after some trial and error, finally decided on something simple and to the point: **Sorry about last night. Can we meet sometime Monday?**

She honestly wasn't expecting a response, but she figured she had to at least try. And as she pulled back out onto the street and in the direction of DC, she tried to imagine how to explain herself to Melissa. What the hell was she supposed to say? *Sorry, sweetie ... but that job that took so much of your childhood away from me is already starting to do the same with my granddaughter, too.*

It was miserable and it broke her heart, but God help her, she worried that it was going to end up being the truth.

CHAPTER THIRTEEN

Kate managed to keep the pull of exhaustion away up until she got on the exit that would lead her into Richmond. There, she let out a yawn so long and deep that she could practically already feel her bed beneath her. She had estimated her time almost perfectly, finally coasting slowly down the streets of Carytown toward her house at 8:40.

Still, despite being somewhere beyond tired, she could not stop thinking about DeMarco. Kate had always had a habit of not wanting to stop working on a case until a final, official, and unbreakable arrest had been made. Naturally, she felt as if she had left the murdered couples' case long before it had been truly wrapped up; she knew it would nag at her until the case was closed. And while she trusted DeMarco to get the job done, Kate Wise had never enjoyed feeling as if she had given up on something.

She found a parking spot close to her house and felt like she was sleepwalking as she walked from her car to her front porch. She was so tired that she had made it all the way up the porch steps before she saw the man on her porch. He was sitting in one of her little faux Adirondack chairs, smiling sheepishly at her.

It was Allen. And despite the thin smile, Kate could tell that he was hurt.

Shit, she thought. *We were supposed to go out for dinner tonight. And I totally forgot.*

She walked over to him and plopped herself down in the chair beside his. They'd sat like this on her porch a few times before. There had usually been a glass of wine in her hand, and a beer in his. But now there was none of that. Now, she knew she had dropped the ball and needed to apologize.

"Allen, I'm so sorry," she said. "I got a call last night from the bureau. They sent me out to Roanoke on this rush thing and...and I just plain forgot."

"It's okay," he said. Allen looked at his watch and added: "I was going to give you until nine and then head back home. I figured it had something to do with your daughter, granddaughter, or work."

"Why didn't you call to remind me?" she asked.

Not that it would have mattered, Kate thought. *All that would have accomplished was making me feel guilty while trying to find a killer.*

Allen shrugged. "Because I knew it wasn't my place. I know that you have a life. A very busy life. I don't say this looking for pity, but I know I'm not on the list of high priorities. And I'm fine with that. It's the sort of relationship I need in my life right now."

"That's not fair to you," Kate said. "How long have you been waiting here?"

"Two hours. But it's cool. It was a nice break. I read some news on my phone, got to play on my Sudoku app, too. At the risk of sounding cheesy, I like it on your porch. It makes me happy. It makes me happier when you're on it with me, but I'll take what I can get."

Kate reached out and took his hand. "Have you had dinner yet?"

"No."

"Come inside. We can whip something up together."

He gave her hand a squeeze and chuckled. "Kate, I'm not sure where you've been and what you've been doing, but you look exhausted. Go in and get some sleep. We can do this some other time."

"No. Look...yes, I'm running on zero sleep for the last day and a half or so. But I want to see you. So why don't you figure out what you want to eat and call it in. I'll grab a shower really quick and we can head out and just pick it up."

"Or we could have it delivered here," he said. "If you don't mind me hanging around, of course."

"That sounds like a plan," she said.

She bit her lip when she nearly found herself inviting him into the shower with her after he made the call for the food. The thought of it excited her but no man had seen her naked since Michael died nearly six years ago. It had been a long stretch of time and while she desperately wanted some kind of physical intimacy again, she wasn't sure if she could be so blatant and inviting about it.

"Go take your shower," he said with more than a hint of suggestiveness in his eyes. "I'll be on the way to pick up our food when you get out. It'll be quicker than waiting for it to be delivered."

"Thanks for understanding," Kate said. She leaned in and kissed him slowly. They had kissed many times—often, actually—but there had never been one that had left her feeling lightheaded. This one did it, but it might have been because closing her eyes reminded her of just how tired she was.

"Are you okay, Kate? You look more than tired. You look...I don't know. Troubled?"

A million things went through Kate's mind in that moment: an image of Michelle on her bed, looking up at her with hopeful and expectant eyes; Davey Armstrong sitting in a holding cell in Roanoke; the bloodstains on the Nashes' living room floor; the hateful and hurt look on Melissa's face as she walked away with Michelle in the car seat.

"I'll be okay," Kate said. "I think the shower will help."

With that, she headed back inside. She felt herself wanting to cry, something that she rarely did. Maybe a shower would wake her up a bit but as far as all of the other things swimming around in her head, no shower of any warmth or length would be able to wash it all away.

Allen was setting the table when she came out of her bedroom. The shower, getting dressed, and making some sense out of her wet hair had taken a little less than half an hour. In that time, Allen had apparently decided to just walk three blocks down to the street to the Italian deli. He knew her order there—a traditional meatball sub—and he had it on her plate when she came in.

The shower *had* helped a bit in terms of how tired she was. But she knew she'd crash soon. It wasn't much of a date but she was glad to see Allen at all, especially after the way the last twenty-four hours of her life had gone.

"I know we have this dinner a lot," Allen said, plopping his pastrami sandwich down on his plate. "But it was getting late and I didn't want you to stay up any later than you had to."

"No, this is perfect," she said. She started eating right away, having not had anything of substance since the pizza at Gino's. And that was already starting to feel like a lifetime ago.

They ate in silence for about three minutes before Allen spoke up. When he did, Kate could tell that he was very hesitant to ask his question. She respected him for going there, for asking the tough questions to make sure she was okay.

"Do you want to talk about it?" he asked. "Whatever it is that had you called away ... I can listen, you know?"

"I know," she said. "But the case isn't closed yet, so I'm not supposed to give out any pertinent information. You understand that, right?"

"Absolutely. So, if it was such a rush sort of job, what brought you back so soon?"

She did her best to explain the situation, letting him know that she was needed for some type of research role to help bring a high-profile local case to a close. As she did, she started to understand how self-obsessed she must seem to him. Leaving her granddaughter and ending her daughter's night out ... dropping everything right away just so she could recapture a feeling of purpose.

God, have I always been like this? she wondered as she finished up her explanation and the table fell to silence again.

With dinner eaten and conversation at a stand-still, Allen stood up and cleared their plates and the take-out containers. "Off to bed you. Do you need a wake-up call in the morning? You look like you're going to sleep pretty hard."

That same spark she'd felt when she had nearly asked him to come into the shower with her reignited. This time, she did not ignore it. Maybe if she had not been so tired she would have put up more of a mental block against it.

"Yeah, a wake-up call would be good," she said. She got up and walked over to him as he put the dishes into the sink. "So at about seven in the morning, I need you to roll over and shake me a bit."

He didn't bother playing dumb. He just gave her a curious look and smiled. "You sure?"

"I am," she said. To punctuate this, she stepped forward and placed her hands on his waist. She pulled him to her and kissed him softly but with a deep passion she had not felt in a very long time.

He responded in kind and somehow, she ended up with her back pressed against the sink. She had to stop the kiss just to catch her breath.

With his face still directly in front of hers, their lips no more than an inch apart, he looked into her eyes. "This will be the last time I ask," he said. "I'm trying to be polite but I'm still a man and all. Are you sure?"

She gently pushed him away from her and walked to the kitchen window. She closed the blinds and then turned to face him. That done, she reached up to the top button of her shirt and undid it. The second one followed. As she started working on the third, she looked up at him with what she hoped was a seductive stare.

"This would go quicker if you would lend a hand."

Allen, as it turned out, was happy to oblige. He walked quickly over to her and in the whirlwind of another of those kisses, helped her finish the task.

Before Michael, Kate had only slept with two men. That made Allen the fourth. And as she stirred awake at three in the morning, she tried to recall if she had ever climaxed as hard as she had the night before. She'd reached it twice and the second one had been so powerful that it had scared her a bit. Thinking back on it in that three a.m. darkness, she smiled to herself. She rolled over and looked at Allen, sleeping as peacefully as she had hoped to.

But sleep had been tricky. First, her nerves had remained on fire when she and Allen had finished. It hadn't lasted long and they had both fallen into bed quite tired. But her body had remained amped up until almost eleven and then she had come awake just after three with the images of the bodies of the Langleys in her mind. She saw them as she had only ever seen them, in the glossy portrait paper within the case files. Bloodied, massacred ... and for what?

Then, for reasons she was not clear on, she started ruminating on the case that had attacked her memory leaving a Carytown shop two days ago. Something about that case would not leave her alone. At the end, a little girl had been saved and a man who had been actively killing people at an alarming speed had been brought to justice.

Only, that really wasn't the case, she thought in the darkness with Allen beside her. Her director at the time had insisted that they had their man even though some of the evidence had been questionable at best. They'd called the case a wrap and then, after that little girl had been returned safely home, two more kids had been found murdered a month later in another state. They'd eventually found the *real* killer, but Kate had never forgiven herself for ignoring her instincts—for not arguing against her former director when she had felt that the man they had apprehended was not the killer.

As quietly as she could, she got out of bed and walked into the kitchen. She got a glass of water and sat in her recliner, thinking back about that case—thinking about DeMarco and a man she was now starting to think was not guilty at all.

"You okay?"

She turned and saw Allen standing in the doorway of the bedroom. He had put his boxers back on but the rest of his body was bare. He looked damned good for a fifty-four-year-old and her mind, if only briefly, jumped away from the darker things she had been dwelling on and to the activities of about five hours ago.

"Yeah. I just couldn't sleep."

"Is it bad? Like, can I make a joke about you coming back to bed and us not sleeping at all?"

She smiled and moved toward him. "Make any jokes you want," she said. "So long as you're ready to back them up."

And before he could make another comment, she was kissing him and leading him back to her bed.

Chapter Fourteen

Seven miles away from where a man named David "Davey" Armstrong lay half-asleep on a cot in a holding cell, another man woke up quickly in bed. He stared at the digital numbers of his alarm clock and saw that it was 5:05. He had an internal alarm that had been waking him up at this time ever since he'd been a child—as early as the age of ten.

Like an automated machine, he got out of bed, took six steps to the rug in front of his bed (six steps which he counted under his breath every morning), and assumed a push-up position. He blasted through one hundred push-ups and then immediately went to the shower. He scrubbed himself and washed his short black hair with the same machine-like mannerisms in which he had gotten out of bed and exercised.

Five minutes later he was toweling off as he walked back into his bedroom. He dressed quickly for the day, a black T-shirt and a faded pair of jeans, and walked into the kitchen. He saw that it was 5:27 and frowned. He was two minutes off. He lived his days by a very strict schedule and even two minutes off could make or break his mood.

And this morning, he was in a very good mood. He felt good—better than he had in quite some time. Maybe that was why he was in the kitchen two minutes early. After all, he'd been on a very busy schedule for the last week or so.

He sat down at his kitchen table with a bowl of cereal and scrolled through Facebook on his iPhone. As usual, he saw nothing of interest. Trump had said something dumb again. Some racist person said something racist. People were posting little videos of cats and cute kids and women in swimsuits that showed everything.

He smirked at it all as he ate his cereal. He cast his thoughts to later in the day—not when he was supposed to head into work, but to some task he had set for himself beyond his monotonous job. He worked at a small plastics factory on the far side of town, pushing buttons, snipping wire, and repeating it a trillion times. He loathed the job but it gave him ample time to think. It gave him the opportunity to think back on his past and figure out where everything had gone so terribly wrong.

Of course, other than his father killing his mother, he could come up with nothing. And he'd been so young when that happened … maybe there had been something else as he'd gotten older.

He spent some of his time at work trying to think of the first time the darkness had entered his mind—when he'd first had those violent and bloody thoughts. But nothing concrete ever came to him.

But he didn't like to dwell there very often. It made him feel like there was something wrong with him. So he turned his thoughts back to all of the wonderful things he had been doing in his spare time lately. That always got him in a much better mood. He figured if he could keep it up and be done with it within a few more days he might actually be able to become a better person. He might finally be able to put the past behind him.

Done with his cereal, he placed the bowl in the sink and headed back to his room. He had fifteen more minutes before he needed to be at work. Usually he would read when he had down time but he had been too busy and distracted to read as of late. Instead of pulling one of his books from the stack along the side of his bed, he reached under his bed and pulled out the shoebox.

Up until recently, the lid of the shoebox had been coated with a layer of fine dust. But he had brushed the dust off two weeks ago and started to dwell on what was inside. As a matter of fact, the things that were inside the shoebox had been consuming his thoughts as of late.

He pried the lid from the box with deliberate care and smiled at what he saw inside.

He took out the stuffed animal, a little gray rabbit with one ear droopy and the other standing at attention. It smiled dumbly up at him with its little glass eyes. And even though he was now an adult, that goofy smile made him feel safe and secure—like there was someone or something in this fucked up world that actually cared for him.

He placed the rabbit on his bed and looked back into the box. There was one more thing in there, which he took out with the same loving care he had showed the rabbit.

He handled the blanket in a way that was childlike, as if he might lie back down on his bed with it and snuggle up to its tattered shape.

Instead, he held it up by its torn edge and started to tear it. It gave way easy, just as it had done the two other times he had torn a strip from it.

He looked at the new fragment of the blanket and smiled. He was tempted to do it now, to do the job in the morning. He could call in sick to work and just do it. But no ... he liked having the day to wait, to build up the excitement.

He placed the box back under the bed with its contents returned. All except that one scrap of fabric which he laid in the center of his bed. He stared longingly at it for a moment before leaving the room to get his day started.

CHAPTER FIFTEEN

It was beyond bizarre to wake up with someone on the opposite side of the bed. Kate took a moment to appreciate the feeling as she quietly got out of bed. She grabbed a pair of underwear and her robe and snuck out of the room while Allen still slept. It made her feel a little immature, but she could not get over how happy she was. She hadn't had a man sleep over since Michael had died. There was something freeing about it—something that made her remember that it was okay to live a little selfishly from time to time.

She walked into the kitchen and started brewing a pot of coffee. She then cracked a few eggs and started making some omelets. As the coffee brewed and the eggs cooked, she impulsively went to the kitchen counter and opened her iPad, pulling up the files on the case in Roanoke. As was her usual approach, she knew she would not be able to stop thinking about the case until it was one hundred percent officially wrapped up.

She looked for any details she might have missed but there were none. She knew that as the coroners finished up their jobs and forensics had everything submitted, there would be more to go on. But for now, she felt that she and DeMarco had done just about everything they could. Still, that did nothing to eliminate the fact that she could not get over the feeling that they were missing something—something that was right in front of their faces.

Kate closed down the files and then opened up her email. She had several, all of which were related to the research assistance she had lined up later in the day. It seemed very cut-and-dried and, if the agents she was overseeing worked well together, they should be able to have their current case wrapped very quickly. She also saw that she was being asked to be in DC by three that afternoon. She read over the case brief that had been put together for her, reading it twice and committing it to memory. It really did seem like a case that was one good theory or lead away from being wrapped up.

She heard footsteps behind her. Before she could turn around, she felt Allen's hands on her shoulders, gently massaging her. He kissed her on the back of the neck, sending a delightful chill through her.

"Good morning," he said.

"Good morning to you, too," she said. She clicked the iPad to sleep as she turned to face him.

"You shut the iPad down right away," he said. "Sensitive information?"

"Sort of," she said. "You hungry?"

He looked to the bar where she had set their plates. She had slightly burned the omelets because she'd been distracted with the case files but she didn't think Allen was the type who would complain about such a thing.

"Absolutely," he said.

He walked to the barstool along the counter, dressed in the same clothes he'd been wearing last night. He had a look on his face that mirrored Kate's own feelings. She was starting to think that Allen very rarely found himself in these sorts of situations, either.

"Are you going back to it all because you miss it or just because retirement isn't your thing?" Allen asked, nodding toward the iPad.

"I ask myself that almost every day," she said. "It's mostly because I miss it. It's all I was ever good at."

"After last night, I beg to differ," he said with a sly little smile.

She turned away a bit as her cheeks flushed. "Anyway, I need to be in DC by three o'clock this afternoon. It'll probably be a pretty quick trip if you want to try to make some plans for tomorrow."

"Yeah, that sounds good to me," he said, cutting into his breakfast.

"Sorry again that I made you wait so long last night."

"Oh, that's okay," he said. "Really. Part of me is a little enamored with what you do. I'd like for you to not tell me any different, but I imagine you kicking in doors and wrestling perps to the ground. It's sort of hot."

She couldn't contain her smile when she thought of tackling Davey Armstrong to the ground yesterday. "Yes, sure," she said. "It's like that for me just about every day. Lots of running and tackling."

"So," he said, forking up the last bit of omelet, "if you're supposed to be in DC at three, I guess you need to get a move on, huh?"

"Yeah, I probably should get ready."

"Am I a terrible guest if I ask if I can use your shower before I head out?" Allen asked.

"Not at all," she said. "Give me some time and maybe I'll join you."

Now it was his turn to hide a little redness in his cheeks. He placed his plate in the sink and took one last sip of his coffee before heading out of the kitchen. He placed a small kiss on the corner of her mouth and headed back toward the bedroom.

Kate did fully intend to join him, but her mind instantly went back to the case. She kept seeing those pieces of fabric, portions of a blanket that had been shoved into the mouths of the victims. She looked to the clock over the kitchen sink, saw that it was 8:37, and decided to call DeMarco.

She answered on the second ring and sounded pleased that Kate had called. "It's feeling pretty lonesome down here in Roanoke," DeMarco said.

"Nothing new?"

"Nothing. I've even gone so far as to check high school records for the Nashes and the Langleys, hoping to find some sort of connection. I also requested all of the forms and paperwork from the county that concern anything to do with the Langleys' foster care process. I'll be getting that today but based on what the Department of Social Services thinks, the Langleys are pretty much perfect. No criminal records or red flags of any kind. So I'm not expecting to find skeletons in their closet."

"And the Nashes were never foster parents, right?"

"Not from what we have. There's nothing that points there, anyway. That *would* be a pretty notable link, though, wouldn't it?"

"Yes, but if it's not there, it's not there." She sighed and then added: "How about Davey Armstrong? Everyone down there still seem to think it's him?"

"Yeah, and there's at least *some* evidence to back it. It's not as strong as I'd like, but it's enough to keep him for a while. For instance, there's a police record from when Davey was seventeen. He locked himself in the Langleys' bathroom with a handgun and was threatening to kill himself. There are also some pretty bad G-chat messages that were just found last night on his computer. He was talking to some friend of his from the community college about his experiences with the Langleys. He talks about some pretty sick sex fantasies about Bethany Langley. He mentioned rape a few times."

"You think you can send them to me?" Kate asked.

"Yeah, if you want."

"Anything else?"

"No, that's about it. I spoke with the college friend about those messages and he swears he doesn't think Davey would have it in him to kill anyone. He *did* say that Davey seemed a little spacey at times, though. To tell you the truth, I can see Duran calling me back up to DC tomorrow if nothing else big breaks on this thing."

"Well, keep me posted," Kate said. "Let me know if you need anything."

They ended the call and Kate instantly tried to think of Davey Armstrong as a teen, living in the Langleys' house and harboring sexual fantasies about his aunt. That added item made the whole thing a little different. Maybe there *was* something Davey wasn't telling them. Maybe he was ashamed not only about the drug use, but about the way he'd felt about his aunt as well.

The idea of it made her uncomfortable. And although she had told Allen she might join him in the shower, any thoughts of sexual activity were erased from her mind with this new update about Davey Armstrong. Instead of joining Allen, she remained at the counter, poring over the files once again and sipping from her coffee.

What the hell am I missing? she asked herself, sure that there was something there right in front of her that had somehow eluded her so far.

Allen didn't comment on Kate deciding not to join him in the shower. He seemed to understand that her mind was usually never on one single track, but all over the place. Kate figured that if they were going to eventually explore a longer relationship later on, this might be something they'd have to tackle head on. But for now, she simply appreciated the fact that he was understanding.

She had started packing when he came out of the bathroom. His pants were on and he was toweling off his hair.

"You okay with this?" he asked.

"With what?" she asked.

He shrugged as he slid his shirt on. "Well, last night was amazing, don't get me wrong. But now the coming and going and your busy life. I don't know. I feel like maybe I used you or something. Maybe I took advantage of your busy schedule and situation. Is that stupid?"

"No," she said, her heart warming for him. "If anything, it's incredibly sweet. No, you did not use me. And I didn't do it out of guilt from making you wait, either. So don't bother going there."

"Good to know," he said. "You mind if I hang around until you leave?"

"Not at all."

Within a few minutes, he was in the kitchen washing the dishes from breakfast. He helped himself to another cup of coffee and sat with her in the bedroom while she packed. They had a pleasant enough conversation about surface-level things: the week's forecast, restaurants they'd like to try, movies they might see together in the theater in the coming weeks. As far as Kate was concerned, it was nice to have such innocent and mundane conversations.

She was packed up and heading for the door by 9:30. That would put her in DC at least two hours before she was due there, but that was fine with her. She figured she might try to catch up with Duran to discuss the case in Roanoke.

Allen carried her one bag out for her and placed it in the trunk of her car. He then reached out and took her hand.

"I like this," he said. "This, of course, not having a definition. Whatever it is that's going on between us ... I like it."

"I do, too," she said. "I'll call you when I'm on the way home."

"You don't have to. I promise I won't wait sadly on your porch until you get back."

"But I want to," she said. She nearly voiced the reasoning behind it, but let it remain in her head instead. *I like the idea that someone is waiting for me, someone who is looking forward to seeing me again.*

With that thought in mind, she also realized that Melissa had yet to return her text. This pained her, but she could not focus on it right now.

Then when? she asked herself as Allen opened the car door for her. *If you want that relationship to work, you need to face it sooner rather than later.*

She got into the car with a heavy sigh, trying to ease the storm in her head.

"You okay?" Allen asked.

"Yeah. Just a lot on my mind. Work...Melissa...I really am just a big mess. You'll figure it out pretty soon, I guess."

He smiled at her, leaned into the car, and kissed her. The kiss carried some heat and it had her buzzing in all the right spots. When he pulled away, God help her, she was lightheaded.

"Be careful out there," Allen said.

"I'll try. See you soon."

He closed her door and gave her a little wave as she started the car. When she pulled off, she looked back and saw him still watching from the sidewalk. She smiled at the sight of him and, for the first time in a very long time, wondered if maybe there *was* something to life other than the niche she had carved out for herself at work. Sure, there were Melissa and Michelle, but there was also this unnamable thing between her and Allen. Not love, not yet anyway, but some sort of tug that felt like being wanted.

That, in tandem with knowing that she would get to watch little Michelle grow up, made her feel an intense joy that caught her off guard. It was something she had not felt in a very long time—something other than her job that actually had her excited for the future.

CHAPTER SIXTEEN

Kate had to admit... it felt good to be back around the mild chaos and business of DC. The moment her eyes fell on the J. Edgar Hoover building, she felt a sense of well-being that she had rarely felt at home following her retirement. She had spent so much time there, had etched out a name and a legacy for herself in that building. It brought back more than memories; it brought back a feeling of purpose and accomplishment that she had been struggling to find back at home in Richmond.

She'd hit a snag in traffic so had not arrived as early as she had hoped. Therefore, she parked in the same parking garage she had parked in for nearly thirty years of her life (of course, it had been updated—modified and added to a lot in those three decades) and headed straight into the building. It was never truly empty, but it was the closest to vacant as it ever was on Sundays. She passed by only five people on her way to the second floor where one of the larger conference rooms had been reserved for the meeting.

When she stepped into the room twenty minutes early, she was pleased to see that a few members of the investigative unit were already there. A projector had been set up and the Keurig on the back table was purring as it filled a cup with coffee. She noticed right away that several of the members of the team looked tired, an indication that they had been putting countless extra hours into this case. She knew the look well; it meant that the case was either on the verge of being cracked or that they were throwing one last Hail Mary attempt at closing it.

"Agent Wise," a tall-statured woman from the front of the room said. "Thank you so much for agreeing to meet with us."

Rather than letting this woman know that Duran had really not given her much of a choice, Kate simply said, "Of course," and shook the woman's hand when it was offered.

The six other agents and assistants in the room also made their way over to her, introducing themselves and giving their thanks. Midway through this, Duran entered the room. He looked like he was in a hurry as usual but also looked satisfied that everyone was present and accounted for a full ten minutes before the meeting was set to begin.

He gave a quick nod around the room and then motioned Kate forward. "Can I see you outside for a moment?" he asked.

She followed him out into the hall, taking note that he closed the door behind them.

"This team is made up of agents who have less than five years of experience each," Duran explained to her. "But they all had tremendous results in the academy and, I believe, have the potential to be great agents with legacies *maybe* as stellar as yours. I tell you all of this so you can understand how motivated they are. They are extremely close to catching this guy and, as I explained earlier, a lot of what they've come up with mirrors the Frank Costello case. You remember the details well enough to help?"

"I remember the details of the Costello case a little *too* vividly."

"Good. Help them out but don't demean them. You're here as support, not as a teacher. But, at the same time, if you could manage to lead them to where you think the path needs to lead ..."

She nodded. "I understand."

When they stepped back into the conference room, the team of seven were sitting around the table. Five of them were on devices—laptops, their phones, or tablets. Two preferred the old-school approach and were at the ready with pen and paper.

"So," she said as she claimed one of the three free seats at the table. "I've read over the case brief and am up to speed on the amazing work you all have done. But who would like to tell me how you got here? How are you this close to bringing this guy in?"

A sleek-looking man who looked to be in his late twenties took the cue. He didn't even let the others *think* about answering her question. Kate tried to decide if he was a kiss-ass or just extremely dedicated.

"Four kidnappings in the last three weeks," this man said. "One in Bethesda, Maryland, two outside of Fredericksburg, Virginia, and the other two in Louisville, Kentucky. There have been no bodies and no letters from the abductor. No demands. Which, honestly, is almost as bad as finding a body."

Kate didn't agree with this, but she understood where he was coming from. If there were no demands being made for the release of the children, there was no telling what they were going through.

As the sleek-looking man paused, the tall woman who had introduced herself to Kate spoke up. "Obviously, the area of interest mirrors the same locations as Frank Costello … not to a tee, but too close to ignore. Also, like Frank Costello, there is no preference of boys or girls. So far, two of each have been abducted."

"Walk me through each potential abduction scene," Kate said.

Another woman took this one. She sounded nervous and tired. "Two were taken from playgrounds, while the mothers were there with them. One of them admits to scrolling through Facebook while her kid was on the monkey bars. She guesses that there was perhaps fifteen to twenty seconds between her peering up from her screen. The third seems to have been taken after straying a bit away from her father in a Walmart in Louisville. The fourth had been walking to her grandmother's house, just six houses down the street from her own home. She'd done it dozens of times, according to her mother."

"Not a single witness at all," the sleek man said. "Somehow, we don't even have this fucker leaving that Walmart on the security cameras."

"How's that possible?" Kate asked.

"Lawn and garden," one of the agents said. "There's only one security camera in the lawn and garden department of that particular Walmart. It faces in from the open air area of the flower section. If someone knew the layout of the store well enough, they would know how to make an exit through lawn and garden without being seen."

Kate's brain was already kicking into high gear, trying to put the pieces together. "Have you checked past employees with knowledge of the camera systems?"

"We've interviewed eleven," the tall woman said. "Two were questioned a second time. In the end, it all came down to nothing."

Kate took a moment, getting out of her seat and walking to the front of the room. "If the presumption is that this man is connected to Frank Costello, it's not even necessarily the locations that would matter—though it *is* very odd about the security cameras. We have to think like Frank Costello thought. Have you all looked at the footage from his interrogations?"

"Several times," a particularly tired-looking man at the back of the table said.

"We've looked at the profiles of the kids, of the families, of even the fucking grandparents," an angry-looking hefty man on the other side of the table said. "But there doesn't seem to be anything."

"The thing that ended up tripping Frank Costello wasn't any of that," Kate said. "You're looking in the wrong place if you think you're going to catch this guy by hoping he's using the same methodologies as Costello. Instead, you have to look at where Costello messed up. And as the files show you, the thing that led him to us in the end was the smallest of details—a small thing that connected each of the families not in genetics or daily routines, but in something so trivial it was never even looked at until it smacked me right in the face."

"You mean the YMCA," the tall female agent said.

"Hey, that's right," the sleek agent said. He now looked very pleased that he was in the room. He was also looking at Kate with the same sort of reverence that most younger agents had when she had been filling out the last of her days as an on-duty agent. "You found out in the end that the parents of those kids all had memberships to the YMCA. Costello was a member, too. But that's really not too remarkable because *tons* of people have memberships to the YMCA."

"Exactly," Kate said. She paused for a moment when she realized that every eye in the room was on her—even the pair in Duran's head. He was smiling approvingly at her as he nodded for her to go on. "Costello used the YMCA as his hunting grounds. He scoped out the gyms—for about seven months, according to his story. He even played a few games of pick-up racquetball with the father of one of his victims."

"So we need to be looking for links outside of the basic family aspects of it all," another of the agents said. "But I don't even know if there *are* any. If so, we would have stumbled across it by now."

"Maybe you have," Kate said. "Maybe it was right there in front of you the entire time but it looked so mundane and ordinary that you looked past it. Frank Costello did not adjust his life when he started abducting kids. He never stopped going to the YMCA and he never quit his job—never took any extra sick days or anything. And if we know that about him and we also know that he was working with someone else..."

"Then they're probably doing the same things," the sleek agent said.

"But why wait nearly twenty years to start again?" the angry-looking agent asked, typing something into his laptop without looking up.

"Maybe it took that long for him to work up the nerve," Duran suggested. "He's never done this on his own before."

"It's pretty much a textbook example of a man who's been left behind by a partner in this kind of thing," Kate said. "When Costello was apprehended and their little adventures came to an end, whatever partner he had likely found himself lost. A *now what?* sort of mentality. But something like abducting and killing kids... that just doesn't go away. So yes... maybe it *was* just a matter of working up the nerve to get back to it. It's likely, even. But we have to think about the sorts of things he might have been harboring or even putting into practice during that time. If he's like Costello, he's likely trying to *not* stand out. He's not interrupting his daily life. And that's a plus for you because that means he should be leaving a pretty big footprint. We just need to know where to start looking."

"Yes, and that's where we're coming up empty," the tall female agent said. "When you've got a guy that moves around like a phantom, it's hard to pin him down. We've checked security cameras, traffic cameras..."

"We even had a team of agents check security camera footage of every gas station within twenty miles of each abduction site for *anything* we could find," the formerly angry man said. "And *nothing.*"

"Have you checked over the sites of Costello's abductions?" Kate asked.

"No use," the sleek-looking agent said. "Of the two for-sure sites, one is a street that has now basically been bulldozed and turned into a high-end community. The other was a small playground that has gone to rot."

"But you know," the female agent said thoughtfully, "you mentioned normal things a moment ago. About looking into things that are so obvious you overlook them until they slap you in the face ..."

She then started to rapidly flip through the pages of a case file in front of her. Without looking up, she said, "Lockridge, do you have the findings from the playground the third victim was taken from?"

"Yeah," the sleek-looking agent said. He clicked around on his laptop for a few seconds and added: "What are you looking for?"

"The waste basket from the corner of the playground. It had been recently emptied, and the man from grounds maintenance believed anything in that can could have not been any older than five or six hours. You have the list of what was in there?"

"Two Coke cans, a flier for a local business, an empty bag of ranch-flavored peanuts, a cracked sippy cup with a picture of Elmo on it."

The female agent pulled a sheet of paper from her pile and slammed it on the table with such force that a few of the others huddled around the table jumped. "Right here," she said, excited. "The fourth victim, taken presumably while she was walking to her grandmother's house. Remember what forensics said they found in the street?"

"Holy shit," one agent said.

"Wait, let's not assume," Lockridge said.

"Nuts of some kind, probably prepackaged," the woman said. "Not cashews but something similar."

Kate had been in rooms where an *a-ha* moment had been reached. The feeling of electricity in the air never got old. She felt it rustling through the conference room in that moment as the team of agents shared looks of acknowledgment or stared at their laptop screens at the information they had accumulated.

Sensing that she had more or less started rolling a small snowball down a steep hill, Kate went on.

"So you start there. Go back to those gas stations and convenience stores. Some of them will likely be able to pull transaction records from as far back as a month. Align each purchase of those nuts to the security footage. That will give you a handful of suspects. After that …"

"They can cross that bridge when they get there," Duran said. "For now, Agent Wise, if you wouldn't mind just giving them a quick criminal profile on Frank Costello."

"Of course," she said. She reached back into her nearly flawless memory and saw the information from the case file. It was one that had stuck with her, as it had been pivotal to her career.

Yet, even as she started detailing the trouble childhood that Frank Costello had endured, Kate's mind went back to Roanoke. She started to once again focus on the murders that were taking place there. She had said something moments ago that was just now setting something ablaze in her mind.

"Maybe it was right there in front of you the entire time but it looked so mundane and ordinary that you looked past it."

This thought swirled at the edges of her mind for the next half an hour as she told the room everything she knew about how Frank Costello had carried out his abductions and murders. Combined with the breakthrough she'd assisted with moments ago, she had no doubts that this highly capable team would have someone in custody within forty-eight hours.

When she called the meeting to a close, the agents got up from the table quickly, anxious to get back out on the trail. Yet as everyone else cleared out, the tall woman hung back. She approached Kate with a look of apprehension as she slung her laptop bag over her shoulder.

"Agent Wise," she said. "I had to take the moment to introduce myself. My name is Rebecca Minor. I've been admiring your work since I first joined the academy. You're the sole reason I wanted to pursue a career as a field agent rather than a lab tech, which is what I was originally going to be."

"Thank you," Kate said, not sure how to take such a compliment.

"I have to admit … I have a lot of your archived case files printed out and in a binder at home. I used them as study guides while I was at the academy."

"Well, it seems that they helped. You're doing a fantastic job from what I can see. You'll have this guy sooner than you think. You're on the right path, you know. Just let it—"

Her phone buzzed in her pocket, interrupting her. She gave an *I'm sorry* look to Agent Minor as she checked it. When she saw that the call was coming from DeMarco, she smiled wanly at Minor and turned away. She marched quickly to the back of the room and took the call.

"Hi, DeMarco. How's it going?"

"Well, it could be better. He did it again."

"The killer?"

"Yeah…"

Kate looked back across the room to where Duran was still standing by the door. He saw her looking and the glance exchanged between them communicated everything. Before she even ended the call with DeMarco, Kate knew that she was heading back to Roanoke.

CHAPTER SEVENTEEN

Kate felt a sense of unease spreading through her as she entered the driveway of the third murder scene. From the sight of the house alone, she could tell that there was something different about this one— that the killer had to have been incredibly motivated to strike here.

First of all, the house was gorgeous. It was an enormous house, done in an altered Colonial style. The grass was perfectly cut and green, bordering the porch like something out of a gardening magazine. Behind the house, she could see the edge of a pond peeking out. The house was situated up on a hill, as if whoever lived inside felt the need to look out on top of the city of Roanoke, which sat to the east as just a tangle of shapes against the trees.

It would have been a beautiful sight indeed if not for the presence of the two police cars and the black sedan. The sedan, she knew, was what DeMarco was driving. Kate parked behind the sedan and walked toward the house. As she made her way up the porch stairs, a policeman came out of the front door. She wasn't too surprised to see that it was Palmetto. He looked tired but managed a smile when he saw her.

"Agent Wise," he said. "Good to see you again."

"Likewise," she said. "You headed out?"

"Yeah. I'm going to see if I can help relieve you guys of some of the monotony. I'm going to see what I can find out from family and friends of the newly deceased. Going to get a few of the local officers to assist. I'll meet back up with you guys later today."

"Thanks for that," Kate said as she headed inside the house.

"Sure." He regarded her with a strange look that made her think he meant to say something else. But he simply returned to his car and started the engine.

Kate made her way into the house and quickly discovered that the interior was just as beautiful as the exterior. The front door led to a tall foyer that showed the full staircase leading upstairs. It was there, looking at her out over the railing, that DeMarco stood. A trail of drying blood led up the stairs to her, stopping at a crumpled shape at DeMarco's feet.

"How long have you been on the scene?" Kate asked, carefully making her way up the stairs. The blood was not in a simple single trail, but splattered here and there. As she reached the landing at the top of the stairs, the puddle grew thicker and darker.

"A little over an hour I guess."

"Anything worthwhile?"

"Not that I could find. There *is* a huge difference here, though—so different that I at first thought this murder was not related to the others. The victim's name is Monica Knight. She's a pretty big-time local lawyer. She also happens to be single. She was married for less than six months but her husband had an affair and left her. That was about twelve years ago, from what I'm being told."

"So not a couple this time?"

"That's right," DeMarco said.

Kate reached the landing and looked down to the body. She was lying on her back, staring up at the ceiling with wide eyes. She had been stabbed multiple times, with most of the attention given to her stomach. One grisly wound etched across her neck and that was where most of the blood seemed to have come from.

"So, what makes it connect to the other murders?" Kate asked.

DeMarco held up a plastic evidence baggie. There was yet another piece of the blanket inside of it. "It was rough," she said. "It was shoved down her throat just like the others. The corner of it was sticking out of the wound in her throat. It had been shoved down in there so hard that one of her front teeth was loose."

"Any connection to the other victims?"

"Nothing apparent. That's what Palmetto is checking for us right now. He's tried reaching out to the ex-husband to warn him that he might be in danger but so far there's been no word."

Kate nodded and hunkered down into a squatting position. She looked closely at the victim's face and frowned. Monica Knight was very pretty, aside from all the blood. It was apparent that she took good care of her blonde hair and her complexion. But Kate also noted that Monica's beauty might come from another factor altogether.

"Hold on. Do we know how old she is?"

DeMarco scanned through some notes she had taken on her phone and said: "Thirty-nine."

"So she's at least ten to fifteen years younger than the other victims," Kate pointed out. "*And* single."

"Yeah, that seemed weird to me, too," DeMarco said. "The piece of fabric in her throat directly ties her to the other victims but that's where the connection ends."

So that eliminates the field of thought that the killer is only targeting couples, Kate thought. *It'll be interesting to see what we find out about the ex-husband.*

She took a closer look at the victim. Based on the trail of blood that led upstairs, there had apparently been some kind of a struggle or a chase. While it seemed odd at first glance that Monica Knight would have chosen to try running upstairs to escape, Kate had seen similar scenarios multiple times over the course of her career. Sometimes the victim had a gun upstairs and chose to try to get to it in order to defend themselves. Other times, the killer blocked the doorway and the victim chose to run upstairs to lock themselves in a bedroom or bathroom—which, in the grand scheme of things—was a pretty good method. In the age of cell phones, it worked more times than not.

Looking over the body, Kate counted at least seven stab wounds in the stomach but it was hard to tell. They were all so close to one another that the area started to look like nothing more than a mess of flesh, cloth from her shirt, and blood. The closeness of the wounds spoke of quick movements, the killer working like a machine. But the one along the throat was not as exact or neat as the others. There was tearing in the flesh as well as slicing. That cut had been done with extreme force, likely out of a deranged anger that was apparently not behind the stab wounds they had seen out of him so far.

As Kate looked Monica Knight's body over, DeMarco's phone rang. She answered it and spoke in a quick and efficient manner. Kate was impressed. DeMarco was able to cut straight to the point without coming off like a bitch or as if she did not care at all about the person on the other end of the line. Kate knew full well just how difficult that was to do.

"Hey, you got something?" DeMarco said as she answered the phone. Her eyes wandered as she listened to the person on the other end. "And someone actually spoke with him? Yeah? Okay...and would he be okay if I called as well? Great. Thanks."

She hung up without a goodbye and looked at Kate. "That was Palmetto," DeMarco said. "Someone on the police force got in touch with Knight's ex-husband. He's alive and well in Nashville, Tennessee. When he was told that his wife had been killed, he was quiet but didn't seem to care too much. But he managed to answer some questions satisfactorily."

"We should still maybe reach out to him when the dust has settled. I don't think it would be necessary to bring him here, but still..."

"Unless there's reason to believe he did it. And if he lives in Nashville and is there *right now,* that basically rules him out. Monica Knight hasn't been dead for much more than eight hours."

Downstairs, someone knocked on the door. "Agents? We good to come in?"

DeMarco nodded at Kate. "Forensics. I sent them packing for a little while when I knew for sure you were on the way."

Kate smiled. DeMarco had been by herself on the case for less than a day but was already running things as if it had been solely hers from the start. She was able to adapt and had the ability to make people respect her from the get-go; again, Kate knew how difficult this could be for a young, attractive woman as she had lived through it herself.

"Yeah, I think we're good here," Kate said to the man at the door below them. She took one final look back at the body, taking a mental picture.

She and DeMarco walked down the stairs as two more members of the forensics team walked into the house. They all passed one another with polite waves as Kate and DeMarco stepped out onto the porch.

"Who discovered the body?" Kate asked.

"Her boyfriend. They've been dating for about a year. His story checked out right away. He was on a plane, touching down in Raleigh, North Carolina, right around the time it's believed she was killed. I already had the flight logs checked and it's all legit."

"Did he name anyone who might have had a beef with her?"

"Well, she was a lawyer. So really, there's no shortage of people that might have *something* against her. But he was at a loss. Couldn't come up with anyone who might have wanted her dead."

"Who is Palmetto going to speak with today?" Kate asked.

"Two of her most recent clients. One was wrongly accused of abuse, or so the story goes. Seems it might be worth at least looking into and besides, Palmetto says he knows the defendant pretty well."

"We know where her parents live?"

"In Charlottesville, which is about an hour and a half away from here. I have them on the list of people to speak with. You think it's worth a visit?"

"I do. It goes back to the blanket. Something about including those scraps—shoving it down their throats—it seems personal in a weird way. I think if we get any leads at all on this, it's going to be from people who knew the victims intimately. More than just a boyfriend of one year or a cheating ex-husband."

And yet again, something she'd said to the assembled team in DC for the child abduction case repeated in her head: *Maybe it was right there in front of you the entire time but it looked so mundane and ordinary that you looked past it.*

"Yeah, that sounds legit," DeMarco said. "I know you just got off of the road and—"

Again, she was interrupted by her phone. She looked at it and said: "Palmetto again." She answered it with her same authoritative yet some-how warm tone. "Something else?"

Kate listened to one side of the conversation for about twenty seconds before DeMarco hung up. "Got something?" Kate asked.

"No. But it turns out we won't have to go to Charlottesville. Her parents are coming to Roanoke to stay with Monica's best friend while they plan for the funeral. They're asking to speak to whoever is in charge of her daughter's murder investigation right away."

"I suppose that would be us," Kate said. She looked back to the home of Monica Knight. There was a skeptical look on her face, as if she thought the house might be keeping a secret from them.

I'm missing something, Kate thought, growing more and more frustrated. *But what?*

Maybe speaking to Knight's parents would push her closer to discovering what it was. Or maybe, just maybe, they were dealing with a killer just crafty enough to leave no trace. Of course, she knew that even the type of mindset that set a killer toward a super-obsessive and neat crime scene could be a clue in and of itself.

Maybe that's where I need to look, Kate thought. *Maybe ...*

"Agent Wise?" DeMarco asked. "You okay?"

"Yeah. Just trailing off with my thoughts," she said. She headed for the car, knowing the house would not give up any secrets it might have. Instead, she was going to have to dig them up herself ... and that just happened to be something she was very good at.

CHAPTER EIGHTEEN

While the parents of Monica Knight gathered their bearings and took care of all of the necessities once they arrived in Roanoke, Kate sat in the conference room she and DeMarco had been given at the Roanoke Police Department. She read through every available file and form the PD had on the Langleys and the Nashes while roughly a dozen pages were being printed out concerning Monica Knight.

She was thinking of the Frank Costello case—of the YMCA in particular. And that got her to thinking about this unidentified partner that could very well be at work, leaving little inconspicuous clues behind in the form of empty nut wrappers and spilled snacks. What was her spilled snack here? What was right in front of her but going unseen?

DeMarco entered the room with the Knight files and handed Kate a copy. They looked through the files together, bouncing findings and ideas off of one another.

"Her college transcripts show that she had originally gone to school to study psychology," DeMarco said. "Namely early child development. Seems sort of creepy when you think of the blanket we're been finding traces of in the victims' throats."

"That *does* seem ominous," Kate said. "But what do you make of the two different requests to have fingerprints taken voluntarily, all within the last five years?"

DeMarco flipped through her pages until she came to this information. "That does seem strange. One of the requests is linked to an additional information request that she also sent to the Department of Social Services."

Kate hung on to that bit of information, sensing that there was something else there, something that could maybe tie it all together. But there was one thing missing—something she could not yet place.

Something in the Langley file ... something similar ...

She started to reach for the Langley file when there was a knock at the door. One of the deputies poked his head in, a frown on his face. "The parents of Monica Knight are here. Should I send them in?"

"Yes," Kate said. "Give us two minutes, please."

The deputy nodded and the moment he was gone, Kate quickly thumbed through the Langley file. It didn't take her too long to find what she was looking for.

"There's a fingerprint request here for the Langleys, too," she said. She tapped at a carbon copy of the fingerprints of Scott and Bethany Langley. "Right here. They had to be fingerprinted when they were going through the process to be approved as foster parents."

"Maybe that's why Monica Knight needed to get fingerprinted?" DeMarco suggested. "It would certainly align with the ties to an information request to DSS."

Kate pondered this for a moment as she gathered up the files in front of her. The last thing she wanted was for a set of grieving parents to come in and see the life of their dead daughter crudely summed up in a series of pages. DeMarco followed suit and stuffed all of the paperwork into her laptop bag.

"Have you had to actively speak with grieving parents before?" Kate asked.

"A few times," she said. "You never really get used to it, though. I mean, when I was working Violent Crimes, there were other agents that did that sort of thing. Agents with a knack for grief psychology. Makes me wonder how doctors manage to do it all the time."

There was another knock at the door. This time when it opened, the same sad-looking deputy led an older couple into the room—Monica Knight's parents. Kate thought the mother might normally look rather young for her age but the act of furiously crying over the unexpected death of a child had taken its toll on her. She looked around the room wildly, as if untrusting of everything.

As for the father, he was a tall gentleman who looked like he was sleepwalking. The redness around their eyes made it clear that they had spent the better part of the last several hours crying over their child. But Kate could also see determination in the father's face; he was determined to be as strong as possible through all of this for his wife.

"This is Dean and Gloria Knight," the deputy said. "With all due respect, Agents, they want to help in any way they can but they also have family local to the area they'd like to get back to as soon as they can."

"We'll be as quick as we can," Kate said. "Thank you, Deputy."

The deputy left, leaving the room in silence. Kate had been down this road a million times and had learned not to dwell too much on the recent loss. It was often best to cut right to the chase, not to dwell on the murders but to start looking for solutions. It not only eliminated the chance of one of the parents breaking down, but it also made them feel assured that they would have answers soon.

"I understand your need to get back to your family as soon as possible," Kate said. "So we'll get right to it. We're looking for a connection between what has happened to your daughter and four other people in the area within the last four days. Up until Monica, we were under the assumption that it was just couples. And there are no direct links between the victims. So we were hoping you might be able to provide us with some insight. Any people that might be upset with Monica or anything she might have mentioned to you recently that threw up a red flag."

"She never really spoke about the negative aspects of her work," Dean Knight said. "But we've been asking ourselves the same thing. With her job, there would be far too many people that might have something against her, right?"

"The local PD is looking into it right now," DeMarco said. "And if no immediate answers are found, we'll also get bureau resources on it. For now, though, we're trying to concentrate on areas that might not be so obvious—things that may make your daughter similar to the others."

"That's right," Kate said. "We know that she was married at one time. And she had no children, correct?"

"That's right," Gloria Knight said. "In fact, I've always believed that's one of the reasons her no good husband ran out on her. Monica *always* wanted kids. She used to joke about how she wanted to start trying to get pregnant as soon as her honeymoon. But her husband was never on the same wavelength."

"She was going to adopt for a while," Dean said. "But I think she started to get far too involved in her career."

"Did she ever *actually* adopt?" Kate asked, starting to feel a thread picking up and knitting itself into the narrative.

"No," Gloria said. "She *did* foster for a while. Just short-terms thing here and there, though."

"How long did she do that?" Kate asked, thinking about those fingerprint requests and DSS paperwork.

"About three or four years, I suppose," Gloria said.

Kate knew what she wanted to do next but measured the possible outcome for a moment. She and DeMarco shared a glance, both aware that they had perhaps stumbled upon something with the foster parent connection. The Langleys, after all, had served as foster parents as well. That still left the Nashes unconnected from it all, but at least it felt like they were getting *somewhere*.

"I'd like to show you something," Kate said. She took the scrap of blanket that she had been holding onto ever since they had first met Palmetto. She did not set it on the table, but held on to it in the event that it *did* look familiar to the Knights. If they responded harshly, she wanted to be able to hide it away as soon as possible.

But she could tell right away that it meant nothing to them. Gloria Knight stared at the scrap of fabric so hard that Kate was pretty sure she was trying to make herself find some connection—anything to find answers about her daughter's death. But after several seconds, she shook her head.

"No. Should it?"

"We don't know," DeMarco said. "But scraps similar to this have been found at all of the crime scenes. So far, it seems to be the only stable connection."

"As for now," Kate said, "I believe that's really all we need. We'll let you get back to your family, but please, if you think of anything—no matter how small or insignificant it may seem—please contact us."

"We will," Dean said as he slowly got up. He took Gloria by the arm and they walked slowly together toward the door. Gloria gave one hopeful look back and said, "Please find out who did this."

She made her way through the door like a woman in a dream. The moment the doors were closed, DeMarco took the files and papers back out on the three different crime scenes.

"There's nothing in the Nashes' history dealing with foster care in any way, shape, or form," she said.

"Well, maybe it's something else, some other connection," Kate said. "What about DSS? Any dealings between the Nashes and the Department of Social Services?"

"I don't think so," DeMarco said. "But I can get someone on the PD to look into it."

"That might be our best bet for now," Kate said.

DeMarco looked at her skeptically and smiled thinly. "Are you sure about that? You look like you're hooked on some other thought."

Kate nodded, not denying it. She was both impressed and a little uneasy that DeMarco already knew her tics and mannerisms so well.

"I'm choosing to focus on the painfully obvious," she said. "We can't find any one thing that connects all of the victims so far. But the killer himself is connecting them for us."

"With the scraps of blanket," DeMarco said.

"Exactly. It's like his calling card. And if it's a children's blanket, maybe it's a relic from his childhood."

"You think the killer knew this victims when he was a kid?"

"Possibly," Kate said.

She'd worked with enough cases stemming from a killer's childhood trauma in the past to know that she was no expert in the field. The good news for Kate, though, was that her career had pointed her in the direction of such experts. And it seemed like it was pointing her that way once again.

Only, with a killer still at large and a set of grieving parents having just left their presence less than two minutes ago, it seemed to be less of a *pointing* and more of an urgent push.

"How's the Internet in this building?" Kate asked.

"Decent. Why?"

"Open up Skype on your laptop," Kate said. "I need to make a call."

CHAPTER NINETEEN

Kate had not expected Dr. Henrietta Yates to answer her Skype call right away. Kate had worked closely with Yates more than twenty times over the course of her career and knew that she was one of the most prominent psychologists in the field of early child development and behaviors. If the blanket held more meaning than Kate was able to decipher, Yates would be able to help.

Kate placed a call to Dr. Yates's office and, after a few back and forth calls with her receptionist, was able to schedule an impromptu face-to-face via DeMarco's laptop. In the time that passed, she took a picture of the ragged fragment of blanket and emailed it to Yates. DeMarco took the opportunity to put in an urgent request with the Records department.

When Yates's face came onto the screen, she was quickly brushing her hair aside with one hand and sipping from a cup of tea with the other. It was apparent that she was in the midst of a busy day, making Kate feel guilty for interrupting her.

"Agent Wise," Dr. Yates said. "It's great to hear from you. It's been what? At least two years, right?"

"Probably more," Kate said.

"I heard through the grapevine that you had retired."

"Yeah, that didn't work out."

"Yeah, I was surprised," Yates said. "The mere idea of retirement doesn't seem to even make sense when I think of you."

"Dr. Yates, I know you're a busy woman and your receptionist told me you had to push some things back to arrange this call. I appreciate that and we will make this as quick as possible."

"No worries," Yates said, though it was clear that there were at least *some* worries. It was apparent she was preoccupied with her own work. "What can I do for you, Agent Wise?"

"I sent you a picture a few minutes ago," Kate said. "It's a torn piece of a blanket. That fragment as well as two others have recently been found at murder scenes. To this point, it's the only evidence that connects the victims. And it's purposefully being left behind by the killer. I was thinking it might have something to do with his childhood...maybe a keepsake or something."

"That's a safe assumption," Yates said. "How are you finding them? Are they carefully set aside or placed on the bodies?"

"They're being shoved down the throats of the victims. Forensics seems to think it's done *after* the murder."

"Well that *does* paint a better picture. You know as well as I do that anything so tangible that is left behind is being left behind for a reason— if not to draw you closer to finding him, then to appease some nostalgic or self-obsessed part of himself. If this blanket *is* from his childhood, then I'd assume the victims are also somehow tied to his childhood. Or at least the killer would think so. Another thing to consider is the throat the fabric was put into."

"I don't follow you."

"I mean, were the victims male or female?"

"That's another interesting thing," Kate said. "The first murders were couples. Two of them. The third scene was a single woman. At the two scenes with the couples, the fabric was—"

"—in the throat of the women, right?" Yates asked.

"Yes, that's right," Kate said, unable to bite back a smile at Yates's intuition.

"Agent Wise, I'd bet just about everything I have on the fact that these murders are based on some sort of perceived wrongdoing from the killer. He likely wasn't nurtured much as a child or maybe he was and he just grew up to have a skewed sense of what nurturing and security meant to him. And going back to the blanket...killers will often leave something behind that is connected to a specific incident or time in their life that deeply affected them."

"So the tendency towards couples and placing the fabric in the throats of the mothers ... you think it's a yearning for a family?"

"Perhaps," Yates said. "But this would be a killer already cemented in a deep state of psychosis. If anything, singling the women out in such a way makes me think he's got some sort of trauma in his past with a mother figure. Blankets in a child's hands are meant to be comforting. And if you look at the mother and father interplay, it's typically the mothers that are viewed as the more comforting."

The Langleys and Monica Knight were foster parents, Kate thought. *I bet if we start looking at lists of kids they fostered, we'll see the killer's name on those lists.*

As if Yates had also already picked up on a similar train of thought, she went on. "Now, I can't be sure, but this looks like it might be fabric from some sort of a child's blanket. Can you confirm that?"

"Basically. I've even spoken the company that likely manufactured it."

As she said this, someone knocked on the conference room door. DeMarco answered it as Yates responded. Kate watched as an officer handed DeMarco a small stack of papers.

"The fact that blankets are often seen as security objects even up into the teen years speaks volumes," Yates said. This killer is bringing something usually seen as something used for comfort into murder scenes. What about the murders themselves? Quick and precise or violent?"

"Violent."

DeMarco was looking over the papers that had just been delivered to her. Slowly, a dawning excitement started to bloom over her face.

On the laptop screen, Yates was nodding her head. "Yes, I'd go so far as to say that this is starting to look like a textbook case of a killer that is blaming something traumatic from his childhood on parents. Maybe parents he did not have."

"Yes, we think there might be a parent element to it," Kate said. "And with that, Doctor Yates, I'm happy to say you can get back to your job. You've given what was a rather lame lead some very strong legs to stand on for right now."

"Good to hear," Dr. Yates said. "Glad to help. And, might I add, it's good to see you working again. Just couldn't stay away, could you?"

"Something like that," Kate said with a smile. "Thanks again, Doctor."

With that, Kate ended the call. She instantly looked over to DeMarco as she still looked through the papers the officer had given her.

"What have you got?" Kate asked.

"Just a bit more information on the Nashes," she said. She slid a Xeroxed sheet over to Kate and added, "It appears that the Nashes also set up an appointment to get fingerprinted at some point in the past. And it appears that it had to do with this."

She slid another sheet over to Kate. Kate looked them over and knew instantly where this was headed. She saw a copy of the Nashes' fingerprints, taken in 2007. With the prints were the typical form requests for a background check. Within the background check information, there was also a request for the information from the Department of Social Services.

The second sheet was fresher; Kate could still feel the slight warmth of it having just come out of a printer. There was a scrawled message at the top, blurred from a recent copy of it being made that read: *Hope this is what you were looking for! – Ruby.* Beneath that scripted message, there was a very simple application form for an organization called Family Friends and Services. It had been filled out by Toni Nash and signed by both Toni and Derrick Nash. The questions on the application were all family or child related—all questions that pointed back to their foster care connection. *How many children have you raised? Why are you interested in caring for children in emergency situations? Do you have ample room within your home to care for a child?*

There were more questions like this, all given appropriate and well-thought-out answers by Toni Nash.

"Have you ever heard of this Family Friends and Services?" DeMarco asked.

"Nope. It's new to me. Sounds a lot like foster care. But the term *foster care* is never used on this application."

"So maybe we pay our new friend Ruby a visit," DeMarco said, pointing to the name at the top of the application.

They got up together, working like a well-oiled machine. It made Kate wonder, if only briefly, what it might have been like to work with DeMarco if she, Kate, were about twenty years younger. They had a connection established between them already that most paired agents could only hope to have after years of working together.

As they left the station, headed for the offices of Family Friends and Services, Kate was once again reminded why she loved this job. It was more than just the thrill of the hunt or putting puzzle pieces together as a case started to come into focus—it was the sense of partnership and camaraderie, too.

It made the discovery of a potential lead all the more exciting. And it also made Kate feel a bit more confident and secure as the endgame slowly came into view.

CHAPTER TWENTY

The central office at Family Friends and Services was a large, brightly lit space. Three of the walls were adorned with canvas prints of smiling children's faces. The fourth wall was filled with a map of the Roanoke area and a large whiteboard adorned with names and dates. Kate and DeMarco sat on one side of a large conference table while the red-headed woman in her early fifties sat down across from them with a mug of coffee. This was Ruby Hendricks, the Director of Operations for Family Friends and Services. She looked bright-eyed and happy but Kate could see nervousness ticking along at the corners of her mouth as well.

"Ms. Hendricks, thank you for meeting with us on such short notice," Kate said.

"Of course. With my position with FFS, I'm rarely out of the office. What is it, exactly, that I can help you with? Is it about the Nashes?"

"You've already heard about them?" DeMarco asked.

"Yes. Cami Nash let me know about it."

"So you knew the Nashes well?" Kate asked.

"Not on a very personal level, but I knew them enough to consider them friends," Ruby said. "I saw them here in the office a few times and they also attended most of our fundraising events."

"Well, as it turns out, we *are* here to ask about the Nashes," Kate said. "We learned today that they were part of Family Friends and Services. However, we really have no idea what you do here."

"Oh," Ruby said, seemingly delighted that she was fielding such an easy question. "Well, I don't know if you are aware of this or not, but the area of Central Virginia has a fairly large foster parent problem. There simply aren't enough people fostering to cover the need for children that

305

are looking for safe homes. The ratio is something like one potential foster home per eighteen kids. What we here at FFS do is step in as a temporary alternate. We consider ourselves a prevention from foster care, actually."

"Is that really a necessary step?" Kate asked.

"Oh yes. Don't get me wrong...there is nothing at all wrong with foster care. I myself am foster approved. But many people abuse the system. And because it is state run, the wait times for paperwork and approvals can take forever. We try to sidestep all of that, and even DSS is starting to realize the need for a service like ours. I can give you an example, actually. Two days ago, we were contacted by DSS. A mother had given birth to her baby and it was discovered in the hospital that the baby was born substance exposed. The mother had done drugs up into the sixth month of pregnancy. Social services removed the baby from the mother but the mother did not want her child getting lost in the foster care system. Instead, she signed the baby over to us and the child is now in the care of one of our Family Friends and Services families. It saves the state the money and hustle of working up an emergency foster situation and gives the mother ample time to clean herself up and get back on her feet. When she *is* a fit mother, we will return her child to her but only after DSS has deemed her suitable."

"And this is all legal?" DeMarco asked.

"Of course. There are actually organizations like this spread out over the country but we don't get much press. Courts only consider cases a so-called victory in a lot of cases if endangered children are placed into foster care because *foster* care is a well-known term. But what we do is essentially the same, only we get no monthly stipend check."

"It's all volunteer?" DeMarco asked.

"Correct. Most of our families are heavily involved in churches or other child care organizations."

"Do the families need to be foster approved?" Kate asked.

"No. And that's another audience we appeal to. Many parents—or former parents, for that matter—don't want to be foster parents but they *do* have a heart for children in need."

"And I assume the Nashes were on your list of participating families?" Kate asked.

"Yes, they were. They had been with us for about ten years or so, I'd guess. Maybe longer. I can pull the records for you, if you like."

"That would be great," Kate said.

"One moment, then," Ruby said as she got up and headed for the door.

When she closed the door behind her, Kate said: "So that explains why the Nashes didn't come up on any foster parent databases."

"And while it's not foster care per se, I think involvement in Family Friends and Services would be close enough—close enough to establish a solid connection between all three families, anyway."

"So now the trick is to see if there are any children that these three families had in common," Kate said. "Was there one single child that all three families kept at some point? And that could lead us straight to the killer."

Both women mulled over this for a moment. It was an exciting thought, but part of Kate thought that it felt just a tad too easy.

Ruby returned two minutes later with a thin binder. The name NASH was typed down the spine. She opened the binder up and turned it so that it was facing Kate and DeMarco.

"Derrick and Toni Nash became part of the Family Friends and Services family in 2007," Ruby said. "They hosted their first child later that year, through Christmas, I believe. Over the last twelve years or so, they've hosted fourteen children, ages six months to fourteen."

"And to become a member of your organization, I assume they had to pass background checks?" DeMarco asked.

"Absolutely. Honestly, anyone applying for FFS has to pretty much undergo the same things as someone working towards becoming a foster parent. The only difference is that I believe with foster care, there are classes you have to take and pass."

"Do you keep a list of the names of the children each family hosts?" Kate asked.

"We do," Ruby said, looking rather uncomfortable. "But ... well, as FBI agents, I'm sure you understand that I can't very well just hand that kind of information over to you. I'd love to ... really, I would. I'm sick over what happened to the Nashes. But we can't give that information out. What I *can* do is direct you to one of the case workers over at Social Services that should be able to get you the entire list."

Kate didn't bother pushing the issue. She knew Ruby was right and while it would slow them down a bit, she understood the safety measures of such a process. "We'd greatly appreciate the number of whichever case worker you feel would act the most urgently on this."

"Of course," Ruby said, scrolling through her phone in search of the contact information.

"Also," Kate said, "with an organization like this, I would assume you see a lot of kids that come through here dealing with varied forms of trauma. Would that be accurate?"

"Yes, unfortunately."

"Is there a local therapist you work with to help with those sorts of cases?"

"Yes, actually. As a matter of fact, she's located just right down the street."

"In that case, thank you for your time," Kate said.

Ruby nodded and grabbed a pen from the table. She jotted down the information of the DSS worker and handed it to DeMarco.

"I mean this when I say it," Ruby said. "Please let me know if there is anything else I can do to help. The Nashes were among the best people I ever met—nice, charitable, and kind. They didn't deserve this."

Kate nodded, keeping in the comment that sprang up in her mind. *That might be so,* she thought. *But someone thought they* did *deserve it. And someone with that kind of skewed mentality might be much more dangerous than we could have ever thought.*

Knowing the rigid process that state judiciary systems put in place to protect the private information of citizens, Kate knew that a direct call to the Department of Social Services would do her no good. They'd ask to speak to her supervisor and they'd work the details out with them. So instead of calling DSS directly, Kate placed a call to Duran. She gave him the information of Ruby's DSS contact and let him know what they were looking for. He ended the call with the promise that he'd get back to her in fifteen minutes with the names of all of the children who had ever been cared for by the Nashes, the Langleys, and Monica Knight.

That little errand allowed Kate and DeMarco enough time to visit the office of the Family Friends and Services' therapist at the other end of the street. Ruby had handed Kate a business card as they had left FFS with the name of Danielle Ethridge and the office address. The same name was on the glass door of the office in white vinyl letters.

Inside, a receptionist sat at a desk, typing something into a laptop. It was a small space, probably a private practice of some sort. The place was well decorated and very homey, reminding Kate of the offices at Family Friends and Services. The receptionist looked up and smiled as they entered.

"Hello, ladies," she said a little too cheerfully. "Can I help you?"

As they approached the desk, Kate showed her ID, as did DeMarco. As they went through their introductions, the woman's good cheer seemed to evaporate. And when they explained that they were there to speak with Dr. Ethridge concerning a rather time-sensitive case, she looked downright scared.

"Of course, of course," the receptionist said. "Unfortunately, Dr. Ethridge is with a patient right now. But I can let her know you are here just as soon as the session is over. It shouldn't be long. Maybe another fifteen minutes."

"Thank you," Kate said. They walked over to a small seating area and when she sat down, the very feel of inactivity made Kate feel like the case was indeed coming together. She'd garnered something of an instinct based on her emotions; when she was at a standstill in a case but it wasn't leading anywhere, she tended to get anxious. On the other hand, as she and DeMarco sat in the waiting area, she felt at peace—as if they were close enough to the end of this thing that they did not have to rush.

Seven minutes into their wait, they each got a text from Duran through a group text. **Emailing a list of names from DSS within 5 mins.**

"That should wrap it up, right?" DeMarco asked. "If we can find one name on these lists that stayed with the Nashes, the Langleys, and Monica Knight, that will be the smoking gun, right?"

"It feels that way," Kate said. "On the other hand, it could also do nothing more than shoot down a lead." Honestly, she did not feel this way but she didn't want to show DeMarco, a younger and still moldable agent, that it was okay to rest on your laurels and simply assume that things were going well.

Kate kept an eye on her phone and when she got the notification that she had a new mail, she opened it right away. Strangely, she felt a stirring of compassion when she saw the lists. The Nashes alone had hosted six children through Family Friends and Services. The Langleys had cared for six, while Monica Knight had housed four foster kids. It was heartwarming to know that there were people in the world who still cared for orphans and troubled children in such a way. It made her think of Michelle and how she would be fortunate to grow up in a home where she would always be loved.

There was a note at the bottom of the lists. It read: *Not a complete list. Some children had their names changed. Some parents had them removed once they resumed care. Others were removed from all lists at their own request after turning eighteen years of age.*

"I see two in common right away," DeMarco said, looking at her own mail.

Kate spotted that, too. And while she hated to instantly eliminate so many other names from the list, it simply made more sense to go with the children whom all of the victims had in common. Seeing these two names, she *did* start to feel a slight bit of anxiousness slipping into her mind.

"Agents?"

They looked up and saw a middle-aged woman in glasses approaching them. Like the receptionist, she smiled widely. She wore a pair of glasses that made her eyes appear very bright.

Kate stood up and shook the woman's hand. DeMarco followed suit.

"Thanks for meeting with us," Kate said. "As I told your receptionist, it's a time-sensitive matter."

"Yes, and I got a text from Ruby that told me you were coming as well. So come on back, Agents, and let me see if I can help."

❧   ❧   ❧

Kate and DeMarco sat on the opposite side of Dr. Ethridge as she slowly lowered herself into the chair behind her desk. "Do you mind if I ask if this matter is about the Langleys and the Nashes?" she asked.

"It is," Kate said, surprised that she knew about one other family that Ruby at Family Friends had not known about. "And if I'm going to be blunt and expect your full cooperation, I suppose I can also tell you that as of this morning, another woman has been killed—Monica Knight."

"Oh my God," she said. "I never really knew her, but heard of her. She wasn't with FSS, correct?"

"Not that we know of," Kate said. "Just foster care."

"We're here," DeMarco said, "because so far the only link we can find between the victims is the fact that they were all connected through the foster system in one way or the other, although we understand the Nashes weren't foster parents, but involved in Family Friends and Services."

"And while we can't go into detail just yet," Kate said, "the killer has been leaving little clues behind that indicate he may have some sort of trauma from his childhood that is still tormenting him."

"I'll help in whatever capacity I can," Ethridge said, "but surely you understand that there will be areas where my hands are tied when it comes to doctor-patient confidentiality."

"Yes," Kate said, fully expecting this. "But I don't think you'll have to divulge too much." She slid her phone over to Ethridge and showed her the list of names. "As you'll see, there are two names that the victims have in common. Two children."

"Yes, I was aware of at least one child that both the Nashes and the Langleys had seen. I don't know if Ruby told you, but I also see quite a few children from DSS cases, particularly after the kids have been moved into foster care. I don't get them all, but I do get many of them."

"So these two children," DeMarco said. "Do the names ring bells? Or, more importantly, do they raise any red flags?"

"Well, Renee Pearson was a handful," Ethridge said, pointing to a name on the list. "I had no idea she had ended up with Monica Knight, though. It might have been just a respite situation where care was only needed for a day or so. Anyway, Renee was always looking for an argument. She'd lash out at people, hitting them in the hopes of getting into a fight. In her first foster home, she was caught holding a pillow over the face of the family's three-year-old son while he slept. The kid was okay, thankfully, but the trouble that Renee got into didn't seem to bother her at all."

"So you'd say she had a tendency toward violence?" Kate asked.

"Yes, that's a safe bet. But...this was nearly...God, almost twelve years ago the last time I saw her. She found a home that sort of fit. Last I heard—and it's been a while—she had gone to college."

"Do you know if she still lives around here?" DeMarco asked.

"Pretty sure. If you'll check with my receptionist on the way out, she might have a current address that we use for Christmas cards and the like."

"Anyone else in that trio stand out?" Kate asked.

Ethridge nodded. "Yeah. Robert Traylor. He was one of those young boys that just...I hate to say it, but you could see the hate in his eyes sometimes. Abandoned as a baby, sexually abused by a foster father when he was four. Robert was cutting himself when he was nine or so—and that was right around the time his uncle finally took him in. That helped for a while from what I can remember, but he got taken in by the cops for the first time when he was eleven or twelve."

"What for?" DeMarco asked.

"Beating up a homeless man. Smashed a liquor bottle right over his head."

"Did he ever threaten you?" Kate asked.

"Oh yeah, almost weekly. He threatened to break into my house and rape me. Pretty harsh words coming from a thirteen-year-old."

"At the risk of jumping to conclusions, do you think he'd be capable of murder?"

Ethridge thought about this for a moment. She steepled her fingers together as she thought, clearly not wanting to take the conversation where it was headed. "I can clearly remember putting notes like *self-harm* and *suicidal thoughts and tendencies* into his evaluations. And that was pretty much over the entire time I saw him as a patient. I suppose he'd be in his late twenties now. Maybe early thirties. And while I am a huge proponent of thinking anyone can change, I just... well, I find it hard to think that he could have changed *that* much."

"Have you seen or heard from him since you last met with him professionally?" DeMarco asked.

"No. And that's been nearly nine years ago."

Kate nodded and got to her feet. As far as she was concerned, they had what they needed. "Well, thanks for your time—again, we certainly appreciate it."

"Agent Wise... do you mind me asking what the killer is leaving behind? You said there were clues he was leaving behind."

"Fragments of what appear to be an old blanket."

"Like a security blanket?"

"That's the hunch I'm going with. Why do you ask?"

Ethridge thought for a moment before answering: "That's a pretty sentimental object." Kate waited for something else, but Ethridge looked lost in thought.

Kate gave a final nod of appreciation and then left the office.

On the way down the hall, DeMarco pulled out her phone. "I doubt someone like Robert Traylor is on the Christmas card list," she said. "I'll put in an information request on his current residence."

"And if Renee Pearson is local, let's pay her a visit, too," Kate said. "Maybe she can offer some insight into how being bounced around from home to home can alter a kid's thinking."

But even while they were making these plans, the last thing Ethridge said remained stuck in her head. It slowly started to glow, as if it might have some meaning to it, some clue to help them break the case.

That's a pretty sentimental object, Ethridge had said of the blanket.

It was a notion that Kate had felt ever since the beginning, but she could not tease out the meaning of it just yet.

Maybe when they encountered Robert Traylor, he'd be able to tell them himself—from the confines of an interrogation room.

CHAPTER TWENTY ONE

Renee Pearson—now Renee Matthews after getting married three years ago—lived just outside of Roanoke, in a neighborhood nestled in a valley that gave a breathtaking view of the mountains. Seeing the neighborhood was, to Kate, an exercise in not pre-judging people based on their history. The neighborhood was a gated community, with houses that would easily go for seven to eight hundred thousand in this part of the country. Dusk was only an hour or so away, the evening light painting the neighborhood in rich colors that seemed to add to the value of the place.

Just as Kate was parking along the curb in front of Renee Matthews's house, DeMarco's phone rang. She answered it right away. Kate continued to admire the neighborhood from behind the wheel as she listened to DeMarco's side of the phone conversation. She was off in less than a minute and although Kate had gotten the gist from DeMarco's end, her partner filled her in.

"So there appears to be no current residence for Robert Traylor," DeMarco said. "The last actual address on file for him was in Blacksburg, Virginia, and that was three years ago. The post office can confirm that he no longer lives there. The best we could get was the address of his uncle. They were apparently fairly tight at one point."

"He local?" Kate asked.

"Just outside of Blacksburg. About an hour and a half away."

"Maybe too late to visit tonight. We can call him when we leave here to see how cooperative he'll be."

They got out of the car and walked up to the porch. DeMarco knocked on the door and it was answered right away by a man carrying a toddler. The kid sucked on a bottle and looked at the agents skeptically.

"Can I help you?" the man asked.

"We're looking for Renee Matthews, formerly Renee Pearson," Kate said.

"That's my wife," he said. He then gave them a skeptical look that mirrored that of his son. "Can I ask who's visiting?"

"Agents Wise and DeMarco, with the FBI," Kate said, showing her ID. "We just need to ask her some questions about some people from her past."

"Ah," the husband said, as if it all made sense now. "Come on in. Renee is in the laundry room. I'll get her."

Mr. Pearson led them into the dining room and offered them both seats while he walked to the back of the house. Kate was glad to see that someone with a marred past had managed to do so well for themselves. Even if it was a case of marrying well, it was something to admire.

Moments later, a pretty woman dressed in a T-shirt and sweatpants came into the dining room. Her blonde hair was done up in a messy bun that made her look about ten years younger. Kate thought she could catch glimpses of the young girl who had once met with Dr. Ethridge.

"Renee?" Kate asked.

"Yeah, that's me," she said. "Chris said you were with the FBI?"

"That's right," DeMarco said, showing her badge.

"Is something wrong?" Renee asked.

"I don't know if you've heard about the Langleys and the Nashes yet," Kate said. "But they've recently been killed."

Renee nodded her head. "Yes. A friend of mine from in town called me. One day after the other, like a double play of terrible news."

"Had you remained close with them over the years?" Kate asked.

"I spoke with Toni Nash every now and then," Renee said. "She would occasionally call to tell me about Olivia being in college. I hadn't spoken to the Langleys in a while, though. They called on my birthday last year and I think that was the last time I spoke with them."

Kate did her best to deliver the next news softly. "What can you tell us about Monica Knight?" she asked.

"A nice enough lady. I stayed with her for about a week when I was fourteen or so and then for a weekend the year after that. She's such a sweet woman, but looking back, I think she was at war with which to give in to: her heart for kids or her career."

"Well, I hate to tell you that she's been killed, too," Kate said. "Sometime last night, we think."

Renee's hand went to her mouth and tears formed in her eyes.

"When did you speak to her last?" DeMarco asked.

"Oh, it's been years. I was married three years ago and she sent me a gift through Amazon. She never called. I invited her to the wedding, but she didn't come."

"How was your time with her when she hosted you?" Kate asked.

"Fine. Nothing special. We got along but nothing really ever clicked, you know? She was very kind and hospitable but there was never any real sense that she wanted to get to know me on a personal level."

"During your time with the Langleys, Nashes, and Monica Knight, did you happen to ever cross paths with a young man named Robert Traylor?"

Renee considered it for a moment before shaking her head. "It doesn't sound familiar. But then again, I was yanked around a lot for several years there."

"We spoke with Dr. Ethridge in Roanoke," DeMarco said. She smiled and added: "It looks like you got things turned around."

"I did," Renee said, wiping a tear away. "I met this college girl at one of the foster homes I was in and she was telling me how awesome college was and how she basically already had a job lined up when she graduated. I decided I'd give it a go. Did some community college to get my GPA up and then went to Virginia Tech. I graduated the same year Chris and I got married. I've been working with the Forestry Department ever since. I think it's a job that'll eventually lead us to West Virginia to live, but we're not quite sure yet."

"Now, just for the sake of us having to do our jobs," Kate said, "would you be able to prove your whereabouts every night for the past week or so?"

Alarmed, Renee sat up rigid in her seat. "Are you seriously suggesting that I—"

"I'm suggesting nothing," Kate said. "However, so far the only thing that these victims have in common is the fact that they were involved in foster care and child protection. And you were a common link among them all."

Renee looked pissed but it was also clear that she understood their approach. "I was here every night for the last week, with the exception of Thursday night. That's our date night. We have a sitter come so Chris and I can go out to dinner."

"And I'm sure that will all check out," DeMarco said apologetically. "Mrs. Matthews, you knew all five of these victims. Is there any reason at all you could think of for someone to want to hurt them? Was there maybe anything that linked them together somehow?"

"I honestly don't know," Renee said. "I can't think of anything. Then again, I was very self-absorbed and wrapped up in myself during that time in my life."

Kate got to her feet, a little regretful that they had driven out here for this brief and uneventful conversation. "Well, over the next day or so, we'd appreciate it if you could give it some thought. If you come up with anything, please let us know."

"Of course."

With that, DeMarco left a business card on the dining room table as Renee walked them to the door.

"You know," Renee said, "foster care is a double-edged sword. For every great family, there's a shitty one. I heard about some pretty bad stories. But I find it hard to believe any of these families would have done something so bad to a child that would cause this."

"Did you ever meet a kid that was abused in the system?" Kate asked.

"A few girls here and there, yeah."

"And would you happen to know any of the names of those abusive families?"

"No … sorry."

"How about you?" DeMarco asked. "Did you ever experience it?"

"No. The Nashes and Langleys were the only actual *homes* I stayed in."

So there goes any hope of singling out the next family on the killer's list, Kate thought.

They thanked Renee one last time and headed back to the car. As Kate cranked the engine to life, DeMarco looked thoughtfully out the window.

"So if this killer *is* a former foster kid with connections to his victims, how can we know when he's done?"

"What do you mean?" Kate asked.

"What if he's like Renee? What if these were the only families he stayed with? What if he's killed them and has quit? He could have already gone into hiding."

"Then let's go find the bastard," Kate said and shifted the car into Drive.

CHAPTER TWENTY TWO

Despite the late hour, Kate was actually glad that the uncle of Robert Traylor agreed to meet with them. His only caveat was that they meet him at a bar in downtown Roanoke. So as the night wound closer to nine o'clock, Kate found herself driving back into Roanoke, following GPS directions to a bar called Shorty's Pub.

They found him at the back of the place, in a corner booth that looked like something that had been torn straight from an old noir movie. A pitcher of beer and a half-empty glass sat in front of him. He was vaguely watching one of the TVs behind the bar, squinting at the highlights on Sports Center.

"Mr. Traylor?" Kate asked as they approached the table.

He looked away from the television and to the two agents. His startled look made it clear that he probably wasn't expecting two women—although Kate was the one he talked to on the phone. An embarrassed look crossed his face, one that he turned toward the pitcher of beer and then back to them.

"Al Traylor," he said. "Nice to meet you. Want a drink?"

Kate would have loved a glass of white wine but she had never been one to drink on the job—not even after hours when she was away from DC.

"No thanks," she said. DeMarco shook her head as well. "Mr. Traylor, I'm Agent Wise and this is Agent DeMarco. As you were told on the phone, we were hoping to speak with you about a case we're working on."

Traylor nodded and sipped from his beer. The glass wasn't quite empty yet but he refilled it from the pitcher in front of him—which was, itself, about half-empty.

"You don't look very surprised," DeMarco said.

"Is it about my stupid fucking nephew?" he asked.

"It is, actually," Kate said. "What made you go there so quickly?"

"Because the boy is an accident waiting to happen. A fuck-up of massive proportions. I'm surprised I haven't been visited by the feds before now." He then chuckled and waved his hand at the glass and pitcher in front of him. "Like I have any room to speak. But, you know, he's the reason I drink so damned much."

Kate and DeMarco sat down on the other end of the booth. "Can you explain that, please?" Kate asked.

"Well, I guess you know he was bounced around in foster care for most of his childhood, right?" When the agents nodded, he nodded right back and then continued. "Well, I was a mess myself for a while. I drank a lot. Got fired from a few jobs because of it. Had three affairs on my wife before she wised up and left me. So yeah ... I was a train wreck even before I met him. And then one day, I get this call from Social Services. They say they've got my nephew and they are looking for a home for him. Apparently, my idiot brother, God rest his miserable soul, skipped town and left his kid behind when he was just a baby—I didn't have a clue because we weren't in touch. He'd been bounced around in foster care until they finally found me. I didn't have him for very long, though, before he was put back in foster care."

"Why did they remove him from your care?" Kate asked.

Traylor pointed to the pint glass in front of him. "I didn't know they do surprise visits. Child Protective Services came by one evening to check on us and I was pretty drunk. Left him playing out in the front yard by himself."

"How old was he at this time?" DeMarco asked.

"Eight or nine. I don't really remember."

"And did he eventually get back into your care?"

"Yes," Traylor said. "I realized that I had wrecked my life, you know. So I cleaned up. Got *almost* sober. Got a steady job. I took the classes for foster care services and everything after I learned that he was just being passed around. There was a rumor that one of the families had been abusing him. So I asked for him back. I passed every class and course they threw at me and he seemed happy enough to be back with me. He lived with me for about a year before he ran away the first time. The cops brought him back three weeks later and he stayed with me again for a few months before he skipped out on me again."

"How was the relationship between the two of you?" Kate asked.

"Shitty at first. But we got to like one another, you know. We watched football on Sundays. Went fishing from time to time... which he hated, but he liked to be outdoors. I asked him, after that first time, why he ran away. He told me he got bored. I asked him where he went and he would never tell me. He got very shady about it."

"After he left the second time, was that the end of it?" Kate asked.

"Oh no. He showed up again when he was sixteen. Scrawny and long grungy hair. Had a girl with him this time. He asked if they could stay with me for a while and I said they could. I'd smell pot coming from his room from time to time. Heard loud sex noises, things like that. I had a talk with him about the girl having to find her own place and that did not go well. He blew up at me but he stayed, you know? He seemed different. Like... he knew how to use people. He was only with me this time for a safe place to stay. I knew that... but..."

He stopped here and took another gulp from his glass. He licked his lips and then continued. "They went out one night and I snooped through his stuff. I wanted to know what he into, where he had been, you know? And there was some dark stuff. Satanic stuff. Violent porn. Things like that. I confronted him about it because, quite frankly, some of the porn had some models that couldn't have been any older than fifteen or sixteen. Needless to say, he went nuts. Pulled a fucking knife on me. I think he would have actually stabbed me if I hadn't punched him first. He stormed out, told me to go to hell."

"Any idea where he went?" Kate asked.

"No. But, because I guess he thought I was a sucker, he came back on Christmas Eve two years after that. He was strung out on something. High as hell, you know? He asked if he could stay and I let him—but only through the New Year. He was doing coke in my house, smoking pot, bringing these fucking creepy people over to hang out, and God knows what else. I gave him until the middle of January to find a job. After he hadn't even tried, I sent him packing. And that's the last time I saw him."

"How long ago was that?" DeMarco asked.

"That's been about three years ago."

"Do you have any idea where we might find him?" Kate asked. "His last listed address is a dead end."

Traylor chuckled. "Oh, I bet it is. And his name probably wouldn't come up under any current address anyway. The moron changed his name. And I found *that* out when I got a letter in the mail last year. Said he had moved, changed his name, and was starting over. He asked for money in the letter—just to get back on his feet. I crumpled it up and threw it away. But yeah, I have his address ... and his new name: Chester Black, and he lives in a trailer out in Whip Springs, back in the woods somewhere."

"You say he pulled a knife on you at one time," Kate said. "Do you think that was him acting out of anger or being high ... or do you think that sort of reaction is just in his nature?"

"I don't follow you."

"Do you think he'd be capable of murder?"

Traylor didn't waste time thinking. He nodded and downed his glass, filling it again from the pitcher right away. "Probably. It was like a gradual decline, you know? He was quiet and brooding when I first had him and then when he came back, there was something darker about him. And then the third time, he'd gone way the hell off the rails. I actually watched him fall apart in stages, you know? That's why I guess I wasn't too surprised to hear from the FBI," he said. "In the back of my head, I've been expecting something to come up concerning *Chester* for quite some time now. That he was either dead or had gotten involved in some shit. I guess he finally snapped completely, huh? Did he actually kill someone?"

"We can't say yet," Kate said, getting to her feet.

"Just as well," Traylor said. "The less I know about him, the better."

As if on cue, he turned his attention back to the televisions behind the bar. He did not look sad, but certainly not upset, either. Kate thought he looked emotionless—as if he had long ago given up on his nephew.

And maybe that's why he ended up the way he did, Kate thought. *Foster families gave up on him, as did his own father and uncle. All of that can build and build until something just flat out snaps ...*

Thinking that, she thought maybe Al Traylor didn't quite look emotionless. Instead, he looked like a man who considered it a defeat that he had not been strong enough to save someone he once cared about—especially now that the someone in question could very well be convicted of multiple murders.

CHAPTER TWENTY THREE

Because Whip Springs was less than half an hour from the bar that Al Traylor had chosen, Kate decided to pay Chester Black a visit despite the time. It was 9:47 when they came to the dirt road that led back to a small cluster of mobile homes. DeMarco had put a call in to Palmetto to get the address, only to hear Palmetto laughing. He wasn't able to give an actual address, but plenty of detail in his directions.

"He says if you fall off the face of the Earth, we've gone too far," DeMarco commented as Kate turned the car onto the dirt road.

Several feet down the road, they came to a small iron square sitting up on a post. The box contained six smaller boxes inside of it, each listed with a last name. It was a crude little PO box of sorts, apparently so the mail carrier didn't have to go all the way down the extremely poorly paved road. Using the flashlight on her phone, Kate saw that Box #4 was adorned with **C. Black**.

It took about another minute or so before the mobile homes came into view. They were derelict structures, one of which was missing a window and was covered instead with a tattered blue tarp. In one yard, two men sat around a small charcoal grill, drinking beer and eating burgers.

Kate parked the car in front of the fourth trailer. She pulled in behind a very old Chevy Cavalier. The back window was adorned with band logos and a pentagram. Given the stories Al Traylor had just told them, as well as the darkened night and isolated locale, Kate was slightly on edge when she and DeMarco got out of the car. She saw that DeMarco was also looking around cautiously, her hand resting by her side where her Glock was concealed beneath her jacket.

The steps leading up to Chester Black's rickety wooden porch were nothing more than concrete blocks that had been strategically stacked to make a crude set of stairs. As they neared them, DeMarco took two quick strides, taking the lead. Several years ago, this might have offended Kate. But now it seemed almost polite—a way to get in front of any potential danger to assist a partner who was twenty-seven years her senior.

When they took the steps, Kate caught a pungent odor. Something rotting ... maybe a dead cat or a deer that had died out in the woods. She wrinkled her nose at it and continued up the wobbly stairs.

The two agents gave one another a nod of readiness before DeMarco knocked on the aluminum screen door.

"Yeah!" a male voice yelled from inside. "Who is it?"

Not wanting to yell, particularly not to be overheard by the men in the yard two trailers back, Kate leaned in as close to the screen door as she could. "Mr. Black, it's the FBI. We need to speak with you, please."

"Bullshit," came the reply, layered with a laugh.

This was followed by footsteps storming toward the door. The door was opened and a pale, thin man looked out at them. His hair was jet black, as was his shirt. His nose was pierced, as was his bottom lip. A tattoo peeked out of the collar of his shirt, running up his neck to the underside of his chin. A tentacle, from the looks of it.

It was clear that Chester Black had thought someone was playing a joke on him. While he stared at them in confusion, DeMarco took the opportunity to show him her badge. "Like my partner said," DeMarco remarked, "we're with the FBI. We'd like to ask you some questions about recent activity in the area."

"What kind of activity?" he asked, vigilant.

He tried staring them down but his eyes were glassy and distant. Kate was pretty sure he was on something. He had the look of someone coming down off of a pretty strong high.

"We'd really prefer to come inside," Kate said.

"That's not going to happen."

"Fine. Then we can talk out here and I can raise my voice a bit so those gentlemen in the yard two trailers up can hear what we need to ask you."

"You think I care what those rednecks think of me?"

"I don't know," DeMarco said. "But I know what *you're* going to think of me if you make me go all the way back to the PD and get a warrant to come into this pigsty. Make it easy on everyone, *Chester.* And we know that's not your real name. We know your real name. We can broadcast that during our conversation on the porch, too."

Black looked at odds, torn in his decision. "Shit," he said. "Fine. Come in. But I clearly wasn't expecting company. Especially not the fucking FBI."

"You high on something right now?" Kate asked.

He only sneered at her as they passed through the doorway.

When they walked inside, the first thing Kate noticed was the smell. It was the same thing she had smelled outside, only stronger. She could not decide if Chester Black simply needed to empty his trash or if some woodland creature had found its way under the trailer and died.

"So what do you want?" Black asked. He was still standing by the door, basically trapping them inside. *Or making sure he has a clear path to escape,* Kate thought, bringing Davey Armstrong to mind.

"You live about fifteen miles away from the Langley family," Kate said. "They fostered you when you were a kid, right?"

"Yeah. For like three months, before they shipped me off to another family."

"Did you know they had been killed?"

Black nodded. "I heard it from one of my neighbors. Murdered, right?" After a short pause, he rolled his eyes and laughed. "Ah, shit. You think I did it?"

"There's no accusation here," DeMarco said. "We're just trying to get as much information as we can. For instance, did you know the Nashes had been murdered, too?"

The look on his face was one of pure shock. But something about it did not sit well with Kate. It didn't seem like he was shocked at the news. It was almost as if someone had discovered some secret and he had not expected it to be revealed.

"No, I hadn't."

"On top of that," Kate said, "a woman named Monica Knight was murdered within the last thirty-six hours."

"You stayed with her for a bit, too, correct?" DeMarco said.

Now there was bewilderment in his eyes. "What the hell? And you're here ... why, exactly?"

"You stayed with all three of them at some point in time. And based on some of the things we've gathered from your family members ..."

"My uncle, you mean?"

Kate ignored this and went on. "Mr. Black, could you provide your whereabouts for each night over the last week or so?"

"I've been all over the place. Roanoke one night. I was at a friend's place last night in Vinton."

"Can you provide proof?"

"Other than word of mouth?"

"That will do for now," DeMarco said. "But we'd eventually need more."

"If you are claiming that you are not the person behind the murders," Kate said, "would you care to tell me what you know about the victims? Is there anything else that might possibly connect them?"

"Other than the fact that I was too much for them to handle?" Black said. "And that Bethany Langley knew how to throw a right-handed slap like a fucking MMA fighter? Yeah, I'm sorry they're dead and all. But fuck them. They gave up on me a long time ago. And the Nashes in particular were so holier-than-thou, it was sickening. Looks to me like it was karma; looks like they got what they deserved."

"That seems a little harsh," DeMarco said.

"Harsh? Harsh! How about that bitch Monica ... dumping me back with DSS after she found out that I had been sexually abused by one of my foster dads. Too much for her too handle. And the Nashes ... when I told them I might be interested in boys ... another family just dumping me off. Getting slapped every time I dared to question the Langleys. Loving homes my ass ..."

While Black went on his little tirade, Kate started to slowly study the trailer. There was a small steak knife sitting on the scarred end table by the couch. At the sight of the knife, the smell of the place grew all the more alarming.

"You may want to put a lid on that kind of talk if you want us to believe that you had nothing to do with the murders," DeMarco said. "You could be one hundred percent innocent, and that sort of talk will get you a nice spot in an interrogation room."

"You going to arrest me for talking bad about someone?" Black yelled.

But Kate barely registered this. Instead, she was looking at part of something white under the couch. She walked over to it and saw that it was the corner of a towel. She reached down and grabbed it.

"What are you doing?" Black asked.

Kate pulled it out and took a quick step back. The towel was crumpled, filthy, and matted with blood.

Fresh blood.

"What's this?" Kate asked.

"I hurt myself earlier," Black said. "Nasty cut. That towel was the first thing I grabbed."

"And why is it shoved under the couch?" DeMarco asked.

"Let me see the cut," Kate said. She felt her right hand inching toward her sidearm.

"It's in an area I'd rather not show some random ass FBI agent," Black said. "And I know my rights. You can't demand that I remove my clothing to show you a wound."

"Then explain yourself," DeMarco said. She was doing a little less to hide the fact that she was thinking of going for her gun.

"Get out of my house," he spat. "Go get that warrant."

"Explain the blood," Kate said. She kept looking back at it. It was a lot of blood, but not too much to automatically make her assume the worst.

"I'm not explaining anything. I said get the fuck out of my house!"

Kate fought her instincts and acted. She was going to lie but she figured that was okay. Black had claimed to know his rights. But for someone dumb enough to quickly shove a blood-soaked towel under his couch, she had to wonder. She figured she could test it just enough to stay out of any legal trouble.

"Apparently, you *don't* know your rights," she said. "That much fresh blood being present at a location where we are questioning someone in an active murder investigation trumps your rights. In fact," she said, showing him her gun but not yet drawing it, "it could be considered threatening materials. Enough for us to draw our weapons and bring you in. Now ... *explain yourself!*"

The way his eyes darted in worry made it very apparent that he had bought her dishonesty. He shook his head nervously and then shrugged. "Fine ..."

And then he threw an elbow hard into DeMarco's chest.

She coughed and stumbled back into the kitchen. She slipped on the linoleum and banged into the fridge. Black then made a mistake in gauging Kate's actions; he took a split second to see how she was going to follow up before he moved. Had he instantly gone for the door and into the night, he might have escaped. But he hesitated, toying with the idea of attacking Kate as well.

Before he could take a single step forward, Kate was rushing at him. It was all too familiar to the scene at Davey Armstrong's apartment. Black's mistake, though, was that in seeing her coming forward, he decided to defend himself.

He reached for the knife on the end table in one deft move. But as his hand fell on it, Kate brought her elbow down on his forearm. Black screamed and went to the floor like a sack of rocks. DeMarco was there with her in an instant, throwing her arms around Black's torso as he tried to fight them off.

But he was far too frail and weak. Kate had him cuffed within five seconds. And as she got to her feet, her heart thrumming, she looked back at the towel.

That blood was very fresh and she'd be willing to bet just about anything that it had not come from Chester Black.

CHAPTER TWENTY FOUR

Kate and DeMarco had searched the area around the trailer for any signs of where the blood had come from but found nothing. DeMarco had found where the stench from within the house had come from, though. There had indeed been a dead cat beneath the trailer. In fact, there had also been a dead dog as well. The dog had been very recently killed, a slit tearing it open from its jaw to its hips.

Kate was thankful that the media had not discovered this grisly tidbit. Somehow, they had learned about Black's arrest; when they arrived at the police department in Roanoke, there were already two news vans parked outside, waiting, with a third roaring down the street in search of a place to park.

As Kate and DeMarco quickly escorted Black into the station, Palmetto came rushing up to them with an apologetic look on his face.

"How the hell did the media find out about this?" Kate barked at him.

"No clue. The chief is pissed. He's got an active hunt for the leak. Sadly, it's happened far too often around here before."

This did nothing to decrease Kate's irritation. She hustled Black into the station through the back door where there were already two reporters jockeying for position. She didn't bother so much as looking at them as they passed by, though she did hear their questions.

"Is this the killer?"

"Why did he do it?"

"Are there more victims out there?"

Inside, things were just as chaotic. There were officers fielding phone calls, basically screaming at the people on the other end as they asked for information regarding the suspect.

Palmetto jockeyed in behind them as they escorted Black down the hall. As they made their way down, the Chief of Police met them coming from the other direction. He looked flustered and tired, but altogether relieved.

"This is him?" the chief asked. "This is the killer?"

"I didn't kill anyone!" Black screamed.

"Just lead us to an interrogation room," Kate said.

Somewhere within her heart, she felt a pang of sorrow—a tearing sensation. She could not make sense of it, but whatever it was made her think of Michelle and Melissa.

"You okay?" DeMarco asked.

Kate nodded. "Hey, follow them to interrogation, would you? I need to take a moment."

"Sure," DeMarco said, looking concerned.

Kate raced back down the hall, to where they had passed a restroom several moments ago. She went in, grateful to find it empty. She gathered her breath and stared at herself in the mirror, wondering just what in the hell was happening to her. Panic attack? Adrenaline surge? No... none of that seemed right.

You know what this is, she told herself. *There's a part of you—the grandmother part, probably—that doesn't think you should be here. That part of you thinks you should be back in Richmond, within a call and twenty miles or so of your daughter and granddaughter. This is guilt ... guilt of not being readily accessible to your family even in your supposed retirement.*

A tear trailed down her cheek unexpectedly. She wiped it away as she pulled out her phone. She toyed with calling Melissa but figured it was too late. Instead, she sent a text. She typed it in quickly, taken aback by this sudden surge of emotion.

Ironically, being back on the job is making me miss you guys even more. I hope you can understand this back and forth with my work. More importantly, I hope you can forgive me. Give that baby girl a kiss from her grandma. Love you.

She pocketed the phone and checked herself over in the mirror. She certainly couldn't question Chester Black looking like an emotional mess.

Confident that she had herself under control, she walked back toward the hallway.

Just as she reached the door, her phone dinged from her pocket. She dug it out and saw that Melissa had already answered her. She imagined her daughter at home, sitting in bed with her husband and maybe scrolling through Facebook on her phone. Michelle would be sleeping in her crib in the bedroom down the hall. The thought brought a smile to her face.

Melissa's response read: **I don't understand it, but that's ok. You're passionate about your job, and that's a good thing. Get out there and get it done, Mom. I have to raise my daughter in this world ... so make it a safer one. Go get the bad guys.**

Kate let out a little chuckle.

Go get the bad guys.

She pushed the restroom door open and walked quickly down the hall to do exactly that.

Kate could tell that the hard façade that Chester Black was putting up was a fake one. There was a terror in his eyes that was much like that of a child staring down the dark cellar stairs during a thunderstorm.

As Kate entered the interrogation room, DeMarco was standing on one side of the table with Black sitting on the other side. "... and forensics is going to tell us pretty quickly where that blood on the towel came from," DeMarco was saying. "So you may as well tell us now."

"You found the animals under the trailer, didn't you?" Black said with a scowl.

"So it was from the dog?" DeMarco said.

"Yes."

Kate thought about the knife she'd seen on the end table. She wondered how much time had passed between his brutal act and DeMarco knocking on his door. Something about the idea chilled her.

"Your uncle told us that he thought you were into some satanic things," Kate said. "Would animal sacrifice be one of them?"

Black glared up at her, that scowl trembling. "No one understands it, but it's not a crime, is it?"

"It can be. You can throw the religious rights stuff at us to keep us tied up for a while but if we really want to pin it on you, we could. Just being honest."

"I did it around eight o'clock," Black said. "The sacrifice. And the bodies... I keep them for about two days."

"So the cat body we found..."

"Last night," Black said.

"Forgive the ignorance, but is there no church?" DeMarco asked. "Do you just do these things solo at home?"

"I meet with others at a location once every month. It's not a *church*, but a gathering."

"And you sacrifice animals there?" Kate asked.

"Yes."

"Dogs and cats?"

"Sheeps and goats."

"Ever do any human sacrifices?" DeMarco asked. She was really digging into him, apparently feeling that even if this satanic stuff was true, Black was very much still the killer.

Kate then realized that about five seconds had passed since DeMarco had asked him about human sacrifices. "Answer the question, Mr. Black," Kate said.

"I've never killed a person before," Chester said. "I'm well aware that satanists have that stereotype, but it's mostly just bullshit."

It didn't quite sit right with Kate. If he was practicing some religious sacrifice, why come at them so aggressively? Did he know he'd be looking at animal cruelty charges at the very least?

Kate was about to continue with her questioning when someone came knocking at the door. DeMarco answered it and a hurried-looking man entered. He held a sheet of paper in his hand. His other was clenched into a fist.

"A moment outside, Agents?" the man said.

Kate and DeMarco walked out of the room with him. The moment the door was closed behind them, the man started in.

"He's our guy," he said. He then seemed to forget who he was and what he was doing. He shook his head and said: "Sorry. I'm Neil Banner, pathology. There are two blood types on the towel we took from his house. One is canine in nature. But the other is human. We don't have a positive ID on the blood and may never get one. It's too contaminated."

"But you're certain it's human?" Kate asked.

"One hundred percent certain," he said, handing her the report.

She nodded and took the paper. "Thank you."

With that, she walked back into the interrogation room. She felt like she was being propelled on a rocket. Though it seemed anticlimactic, they'd gotten him. Their killer was sitting right in front of them.

"You have one chance to change your story, Mr. Black. You're certain there's just dog blood on that towel?"

"Yes!" He nearly screamed it.

Kate placed the report on the table. She was sure he wouldn't be able to understand any of it, but she wanted him to know that they now had proof.

"That was your last chance. The bad news for you is that an officer will come in here very shortly and read you your rights. You will be under arrest for probable murder. The good news is that I won't be the one doing it. Because the things I've seen these last few days … if it was you that did them, I kind of want to hurt you right now."

There was plenty more she wanted to say, mainly because there was still some seed of doubt in the back of her mind. It seemed too easy, almost like it was handed to them. But the report on the table showed human blood on that towel … a towel Chester Black had tried to hide from them.

You're overthinking things again, she told herself. *You got him. Consider it a job well done and get home. Go see Melissa and Michelle.*

"Anything else to add, Agent DeMarco?" Kate asked.

"No. I'm good."

"Enjoy your time in prison," Kate told Black. "I'm sure you'll get life, but I doubt the judicial system will let you live it. Five victims … gruesome murders. You do the math."

"I don't know what the fuck you're talking about!" Black screamed.

And damn if Kate didn't see genuine confusion and horror in his eyes.

Don't go there, she said. *This is your guy. He's partially insane and the report right there on the table spells out his guilt.*

That thought was enough to allow her to leave the room. DeMarco followed her out and cut her off in the hallway.

"Agent Wise... Kate... are you okay?"

"Yeah, why?"

"I've never seen you so pissed at someone before. That got raw. Just checking in on you."

"Yeah, I'm fine. Honestly... I just want to go home."

"Let's do that," DeMarco said. "We got our man. Maybe we can sneak out before paperwork starts. I think the local PD can handle that on their own."

"Sounds good to me," Kate said.

They walked down the hallway toward the front of the police department. When Kate realized she could faintly hear the screams of Chester Black proclaiming his so-called innocence, she was surprised at just how easily she was able to tune it out.

CHAPTER TWENTY FIVE

Neither of them even considered staying in a motel in Roanoke. Kate and DeMarco figured they could take shifts driving if the other got tired. They did indeed switch out, DeMarco taking the wheel a little less than halfway through the trip so Kate could doze. Kate was stirred awake by DeMarco tapping on her shoulder.

Kate opened her eyes, instantly noticing the pain in her neck from sleeping in the passenger's seat.

"You're home," DeMarco said.

Sure enough, Kate looked out of the window and saw her house. She checked her watch and saw that it was 4:05 in the morning.

"Thanks," Kate said. "Now, come on in. I'm not letting you drive back to DC or try checking into a motel at such an hour."

"You sure?"

"Positive," Kate said. She got out of the car and started toward her steps before DeMarco could argue.

Kate didn't see the point in being formal. With what she and DeMarco had been through—not just with this case but with the one they'd shared two months ago—they were, as far as Kate was concerned, quite close.

"Guest bedroom is down the hall, last door on the right," she said. "The bathroom is right beside that. Make yourself at home. And if you wake me up early for anything, you might just get shot."

DeMarco smiled and headed down the hall. She turned back to Kate and smiled. "Seriously," she said, "thanks. It's been an absolute pleasure and thrill to get to know you, Agent Wise."

"I'll return the sentiment in the morning," Kate said. "For now ... sleep."

With that, Kate walked down the same hallway and entered her bedroom. She stripped down, quickly ruled out a shower, and fell into bed. She had just enough time to wonder if DeMarco would be comfortable in her house before sleep reached up and snatched her.

While DeMarco did not wake up Kate up the next morning, the smell of brewing coffee did. Kate tried to ignore it, but she had always been as sucker for a good cup of morning coffee. She looked at the alarm clock on her bedside table and saw that it was 9:45. She figured six hours of sleep was enough for now; she could easily make up for it tonight.

She rolled out of bed, threw on her around-the-house clothes, and headed out to the kitchen. DeMarco was already showered and dressed. She sat at the kitchen bar, scrolling through her phone with a cup of coffee sitting beside her. When she saw Kate enter the kitchen, she looked up and gave a nearly apologetic look.

"Sorry," she said. "You told me to make myself at home. I figured that meant coffee was included."

"Yes. And thank you for brewing it. How long have you been up?"

"About an hour. I called Duran and filled him in on everything."

"We did that last night…"

"Oh, I know. I mean I told him I crashed here because of the late hour. He seemed cool with it."

"Oh. Okay."

"If you don't mind, I'm going to finish up my coffee and get out of your hair."

"You're not in my hair. It's nice to have the company."

"Oh, I don't really have a choice. Duran wants me there this afternoon to give a briefing."

"You need me to come?" Kate asked.

"That's not necessary. Consider it one of the perks of your current position."

Kate knew that DeMarco meant it as a funny little jab with no ill intent but it stung nonetheless. She went to the coffeemaker and poured herself a cup. She was quite happy to find that it did not feel odd to be sharing her home with DeMarco. In fact, it felt natural.

"When you get back, will you keep me posted on how it goes down? I'd really like to see this one to the end."

"Of course." DeMarco sipped from her coffee with a thoughtful look on her face. "You don't feel comfortable leaving now, do you? You don't think it's Black."

"I don't know. It fits ... especially the human blood on that towel. The whole satanic thing just feels too ... convenient. I'd love to see what the lab results come back reading."

"Yeah. I thought so, too."

They left it at that, the question hanging in the air above them. As Kate joined DeMarco at the bar with her coffee, she thought of Black trying to escape his trailer. She thought of the terrible smell, of the blood and the animal carcasses under the trailer.

It's him, she thought. *Sometimes life hands you an answer and you just have to take it.*

Yes, some other more stubborn part of her thought. *But sometimes life forces those answers on you whether you want them or not.*

DeMarco was gone by 10:30, leaving Kate alone with her thoughts for the first time since DeMarco had knocked on her door to start the case off a few nights ago. Unsurprisingly, those thoughts led to Michelle and Melissa. She sat on her front porch, enjoying the quiet hum of the Carytown district and the morning's third cup of coffee, and doing her best to figure out how to manage her life from here on out.

It started by having a chat with Melissa. It wasn't something she dreaded, but it also wasn't something she was particularly looking forward to, either. She figured she may as well get it over with. Besides ... she tended to blow things out of proportion when it came to Melissa. For all she knew, her daughter might not be too upset with how things had gone down at all. She'd basically said as much during their brief text exchange the night before.

Go get the bad guys, Melissa had texted.

Again, Kate thought of Chester Black and started to feel any certainty she'd had wavering.

Before it could consume her mind, she picked up her cell phone and placed a call to Melissa. Melissa answered on the second ring. When Kate said "Hello," she could hear Michelle babbling in the background.

"Hey, Lissa. Thought I'd let you know I'm back home."

"Oh, good. Did you get the bad guy?"

"We think so. Thanks for that text, by the way. I know that conversation could have gone very differently. I appreciated the kindness."

"Don't mention it. Mom ... please don't take this the wrong way, but I'm used to it. You were always like this when I was a kid, you know? I didn't automatically think some switch was going to flip when you became a grandmother."

"Well, maybe you should have."

"Don't be too hard on yourself, Mom. Yes, I was pissed when you called at the last minute to tell me that we had to cut short our first night out in two months because you'd been called into work. But it rolled off my back—eventually."

"Thank you, Lissa."

"Of course. But listen. You have to understand that I need to start planning accordingly. Until you can *really* retire, I don't think I'm going to ask you to babysit anymore." She stopped here, perhaps waiting for some protest. Kate felt one coming, but wanted to give Melissa a chance to explain first. "We're going to look for one of those certified babysitters, you know? Our five-year anniversary is coming up in three months and we're thinking of taking two days to ourselves. And I love you, Mom ... but until the job comes second, I don't feel like I can ask you to keep Michelle."

"That hurts, but it's fair."

"Don't get me wrong. Michelle and I would love to come over and visit—a lot. I want her to know you. I really do. I keep telling her you had to bail because even in retirement, you're being a badass."

"That's a rosy way to paint it, I suppose."

"Don't sweat it, Mom. Look, how about Michelle and I come over on Saturday. We'll do lunch and I'll let you change some of these disgusting diapers."

"Sounds like a plan," Kate said. With the conversation coming to a close, the weight of it was indeed starting to sting.

She doesn't see me as reliable enough to keep my own granddaughter, she thought. *And the hell of it is that she has a good point.*

She stared out to the street, watching the pedestrian traffic and thinking about their individual lives. They'd all go home at some point today and either lift up or tear down their friends and family members. They would go home to feel loved or feel as if they weren't quite good enough.

That's every life, she thought. *The idea of being happy is probably different for each one of them. For some it rests in work; in others, friends, family, or lovers. In others, some unnamable thing.*

It was a thought that made her realize that if she was ever going to balance her life in a way that allowed her to keep her feet in the pools of the FBI while still being a reliable mother and grandmother, she was going to have to finally scrutinize that part of her own life. What was it that made her truly happy? And if it was more than one thing, what did she need to do to bring those two worlds together?

With this heavy thought on her mind, her cell phone buzzed at her. She checked it and saw that it was a text from Allen.

Are you back in town? Want to do dinner again? All the stuff that happened after dinner last time not expected. J

Kate couldn't suppress the giggle that came out of her in response to the little smiley face and the innuendo of how their last date had ended. She thought for a moment, smiled, and then sent a response.

I am home. But tired … got in late and need to catch up on sleep. How about dinner tomorrow? The only stipulation being that all the stuff that happened after dinner last night is also included.

It felt good to be back in the dating saddle, she had to admit. It had been a very long time since she had spoken to a man in such a way. It made her feel about twenty years younger.

Allen responded right away. **Jeez, twist my arm why don't you? Sounds good. See you at 6?**

She quickly returned a text to confirm the time and then headed back inside. She looked around the empty house and felt a little surge of warmth. She had a date lined up for tomorrow, lunch with Michelle and Melissa next week, and she had just come back from presumably wrapping a gruesome murder case. Life was looking pretty sweet.

Then why does something feel off?

It was a good question. And the reason it unsettled her so much was because in asking herself the question, Chester Black kept coming to mind.

What if it's not him?

And it was that question that had her sitting in her armchair, staring at the walls. She sat there for a very long time and with each second that passed, she started to wonder if she and DeMarco had left Roanoke too soon.

CHAPTER TWENTY SIX

Even though she'd told Allen their date would have to wait until tomorrow because she was so tired, Kate ended up making full use of her afternoon. As three o'clock rolled around, she walked several blocks down the street for Chinese takeout. Then, over orange chicken and cheese wontons, she pulled the case files up on her computer and took out the few printed materials she had collected while in Roanoke. She made herself a little workstation at the kitchen table and went to work, trying to alleviate the nasty feeling that Chester Black was not their man and the case was still wide open.

The thing that was really hanging her up was the blanket. And that made no sense to her. It was clear that it had meaning to the killer. It took a lot of extra effort to cram it into the throats of his victims and it was clear that he was doing it on purpose.

But the question remained: *Why?*

She thought of Chester Black again. She thought of the personality he projected and the things they had seen and experienced in his trailer. Kate was far from a psychologist but she didn't seen any outright signs from him of someone who might still be clutching to some long-lost memories of his childhood that involved a blanket.

She recalled what Danielle Ethridge had said, about how the blanket had once likely been a comfort object. And as far as Kate was concerned, Chester Black did not seem like the type to obsess over a comfort object.

The crimes Chester Black had committed, while absolutely deplorable and poorly thought out, were of what he felt was necessity—crimes that were tied into his abnormal religious beliefs. That in no way made him a killer.

But they found human blood on that towel. What about that?

That was the one roadblock in keeping Kate from thinking Chester Black was innocent. If she could get around that, she would have to face the fact that she was pretty sure she and DeMarco had left for home, leaving the wrong man in a holding cell in Roanoke.

If the blanket was a comfort object ... what does that say about the killer when he was a kid?

She dwelled on this for a moment, sensing there was something worth digging into. If the killer held onto a security blanket as a child, it likely meant that he'd been insecure. Maybe even quiet. Again, she was not a psychologist, but she had been involved with enough cases to make extremely educated guesses—which usually turned out to be right.

Yet they had spent their time looking for someone who was violent by nature. They had been looking for a child who had dealt with issues from a young age. But what if their killer had never truly seemed violent until just recently? What if their killer had been a quiet and mostly harmless kid, dragging a blanket around behind him?

She'd been digging through the files for any evidence of this for a little over an hour when her cell phone rang. She saw that it was DeMarco and answered it right away.

"All wrapped up?" Kate asked.

"On this end, yes. But I got a call during the meeting. It was Palmetto, from Roanoke."

"The human blood on the towel..."

"That really has been bothering you, huh?" DeMarco said.

"It has. Anyway ... what were the results?"

"The blood was from a woman named Abby Warren. Roanoke PD ran a search and found her alive and well. She happens to be Chester Black's girlfriend. And she admitted to the two of them engaging in some consensual blood-letting during sex."

"Cutting one another?"

"Yeah. She has the scars to prove it. Chester figured he'd be charged for something because he was the one doing the cutting, so he never said anything. But it all checks out. And based on all of this ..."

"He's free to go."

"Well, he's looking at some animal cruelty charges, but it's not looking like he's our killer."

"So what now?"

"What now is you rest up. I'll pick you up around nine in the morning tomorrow and we're heading back to Roanoke."

"We have to start with Dr. Ethridge," Kate said. "I think we've been looking for the wrong kind of killer." She then told DeMarco about her breakthrough concerning a quiet kid that, for some reason or another, had become violent more recently rather than always having an appetite for it.

"Sounds like a plan," DeMarco said. "Just … well, this isn't going to mess up any babysitting plans again, is it?"

"No. Just a date." She frowned when she thought about having to cancel on Allen again. At least this time she'd have the awareness to inform him beforehand.

"You okay heading back out there?" DeMarco asked.

Kate appreciated the respect and courtesy but once again felt that she was being handed certain privileges. She knew that if she elected not to return to Roanoke to put a bow on this case, Duran would likely not come down too hard on her. But she *wanted* to go out there, to help DeMarco find the killer before he could strike again.

"Absolutely," she said. "I'll have coffee waiting when you pick me up."

They ended the call and rather than call it a day, Kate went directly back to her case files. Maybe there was something they had missed. Maybe if she now looked at it through the lens of looking for a killer who had been quiet and introverted as a child, something new would present itself.

She wanted to be in the know, the details of the case like the lyrics to a well-worn song in her head. Because if she had her way, they were going to catch the bastard this time.

Maybe even quickly enough so that she could keep her date with Allen.

CHAPTER TWENTY SEVEN

True to her word, Kate had coffee waiting the next morning. She knew that DeMarco took it black, so she went ahead and poured some into an insulated cup. DeMarco arrived twenty minutes late but Kate was fine with that. She realized the ungodly hour DeMarco had to leave DC in order to arrive at her house so early, so she was willing to overlook the tardiness. Not that she had any authority to give her grief over it anyway.

DeMarco seemed troubled almost right away. Kate volunteered to drive, allowing DeMarco to wrestle with her thoughts. But after a while, it was just too much to bear. They were comfortable enough with one another now where silence among them was perfectly okay, but this one was thick and filled with anxiousness.

"What's on your mind?" Kate asked.

"Chester Black. I was so sure it was him."

"It was a safe assumption," Kate said. "And you know what? I felt unsure about him from the start. I should have said something."

"Yeah, but even if you had, we'd be right back here ... right where we are now. Chasing our tails and not sure where to look. All you would have saved was a night in an interrogation room for Chester Black. And let's face it—he sort of deserved it."

"Is this the first time you've been wrong about something on a case?" Kate asked.

"God no."

"And it won't be the last, either. Don't let it bother you so much."

DeMarco nodded, but still gazed out the window with a brooding look on her face. Kate understood it. She, too, was beating herself up by not fully investing in the bit of hesitation she had felt when they left

Roanoke. But she had also experienced this enough in her career to know that it was useless to ponder on it and keep looking back. If they obsessed over things that happened in the past, that gave the killer an edge in the present.

And this killer already seemed to have more than enough of an edge.

Dr. Ethridge appeared a little rushed when Kate and DeMarco showed up at her office at 1:40. She had been expecting them, as DeMarco had called on their way down to Roanoke to keep her abreast of what was happening. But there was a sense of urgency to the doctor now, as if she too could feel the absolute intensity and importance of the situation.

"I've blocked off the next two hours in my schedule to help any way I can," Ethridge said. "I've looked through all of my records over the past fifteen years and pulled any file that seemed like it would be a match. Unfortunately, there's quite a bit."

She pointed to a pile of folders on her desk. It sat about a foot and a half tall. It was certainly quite a bit of material to sift through, but not as bad as Kate had been expecting. "That doesn't look too bad," she commented.

"Oh, this is only the physical records," she said. "This is everything from 2003 back. Everything from 2004 to current day is saved digitally on the server. There's this physical pile and then about thirty more on the server."

"Will you allow us access to the server?" DeMarco asked.

"Normally, I'd put up a fight. But this situation is getting out of hand."

"Thank you," Kate said. "Agent DeMarco, would you like to take the digital files while I go through the folders?"

"That works."

"Dr. Ethridge, I'd like to have you on hand to answer any questions that might arise."

"Of course. Now, these files that I have pulled—as well as the digital ones I have already flagged for you—are based on the profile you gave me. A kid who was very quiet and introverted. The type that might seek comfort from something like a blanket or a stuffed animal."

"That's correct," Kate said.

"It's worth noting that most children that fit that profile are going to be the type who would respond more to a mother-figure rather than a father-figure. Because of that, I pulled files with patients with that characteristic as well."

"Incredible work," DeMarco said. "Now, is there a computer I can work from?"

"Yes, you can use my personal laptop," Ethridge said. She went to her desk, opened it up, and logged DeMarco in.

The next half an hour felt very much like an intense study session to Kate. It reminded her of her earlier days with the bureau when she had often been stuck with painstaking research assignments. Even back then, though, she'd been seen as an excellent profiler. It was one of the reasons it was bothering her so badly that she could not easily pin down the killer in this case. Even as she went through Ethridge's files and started ruling patients out based on the date of service, she knew full well that the answer may not be here.

She fished through the folders as DeMarco clicked through the files on Ethridge's laptop. Most of the files contained at least one Polaroid picture of the patient. Many of them looked into the camera without much of an expression, though some had bright smiles on their faces. She nearly asked Ethridge why she kept these pictures but remembered somewhere along the way in her profiler training that psychologists often used this technique to show their patients how an expression could speak volumes. It was a great conversation starter. *Why do you feel this way today? The little boy in this picture doesn't look very happy, does he?*

Kate also noticed that in a few of the thicker folders, Ethridge had kept drawings that the children had made. Some were quite pretty in a childlike way—perfectly square houses with triangular roofs with big fluffy clouds and bright suns in the skies. But there were some that were clear cries for help: stick-figure kids with frowning faces, crimson pools around little feet, hard red and black lines everywhere.

"Do you have every child draw something for you?" Kate asked.

"Most of the time," Ethridge answered. "It really all depends on the level of trauma they are dealing with. Simple little drawings are a great way for me to really get a quick judge of their emotional state. It gives me topics to start from without having to guess."

"How often do you get ones like this?" Kate asked. She held up a picture of a little girl in pigtails. Behind her, a little dog had been drawn upside down. Something was on fire behind all of it. The little girl's mouth was a big black O and tears were coming out of her eyes in big exaggerated drops.

"About half the time."

"Is there any correlation between these types of drawings and the kind of kid we're looking for in all these files?"

"Sometimes. The kids that are quiet and reserved tend to draw somber pictures, but nothing violent. Of course, that's not *always* the case. While the diagnoses can be the same, there are no two kids that are one hundred percent alike in how they handle their emotions. So one introverted child might draw rain clouds or big storm clouds with lightning while another might draw a man with a knife or a dead animal. There's no right-down-the-middle with this sort of thing."

Kate nodded, putting the drawing back with a little chill creeping down her spine. DeMarco then called Ethridge over to the computer with a question. As the two of them chatted, Kate continued to go through the folders. She saw ruined childhood after ruined childhood and she started to get sentimental. Any one of these kids could be Melissa. No kid was guaranteed a safe childhood. No child could be promised a healthy and happy life.

This stark realization came to a grinding halt when Kate opened the next folder in the pile. Like a few others, the child's Polaroid was up front, paper-clipped to the primary summary file. It was a picture of a boy giving a very thin smile that was clearly being forced. Kate guessed him to be about eight years old. Maybe nine at most.

She skimmed the file but when she realized it was quite thick, she looked up at Dr. Ethridge. "What can you tell me about this patient?" she asked.

Ethridge came over and looked at the file. She fingered the Polaroid in a loving sort of way and frowned. "That's Jeremy Neely. I saw him for about three years."

"Was he an orphan?"

"He was bounced around a few foster homes in his youth, yes. Poor kid … he was seven years old when he watched his father kill his mother. He hit her in the head with a bat right in front of Jeremy. He walked around his dead mother's body for almost an entire day before anyone knew what had happened."

"My God," Kate said.

DeMarco had taken interest now as well. She was looking up from her laptop, sensing that something might be taking shape. Kate waved her over to join her, feeling that this was finally the break they had been looking for.

"Dr. Ethridge, can you get me the list of foster families he stayed with?"

"I don't have the complete list. You'd have to contact Social Services to get the entire list."

"You have the appropriate clearance to get it, right?"

"I do," Ethridge said slowly. She grabbed her cell phone from her desk as understanding started to bloom in her eyes. She turned her back to the agents and placed the call.

Kate nodded, expecting as much. She then pointed to the picture of Jeremy Neely, making sure DeMarco was seeing the one peculiar thing she had seen.

"Look familiar?" Kate asked.

"Oh my God," DeMarco said. "This is him, isn't it?"

Kate didn't have to answer.

In the picture, little Jeremy Neely held something in his right hand. He clutched it tightly to his side in a tight fist.

A blanket. A blanket with a pattern that Kate and DeMarco had gotten to know quite well.

Ethridge joined them again. There was an annoyed look of panic in her eyes. "They're going to call me back. That's considered private information and even in a situation like this, it has to be cleared. If he was wrapped up in a special-needs domestic abuse or criminal case of any kind, that might be why his name wasn't on the original list of kids— if, that is, he stayed with Ms. Knight, the Nashes, and the Langleys. I pushed hard, though. What would usually take a day or so to get, we should have in a few hours."

"Are you kidding me?" DeMarco said.

"It's a trade-off," Ethridge said. "On the one hand, it's amazing that the government is so dedicated to protecting such information. But on the other hand, they don't bend their rules for much of anything."

"You said you have a partial list, right?" Kate asked.

"Yes, it should be there in the files…"

Ethridge reached in over Kate's shoulder and flipped through the pages. She stopped six pages in and pointed to a section near the bottom. "Right there. It shows where there was a transfer from the Langleys to a group home. But that's all I have. That must have been his first foster home."

The Langleys, Kate thought.

It was more than enough to directly tie the Nashes and Monica Knight.

"If we haven't heard from DSS by the end of the day, I'll get our director to give them a call," Kate said. "As for now, we have a name and that's more than enough. Let's find out where Jeremy Neely lives and pay him a visit."

CHAPTER TWENTY EIGHT

He sat on a large rock, just along the tree line. He stared at the house intently, but patient. He supposed if someone stood on the back porch and stared out in his direction, there was a slight chance that he'd be seen. But he knew their routines well. The only time they ever went out onto the back porch was for their morning coffee and when they grilled something for dinner.

But he knew they were not grilling tonight. In fact, they weren't even home. They'd left two hours ago. He'd barely heard their voices as they'd made their way to the car, arguing between Mexican or Thai for dinner.

Since then, he'd been waiting. He'd sat on the rock, motionless. He was rooted there by the anticipation of what would be happening later. He knew he had a few hours left to wait but that was fine with him. He'd waited nearly twelve years so far … so what was four or five more hours?

This wasn't the first time he'd sat on this rock, watching the house. He'd been here countless times before, watching and learning the ways of their lives.

The Colemans. Harry and Ruth. He had lived under their roof—the very roof he was currently staring at—for about five months at one time. They had been nice enough but, in the end, had not been able to keep him. He supposed he had been too much for them, too much of a hassle for their pretentious well-to-do lives. They'd had busy lives both in and out of the house. When he had come along, though, all of that had changed for them. Their weekend tennis matches: gone. Their Wednesday nights out with friends: also gone.

His eyes traveled from window to window. The one on the right on the second floor was their bedroom. He knew this because one night, they had neglected to shut the blinds as they had readied for bed. He had seen Ruth Coleman's naked body standing right in front of the window for about ten seconds before she had been alert enough to close the blinds. There had been about fifty yards between them but he'd still been able to make out her shape, her curves, the smallish globes of her breasts.

For a woman pushing fifty, it had been quite nice. It was not the first time he had thought of Ruth in a sexual way. There had been one night, when he had lived with them—he had been about ten years old or so at the time—when he had stirred awake from a bad dream. He'd walked down the hall to their room to ask if he could sleep there but had stopped in the doorway when he saw the movement in the bed. Ruth had been sitting up on her knees with Harry beneath her. She'd been making noises that had sounded as if she was in pain but as they moved faster together, he realized that they were sounds of pleasure.

He had watched from the doorway, the door open about a quarter of the way, until they had finished.

He'd held on to that memory, often revisiting it whenever he'd felt the darkness invading his mind. It had almost been enough to make him change his mind about what he had to do.

His thoughts of Ruth's naked body were broken up by the sound of an approaching car. He looked to the driveway and saw their Chrysler rolling in. They parked and got out, laughing. Harry waited for Ruth at the front of the car and took her hand. They walked into the house, giggling.

In the woods, he smiled. Maybe they'd had a few drinks with dinner, maybe just enough to be giddy and horny. Maybe they'd make love sometime in the coming hour or so. He hoped so. Maybe he'd find some way to sneak to a window and watch. Also, if they had been drinking, they'd be good and tired, depleted and conked out by the time he walked out of the tree line and up to their house.

He'd enter through the back door. He knew where the spare key was. He'd spent two hours looking for it one afternoon when he knew they had left for a weekend trip to see Harry's brother in Charlotte, North Carolina. It was in the backyard, underneath one of the boards that served as the border of Ruth's tiny herb garden.

He wanted to go now. He wanted to sneak in and maybe catch them in the act. He had never had sex and had never seen the appeal of it. But all the same, seeing Ruth's body at the window that night had reminded him of his urges. He thought the act itself had to be gross but then again...

No. He had to wait. He knew that. He'd waited this long. No sense in screwing it all up now. He had to wait until it was dark.

As if to tide himself over, he looked into the little rucksack he had set on the ground next to the rock. It had little spatters of dried blood on it. He wasn't sure who it belonged to. Honestly, the last two weeks had been a bloody blur.

He reached into the sack and stroked the handle of the knife.

He took out the scrap of old blanket and nuzzled it to his cheek. There was something reassuring about the feel of it, something that told him that everything was going to be okay.

Fully believing that, he placed the scrap back into the sack and waited.

CHAPTER TWENTY NINE

The address Kate had gotten for Jeremy Neely was just on the out-skirts of Roanoke, in a tiny little town called Deerborne. The drive itself only took about twenty minutes but because they had spent several hours in Dr. Ethridge's office, it was closing in on 5:30 when Kate and DeMarco pulled up in front of Jeremy Neely's home.

The house was an older two-story house. It was in a low-income neighborhood, the streets uncared for and the lawns mostly dead and gray. An air conditioner unit stuck out of one of the side windows like a rotten tooth about to fall out. It was running, making an awful racket as it leaked a trail of water down the side of the house.

They walked up the concrete stairs and onto the porch. As Kate neared the door, her right hand hovered over the handle of her Glock. She knocked with her left hand. Beside her, DeMarco had locked her legs, ready to spring if necessary.

After ten seconds, no one had answered the door. Kate knocked again, this time saying, "Mr. Neely? Are you home?"

"No car along the street," DeMarco pointed out.

Kate had noticed this as well. She looked up and down the street, weighing their options. They had more than enough reason to believe that Jeremy Neely was their killer. And this had been confirmed as his address. Under any normal circumstances, she might just wait in the car until Neely arrived home. But they were working against a clock here, with no idea whether or not Neely intended to kill again.

"Agent DeMarco, my knees aren't quite what they used to be. Would you mind ...?"

DeMarco looked both surprised and honored to have been asked. She drew her Glock, took a step back, and then delivered a hard kick to the door. It sprung open, taking a small portion of the frame with it.

They entered the house in perfect step with one another. Kate took the lead with DeMarco close behind. They stepped quietly, allowing each other to hear the silence of the place. Within a few seconds, Kate felt certain that they were alone; Neely was not here.

Still, they investigated the house with caution, guns at the ready. The living room was sparsely furnished and meticulously cleaned. It offered no clues of any kind. The kitchen was equally useless, revealing nothing more than the fact that Neely needed to do his dishes.

Being that they felt as if every moment wasted was a potentially deadly one for Neely's next target, they skipped everything else in the house and headed directly for the bedroom. Nine times out of ten, that's where clues about any case or suspect were found.

Like the living room, Neely's bedroom was mostly clean and without much furniture or belongings. A queen-sized bed sat along the center of the far wall and a small desk sat beside the bed. Other than an old dresser, that was all there was. Kate checked the closet and found nothing but a few hanging shirts and an empty Amazon box.

When she turned away from the closet, she saw DeMarco crouched on the floor. She was looking under the bed. Apparently, she had found something because she started to reach under it.

"What have you got?" Kate asked.

"A shoebox."

"Careful..."

DeMarco pulled the box out from under the bed. It was unremarkable, identical to just about every other shoebox that had ever been slid under a bed. Kate had done this for her entire life, keeping toys and love letters in it as a girl, and bills and checks as an adult.

They shared an uneasy look as DeMarco opened up the box.

There was only one thing inside.

"Holy shit," Kate breathed.

It an old blanket—a blanket that had clearly been torn from along the sides.

The pattern and fabric was identical to what had been pulled from the throats of the victims. It was also the exact same as the blanket that had been held by Jeremy Neely in the photograph in Ethridge's files.

"Call Duran," Kate said. "We need him to bully whoever the hell is in charge of standing on that foster care information and we need him to do it *now*."

DeMarco pulled her phone from her pocket and did just that. Kate, meanwhile, checked under the bed for anything else but there was nothing to be found.

But the blanket was enough. They had their man now. The only question, of course, was where the hell was he?

You know where he is, she told herself. *He's out targeting his next victim ... some other family that tried to help him at some point in their lives and now are being rewarded by being killed.*

On the phone, DeMarco was getting loud with Director Duran's receptionist. "This is an emergency ... one he will slaughter you for if you don't get him right now. I don't care *who* he is meeting with!"

That apparently did the trick, as DeMarco was put on hold. She was fuming, pacing around the room in order to do *something* with the pent-up excitement that was rocketing through her body.

Kate felt it, too. The excitement of knowing you were about to break a case ... that the endgame was on the horizon.

And knowing that just one phone call separated them from not only apprehending the killer but also potentially saving two lives made it a maddening experience.

She looked back to that tattered blanket as a feeling of dread started to spread through her. Mingled with the excitement, it almost made her feel lightheaded. But the blanket actually helped to ease her mind, to steady her focus.

We've got him, she thought. *We know his name, we know where he lives ... we just need to know what other families cared for him as a kid.*

All they could do was wait.

And hope that while they waited, two more people weren't being killed.

Kate and DeMarco remained in Neely's house while waiting for the call from Duran. Every minute that passed was excruciating. They both paced the floors, remaining mostly in the bedroom. Kate racked her brain for any other ways to find out who else might have kept Jeremy Neely but could come up with nothing.

"I just don't understand how so many families kept him and no one saw this coming," DeMarco said. "You'd think a murder spree like this one might have been prevented if someone had maybe just paid more attention to the way he acted as a kid."

"You heard Ethridge," Kate said. "No two kids are ever one hundred percent the same. For all we know, Jeremy Neely never showed any signs of doing anything like this."

It reminded Kate of the old adage: It's the quiet ones you need to watch.

Of course, in this scenario, that was absolutely correct.

When Kate's phone rang, both agents went absolutely still for a moment. It had the same effect as a gunshot from the next room. Kate answered it with a jolt of adrenaline blasting through her body.

"This is Agent Wise."

"Wise, it's Duran. I got the list of families. You ready?"

"Shoot."

"In order of appearance, we've got the Langleys, the Nashes, a single woman named Monica Knight, the Colemans, and the Vaughns. But he was only with the Vaughns for two days. He stayed with the Colemans for about five months."

"You got names for the Colemans?" Kate asked.

"And an address. 174 Angler Drive, Moneta, Virginia."

Shit, she thought. *Not local.*

Kate covered the mouthpiece on her phone and looked at DeMarco. "Plug Moneta into your GPS and see how far away it is."

DeMarco did as she was asked. Kate turned her attention back to Duran and asked: "Is that all? No other families?"

"That's it. You think the Colemans are next?" Duran asked.

"It's an incredibly good chance."

DeMarco showed Kate her phone. She had typed Moneta into her map app search bar. It was apparently a little lakeside town about thirty minutes away.

"Moneta is about half an hour away from us," Kate said. "We're headed there now."

"Perfect. Good luck, Wise."

With a nod of understanding between them, Kate and DeMarco sprinted out of the bedroom, through the house, and back outside. As she got behind the wheel, she heard DeMarco on her phone as she got into the passenger seat.

"Palmetto, it's Agent DeMarco. I need you and a few officers to get over to Moneta as soon as possible. Agent Wise and I are headed there now with a strong suspicion that our killer's next target is there."

Kate pulled out into the road and sped forward while DeMarco filled Palmetto in. Dusk was slowly settling down, the horizon holding most of the day's remaining light. When she came to the end of the street, she took a hard right, the back end of the car fishtailing. She felt like she was racing a clock and as far as she was concerned, her time would run out when night fell.

But with a killer so close to her grasp, she'd be damned if she'd let that happen.

CHAPTER THIRTY

Had she not been in a rush to potentially stop a killer, Kate thought she might have enjoyed the quaint and scenic little town of Moneta. It sat alongside Smith Mountain Lake, a lake cupped almost perfectly within the Blue Ridge Mountains. The fact that the sun had pretty much set behind the mountains added a whole new tone of beauty to the place.

As she passed by the central intersection of the town, Kate spotted the two police cruisers in the gas station parking lot to her right. Palmetto had called ahead to Moneta PD and asked for two units to be available for backup while the State PD hurried along. Kate flashed her lights at them as she passed through the intersection and they fell in behind her.

Angler Drive was located within a small subdivision that was separated from the lake by only a thin strip of woodland that grew in size and spread out the closer it got to the mountains. As they crept closer and closer to the Coleman residence, Kate decided on the best approach in her mind. She figured that if Jeremy Neely was indeed there or on the way, there was no sense in scaring him away with blazing sirens and police cars pulling into the driveway. Given that, she elected to park her car along the side of the road just out of eyesight of the Colemans' paved driveway. Behind her, the police cruisers did the same.

When she got out of the car and met one of the officers from the first car as he got out, she realized just how dark it had gotten. She could still see without the aid of a flashlight, but that wouldn't last much longer.

"Thanks for the assist," Kate said. "Agent DeMarco and I will go to the door. If everything is fine and good, that'll be the end of it. We'll inform them of the situation and then ask you to stay here until State PD arrives. You guys can work out the surveillance among yourselves. But if we get in there and find out that we were too late, we'll call for backup."

"Officer Palmetto said this guy has killed five people," the cop said. "Is that true?"

Kate nodded, but thought: *Let's pray it's only five ... and not seven.*

They made their way down the paved drive in a quick walk. They did not want to appear too rushed, nor did they want to seem too casual. As they closed in on the house, Kate noted that a light was on downstairs, shining through the largest window along the front of the house as well as one on the side. Probably the living room. Another one was on upstairs.

There's one good sign, at least, Kate thought.

They ascended the stairs at that same pace but took a moment to collect themselves before Kate knocked on the door. She raised her hand to do just that but was stopped by a noise from somewhere inside.

It was a scream. A man's scream.

Kate tried the front door and found it locked. This door was locked by an electrical lock with a numerical pin—one of the fancier models she'd seen. It was not going to be as easy as knocking the door down at Jeremy Neely's house. Still, DeMarco gave it a try. Her foot slammed into the door and it trembled quite a bit, but it did not pop open.

So much for the element of surprise, Kate thought.

As she leveled her Glock at the lock, another of those screams sounded out. This one was followed by a second sound, more like a low moan, and this one from the throat of a woman.

Turning her head away from the door, she fired off a single round that tore through the lock and the door itself. DeMarco immediately threw another kick, this one blasting the door open.

They entered the house through a small foyer that opened up into the kitchen. And it was right there, in the space between the kitchen and the opening to the living room, that Jeremy Neely was crouched on the floor. In one hand, he held a knife. In the other, he gripped the neck of the man who was pinned under his knees. The man lay beneath him, struggling to get free, but there were a series of cuts on his arms that had weakened him. Already, a pool of blood had started to form on the floor.

A woman lay on the floor as well. She was on her side, blood everywhere, trying to get up but unable to do so.

It took Kate about two second to see all of this and by the time she had taken it all in, DeMarco had sprung to action. Kate was amazed by how fast the woman was. She took two huge strides forward and was then in a crouched position, like an NFL lineman prepared to bowl over the opposition.

DeMarco threw herself at Neely, her aim spot on. Her shoulder checked his chest and they both went to the floor in a heap. However, as they fell, DeMarco's left arm jammed down on Neely's knife. Kate saw it happen and she rushed forward, grimacing and hoping that the blade hadn't nicked any arteries.

Neely took advantage of DeMarco's shock and kicked her away. He then raised the knife to plunge it down through DeMarco's chest, but Kate reached him just in time. She drew her knee up hard, connecting with the underside of Neely's jaw. He rocked back, nearly falling over but catching himself on the edge of the kitchen bar.

He started to surge forward again but Kate had locked her knees into place and stood in a perfect shooter's stance less than three feet from him.

"Move and I'll take out your knees," she said.

Neely seemed to think about it for a moment. In the seconds that hung in the air, Kate desperately wanted to take stock of the situation. She was afraid the woman—apparently Mrs. Coleman—would be dead in a handful of moments. She also had no idea how badly DeMarco was injured. She saw DeMarco getting to her feet out of the corner of her eye. Even without taking her eyes away from Neely, she could tell that DeMarco was holding her cut arm close to her body.

"Drop the knife, Jeremy," Kate said. "We know what you did to the other families. Anything you do from this point on is just going to make it worse for you."

He smiled, as if this was great news. And then he swung the knife around in a flash, aimed directly for DeMarco.

Kate lowered her aim and pulled the trigger. The shot took Neely directly above the knee. His leg crumpled as he went to the floor. DeMarco wasted no time in throwing her full weight into his back.

As Kate dropped to her knees to pull his arms back and handcuff him, the policemen who had been waiting at the top of the driveway came rushing through the door with their guns drawn. Kate assumed they'd been alerted by the first gunshot when she'd blasted through the lock.

It couldn't have taken them more than twenty seconds to run down here, Kate thought. *Is that really all the time that passed between now and then?*

"I'm good here for now," Kate said, snapping the cuffs closed. "Get an ambulance out here. We've got a woman in what looked like critical condition, and a wounded FBI agent."

Kate looked at DeMarco to gauge her situation but saw that the younger agent was kneeling down by Mrs. Coleman. Meanwhile, Mr. Coleman was looking around as if in shock. Kate didn't think he had been cut badly enough to the point where his life was in danger, but the ordeal had certainly unglued him.

"Why?"

The question came from the floor, from the mouth of Jeremy Neely.

"Excuse me?" Kate said.

"Why? Why did they not love me?"

For reasons she could not even start to understand, a wave of pity washed through her. She had to turn away from Neely. Instead, she focused on DeMarco. Her left arm was bleeding heavily, the wound located on the backside of her upper arm.

"We need to stop the bleeding," DeMarco said.

"I will," she said. "But we need to help her first."

Mrs. Coleman's eyes were open but they seemed to be looking some-where very far away, some place on the other side of the ceiling. There was blood everywhere—splashed along her cheeks, covering her chest, on the floor.

"Ruth..."

Her husband was starting to come around. Kate tried to turn her attention to him, to break his focus before he saw the state his wife was in.

As it turned out, she was about half a second too late. Mr. Coleman saw his wife and something inside of him broke. It was a haunting sound that tore through the house even as Kate, DeMarco, and the local officer did what they could to stop Ruth Coleman's bleeding.

The husband's screams were piercing and filled with torment. They filled the house and Kate's head until the sound of approaching sirens and the wails of ambulances drowned him out five minutes later.

CHAPTER THIRTY ONE

Kate sat in the little sterile hospital examination room with DeMarco, looking at her phone. It was 8:55 and she was staring at a blank text screen with Allen's name above it. She had been thinking of what to say for the last minute or so and finally decided on: **So I'm terrible. Work called again. Same case. But we wrapped it. That means no dinner. I'm so sorry.**

She sent it and then looked at DeMarco. She was sitting on the very edge of the little examination bed. There was a gauze wrapping around her left arm where she had been cut. She hadn't lost too much blood and although the wound had been rather deep, it had been easily fixed with sixteen stitches.

"Was that to your daughter?" DeMarco asked.

"No. Boyfriend."

DeMarco nodded with a frown. "It's been rough on you, huh? Trying to balance all of this."

"Yeah. But I'm getting the hang of it. I just have to stop disappointing those around me who live normal lives. And I... wait. Hold on. You're the one that got stabbed in the arm. What the hell are you doing worrying about me?"

DeMarco shrugged and looked at the floor. "My mom used to tell me stories when I was young about how she almost didn't go the family route. She was playing guitar and singing in this band that nearly made it. She told me how she always admired Stevie Nicks... you know, the singer from Fleetwood Mac?"

"Yes, I know who she is."

"Well, my mom looked to Stevie on how to act, how to play the role of a female lead in a band. And oh my God, this is going to come out way cheesier than I intended but...you're my Stevie Nicks, Kate. The moment I made it as an agent back in the Violent Crimes Unit, I started researching your older cases, learning from you and digging through your files. So yes...I am going to worry about you. The fact that you came back out of retirement to do things like we did tonight floors me."

"Thanks for that," Kate said, feeling tears welling up.

If only Melissa thought of me in that same way.

Her phone buzzed in her hand. She looked down and saw that Allen had returned her text. **I understand. Raincheck. Call me when you get in.**

She was relieved that he had taken it so well but she also felt like she was taking advantage of him. She thought about texting Melissa to fill her in but decided against it. Melissa didn't even know she had been called back out to Roanoke anyway. Thinking of them both so closely together, it then occurred to Kate that Melissa didn't even know about Allen.

It can't be a good thing that DeMarco already knows more about my personal life than my own daughter does, Kate thought.

Still slightly reeling from DeMarco's comments, Kate tried to think of something equally sentimental to tell DeMarco, but was interrupted by a knock at the door. After a second or two, it opened and Palmetto walked in.

"How's it going?" he asked.

"DeMarco is a hero," Kate said, using that as her return compliment.

"Sixteen stitches does not make me a hero," DeMarco argued. "Although it does add a scar and scars are sort of badass."

"I'm just glad it wasn't worse. You truly did save the day, Agent DeMarco. So thanks for that."

"Anyway, I just wanted to drop by and fill you guys in," Palmetto said. "Neely confessed to all of it. He's blaming it on everyone's inability to love him as a child. When they searched him, they found a scrap of the blanket in his back pocket. He openly admitted that it had been intended to go down Ruth Coleman's throat. He said he got the idea from watching his dad kill his mom so easily, like it was nothing. First reactions from the cops are that he's likely going to go for an insanity plea."

"You think he'll get it?" Kate asked.

"Beats me."

"Why the blanket, though?" DeMarco asked.

"That's where more of the crazy comes in. He says it was the only thing he had as a kid that made him feel safe and comfortable. But as he got older and saw how these people who were supposed to love him didn't love him the way he thought they should, the blanket started to take on this whole new meaning. He hated it. Wanted to use something he had once thought of as safe to aid in the murders."

"That's terrible," DeMarco said.

"As for Ruth Coleman, she lost a lot of blood and there were two major arteries that were nicked. One stab wound missed her heart by less than an inch. She also has a punctured lung. She's listed as being in critical condition, but I spoke with the doctor that oversaw her when she came in. It may not be as hopeless as her appearance makes it seem."

"That's fantastic news," Kate said.

"It is," Palmetto agreed. He then looked at DeMarco and said: "Do you mind if I steal Agent Wise away for a second?"

"Not a problem," DeMarco said.

Palmetto opened the door and led Kate out into the hall. He started walking slowly forward and had a thoughtful look on his face.

"What is it?" Kate asked. "Is everything okay?"

"Yes, the case is basically wrapped thanks to you two. But I had something else ... something I needed to ask you. I know you're from out of DC and all but I figured it couldn't hurt to ask if you wanted to try to grab dinner or something before you headed back."

It was totally unexpected and she supposed the look on her face said as much. Palmetto's look of thoughtfulness turned to one of apology as she looked for the right words to use.

"Sorry," Palmetto said. "I noticed there's no ring on your finger. I thought it would be okay to ask."

"Oh, it is. And I'm flattered but I'm seeing someone back home. And honestly, between you and I, even if I wasn't, I don't know that I would. My life is sort of a mess right now. There's a balance I need to find and..."

"What?"

"Nothing," she said with a chuckle. "I nearly just dumped a whole lot of complaining on you."

"That would have been okay."

"As for the dinner, I'll have to decline. But seriously... thanks for asking. Sometimes that's all a woman needs to feel worthwhile."

"You're pretty incredible, Agent Wise. I don't see you as having issues with feeling like you're worthy."

If she didn't have Allen back at home waiting for her, she would have kissed him right there and then. Not out of an attraction or strong desire but because those were pretty close to the exact words she'd needed to hear ever since pulling herself out of the dark period she'd lived through after her husband, Michael, had been killed.

"Thank you," Kate said. "For the comments and your help on the case."

He nodded, understanding that her comment had ended the talk of relationships and placed them back on official business. "It was a pleasure meeting you, Agent Wise. DeMarco, too. Be safe getting back home."

With that, he continued down the hallway. Kate watched him go for a while before heading back to DeMarco. When she returned to the room, the nurse had returned and was handing DeMarco the outpatient paperwork.

"What did Palmetto want?" DeMarco asked, looking up from the forms.

"Nothing."

"Everything good?"

Kate smiled. She looked at DeMarco's arm. She thought of Melissa, Michelle, and Allen back at home. She thought of the Colemans, both together and alive elsewhere within this very same hospital.

"Yeah," Kate said with a genuine smile. "Everything is good."

⚜   ⚜   ⚜

After they left the hospital, Director Duran had called to touch based and requested that Kate come back to DC for a brief meeting. She had been looking forward to getting back to Allen as soon as she could but agreed to make the trip. That was how she ended up taking the elevator up to Duran's office on Monday afternoon. Part of her was very nervous, wondering if perhaps she had crossed some lines or had overstepped her bounds in catching Jeremy Neely.

Could be some sort of a complaint or grievance that was filed against me during this last case, she thought. Then, behind that thought came another: *Where is all of this negativity coming from? You never questioned yourself this much before you retired...*

"Agent Wise, welcome back. I'm glad you and Agent DeMarco made it back relatively unscathed. Have you spoken to DeMarco today?"

"I have. She thinks it's ridiculous that she's having to stay at home for a week because of a nick on her arm."

Duran smiled. "You know, Agent DeMarco reminds me of another agent that I know rather well."

"She's much smarter and braver than me," Kate said.

"So you like her as an agent?"

"I do. If I didn't know the situation and you told me she'd only been with the bureau for a little over two years, I wouldn't believe you."

Duran tapped his fingers anxiously on the folder in front of him and slid it over to Kate. "Take a look at this and let me know what you think."

She took the folder and opened it up; there were only two pages inside. And within five seconds of skimming the top one, she understood what she was looking at. She looked up at Duran, making sure he wasn't playing a joke on her.

"Reinstatement?" she asked.

"It's the closest we could come up with based on the fact that you retired. You did not quit and you were not fired. But we also wouldn't be hiring you as a new employee. So yes... consider this the bureau's official request that you come back as a full-time agent. And based on what you've told me today, I'd like to enlist Agent DeMarco as your full-time partner."

Kate looked the forms over and was filled with the same emotions she'd felt when Palmetto had so generously complimented her in the hospital hallway. It made her feel valued. It made her feel wanted.

But she knew she couldn't. Could she?

"I can't move back to DC," she said. "I'm in Richmond for the long haul. My family is there ... a new granddaughter and everything."

"We can work around that," he said. "It's not just me, Agent Wise. Even those above me think you're still a valuable asset. I know lots of agents retire and come back to help with research and teaching. And while you'd be great at that, your skills would also be going to waste. I felt it when I was there at the meeting last week where you guided those younger agents towards an answer in the child abduction case—an answer, I might add, that led to an arrest this morning."

She sighed and closed the folder. "Can you give me some time to think it over?"

"Absolutely. Take your time. And again, I truly do appreciate the work you've put in for these last two cases."

"Thanks."

"That's all for now," Duran said. "Sorry to make you come back to DC for this brief meeting."

"It's okay," she said, gripping the edges of the folder. "It was worth it."

CHAPTER THIRTY TWO

It was the first time she'd made pesto from scratch and Kate did not mind saying that it was damned good. She poured it from her pot into a ceramic bowl and placed it on the table by the salad. The entire house smelled of baked ziti and garlic bread. Her back door was open, the screen door allowing a breeze inside. As she stood at the table, making sure she had not missed a beat, the breeze that came through froze her for a moment.

I'm happy here, too, she thought.

She smiled and went to the wine rack in the kitchen. She plucked one bottle of white and one bottle of red from the rack. She set them down on the table just as someone knocked on her front door.

"Come in!" she called.

The door opened and Allen came walking through. He was carrying a small plastic bag and a six-pack of beer. He hefted it up and shrugged. "I didn't know if this was a wine sort of thing or a beer sort of thing."

"Both is fine," Kate said.

She met him at the door, took the plastic bag, and gave him a kiss on the lips. It was a quick one, but Allen took her by the arm with his now-free hand and pulled her back to him. He kissed her again, this time lingering. When they pulled apart, Kate found herself pleasantly dizzy.

"Honestly," Allen said, "I brought the beer for me. I figure if the conversation gets awkward, I can sneak off, chug two of them, and come back in a much looser mood."

"I don't think that will be necessary," she said and then gave a little smirk. "You're meeting my daughter and granddaughter ... not my parents."

"That's true, I guess. Still..."

"Why don't you go ahead and start on one now and we'll see how it goes."

"Yes ma'am," he said, taking one of the beers out and popping the top off. "Anything I can do for you?"

"Wine glasses. In the cupboard."

Allen set about helping her, getting the glasses and then taking the cupcakes out of the plastic bag he had brought. He'd gotten them because Kate had told him that Melissa had a soft spot for cupcakes.

"You going to tell her about the offer your director gave you?" Allen asked.

"I think I am," Kate said as she took the ziti out of the oven. "She'll be fine with it. I want to tell her and her husband about it so we can all work together and find out some way that I can balance it all."

Before Allen could respond, there was another knock at the door. This time, it opened without Kate answering. Melissa and Terry stepped inside, Terry carrying Michelle on his shoulder. He took two steps in and his eyes grew wide.

"Man oh man, it smells delicious in here!"

Kate walked over to relieve Terry of Michelle. The baby went to her without any fuss, giving a little smile of recognition. When Kate offered Michelle her finger, the baby took it and gave a little squeeze.

"Sorry," Melissa said as she approached Allen. "My mother sees Michelle and the world just fades out. I'm Melissa."

Allen extended his hand and they shook. "I'm Allen. I've heard a lot about you *and* Michelle, so it's finally nice to meet you."

Terry was next, shaking hands with Allen. Allen offered Terry a beer, which Terry accepted, and that was just about all it took for the two of them to break the ice.

Kate walked back into the kitchen with her granddaughter in her arms. Melissa and Terry were asking Allen several questions, none of which were too pressing or private. Kate joined in as Michelle started swatting at her chin with her chubby little hands.

"You guys ready to eat?" she asked.

"It looks amazing, Mom," Melissa said. "Thanks."

As they all took their seats, Allen passed by her and planted a quick kiss on her cheek. It felt natural. It felt nice and comfortable. She saw that Melissa had seen this and was smiling at her.

Yeah, this is worth keeping, she thought. *This is worth fighting for balance.*

The truth of the matter was that her job fulfilled something within her that her family did not. It seemed like an ugly truth, but it was still the truth. But it had taken her this long, after losing a husband and continuously straining her relationship with Melissa, to understand that the opposite was also true.

Her family offered something that her job never could. Love, support, and a sense of home that came with no goals or expectations.

Kate fully grasped that now. And she knew that she could learn to balance it all.

And with that balance, perhaps she could even be a better agent.

Of course she was going to take Duran up on his offer. She could deny it all she wanted, but she was an FBI agent to her core—and would be until she was a bedridden old lady.

As far as Kate Wise was concerned, she was no longer going to look back on her career with nostalgia and longing.

She had not put it all behind her after all.

IF SHE RAN

(a kate wise mystery—book 3)

BLAKE PIERCE

ONCE STALKED (Book #9)
ONCE LOST (Book #10)
ONCE BURIED (Book #11)
ONCE BOUND (Book #12)
ONCE TRAPPED (Book #13)
ONCE DORMANT (book #14)
ONCE SHUNNED (Book #15)

MACKENZIE WHITE MYSTERY SERIES
BEFORE HE KILLS (Book #1)
BEFORE HE SEES (Book #2)
BEFORE HE COVETS (Book #3)
BEFORE HE TAKES (Book #4)
BEFORE HE NEEDS (Book #5)
BEFORE HE FEELS (Book #6)
BEFORE HE SINS (Book #7)
BEFORE HE HUNTS (Book #8)
BEFORE HE PREYS (Book #9)
BEFORE HE LONGS (Book #10)
BEFORE HE LAPSES (Book #11)

AVERY BLACK MYSTERY SERIES
CAUSE TO KILL (Book #1)
CAUSE TO RUN (Book #2)
CAUSE TO HIDE (Book #3)
CAUSE TO FEAR (Book #4)
CAUSE TO SAVE (Book #5)
CAUSE TO DREAD (Book #6)

KERI LOCKE MYSTERY SERIES
A TRACE OF DEATH (Book #1)
A TRACE OF MUDER (Book #2)
A TRACE OF VICE (Book #3)
A TRACE OF CRIME (Book #4)
A TRACE OF HOPE (Book #5)

TABLE OF CONTENTS

CHAPTER ONE

Her nerves were on fire and she felt like she might get sick at any moment. The boxing gloves on her hands felt foreign and the head gear was suffocating. Neither of these things were new to Kate Wise—she had been training for about two months now, but this was her first time sparring with an actual partner. While she was aware that it was all in good fun and just part of the workout regimen, it was still making her nervous. She'd be throwing actual punches at someone's body and that was not something she had ever taken lightly.

She looked across the ring at her sparring partner, a younger woman whom she was trying her best not to view as an *opponent*. She was another member of the small gym who had been undergoing the boxing program. The woman's name was Margo Dunn and she was taking the course for the same reason as Kate; it was a great full body exercise that, at its core, didn't involve too much running or weightlifting.

Margo grinned at Kate as her trainer slipped in her mouth guard. Kate nodded back in response as her trainer slid hers in as well. When it fell in perfectly around her teeth, Kate felt as if a switch had been flipped. She was in boxing mode now. Yes, the nerves were still there and she was uneasy with the whole situation, but it was time to go. It was time to work. There was only an audience of seven—made up of trainers and two other gym members who were just curious.

By the side of the ring, someone rang the little bell to signify the start of the fight. Kate walked out to the middle of the ring, where she met with Margo. They tapped gloves and took two respectful steps back.

And then it was on. Kate circled a bit, finding the rhythm with her feet she had been taught to remember as if she were dancing. She stepped forward and threw her first jab. Margo blocked it easily, but it was good to just get warmed up. Kate jabbed again, a little rabbit punch with her left hand. Margo blocked this one and then countered with a left that caught Kate right along the side of the head. The punch was soft by design—this was, after all, just a sparring match—and fell right along the cushion of the head gear. But still, it was enough to rock Kate a bit.

You're fifty-six, she thought to herself. *What the hell were you thinking?*

She considered the question as Margo threw a right-handed hook. Kate sidestepped it. Dodging it so easily gave her more confidence. When she also managed to effortlessly block the jab Margo followed with, it stirred up the need to excel.

You know why you're doing this, she thought. *Nine weeks in and you've lost eighteen pounds and have the best muscle tone you've had in your life. You feel about twenty years younger and let's be real ... have you ever felt this strong?*

No, she hadn't. And while she was nowhere near mastering the art of boxing, she knew that she had the basic skills down.

With this mentality locked in place, she stepped forward in a near-strafing position, faked a left jab, and then delivered a right hook. When the hook landed right along Margo's chin, Kate sent out the left jab ... and then another. Both landed true, rocking Margo a bit. A light of surprise shone in her eyes as she staggered back against the ropes. She grinned, though. Like Kate, she knew this was more or less just practice and she had just learned a lesson: be on the lookout for hard fakes at all times.

Margo responded with two jabs to the body, one that connected with Kate's ribs. The wind went rushing out of her for a moment and by the time she had caught it again, she saw the heavy right hook coming from her left. She tried moving but hadn't caught it in time. It slammed into the side of her padded head and shook her backward.

She was dizzy for a moment. Her vision blurred and her knees felt a little weak. She thought about falling, just to catch a break.

Yeah ... too old for this.

But then the counter to that was: *You know any other women over fifty who could take this punch and remain standing?*

Kate responded with two jabs and then a blow to the body. Only one of the jabs landed but the body blow struck its target. Margo went back into the ropes, staggering a bit. She then came back off of the ropes and threw an impatient uppercut. It was not designed to land. It was just meant to cause Kate to bring her arms up to block it so Margo could then deliver jabs to her exposed core. But Kate saw the slight hesitation in the delivery, knowing the purpose behind it. Instead of blocking the punch, she stepped hard to the right, waited for the full delivery to swing through, and then threw a hard right-handed jab that connected with the side of Margo's head.

Margo went down right away. She fell on her stomach and rolled over quickly. She slid back to her corner and popped out her mouth guard. She smiled at Kate and shook her head in disbelief.

"I'm sorry," Kate said, kneeling down in front of Margo.

"Don't be," Margo said. "It honestly makes no sense how you manage to be that fast. I feel like I need to apologize. Because of your age, I assumed you'd be ... slower."

Kate's trainer—a grizzled sixty-something man with a long white beard—climbed between the ropes, chuckling. "I made that same mistake," he said. "Had a black eye for about a week because of it. Caught the exact same punch that just knocked you down."

"Don't feel so apologetic," Kate said. "That one to my head was huge. It almost got me."

"It *should* have gotten you," the trainer said. "Honestly, it was a little harder than I like to see in these simple sparring matches." He then looked to Margo. "Up to you. You want to keep going?"

Margo nodded and pulled herself up. Again, her trainer put her mouthpiece in. Both women returned to their respective corners and waited for the bell.

But it was not the bell that Kate heard. Instead, she heard the ringing of her phone. And it was the assigned ringer she used for all calls that came from the bureau.

She pushed her mouthpiece out of her mouth and held her gloved hands out to her trainer. "Sorry," she said. "I have to take that."

Her trainer knew about her part-time job as a special agent. He thought it was hard-ass (his word, not hers) that she refused to entirely retire from such a job. So when he untied her gloves for her, he did so as quickly as possible.

Kate slid between the ropes and ran to her gym bag, which was sitting by the wall. She always kept it out and not in the locker room just in case she got such a call. She grabbed the phone and her heart surged with excitement and despair all at once when she saw Deputy Director Duran's name on the display.

"This is Agent Wise," she said.

"Wise, it's Duran. You got a second?"

"I do," she said, glancing back at the ring with longing. Margo's trainer was working with her on how to avoid fake-outs. "What can I do for you?"

"I was hoping you could come in on a case. It's effective immediately, and I'd need you and DeMarco to fly out tonight."

"I don't know," she said. And that was the truth. It was very sudden and she had spoken to Melissa, her daughter, several times in the last few weeks about not being so readily available for the last-minute jobs. She had been spending much more time with Melissa and Michelle, her granddaughter, over the last month or so and they finally had a good thing going—something like a routine. Something like a family.

"I appreciate you thinking of me," Kate said. "But I don't know if I can come in for this one. It's very last minute. And flying out...that makes it seem like it's pretty far away. I don't know that I'm prepared for a long trip. Where is it, anyway?"

"New York. Kate...I'm pretty sure it has ties to the Nobilini case."

The name sent a chill through her. Her head started ringing, and it wasn't from the blow Margo had delivered moments ago. Flashes of a case from nearly eight years ago cascaded through her head—leering, taunting.

"Kate?"

"I'm here," she said. She then looked back to the ring. Margo was stretching and lightly jogging in place, ready for their next bout.

It was a shame she wouldn't get it. Because as soon as Kate heard the name, she knew she'd take the case. She had to.

The Nobilini case had gotten away from her eight years ago—one of the true defeats she'd ever had in her career.

This was her chance to close it—to bolt shut the one case that had truly bested her.

"When's the flight?" she asked Duran.

"Dulles to JFK, leaves in four hours."

She thought of Melissa and Michelle, her heart sinking. Melissa wouldn't understand, but Kate could not turn this opportunity down.

"I'll be on it," she said.

CHAPTER TWO

Kate managed to pack and make it out of Richmond in less than an hour and a half. When she met her partner, Kristen DeMarco, outside of one of the many Starbucks in Dulles International Airport, they had only ten minutes remaining before takeoff; most of the plane's passengers had already boarded.

As DeMarco started power-walking toward Kate with her coffee in hand, she smiled and shook her head. "If you'd just go ahead and move to DC, you wouldn't be rushing and borderline late all the time."

"No can do," Kate said as they joined together and starting hurrying for the gate. "It's enough that this so-called part-time job is keeping me away from my family more than I'd like. If it was a requirement that I live in DC, I wouldn't be doing it at all."

"How *are* Melissa and little Michelle?" DeMarco asked.

"They're doing well. I spoke with Melissa on my way here. She said she understood and wished me luck. And for the first time, I think she actually meant it."

"Good. I told you she'd come around. I assume it would be cool as hell to have a bad-ass for a mother."

"I'm far from a bad-ass," Kate said as they reached the gate. Still, she thought of what she had been doing when she received the call and thought it might be okay to accept that moniker ... at least a little.

"Last I heard," Kate said, "you were working a triple murder case out in Maine."

"Yeah, I was. We wrapped it about a week ago—about six agents in all on that thing. When I got the call from Duran about this case, he told me he planned to send you out and asked if I wanted to partner with you.

I, of course, jumped at the chance. I told him I'd like to be partnered with you whenever possible in the future."

"Thanks," Kate said. She left it at that, though. It actually meant a lot to her but she didn't want to get sappy on DeMarco.

They boarded the plane together and took their seats, right beside one another. When they were settled, DeMarco reached into her carry-on and pulled out a thick folder crammed with papers and documents.

"This is everything on the Nobilini file," she said. "Based on your history with it, I assume you know it inside and out?"

"Probably," Kate said.

"It's a pretty quick flight," DeMarco pointed out. "I'd much rather hear it from you instead of notes and files."

Kate would have felt the same way. What surprised her was how eager she was to share the details of the case with DeMarco. The case had been like a nagging itch at the back of her mind over the years but she had always managed to push it away, not wanting to focus on the one true failure of her career.

So as the plane started to position itself toward the runway, Kate started to go back over the specifics of the case. As she did, stopping for the annoyance of the pre-flight announcements, she realized that it all felt new now. Maybe it was all the time that had passed since she had last truly dwelt on it, or the almost-retirement (or both), but the case now felt alive and active.

She told DeMarco the details of the case in a high-end suburb just out of New York City. Just one body, but the case had been pushed by some-one in Congress, as the victim was closely linked. No prints, no clues. The body, one Frank Nobilini, was found in an alley in the Midtown dis-trict. The best guess was that he had been headed for work, walking the single block from the parking garage to his office. Just a single gunshot wound to the back of the head. Execution style.

"How could it be execution style if someone clearly abducted him and dragged him into the alleyway?" DeMarco asked.

"That's another unanswered question to the case. It was assumed that Nobilini was roughed up a bit, forced to his knees, and then shot in the back of the head. Blood and bits of skull were all over the side of the wall of the building beside the body. His BMW keys were still in his hand."

DeMarco nodded and allowed Kate to continue.

"The victim was from a small town, a well-to-do little suburb called Ashton," Kate said. "It's the sort of town that draws in visitors for its pretentious antique stores, overpriced dining, and immaculate real estate."

"And that's the thing I don't get about it," DeMarco said. "A place like that, people tend to gossip, right? You'd think *someone* would have known something or heard rumors about who the killer was. But there's nothing in these files." She said this last bit as she thumped her fingers against the folder.

"That always unnerved me," Kate said. "Ashton is an upscale place. But outside of that, it's also a very tight community. Everyone knows each other. For the most part, everyone was polite to one another. Neighbors helping neighbors, big turn-outs for school bake sales, the whole nine yards. The place is squeaky clean."

"No motives for the killer?" DeMarco asked.

"None that I ever knew about. Ashton has a population of just over three thousand. And sure, while it does attract its fair amount of people from New York City and other outlying areas, it has an incredibly small crime rate. So even though the murder didn't actually occur in Ashton, it's why the Nobilini murder was such a big deal eight years ago."

"And there were never any other murders like this one?"

"Nope. Not until today, apparently. My theory is that the killer noted the FBI presence and got spooked. In a town that size, it would be easy to notice the presence of the FBI." Kate paused here and took the file folder from DeMarco. "How much did Duran tell you?"

"Not much. He said we were in a rush and asked that I read over the case files."

"Did you see what sort of gun was used for the murder?" Kate asked.

"I did. A Ruger Hunter Mark IV. Seemed weird. Seemed *professional.* That's an expensive gun for some random murder with no apparent motive."

"I agree. The bullet and the casing we found made it an easy one to recognize. And despite the expensive and very nice gun that was used, the fact that it was used at all told us all we needed to know: it was someone that knew jack shit about killing people."

"How's that?"

"Anyone that knew what they were doing would know that the Ruger Hunter Mark IV would leave behind a casing. Which makes it a terrible choice."

"I assume this latest man was killed by a similar weapon?" DeMarco asked.

"According to Duran, it's the exact same weapon."

"So this killer decided to do it again eight years later. Weird."

"Well, we'll have to wait and see about that," Kate said. "All Duran told me was that the victim looked as if he had been set up like a prop. And that the weapon used to kill him was the same kind that killed Frank Nobilini."

"Yeah, and this one is in Midtown in New York City. I wonder if this latest victim is also connected to Ashton."

Kate only shrugged as the plane experienced a bit of turbulence. It had done her a great deal of good to go through the case details. It had essentially knocked the cobwebs off of the case and made it feel new again. And maybe, Kate figured, eight years of space between her and the original case might allow her to look at it with fresh eyes.

It had been a while since Kate had been to New York. She and Michael, her late husband, had come here for a weekend getaway not long before he died. The congestion and absolute busyness of the place never ceased to awe her. It made the gridlock of Washington, DC, seem trivial by comparison. The fact that it was nearing nine o'clock on a Friday night was not helping matters.

They arrived at the scene of the crime at 8:42 p.m. Kate parked their rental car as close to the crime scene tape as she could. The scene was in a back alley located on 43rd Street, the hustle and bustle of Grand Central Station a few blocks over. There were two police cars parked nose to nose in front of the alley, not blocking the yellow crime scene tape or the alley itself, but making it known to anyone who wanted a peek at what was going on that there would be repercussions for their curiosity.

As Kate and DeMarco reached the alleyway, a bulky policeman stopped them at the crime scene tape. But when Kate showed her badge, he shrugged his shoulders and lifted the tape for them. She noted that he made no real attempt to check out DeMarco when she bent down to go under the tape. She wondered idly if DeMarco, an openly homosexual woman, took offense when a man checked her out or if she considered it a compliment.

"Feds," the officer said with a huff. "I heard they called you in. Seems a bit much to me. Pretty open and shut case from the looks of it."

"Just checking on something," Kate said as she and DeMarco walked into the dark alley.

The police cars at the mouth of the alley had been parked at a light angle to allow the headlights to shine into the darkness. Kate's and DeMarco's elongated shadows added an air of eeriness to the scene.

At the back of the alleyway—which dead-ended along a brick wall—there were two policemen and a plainclothes detective standing in a small semicircle. There was a slight lump against the wall in front of them. The victim, Kate presumed. She approached the three men and introduced herself and DeMarco as they again showed their ID.

"Nice to meet you," one of the officers said. "But if I'm being honest, I don't quite know why the FBI was so insistent on getting someone out here."

"Ah, Jesus," the plainclothes detective said. He looked to be in his forties and a bit grungy. Long dark hair, five o'clock shadow, and a pair of glasses that reminded Kate of every picture she'd ever seen of Buddy Holly.

"We've been through this," the detective said. He looked at Kate, rolled his eyes, and said: "If it's a crime that's older than a week or so, NYPD doesn't want to touch it. It blows their minds that anyone would want to dig back up an unsolved murder case from eight years ago. I was actually the one that called the bureau. I know they were hot and heavy on the Nobilini case when it was active. Some sort of friendship with someone in Congress, right?"

"That's right," Kate said. "And I was the lead agent on that case."

"Oh. Good to meet you. I'm Detective Luke Pritchard. I sort of have an obsession with cold cases. This one pinged my interest because of the weapon that seems to have been used as well as the fact that it was carried out execution style. If you look closely, you can see scuff marks on the forehead where the killer apparently had him lean against the brick wall right here." He placed his hand on the side of the building to their right where there was dried blood splattered everywhere.

"May we?" Kate asked.

The two policemen shrugged and stepped back. "By all means," one said. "With a detective and the bureau on this, we'll happily leave you to it."

"Have fun," the other cop said as they turned away and headed back to the mouth of the alleyway.

Kate and DeMarco crowded in around the body. Pritchard stepped back to allow them some extra room, but kept close.

"Well," DeMarco said, "I'd say the immediate cause of death is pretty clear."

This was true. There was a single bullet hole in the back of the man's head, the hole rather clean but the rim of it charred and gory—just like Frank Nobilini's. It was a man, in his late thirties or early forties if Kate had to venture a guess. He was wearing high-end athletic wear, a thin zip-up hoodie, and nice jogging pants. The laces of his expensive running shoes were tied perfectly and the Apple ear buds he had been listening to sat neatly to his side, as if placed there intentionally.

"We have an ID yet?" Kate asked.

"Yeah," Pritchard said. "Jack Tucker. The ID in his wallet places his residence in the town of Ashton. Which, to me, was an even stronger connection to the Nobilini case."

"Are you familiar with Ashton, Detective?" Kate asked.

"Not very. Been through there a few times, but it's not my kind of place. Too perfect, too quaint and sickeningly sweet."

She knew what he meant. She couldn't help but wonder what he was going to feel like, having to return to Ashton.

"When was the body discovered?" DeMarco asked.

"Four thirty this afternoon. I arrived on the scene at a quarter after five and made all those connections. I had to beg them not to move the body until you guys got here. I figure you'd need to see the scene, body and all."

"I bet that made you popular," Kate commented.

"Oh, I'm used to it. I wish I was joking when I tell you that a lot of the cops around here call me Cold Case Pritchard."

"Well, I think on this one, you made the right call," Kate said. "Even if it turns out not to be connected, there's still someone out there that shot this man—someone that we need to find just in case this isn't an isolated incident."

"Yeah, no clue on my end," Pritchard said. "I have a few voice memos with my observations if you'd like to check them out."

"That could be helpful. I assume forensics has already snapped pictures?"

"Yeah. The digitals are probably already available."

With that, Kate got to her feet, her eyes still on Jack Tucker's body. His head was tilted to the right, as if he were staring longingly at the earbuds that had been so carefully placed by his side.

"Has the family been notified?" DeMarco asked.

"No. And I fear that because I asked the PD to hold off on moving the body and getting the case moved along, they're going to task me with it."

"If it's all the same, I'd prefer to do it," Kate said. "The fewer channels the details are being processed through, the better."

"If that's what you want."

Kate finally looked away from the body of Jack Tucker and then to the mouth of the alley where the two cops were congregating with the cop who had lifted the tape. She had delivered such devastating news more times than she cared to count and it was never easy. In fact, somehow, it seemed to get harder and harder.

But she had also learned that strangely enough, it was in the sharp and agonizing throes of grief that those suffering loss seemed to be able to remember the most minute of details.

Kate hoped it would hold true in this case.

And if so, maybe an unsuspecting new widow could help her close a case that had haunted her for nearly a decade.

Chapter Three

It was only a twenty-minute drive from midtown to Ashton. It was 9:20 when they left the crime scene and the Friday night traffic remained stubborn and grueling. As they came out of the worst of the traffic and onto the freeway, Kate noticed that DeMarco was unusually quiet. She was in the passenger's seat, staring almost defiantly out the window at the passing cityscape.

"You okay over there?" Kate asked.

Without turning toward Kate, DeMarco answered right away, making it clear that something had been on her mind since leaving the crime scene.

"I know you've been at this awhile and know the ropes, but I've only ever had to break the news of a dead family member one time before. I hated it. It made me feel awful. And I really wish you had checked with me before volunteering us for it."

"I'm sorry. I didn't even think about that. But it *is* part of the job in some cases. At the risk of sounding cold, it's best to start getting used to it right off the bat. Besides . . . if we're running the case, what's the point in delegating this miserable task to that poor detective?"

"Still . . . how about a little heads-up on things like that in the future?"

The tone in her voice was one of anger, something she had not heard from DeMarco before—not directed toward her, anyway. "Yeah," she said, and left it at that.

They drove the rest of the way into Ashton in silence. Kate had worked enough cases where she had to break the news of a death to know that any tension between partners was going to make the matter so much worse. But she also knew that DeMarco wasn't the type who was going to listen to any lessons she had to deliver while she was pissed off. So maybe this one, Kate thought, would be something she could simply learn by living it out.

They arrived at the Tucker residence at 9:42. Kate was not at all surprised to see that the porch light, as well as just about every other light in the house, was on. From the looks of Jack Tucker's attire, he had been out for a morning jog. The question of why his body had been in the city, though, presented many questions. All of those questions presumably led to one very concerned wife.

A concerned wife who is about to find out she's now a widow, Kate thought. *My God, I hope they don't have kids.*

Kate parked in front of the house and got out of the car. DeMarco followed suit, only slower, as if to make sure to let Kate know that she was not at all happy about this particular detail. They walked up the flagstone walk toward the steps and Kate watched as the front door opened before they even made it to the porch.

The woman at the door saw them and froze. It looked as if she were working very hard to come up with what words she wanted to speak. In the end, all she could muster was: "Who are you?"

Kate slowly reached into her jacket pocket for her ID. Before she could even fully show it or give her name, the wife already knew. It showed in her eyes and the way her face slowly started to crumple. And as Kate and DeMarco finally reached the porch steps, Jack Tucker's wife went to her knees in the doorway and began to wail.

As it turned out, the Tuckers *did* have kids. Three of them, in fact, ages seven, ten, and thirteen. They were all still awake, lingering in the living room while Kate did her best to get the wife—Missy, she managed to introduce herself through her wailing and sobs—inside and sitting down. The thirteen-year-old came rushing to her mother's side while DeMarco did her best to keep the others away while their mother came to terms with the devastating news that she had just been handed.

In a way, Kate realized that maybe she *had* jumped the gun on DeMarco. The first twenty minutes she spent in the Tucker home that night were gut-wrenching. She could only think of one other moment in her career that was as heartbreaking. She looked over at DeMarco, both during and after she had tried to corral the kids, and saw the defiance and anger there. Kate figured this might be something that DeMarco held against her for a very long time.

Somewhere in the midst of it all, Missy Tucker realized that she was going to have to find someone to sit with her kids if she was going to try to be of any help to Kate and DeMarco. Through thin wails, she called her brother-in-law, having to break the news to him as well. They also lived in Ashton and his wife left almost immediately to come sit with the kids.

In an effort to give Missy and the Tucker children some privacy to deal with their grief, Kate got Missy's permission to look around the house for any signs of what might have occurred to have resulted in someone wanting to murder her husband. They started in the master bedroom, searching through the Tuckers' bedside tables and private items to the sound of a sobbing family downstairs.

"This really sucks," DeMarco said.

"It does. I'm sorry, DeMarco. I really am. I just thought it would be easier for everyone involved."

"Is that really what it is?" DeMarco asked. "I know I don't know you all that well yet, but one of the things I *do* know about you is you have a tendency to go out of your way to put as much pressure on yourself as you can. It's why you can't figure out the rather simple struggle of balancing your time with the bureau with the time for your family."

"Excuse me?" Kate asked, feeling a flare of anger.

DeMarco shrugged. "Sorry. But it's true. Local cops could have done this and we could have probably already been elsewhere, digging into this case."

"With no witnesses, the wife is the best bet," Kate said. "It just so happens she's also having to deal with the death of her husband. It sucks for everyone involved. But you have to get over your own discomfort. In the grand scheme of things, who is more uncomfortable right now? You or the freshly grieving widow downstairs?"

Kate wasn't aware of her loud and irritated tone until the last few words were out of her mouth. DeMarco stared her down for a moment before shaking her head like some spoiled teenager with no rebuttal, and left the room.

When Kate also left the room, she saw that DeMarco was looking through an office and miniature library just down the hallway. Kate left her to it, opting to head outside to look for any clues. She wasn't expecting to find anything as she skirted around the house but knew it would be irresponsible not to go through the routine.

Back inside, she saw that Jack Tucker's brother and wife had come. The brother and Missy were in a trembling embrace while the wife knelt by the kids and gave them all a hug. Kate saw that the thirteen-year-old— a girl who looked very much like her father—had a blank look on her face. Seeing it, she didn't fault DeMarco for being pissed at her.

"Agent Wise?"

Kate turned as she was about to head back up the stairs and saw Missy coming down the hallway toward her. "Yes?"

"If we're going to talk, let's do it now. I don't know how much longer I can hold it together." Already, she was starting to let out little whines and moans again. Being that the news of her husband's death was barely one hour old, Kate admired her for her strength.

Missy said nothing else, but walked up the stairs with a quick glance back toward the living room where her kids and relatives were gathered. DeMarco joined them from where she was checking the medicine cabinet in the upstairs bathroom and the three of them went into the master bedroom—the bedroom Kate and DeMarco had already checked.

Missy sat on the edge of the bed like a woman waking up from a very bad dream, only to realize the dream was still taking place.

"You asked me earlier why he was in New York City," she said. "Jack worked as a senior accountant for a pretty big firm—Adler and Johnson. They've been working night and day on this big overhaul for a nuclear decommissioning company in South Carolina. On the really late nights, he's just been staying in the city."

"Were you expecting him back tonight or were you thinking he'd be staying in a hotel?" DeMarco asked.

"I talked to him at about seven this morning, before he left for his morning run. He said not only did he plan on being home today, but probably pretty early—maybe around four or so."

"I assume you started trying to call or text him at a certain point when you realized it was getting late?" Kate asked.

"Yeah, but not until seven or so. When those guys get deep into their jobs, time sort of goes out the window."

"Mrs. Tucker, the FBI was called in on your husband's murder because the situation reflects the details and circumstances of a case from eight years ago. The victim was another man who lived here in Ashton, also killed in New York," Kate explained. "There is no *hard* evidence to support it, but it's close enough to have alarmed the bureau. So it is very important that you try to think about any people that your husband might have made enemies with."

Kate could tell that Missy was once again fighting with tears. She gulped down the need to let out the grief, trying to get through it.

"I can't think of anyone. I'm not just saying it because I love the man, but he was extremely kind. Outside of a few little arguments at work, I don't think he ever had a heated argument his entire life."

"What about any close friends?" Kate asked. "Are there any friends, men in particular, that he hung around with who might have seen another side of him?"

"Well, he was a little silly with this group of friends out at the yacht club, but I don't think they'd describe him as anything negative."

"Do you have the names of some of these friends that we could talk to?" DeMarco asked.

"Yes. He had this core group…him and three other guys. They get together at the yacht club or hang out at the cigar bar and watch sports. Football, mostly."

"Do you happen to know if any of them have people they might consider enemies?" DeMarco asked. "Even jealous ex-wives or estranged family members?"

"I don't know. I don't know them that well and—"

395

The sound of uncontrollable sobbing from downstairs interrupted her. Missy looked in the direction of the bedroom door with a frown that made Kate's heart ache.

"That's Dylan, our middle child. He and his father were..."

She stopped here, her lip quivering as she tried to keep herself together.

"It's okay, Mrs. Tucker," DeMarco said. "Go to your kids. We've got enough to get started."

Missy got up quickly and sprinted for the door, already starting to cry. DeMarco followed behind her slowly, casting an angry look back at Kate. Kate stood in the bedroom a moment longer, getting a grip on her own emotions. No, this part of the job never got truly easier. And the fact that they had gotten very little information from the visit made it even worse.

She finally headed back out into the hallway, understanding why DeMarco was mad at her. Hell, she was a little angry with herself.

Kate walked back downstairs and head out the door. She saw that DeMarco was already getting into the car, wiping tears from her eyes. Kate closed the door softly behind her, the grief and weeping of the Tucker family pushing her along like an usher that led her deeper and deeper into a case that already seemed lost.

CHAPTER FOUR

By nine o'clock the following morning, news of Jack Tucker's murder had started making the rounds around Ashton. It was the main reason why it was so easy for Kate and DeMarco to get in touch with Jack's friends—the names and numbers of which Missy had given them last night. Not only had his friends already heard the news, they had started to come up with plans on how to help Missy and the kids as they dealt with their loss.

After a few quick phone calls, Kate and DeMarco had set up a meeting with three of Jack's friends at the yacht club. It was a Saturday, so the lot was already starting to fill up, even at nine in the morning. The club was located right along the Long Island Sound and had what Kate thought was probably the best view of the sound without all of the pretentious boat traffic getting in the way.

The club itself was a two-story building that looked nearly Colonial in style, with a modern twist, particularly to the exterior and landscaping. Kate was greeted by a man who was already standing at the doors. He was dressed in a simple button-down shirt and a pair of khakis—probably what passed for weekend casual for someone who belonged to a yacht club like this one.

"You Agent Wise?" the man asked.

"I am. And this is my partner, Agent DeMarco."

DeMarco only nodded, her anger and bitterness from the previous night still very much present. When they had parted ways at the hotel last night, DeMarco hadn't said so much as a single word. She *had* managed a simple "good morning" over their quick breakfast but that had been it so far.

"I'm James Cortez," the man said. "I spoke with you on the phone earlier this morning. The other guys are out on the veranda, ready and waiting with coffee."

He led them through the club, its high ceilings and warm environment utterly charming. Kate wondered how much it cost to be a member here for a year. Out of her price range for sure. When they stepped out onto the veranda that overlooked the Long Island Sound, she became certain of this. It was beautiful, looking directly out onto the water with the tall shapes and haze of the city on the other side.

There were two other men sitting at a small wooden table that held a large plate of pastries and bagels as well as a carafe of coffee. Both men looked up at the agents and got to their feet to greet them. One of the men looked rather young, certainly no older than thirty, while James Cortez and the other man were easily in their mid-forties.

"Duncan Ertz," the younger man said, extending his hand.

Kate and DeMarco both shook the men's hands as they went through a quick round of introductions. The older man was Paul Wickers, freshly retired from his job as a stockbroker and more than willing to talk about it, as it was the second thing that came out of his mouth.

Kate and DeMarco took a seat at the table. Kate took one of the empty coffee cups and filled it, doctoring it up with the sugar and cream that sat by the plate of breakfast pastries.

"It hurts to think about poor Missy and those kids this morning," Duncan said, biting into a Danish.

Kate recalled the trauma of last night and felt that she needed to check in on the poor woman. She looked across the table at DeMarco and wondered if she needed to check in on her, too. Removed from the situation, Kate was starting to understand that perhaps DeMarco had taken it so hard because of something in her past—something she had still not gotten over yet.

"Well," Kate said, "Missy specifically mentioned you gentlemen as those closest to Jack outside of his family. I was hoping to get some insights into the sort of man he was outside of his home and work."

"Well, that's the thing," James Cortez said. "From what I know, Jack was the same man no matter where he was. A straight shooter. A kind soul that always wanted to help others. If he had any flaws, I'd say it was that he was a little too involved with his work."

"He was always good for a joke," Duncan said. "They weren't funny most of the time, but he loved to tell them."

"That's for sure," Paul said.

"There were no secrets he told you guys about?" DeMarco asked. "Maybe an affair or even thoughts of an affair?"

"God no," Paul said. "Jack Tucker was insanely in love with his wife. I'd feel safe saying that man loved everything about his life. His wife, kids, work, friends…"

"That's why this makes no sense," James said. "I mean this in the most respectful way possible, but from an outsider's perspective, Jack was a pretty standard guy. Boring, almost."

"Any idea if he might have any connections to the victim of a murder that occurred eight years ago?" Kate asked. "A guy named Frank Nobilini who also lived in Ashton and was killed in New York."

"Frank Nobilini?" Duncan Ertz said, shaking his head.

"Yeah," James said. "Worked for that big-ass ad agency that does all the sneaker jobs. His wife was Jennifer… your wife probably knows her. Nice lady. Into community beautification projects and is very active with the PTA and things like that."

Ertz shrugged. Apparently, he was the newbie of the group and knew none of this.

"You think Jack's murder is linked to Nobilini's?" Paul asked.

"It's far too early to know that just yet," Kate said. "But given the nature of the murder, we have to look at it from that viewpoint."

"Do any of you happen to know the names of anyone Jack worked with?" DeMarco asked.

"There's only two people over him," Paul said. "One of them is a guy named Luca. He lives in Switzerland and comes over three or four times a year. The other is a local guy named Daiju Hiroto. I'm pretty sure he's the supervisor over the Adler and Johnson NYC offices."

"According to Jack," Duncan said, "Daiju is the kind of guy that practically lives at work."

"Was it common for Jack to have to work weekends?" Kate asked.

"Here and there," James said. "He'd done it a lot lately, actually. They're in the middle of some huge job to help bail out a nuclear decommissioning company. Last time I spoke with Jack, he said if they straightened it all out in time, there could be a *lot* of money involved in it."

"I'd bet good money you'll find almost the entire crew working today," Paul said. "They might be able to tell you some things we don't know about."

DeMarco slid one of her business cards over to James Cortez and then picked a cherry Danish from the plate in front of them. "Please give us a call if you think of anything else over the course of the next few days."

"And maybe keep the idea of the case from eight years ago to yourself," Kate said. "The last thing we need is for the people living in Ashton to get into a frenzy."

Paul nodded, sensing that she was speaking directly to him.

"Thanks, gentlemen," Kate said.

She took one more long sip of her coffee and left the men to their quiet breakfast. She glanced out at the sound where a sailboat was slowly coasting out into the water, as if tugging in the start of the weekend behind it.

"I'll get the address to Jack Tucker's office at Adler and Johnson," DeMarco said, pulling out her phone. And even in that, her tone was distant and cold.

She and I are going to have to hash this out before it gets out of hand, Kate thought. *Sure, she's a hard-ass but if I have to put her in her place, I won't hesitate to do so.*

The offices of Adler and Johnson were located in one of the more glamorous-looking high rises in Manhattan. It was located on the first and second floors of a building that also contained a law firm, a mobile applications developer, and a small literary agency. As it turned out, Paul Wickers had been correct; most of the team Jack Tucker had worked with was in the office. The workspace smelled of strong coffee and though there was a great deal of busyness among the eight people working, there was a somber mood as well.

Daiju Hiroto met with them right away, escorting them into his large office. He looked like a man torn—perhaps between his need to get this massive project finished on time and the humane reaction to the death of a co-worker and friend.

"I learned the news this morning," Hiroto said from behind his large desk. "I had been at work since six this morning and one of our workers—Katie Mayer—came in with the news. There were fifteen of us here at the time and I gave them all the option of taking the weekend off. Six people thought it best to leave to pay their respects."

"If you did not have this team to oversee, would you have done the same?" Kate asked.

"No. It is a selfish answer, but this job has to be done. We have two weeks to finish everything and we are a bit behind. And more than fifty people's jobs are at risk if we don't pull it off."

"Of your team, who do you think would have known Jack the best?" Kate asked.

"Probably me. Jack and I worked very closely together on several large jobs over the last ten years or so. We've traveled all over the world together and pulled late nights and meetings that the rest of the team didn't even know about."

"But you said someone else knew about his death first?" DeMarco asked.

"Yes, Katie. She lives in Ashton and is fairly good friends with Jack's wife."

Kate wanted to say something about how it seemed a little offensive that Hiroto was not calling it a day so that he, as well as the others who had dutifully stayed behind, could grieve. But she knew the demons that sometimes drove men who were possessed by their work and knew that it was not her place to make such a judgment.

"In all of your time with Jack, did you ever know him to keep secrets?" DeMarco asked.

"Not that I can think of. And if he did, I apparently wasn't someone he wished to divulge them to. But between the three of us, I find it very hard to believe that Jack had a secret life. He was on the straight and narrow, you know? A good guy. Polished around the edges."

"So you can't think of any reason someone might have wanted to kill him?" Kate asked.

"No. The idea is insane." He paused here and looked out through the glass walls of his office and to the rest of his team. "And it was here in the city?" he asked.

"It was. Did you not call him when you realized he had not come in?"

"Oh, I did. Several times. When he didn't answer by noon or so, I let it go. Jack was always very sharp, very smart. If he needed a few hours just to get away—which he did from time to time—I let him have it."

"Mr. Hiroto, would you mind if we spoke to some of the others out there?" Kate asked, nodding toward the other side of the glass walls.

"By all means. Help yourself."

"And could you get the contact information of those that decided to leave?" DeMarco asked.

"Certainly."

Kate and DeMarco ventured out into the workspace of cubicles, large desks, and rich coffee. But even before they had spoken to a single person, Kate got a pretty good feeling that they were going to get more of the same. Usually, when more than one person described someone else as being very plain and uneventful, it usually turned out to be true.

Within fifteen minutes, they had spoken with the eight other workers currently in the office. Kate had been right; everyone described Jack and sweet, kind, not one to rock the boat. And for the second time that morning, someone referred to Jack Tucker as boring—but in a good, non-offensive way.

In the back of her head, Kate felt something stir, some memory or saying that she had heard somewhere along the roads of her life. Something about watching out for a bored wife or spouse—how the boredom might make them snap. But it wouldn't come to her.

After stopping by Hiroto's office one last time to get a list of the people who had elected to leave work, Kate and DeMarco headed back out into the gorgeous New York City Saturday morning. She thought of poor Missy Tucker, sitting under the weight of this beautiful day, trying to adapt to a life that, for a while anyway, might not seem so beautiful at all.

They spent the rest of their morning visiting with the ones who had decided to leave work. They encountered many tears and even a few who were enraged that a man as innocent and as kind as Jack Tucker would have been murdered. It was exactly the same as speaking to the others in the office, only not as stifling.

They spoke with the last person—a man named Jerry Craft—shortly after lunchtime. They arrived at his home just as Jerry was getting into his car. Kate parked behind him in his driveway, catching an irritated look. She stepped out of the car as Jerry Craft approached them. His eyes were red and he looked quite melancholy.

"Sorry to bother you," Kate said, showing her ID. DeMarco stepped up beside her and did the same. "We're agents Wise and DeMarco, FBI. We were hoping you might have some time to speak with us about Jack Tucker."

The irritation quickly left Jerry's face and he nodded and propped himself up against the back of his car.

"I don't know what I could offer than what I'm sure you've already heard from everyone else. I assume you spoke with Mr. Hiroto and everyone else at the office?"

"We have," Kate said. "We're now speaking with those that left today—as it would seem they had a closer connection with Jack."

"I don't know if that's necessarily true," Jerry said. "There were only a few of us that ever really hung out outside of work. And Jack usually wasn't among them. A few of them probably took Hiroto up on his offer just to get a day off."

"Any idea why Jack wasn't one to hang out after work hours?" DeMarco asked.

"No reason, I don't think. Jack was something of a home body, you know? He'd rather be at home with his wife and kids in his free time. The job had him working crazy hours as it was—no sense in hanging at a bar with those same people you just left work with. He loved his family, you know? Always doing extravagant things for birthdays and anniversaries. Always talking up his kids at work."

"So you also think he had the perfect life?" Kate asked.

"Seemed that way. Although, really, can any of us have a *perfect* life? I mean, even Jack had some strain with his mother from what I know. But don't we all?"

"How's that?"

"Nothing big. There was this one day at work where I heard him talking to his wife on the phone. He was out in the stairwell for privacy, but I was using one of the older workstations right by the stairwell door. It stands out because it was the only time I heard him speaking to or about his wife with anything but happiness in his voice."

"And it was a conversation about his mother?" Kate asked.

"Pretty sure. I sort of teased him about it when he came back in but he wasn't in a joking mood."

"Do you know anything about his parents?" Kate asked.

"No. Like I said, Jack was a great guy, but I wouldn't really call him a *friend*."

"Where are you headed right now?" DeMarco asked.

"I was going to go grab some flowers for his family and drop them by their house. I met his wife and kids a few times at Christmas parties and company barbecues, things like that. A great little family. It's a damned shame what happened. Makes me a little sick, you know?"

"Well, we won't keep you any longer," Kate said. "Thank you, Mr. Craft."

Back in the car, Kate backed out of Jerry's driveway and said: "You want to grab Jack's mother's information?"

"On it," DeMarco said a little coldly.

Kate again found herself fighting to stay quiet. If DeMarco was going to draw out her little irritation about last night's events, that was her choice. Kate sure as hell wasn't going to let it affect her progress on this case.

At the same time, she also found herself having to bite back an ironic smile. She had spent so much time wrestling with whether or not her new position was keeping her away from her family yet here she was, working with a woman who reminded her so much of Melissa at times that it was scary. She thought of Melissa and Michelle as DeMarco was bounced back and forth along the departments within the bureau, searching for information on Jack Tucker's mother. She thought of how Melissa had behaved and acted the first time she, Kate, had been so enthralled in the Nobilini case. That had been eight years ago; Melissa had been twenty-one, still slightly rebellious and pretty much against anything her mother wished of her. There had been one stretch of time where Melissa had tried out coloring her hair purple. It had actually looked quite good but Kate had never been able to bring herself to say it out loud. It had been a trying time in their lives, even when Michael, her husband, had still been alive and there to help her do the parenting as Melissa had gotten older.

"That's interesting," DeMarco said, pulling Kate out of her trip down memory lane. She was setting her phone down and looking ahead with an excited little sparkle in her eyes.

"What's interesting?" Kate asked.

"Jack's mother is one Olivia Tucker. Sixty-six years old, lives in Queens. A squeaky clean criminal record, but with one minor ding."

"What's the ding?"

"She had the cops called on her two years ago. The call was placed by Missy Tucker, on the same night Olivia Tucker was trying to force her way into their house."

They shared a look and in it, Kate could feel some of that tension between them start to melt away. Good leads, after all, had a tendency to bring even the most estranged partners together.

Feeling as if she was finally getting somewhere, Kate turned the car around and headed toward Queens.

CHAPTER FIVE

Olivia Tucker lived in a basic run-of-the-mill apartment in Jackson Heights. When Kate and DeMarco arrived, she was being visited by a local preacher. It was the preacher who answered the door, a tall black man who looked very somber and sad. He regarded the agents skeptically and sighed softly.

"Can I help you ladies?"

"We need to speak with Mrs. Tucker," DeMarco said. "Who might you be?"

"I'm Leland Toombs, the pastor of her church. And who might you be?"

They went through the usual routine of showing their IDs and introducing themselves. Toombs took a tentative step back and gave them a disapproving look.

"You understand she is in a very distressed state, right?"

"Of course," Kate said. "We're trying to find her son's killer and we are hoping she might be able to shed some light to help."

"Who is that?" a shaky voice called from elsewhere in the apartment. A woman stepped into view from another room and started for the door.

"It's the FBI," Leland told her. "But Olivia, I'd suggest you take a moment to think about if you are ready to speak with them."

Olivia Tucker came to the door looking an absolute mess. Her eyes were bloodshot and it looked like she was even having trouble walking. She looked at Kate and DeMarco and then placed a reassuring hand on Toombs's shoulder.

"Yes, I think I need to," she said. "Pastor Toombs, would you give me a moment?"

"I think maybe I should be here when they speak with you."

She shook her head. "No. I appreciate it, but I need to do this part on my own."

Toombs frowned and then looked at Kate and DeMarco. "Please be kind. She is not taking this well." He then gave Olivia one final look and stepped out of the door while calling over his shoulder, "Please call me if you need anything, Olivia."

Olivia watched him go and then slowly closed the door behind her. "Please, come on into the living room."

Her voice was soft and ragged and she still walked as if her legs weren't quite sure what they were doing.

"Did you know," she said as they entered the living room, "that the cops called me and told me what had happened a full six hours after his body was found?"

"Why so long?" Kate asked.

"I suppose they assumed Missy would call and tell me. They told her first, of course. But it was later, after Missy had refused, that the police finally called."

"Are you sure she *refused*?" DeMarco asked. "Given the nature of what happened, do you think she simply forgot?"

Olivia shrugged, but not as an *I don't know* gesture. It was more of an *I don't care*.

"Do you mean to tell me that you think Missy would have done something like that on purpose?" Kate asked.

"Honestly, I just don't know. The woman is vindictive as hell. I wouldn't put much of anything beyond her. She probably *forgot* so she wouldn't have to speak to me or, God forbid, *see* me."

"Want to tell us why you seem to dislike her so much?" DeMarco asked.

"Oh, I never liked her, not really. She was quite charming at first, when she was trying to earn my good graces. But the moment Jack put that engagement ring on her finger, she became some other person. Controlling. Manipulative. She has never appreciated the plush little life she has. She may have loved Jack deep down in some sick, twisted way—I don't doubt that. But she never appreciated him."

"Can you explain that a bit more?" Kate asked.

"She was always wanting something else—wanting more. And she made no secret of it. Everything she had, no matter what it was—kids, wealthy husband, beautiful house, you name it—it was never enough. Nothing Jack ever did was good enough for her."

Kate noticed the look of absolute venom in Olivia's face as she spoke. She believed every single word she was saying. But from the little bit of time Kate had spent with Missy Tucker, she found it all very hard to believe.

"Do you know if Jack felt this way about her?"

"God, no. He was so blinded by it all. By her and her little act."

"So you'd comfortably rule out the idea of him being involved in an affair?"

Her look of shock was all the answer Kate needed. But Olivia had some choice words, too. "Given what I've been through the last few hours, how dare you ask such a stupid question? Are you *trying* to be insensitive and rude?"

"I ask only because that would at least give us somewhere to start looking. If he was involved in something like that, it would give us a series of leads to pursue. Because quite frankly, as of now, we have no witnesses and no suspects."

"Suspects? Honey, I've already told you who did it. It was his hateful wife."

Kate and DeMarco shared an uneasy glance. Whether Oliva Tucker's statement was true or not, this case was going to get quite awkward before it was brought to a close.

Kate let the comment hang in the air for a moment before going on. When she did, she was sure to use her words carefully, choosing each one with great purpose.

"Are you sure you want to make such a bold statement?" Kate asked. "If you're serious about that, I have to consider it a lead and start pursuing Missy Tucker as a potential suspect."

"You do your job the way you want," Olivia said. "But I know that woman. She wanted something different. She wanted out, but without the risk of losing everything in the process. Now you tell me some easier way to go about doing that than killing your husband."

Throughout all of her career, Kate didn't think she'd ever met anyone who was so blinded with hatred for someone else—in-laws, estranged siblings, and so on, she'd seen it all. But Olivia Tucker took things to a whole different level.

"I have to point out," DeMarco said, "that a great deal of time on our trip out here was spent going over everything there was to know about both Jack *and* Missy. While we don't have full reports by any means, there was more than enough to see that there was no marital discord strong enough to ping any legal issues."

"That's right," Kate said. "Additionally, there were no financial troubles, no marks on her criminal record, nothing like that. You, on the other hand, do have a slight mark on your record. Do you want to tell me about the night Missy had to call the cops because you were trying to get into their home?"

"Jack was having a hard time at work. He'd had a panic attack. I called to check on him and to talk to my grandkids, but Missy wasn't allowing it. She told me that Jack was too nice to say anything, but that *I* was part of the reason for his panic attack. She hung up on me when I called so I decided to go to their house. We had it out and she shoved me out the door, refusing to let me into the house. After that … well, I let my temper get the best of me and she called the police."

"If we need to, we'll look into that," Kate said "But honestly, there is nothing we have seen and nothing in the records to indicate that Missy would have had any reason at all to kill her husband. There's no motive that we can see."

"Well, if you're that convinced, why the hell are you even here to speak with me?"

"Honestly?" DeMarco said. "It's because your name came up. One of Jack's co-workers overheard him having a heated conversation with his wife about you. We checked your records just to cover our bases and found out about the police call."

Olivia smiled the sort of smile often seen on tired villains in movies. "Well then, it seems you already have your mind made up about me."

"That's not the case at all. We just—"

"If you ladies don't mind, I'm going to politely ask you to leave. I'd like to properly grieve my son."

Kate knew that their time with Olivia Tucker was over; if she kept pressing, the woman would only shut down. Besides that, she had been useless for information—unless the vile feelings she had toward her daughter-in-law could be seen as truth. And Kate doubted there was anything to it.

"Thank you," Kate said. "And we are truly sorry for your loss."

Olivia nodded, got up, and walked out of the room. "I'm sure you remember where the door is," she said, before disappearing elsewhere into the house.

Kate and DeMarco took their leave, no closer to a solid lead but having been thoroughly rattled by Olivia Tucker's views on Missy.

"You think there's a shred of truth to any of it?" DeMarco asked. She seemed to be coming out of her funk, apparently motivated by the case.

"I think in this moment, while she's searching for answers to what happened, she thinks some of it is true. I think she's taking little nuggets of fears she's had over the years and amplifying them just to have some object to place her blame and rage on."

DeMarco nodded as they got into the car. "Whatever it was, it was ugly."

"And I think it rules her out of any foul play. We may want to keep an eye on Missy, though, just to keep her safe. Maybe even let local PD know how unhinged Olivia seems to be."

"And then what?"

"And then we regroup. Possibly over a glass or two of wine back at the hotel."

It sounded like a good idea but Kate continued to think of Missy Tucker and how her world was now very much an empty shell of what it had once been. Kate remembered all too well what it felt like to lose the man you loved, the man who knew you like a book he'd read millions of times. It was heartbreaking beyond words and drained the life out of you.

Revisiting that feeling in that moment, as she headed toward the hotel, made her more motivated that ever. It made her reach back into her memories to where details of the first case rested, back where the Nobilini case had started.

Her mind tried to latch onto a name—a name she knew well but that had faded into the deeper regions of her memory. It was a name she was reminded of earlier in the day, when they had met with Jack Tucker's friends at the yacht club.

Cass Nobilini.

You know there are answers there, Kate thought.

There might be. And she'd go looking for them if it came to that.

But she really hoped it wouldn't. She hoped she could make it the rest of her life never seeing Cass Nobilini again. But she also knew the chances of that were very slim—that she may, in fact, be seeing her sooner rather than later.

CHAPTER SIX

They settled in at the hotel's bar just as the dinner rush started to pack the place out. While the prospect of a glass of wine was indeed promising, Kate found that she was a bit more excited about the burger she ordered. Usually when on a case, she'd somehow forget to eat lunch, leaving her ravenous at the end of the day. As she sank her mouth into the burger for the first bite, she saw DeMarco giving her a small smile. It was her first authentic smile of the day.

"What?" Kate asked through a mouthful of burger.

"Nothing," DeMarco said, picking at her grilled chicken salad. "It's reassuring to see a woman of your size and age eat like that."

Swallowing down the bite, Kate nodded and said, "I was gifted with an amazing metabolism."

"Oh, what a bitch."

"It's worth it to be able to eat like this."

A brief silence passed between them, which was shattered by both of them laughing together at the exchange. It felt good to be able to lower her guard around DeMarco after the tense day they'd shared. DeMarco seemed to feel the same way, based on what she said after sipping from her glass of wine.

"Sorry I was so bitter all day. The whole thing of breaking news like that to a family…it's hard. I mean, I know it's hard, but it's especially hard on me. I had this thing happen in my past that jarred me. I thought I was over it, but apparently, I'm not."

"What happened?"

DeMarco took a moment, perhaps considering whether or not she wanted to delve into the story. With another large sip of wine, she decided to go ahead with it. She let out a sigh and began.

"I knew I was gay when I was fourteen. I had my first girlfriend when I was sixteen. When I was seventeen, my girlfriend Rose and I—she was nineteen—decided that we were going to go ahead and come out. We both had kept it a secret, particularly from our parents. So there we were—about to break the news. I was supposed to meet her at her house and we were going to tell her parents, who, I might add, assumed that Rose and I were just really good friends. I was always at her house and vice versa, you know? So I'm sitting there on her parents' couch when I get a phone call. It's from the police, telling me that Rose was in a car accident and that she had died right away, upon impact. I was called rather than her parents because they found her cell phone and saw that I took up about ninety percent of her call history.

"So I break down right away and her parents are sitting there, wondering what the hell happened—why I'm suddenly in tears, on my knees in the floor. And I had to tell them. I had to tell them what the policeman had just told me." She paused here, poked at her salad a bit, and then added, "It was the absolute worst moment of my life."

Kate found it hard to look at DeMarco; she was delivering the story not as an emotional part of it, but as if she were a robot, reciting back a series of events. Still, the tale was more than enough to explain DeMarco's attitude the previous night when she, Kate, had volunteered them to break the bad news to Missy Tucker.

"If I'd known any of that, you know I wouldn't have volunteered us," Kate said.

"I know. And I knew it then. But my emotions strangled any reason or logic. Quite honestly, I just needed to sit and stew in it for a while. Sorry you caught the brunt of it."

"Water under the bridge," Kate said.

"Have you done that a lot in your career? Breaking news like that?"

"Oh yes. And it never gets easy. It becomes easier to detach yourself from it, but the act itself is never easy."

The table fell into silence again. The waiter came by and refilled their wine as Kate continued to work on her burger.

"So how's your man?" DeMarco asked. "Allen, right?"

"He's doing good. He's just about to the point in the relationship where he worries about me still being involved in the FBI. He'd prefer that I take a desk job. Or stay retired."

"So it's getting serious, huh?"

"It feels that way. And part of me is excited for it. But there's a small part of me that feels like it would be a waste of time. He and I are both quickly approaching sixty. Starting a new relationship at that age feels ... odd, I guess." Sensing that DeMarco would latch onto the topic if she was allowed to do so, Kate quickly redirected the conversation.

"How about you? Has the love life picked up at all since the last time we had this awkward conversation?"

DeMarco shook her head and smiled. "No, but that's by choice. I'm still enjoying the Land of One-Night Stands while I still can."

"Does that make you happy?"

DeMarco seemed genuinely shocked by the question. "It sort of does. I don't need the responsibilities and requirements that come with a relationship right now."

Kate chuckled. She had never been in the Land of One-Night Stands. She'd met Michael while in college and married him a year and a half later. It had been the kind of relationship where she had started to understand that they would spend their lives together as soon as their first kiss.

"So where's the next step in this case?" DeMarco asked.

"I'm thinking about revisiting the initial case rather than just using it as a reference. I'm wondering if there's new information that might have come up within the Nobilini family. But ... well, like your story about your girlfriend being killed while you sat on her parents' sofa, it's not territory that is easily ventured back into."

"So more awkward visits and conversations tomorrow?"

"Maybe. I'm not sure yet."

"Is there anything worth filling me in on before I step blindly into it?"

"Probably. But trust me ... it would be better saved for the morning. Going into it right now is only going to keep us up late and screw with my sleep."

"Oh. *Those* kinds of stories."

"Exactly."

They finished their current glasses of wine and paid their checks. On the way up to their rooms, Kate thought about the story DeMarco had just told—of that sad glimpse into her past. It made her very aware that she knew very little about her partner. If they were working in a normal relationship, seeing one another nearly every day rather than once or twice every few months, that would certainly be different. It made her wonder if she was doing her part to truly get to know DeMarco.

They parted ways at their rooms—Demarco's directly across the hall from Kate's—and Kate felt the need to say something. Anything, really, to let her know that she appreciated DeMarco's willingness to open up.

"Again, I apologize about last night. It's dawning on me that I don't know you well enough to be making decisions like that for both of us."

"It's fine, really," DeMarco said. "I should have told you about it last night."

"We need to be intentional about getting to know one another. If we're trusting each other with our lives, it's kind of necessary. Maybe outside of work sometime."

"Yeah, that would be nice." DeMarco paused here as she opened her door. "You said you had some thinking to do ... about the old case. The Nobilini case. Let me know if you need someone to ping ideas off of."

"I'll do that," Kate said.

With that, they entered the rooms, ending the day between them. Kate kicked off her shoes and went directly to her laptop. As she booted it up, she called Director Duran. As she'd expected, he did not answer his phone but the line was then redirected to his assistant director, a woman named Nancy Saunders. Kate put in a request to have digital copies of the Nobilini files sent to her email as soon as possible. She knew that DeMarco had brought a few, but it was just the overview of the case. Kate felt the need to get back into the grittiness of the case, right down to the finer details. Saunders committed to getting it done, letting her know she'd have them by nine o'clock the following morning.

Cass Nobilini, Kate thought.

She'd thought of the woman almost right away, after Duran had told her about the possible connection. She'd thought of her again when she'd heard the wails and screeches of Missy Tucker as she grieved her murdered husband, and then again while talking to Jack Tucker's friends.

Cass Nobilini, the mother of Frank Nobilini. The woman who had found it insulting and darkly improper for the media to latch onto the event of her son's murder just because he had once worked closely with a few popular men in Congress as a financial advisor. Kate felt that she had been a fool to even pretend that this case was not going to lead her back to Cass Nobilini in some way.

It was that thought that remained with her for the remainder of the night, clinging to the forefront of her mind as she eventually lay down in bed and drifted off to sleep.

She could still see the crime scene in her head. The wear and tear of memory made it a little faded and rusty, but the haziness was stripped away whenever she dreamed about it. In her dreams, it was as clear as if she were watching television.

And she saw it that night, managing to fall asleep shortly after nine yet twitching and moaning slightly in her sleep as the midnight hour approached.

The scene: Frank Nobilini, killed in the alley and still holding his BMW keys. The case had eventually led her back to his home, a four-bedroom house in Ashton. She'd started in the garage, which had smelled faintly of lawn trimmings from a recent grass-cutting. She'd felt like she was in some haunted place, like Frank Nobilini's spirit was there somewhere, waiting for her. Maybe in the empty space where his BMW was supposed to be but, at that time, had sat in a parking lot several blocks away from where his body had been found. The garage had been cold and like some weird tomb. It was one of the handful of scenes from her past that always came back vividly for reasons she had never understood.

There had been no clues of any kind at the house, no signs of why someone might want to kill him. One would think that maybe it was for his very nice car, but the keys had been in his hand. The house had been clean. Almost eerily so. No paperwork trails, nothing of note in the address books or the mail. Nothing.

In her dream, Kate was standing there, in the alley. She was touching the still-sticky smear of gore on side of the wall in the same experimental way a child might touch a stray drop of syrup on the kitchen table. She turned and looked behind her, wanting to look down the alleyway, but saw the interior of the Nobilinis' garage instead. As if she had been invited inside, she walked to the wooden stairs that led to the door that would take her into the kitchen. She then moved in the way that only dreams allow, fluidly, almost being projected rather than moved by her legs. She somehow ended up in the bathroom, looking to the large tub/ shower combo installed in the wall. It was filled with blood. Something was moving beneath the surface, causing little bubbles to rise to the top of the blood. When one would pop, it would send tiny droplets against the porcelain side of the wall.

She backed away, stepping through the bathroom doorway and into the hall. There, Frank Nobilini was walking toward her. Behind him, his wife, Jennifer, simply watched. She even gave Kate a harmless little wave as her dead husband lurched down the hallway. Frank walked very zombie-like, slowly and with an exaggerated gait.

"It's okay," someone said from behind her.

She turned and saw Cass Nobilini, Frank's mother, sitting on the floor. She looked tired, defeated... as if she were waiting for an executioner's blade.

"Cass...?"

"You were never going to solve it. It was over your head. But time... it has a way of changing things, doesn't it?"

Kate turned back to Frank, still advancing. As he came by the bathroom door, Kate saw that some of the blood had come out of the tub and into the floor, seeping out into the hallway. When Frank stepped in it, it made a wet sucking sound.

Frank Nobilini smiled at her and raised his hand to her—slightly decayed and mottled. Kate slowly backed away, raising her own hands to her face, and let out a scream.

She woke up, feeling the scream lodged in her throat.

That damned house. She had never understood why it had rattled her in such a way. Maye because of Jennifer Nobilini's screams and wails, laced with the picture-perfect house … it had all seemed surreal. Like something out of an artsy horror movie.

Kate sat up and slowly inched her way to the edge of the bed. She collected a few deep breaths and looked at the clock: 1:22. The only light in the room came from the numbers on the alarm clock and the faint glow of the security lights outside, barely shining in through the closed blinds.

She'd had dreams concerning Cass Nobilini and that first case before, but this one had been a doozy. Her heart was still hammering in her chest as she got out of bed and walked to the mini-fridge for a bottle of water. She sipped some down as she walked over to the bedside table where she had set her laptop up.

She flicked on the bedside lamp and logged into her email. She had only one new one, and that had come from Assistant Director Saunders. She'd tasked an agent with digging up the Nobilini files and they had been delivered to her shortly before midnight.

She knew that there was no way she'd return to a deep sleep, so she opened them up one by one, a bit uncomfortable by how natural it seemed and how familiar those old files felt. She looked through them briefly at first, in the same way someone visiting a somewhat familiar location might give the area a once-over before truly starting to study the place. When she came to the last of the twenty-six pages, she went back to the beginning. But before getting deep into it, she went to the little complimentary coffee maker and set a pot to brew. As it started to percolate, she made the bed, relocated the laptop to the small table against the far wall, and made herself a little workstation.

Within five minutes, she was reading each of the files line by line and sipping on a cup of very dark, very cheap coffee. The account of Frank

Nobilini felt like an old friend, the sort of friend that only called with bad news. The case detailed every conversation she'd had with neighbors and friends in Ashton. As she read over them all, she was unsettled with how similar they all were to the conversations she'd recently had concerning Jack Tucker.

The only thing that had even remotely resembled anything of merit had come from twenty-two-year-old Alice Delgado, a nanny for a family in Ashton who had cared for two kids, ages eight and eleven. Alice had admitted to making sexual advances toward Frank Nobilini when they had crossed paths at a local park. Frank had responded with flattery and polite rejection. While that had been the extent of it, the news of Frank's death had made Alice feel incredibly guilty—so guilty that she had contacted Jennifer Nobilini to confess. Jennifer, the caring and apparently flawless woman she was, had forgiven her almost right away.

Aside from that one detail, there had been nothing. Not in conversations, not at the crime scene, not in the Nobilinis' home. And nothing in the criminal records for Frank or Jennifer—no history of criminal activities, no enemies to speak of ... nothing.

Kate had remained on the case for six months, then took a step back, working on it only as a background project for another eight months before the case was totally given up on. It had not been the only unsolved case in her career, but it *had* been the only unclosed case with such a degree of strangeness to it.

As she read through, she did her best to apply Jack Tucker's death to it. And the more she read and reacquainted herself with the case, the more certain she became that Jack's murder was linked. It was either done by the exact same killer or a copycat.

It was 4:10 before she felt she had given the notes and files their proper attention. She stared at her second cup of coffee for a moment and then slowly picked up her cell phone. She placed a call to the twenty-four/ seven resource line at the bureau. It was a bit slower than a direct call to Saunders or Duran during the day but it was better than nothing.

After giving her name and badge number, she was greeted by a voice that was far too warm and pleasant for a quarter after four in the morning.

"Agent Wise, how can we help you?"

"I need the current address and phone number for a woman that probably lives somewhere in New York. Cass Nobilini."

"Okay, and is this going to be the best number to send that information to?"

"It is. Thanks."

But even before she ended the call, Kate felt guilty as hell. There was a very large part of her that hoped Cass Nobilini had decided to move. If Kate could make it through this case without having to cross paths with Cass, she'd consider herself fortunate.

You know that won't happen, Kate thought. *You're just not that lucky.*

She got her answer twenty minutes later when she got a return call from the bureau. After giving the phone number for one Cass Nobilini, the address confirmed it.

"127 Harper Street. Ashton, New York."

CHAPTER SEVEN

Kate was wired on nerves and late-night coffee as she and DeMarco loaded up into the car the following morning. They'd had a quick complimentary breakfast within the hotel before leaving, but Kate had not been able to eat much. Her stomach felt even more unstable as she pulled the car out into Sunday morning traffic, realizing that she was going to have to try to explain her history with Cass Nobilini to DeMarco.

"Here's the thing," Kate said. "I don't want you feeling like I'm keeping things from you and I certainly don't want you to feel like I'm expecting you to go into this blindly. So I need to tell you about Cass Nobilini. I need to tell you how, even above the unsolved murder of her son, dealing with her was the hardest part of this case."

"Was she confrontational?" DeMarco asked.

"No. Not quite. But ... well, it's hard to explain."

"We've got a twenty-minute drive out to Ashton. Try."

Kate knew she had to get it out—if not to inform DeMarco, then to simply expel it from her mind so it would quit nagging at her. She was pleased to find that once she got started, it really wasn't that difficult at all.

"Eight years ago, when Frank Nobilini was killed, I met Cass Nobilini—Frank's mother. She had been told the news about a day or so before the FBI arrived. She was grieving, sure, but she was also ... *determined*. That's the best word I can think to use. She was determined to figure out who had killed her son. She was extremely helpful when we spoke with her but as far as she was concerned, everyone was a suspect. Everyone from the guy that got his order wrong at the deli to the mailman. I wish I was exaggerating here, DeMarco, but I'm not. She would call at least four or five times a day to ask me if I had considered someone in particular. And the longer we went without finding a killer, the more persistent she became. The more time that went by without us coming up with a suspect, the more insistent she became that she could figure it out herself... that we were very bad at our jobs. And because I was the lead on it, I got the brunt of it all."

"Was it like a coping mechanism?" DeMarco.

"That's what the bureau psychiatrist said. And honestly, it's not that uncommon in cases where the death is sudden and the killer is never found. But Cass went above and beyond. There was one day where I had to sit down with her and get a little mean; I had to tell her to back off and let the bureau do their job. She responded in an honest way, telling us that if we were doing our jobs the right way, we'd have her son's killer in custody.

"She obeyed for the most part, though. At first. When we were quietly taken off of the case and just sort of had it running the background, I got a call one night. A call from Cass Nobilini. This was about five months after we'd stopped running hard after the case. She called me and told me that she knew who had killed her son. She said the FBI needed to come back to Ashton. And I had to tell her the truth—that unless she had hard evidence to support her claims, the bureau couldn't become active on it again. Of course, she never had that evidence. So she called me one more time a few weeks later to let me know that she would forever blame the FBI—me, in particular, as the lead agent on the case—for not bringing her son's killer to justice."

"That's a little unfair," DeMarco said.

"It is. And unrealistic, too. But for some reason, that always stuck with me. At the risk of sounding like a diva, I always took failure very hard. The fact that I could never find such a blatant killer *and* was being blamed by a mother of the victim for never finding the killer... well, that's haunted me for years."

"And we're about to pay her a visit," DeMarco said. She rubbed at her head and gave a lopsided grin. "Now I feel *really* bad for giving you such a hard time about Missy Tucker. Did you call ahead?"

"No. I probably should have. But I didn't want to give her any warning. I have no clue how she'll respond to seeing me."

"Since she lives in Ashton, I'd assume she's already heard about the murder. Any chance you think she might be *expecting* you to show up?"

To that, Kate had no answer. What she didn't dare say, though, was that she was actually hoping Cass Nobilini would not be home.

It was the same house Kate had been inside eight years ago. She was pretty sure the porch had been repainted and that most of the landscaping was new, but it was eerily familiar otherwise. As she and DeMarco stepped up onto the porch steps, Kate felt a little foolish at the fact that her heart seemed to be trying to beat right out of her chest.

"You good?" DeMarco asked.

Before she could even think about the answer, Kate knocked on the door with a hard, rapid motion.

Almost right away, there was a response from inside, a sing-song *"Coming! One second!"*

The past came roaring back to Kate. Being blamed for not finding the killer, having to tell Cass to calm the hell down and stay out of the way of the FBI. It all hit her as she heard the footfalls approaching and for a moment, she nearly wanted to make a run for it. But then the door was opening in front of them and a woman straight out of Kate's past looked out at them. Most of her hair was now gray and there was an abundance of wrinkles on her seventy-year-old face, but she looked remarkably upbeat, all things considered.

It was clear that Cass recognized her right away. She looked from Kate to DeMarco and then back to Kate. The slow smile that crept onto her face seemed genuine enough.

"Agent Wise," Cass said. "It's ... well, I guess it's nice to see you."

"You, too."

"I thought you'd show up sooner or later. You're here in town about Jack Tucker, I take it?"

"Yes."

Cass nodded and let out a sigh. She stared at Kate for a moment, just long enough for a thick tension to worm its way back into Kate's heart.

"Well, come on in," she said. "I've got some cinnamon rolls that just came out of the oven. And coffee ready to go."

Cass led them into the house, walking casually ahead of them. The smell of freshly baked cinnamon rolls beckoned like a ghostly finger, pulling them forward.

"Looks like you were right," Kate whispered softly to DeMarco as they walked down the hallway. "It *is* almost as if she was expecting me. I'm a sucker for a good cinnamon roll."

Cass led them into her kitchen. Kate thought it, like some of the exterior of the house, had seen some TLC since the last time she visited. As she perched herself on a barstool along the kitchen counter, the entire scene from eight years ago flashed in her head.

I was standing, leaning against the counter by the stove, when Cass nearly fainted from the grief of losing her son. Her husband had died two years earlier. Prostate cancer. She cried out to him in her anguish and pleaded with me to explain it all to her.

Kate shook the thought away, not allowing herself to go back there. Besides, Cass looked well. Perhaps whatever skewed motivations had pushed her all those years ago had died. Maybe she was now a perfectly healthy and rational woman. Time healed all wounds, right?

"Mrs. Nobilini, this is—" Kate started.

"Oh, I think you and I have been through enough where you can call me Cass."

With a smile, Kate tried again. "Cass, this is my partner, Agent DeMarco. I've informed her of our history."

"All of it?" Cass asked as she took cinnamon rolls out of a still-steaming pan and placed them on plates she took from the cupboard.

"Yes. Even the things you probably wouldn't want a stranger to know."

Cass nodded as she brought the agents each a cinnamon roll. "I'm not particularly proud of that time of my life. I dealt with my pain in sorrow in some very questionable ways. I always meant to call you … to apologize …"

"It's okay," Kate said. "How are you?"

"I'm okay now. But that period went on for years. I...well, I nearly broke the law a few times if I'm being honest. Surveilling people, coming close to breaking and entering a few times." She sat down on the other side of the bar on her own stool and joined them with her own roll. "I devoted my life to it for several months. The final straw was when close friends of mine called the police on me. Not for breaking any laws, but because they feared I was a danger to myself. I went to therapy and worked it all out."

Kate wasn't sure what to say. She couldn't imagine going through that sort of pain, even after losing her own husband several years ago to dubious circumstances.

"Well, as you said at the door," DeMarco said, apparently sensing Kate's hesitation, "we're in the area to try to solve another murder. Jack Tucker. A murder that seems to be eerily similar to your son's."

"Can I ask how similar?" Cass asked. But her tone indicated she might not be prepared to hear it.

"Same type of gun. Same execution style. Another resident of Ashton who appears to have been a very happily married man with a perfect life, found in an alleyway in New York City."

"My God," Cass said.

"I wonder, though," Kate said. "In all of that time you spent working towards trying to find answers, did you come across *anything* that, even now, felt like it might lead somewhere?"

"No. Nothing." Cass looked away, poking at her cinnamon roll in embarrassment. "And after a while, it occurred to me that anyone that was able to kill Frank in such a blatant and egregious way...well, they're probably long gone by now."

"It would be a reasonable thing to assume," Kate said. "In terms of Jack Tucker, did you know him or his family by any chance?"

"I didn't personally," she said. "But something occurred to me yesterday that seems odd. It might be nothing, but...it doesn't feel like it."

"What's that?" Kate asked.

"Do you remember Alice Delgado?"

The name popped up in her head as if it had been waiting all along. The fact that she had revisited that name on the old case files the night before no longer seemed by chance. "I do. She admitted to making advances towards Frank and was so stricken with guilt that she visited Jennifer and told her about it."

"Right. As I understand it, Alice worked with Missy Tucker a few years back. It was a small job, just manning a register at a local boutique shop that closed almost as quickly as it opened up."

"How long ago was this?"

"Maybe four years ago, give or take. The place was only open for like a year and a half. Everything in there was just too damned expensive."

"Have you reached out to Jennifer since Jack Tucker's murder?" Kate asked. "I imagine it brought a lot of new stuff up. New pain and questions."

"No. I thought about it. But I didn't want to assume that the Tucker murder would automatically bring up Frank's murder in her head. She may not even be aware of the way in which Jack was killed. She sort of clammed up after Frank died. We don't really talk much. Her entire life is completely centered around her children now. Well, that and community projects. She's very ... *intimidating*. A lot of people see her as the poor widow, you know? But she's very involved. Community projects, school stuff for the kids. I think she's really active with the PTA."

"They had two, right?"

"Yes. Carter and Elisa. Jennifer *has* managed to sort of pick up the pieces ... starting a new life and all that. But you know ... I hate to throw her under the bus but even though she's a bit older now, she hangs around with younger ladies. I think it's because of the PTA at the middle school. There's a tight-knit group of ladies involved in the middle school PTA."

"How's that throwing her under the bus?" DeMarco asked.

"It's a small town, dear," Cass said. "People gossip all the time, especially the women. Maybe even more so with the women on the PTA. I know it might sound fickle, but that's Ashton for you. If there were rumors or gossip or anything related to Jack Tucker or the brief little working relationship between Missy Tucker and Alice Delgado, I guarantee you it was circulated in that little group."

"Are you not part of the group?" Kate asked. She took a huge bite of her cinnamon roll as she waited for an answer.

"Oh, I'm too old. I only know these women because you get to know everyone in a town like this."

Kate finished up her cinnamon roll, starting to get a good idea of where they'd have to go next. It would be yet another step back into her past but that was okay; if this visit with Cass Nobilini had turned out smooth, she figured anything was possible. Still, she felt a sense of foreboding as she thought about digging those old skeletons up, picking at those old scabs. It was also surreal to sense that in order to dig up any leads on her current case, she was going to have to keep revisiting an old one—an old one that had managed to escape her and taunt her for years afterward.

"Agent Wise, are you okay?"

Kate blinked, the sound of her name coming from Cass Nobilini jarring her out of her train of thought. "Yeah…I was just lost in my own thoughts for a second."

"Were you?" Cass asked, as if she understood perfectly. "Or were you—like me—stuck on trying to figure out how to escape that one certain part of your life you wish you could go back and change?"

To that, Kate could say nothing. It was as if the old lady had crawled into her mind and starting moving things around.

Would that be so bad? Kate wondered. *While she's in there, she can have these memories from her son's case and take them with her. I sure as hell don't want them anymore.*

But that wasn't exactly true. Because the longer she sat in Cass's kitchen, the more certain she became that crumbs from that old case would be what it took to close the Jack Tucker case.

CHAPTER EIGHT

It took quite a while for Kate and DeMarco to track down Alice Delgado. When they found that she was not at home, they requested her number from the bureau. The number went straight to voicemail. Kate then called the head office of the school that her son, Patrick, attended to see if they had any secondary contact information on file, since, like Jennifer Nobilini, Alice was actively involved with the PTA. That's where they hit pay dirt. The secondary information was not necessary, as Alice was currently at the elementary school, speaking with a local DJ about the set-up and playlist for the upcoming Fall Festival.

Kate and DeMarco entered the school, heading for the office first in order to be properly buzzed in. It was alarming to Kate to see that schools these days had to be so security-based. It had been twelve years since she had stepped foot in a school, and that had been to attend Melissa's graduation. While she had heard about some of the security measures taking place at even the smallest rural schools, seeing it firsthand was something very different—especially within an elementary school.

They found the gymnasium with no problem, following the sound of a few skidding sneakers and a bouncing basketball. When they got there, they saw some kids playing a game of five-on-five. On the right side of the gym, a gym teacher or coach of some sort watched the game. At the far end of the gym, a middle-aged woman was speaking to a tall man who seemed to be very interested in a particular corner of the gym. Kate assumed this to be the DJ that Alice was working with.

They walked to the far end, toward the DJ and the woman Kate assumed to be Alice. While she did not remember Alice Delgado nearly as well as Cass Nobilini, she assumed she would recognize the woman's

428

face. She saw each and every face from that case at least once or twice a month in her head. It had gotten better over the years, but those faces and their expressions always seemed to find a way to come back to haunt her.

As they got closer, she saw that it was indeed Alice Delgado. She was still quite pretty, a woman having just crossed the border of thirty that could easily pass as twenty-one with a little extra time in front of the mirror. And as Alice's face came into view, Kate started to recall how unpleasant the woman had been. Once she'd confessed to her attempt at seducing Frank Nobilini, she'd been honest and genuine in her remorse, but the guilt that had swept down on her had also turned her into something of a bitch. During follow-up visits and conversations, Alice had been confrontational and very heard to speak to.

The look Alice gave her when she noticed the two agents coming across the gym made Kate think that not only did Alice remember her quite well, but that she still held a grudge. Kate was reminded of Melissa who, on a few occasions, had referred to her own angry expressions as RBF, or "resting bitch face." And that's exactly what Kate was getting from Alice as she and DeMarco approached her.

"Ms. Delgado, can we have a minute of your time?" Kate asked.

Alice looked surprised, completely off of her game, but did her best to hide it with that stern and bitter look of anger.

"I'm in the middle of something," Alice said. But already, there was curiosity in her tone. In her eyes, too. Her disappointment and anger was quickly being overruled with her need to know why an FBI agent she met eight years ago had suddenly reappeared in the elementary school her seven year-old son was attending.

"I understand," Kate said. "But this will only take a moment and it's rather time sensitive."

She sighed, placed her hands on her hips, and looked to the DJ. "Could you give us a second?" she asked.

He nodded and walked away, heading over to check out the game of five-on-five. When he was safely out of earshot, Alice Delgado started speaking before Kate or DeMarco ever had the chance.

"Yes, I know about Jack Tucker. And I know that his murder was basically the same as Frank Nobilini's."

"Well, we're still lacking any sort of clues," Kate said.

"Just like last time, then?"

It was a biting remark. Kate was thrown off her game for a moment but was equally surprised when DeMarco took a single step forward and stood up for her. "No, not like last time. There are others dealing with their own grief right now. A woman named Missy Tucker—a woman we understand you worked with for a short time. So unless you wish what happened to Cass and Jennifer Nobilini eight years ago onto another widow, we'd appreciate your cooperation."

The look on Alice's face was one of utter disbelief. DeMarco might as well have just reached out and slapped her.

"Yes," Alice said, slowly starting to check her attitude. "We worked together for a small amount of time. The two of us and one other woman ran a little shop in town for a while."

"Did you get to know her well?" Kate asked.

"Fairly well, I'd say. We never really became close friends or anything like that, but we chatted quite a bit." She paused here and then added: "I'm sorry, but how does learning about Missy help you to find Jack Tucker's killer?"

"Because it's good to know if there was ever anything that came up in casual conversation that might have seemed odd to you," Kate said. "Anything that might have marred your opinion of their marriage."

Alice chuckled at this, shaking her head. "No. Good grief, they were like the picture of a perfect marriage. He was always doing things for her, always doting over her and the kids. I got pregnant very shortly after the FBI ditched Frank Nobilini's case. Married the father. And honestly, we always looked at the Tuckers' marriage as something to shoot for."

"Would it surprise you to know that Jack's mother was not the biggest fan of Missy?"

"It would not. That woman has issues. From what I understand, Jack was very close with his mother. This is just my own theory, but I think she took it as a competition when Jack got married and all of his attention went to his bride and their children. Shit... I knew that back when I first started working as a nanny in Ashton. Word gets around, you know.

Apparently, Jack's mother was competitive … wanted her little boy under her thumb at all times."

It was clear that Alice was still a little uncertain about talking to them. Like Kate, it was clear that she had issues from the case eight years before that she had not quite resolved yet. Maybe the guilt or the hurt of confessing to Jennifer Nobilini. Kate started to feel bad for her in that moment. More than that, she started to feel guilty all over again for having never found Frank Nobilini's killer.

"We spoke with Cass Nobilini this morning," Kate said. "She indicated that a lot of mothers of school-age kids might be part of social circles that tend to hear things other people might not be privy to."

"You mean gossip?" Alice asked.

Kate said nothing, hoping her silence would speak for itself.

"You're not wrong," Alice said with a hint of annoyance. "But I stand by what I said. There was absolutely nothing to say about Jack and Missy Tucker. They were perfect. Some of my friends sometimes use him as measuring stick—how they wish their husbands would love on them the way Jack loved on Missy. Let's face it, Agent Wise. Back in the day, when you and I first met, I was attracted to Frank Nobilini for a reason. I made a fool of myself for a reason. He was a good man, just like Jack. A kind and generous man and who was attractive as hell to me. It's attractive as hell to a lot of women, you know?"

"Any chance the Tuckers might have been just posturing it all?" DeMarco asked.

"If they were, they should be actors. In a town like Ashton, if you can somehow stay out of the grapevine, you're doing something right. So, no … the Tuckers were solid. If they were hiding secrets, they were pros about it."

"How about friends?" Kate asked. "While you were working with Missy, did she tend to talk about certain women that she hung out with?"

"Missy has one very good friend, a woman named Kelly Osman. There's another woman they tend to hang out with but I don't know her well. Jasmine Brooks is her name. They'd know a lot more about Missy and her life than I do. They're on the PTA as well, but they have kids in middle school. And that's the PTA Missy spends most of her time on. They tend to need the most help."

"Cass tells us that Jennifer Nobilini also serves with the PTA. Is that right?"

"Yes. She's pretty active, especially with art-related things. She sort of hops back and forth between this school and the middle school. She'll sort of poke her head into our little PTA circle of friends, but I think the gossip and small talk bothers her sometimes. She's extremely helpful with all things PTA but when the meetings and functions end, she mostly sticks to herself. Even when she helps out with her little community projects around town, she keeps a low profile. Doesn't want the attention, and keeps to herself."

"Are things...awkward between the two of you after what happened?"

Alice shrugged. "Maybe a bit. We don't really talk, you know? Even when we *are* in the same PTA meetings, we don't force it. We don't pretend nothing happened, but we're not hateful to one another, either. I have nothing against her. If anything, I respect the hell out of her."

"Thanks for the information," Kate said. "We'll let you get back to your project."

"Agent Wise...I think I speak on behalf of Cass Nobilini and Missy Tucker when I say that I hope you find the sonofabitch this time. Why come back and do this to someone else eight years later?"

"We're doing our best," Kate said.

A lopsided frown crossed Alice's face as Kate and DeMarco turned away. It was a frown that seemed to mock, to say: *Are you really?*

DeMarco fell in close to Kate as they exited the gymnasium. "Don't do that," she said.

"Don't do what?" Kate asked.

"Beat yourself up about the past. Leave the past where it is. You keep looking behind you and the present is going to sneak up on you and kick you in the teeth."

Kate nodded but in her head, she couldn't help but think: *I'm afraid it already has.*

❧ ❧ ❧

Kelly Osman was not nearly as difficult to find as Alice Delgado had been. Kelly worked at a bed and breakfast in Ashton, a business she and her husband owned and operated. It was tucked away in the far end of town where the sparkle of the Hudson River could just barely be seen from the expansive side lawn. When Kate and DeMarco arrived at the Ashton Views Bed and Breakfast, Kelly Osman was outside, tending to the rather gorgeous flower garden. After the slight shock of the sudden appearance of a pair of FBI agents, Kelly led them to a nearby sitting area on the other side of the flower garden. A few butterflies flitted back and forth among several hydrangeas as Kate and DeMarco sat on a bench. Looking quite uncomfortable, Kelly took a seat in a lazy Adirondack chair.

"I spoke with Missy this morning," Kelly said as she continued to gauge the agents. "And I was at her house yesterday, just being there for her and delivering a casserole. I can't... God, I can't even start to figure out how to support her in this. She loved Jack so much..."

"That's one of the things we wanted to talk to you about," Kate said. "As her friend, I understand that it might be hard to think of such things, but we need you to think about anything from their past that might have put a crack in what seemed like their perfect marriage."

"You're looking for motive for someone to kill him, right?" She trailed off here, looking out in the direction of the Hudson River. "You can look all you want, but I don't think you're going to find much of anything. If Jack had *any* enemies, it might have been from his work. He was an accountant. A big shot. You know that, right? He had some really big-name clients, too. From what I understand, he was like a savant at it. He was that kind of guy. Good at everything he touched. And Missy was always very quick to let everyone know it."

"She never said a cross word about him?" DeMarco asked.

"Not one that I ever heard. *Maybe* one time she griped about how he had a bad habit of always leaving his shoes by the coffee table, but that's about it."

"Did you know any of Jack's friends?" Kate asked.

"Well, he had a close-knit little group at the yacht club ..."

"Yes, we've already spoken to them."

"You know ... while I don't think I'd call them *friends*, my husband knew Jack pretty well at one point. A few years back, they'd meet with some of Jack's accounting associates and play a few rounds of tennis. And they also always attended what my husband called Dude Group—a group of dads that met maybe twice a year to smoke cigars and come up with plans to raise money for the schools. Fundraising and all that. The PTA without being the PTA."

"Do you think your husband would be willing to speak with us?" Kate asked.

"Sure. He's right inside, helping the cleaning crew. One second."

Kelly got up and ran into the two-story bed and breakfast. When she was gone, Kate sighed and rested her head against the back of the bench. "It was like this last time, too. There was never anything out of sorts or messed up about Frank Nobilini or his family. Not a single thing. No shady pasts, no real enemies to speak of. Just kind, everyday people with good lives."

"Maybe that's the connection right there," DeMarco suggested. "Clean living, good lives. Success, maybe? Good marriages?"

"I don't know. Thinking back to that original case, with the Nobilinis ... something about the way he was in the fetal position, his brains all over the wall. I always wondered if the killer was trying to tell us something ... to almost make fun of them somehow."

They both dwelled on this as Kelly came back out of the bed and breakfast. Her husband walked behind her, a tall African-American man with plain good looks. He joined them in the sitting area, taking up another Adirondack by his wife.

"Lamont Osman," he said, extending his hand and shaking Kate's and then DeMarco's. "Kelly says you want to ask me some questions about Jack Tucker?"

"Yes. How close were you, exactly?"

"Not very. I mean, it was more than just a nod-and-wave sort of thing as of late, but we hung out here and there several years ago. The most time I ever spent with him was playing tennis a few years back. But when he made that job transition, that sort of dried up."

"And he never said or did anything that made you think that maybe the perfect life scenario was a ruse?"

"Nothing jumps out at me," he said. "But then again, it's different with men. We don't exactly get together and dish out gossip." He playfully nudged Kelly as he said this.

"Hey," she said, though there wasn't much defensiveness to it.

"Any gossip about the Tuckers you'd care to share?" DeMarco asked, lightly prodding.

"Nothing worth mentioning," Kelly said. "Whenever Jack's name came up, it was to compare with someone else's husband. Honestly, I think a few ladies in the Ashton circles had a little crush on him."

Just like with Frank Nobilini, Kate thought.

"Would anyone act on such a thing around here?" Kate asked.

"Doubtful. And even if a woman had the audacity to act on something like that, it's pretty well known that Jack Tucker isn't that sort of guy."

"We keep hearing that," Kate said. "How can you be so sure?"

"I know it sounds mean," Lamont said, "but Jack wasn't a very exciting dude. Yes, he was kind and yes, he was the sort to keep a clean nose and stay out of trouble. But because of all of that, he would sort of fade into the background, you know? The type of guy that, if he went to a party, you'd have to think really hard the next day about whether you saw him there or not. A good guy for sure but ... well, if I'm being honest, sort of boring."

Boring, Kate thought. *There's that word again.*

Kate wracked her brain, trying to think of what else to ask, but she knew she'd end up coming to the same conclusion. That Jack Tucker was a nice guy, a real sweetheart, but sort of drab and plain.

Boring.

And then it dawned on her that maybe being boring, in and of itself, could potentially be a front for something else. And if a man could become very good at appearing boring, there was no telling what sorts of things he might become capable of hiding.

CHAPTER NINE

The day went by far too quickly as far as Kate was concerned. They'd gone from house to house—from family member to acquaintance and back again—and Kate felt that they had still gotten nowhere. It was the sort of case where she was practically just waiting for another body to show up. And God help her, she almost wanted that. It would at least present them with another opportunity to find evidence or clues.

They even revisited the alleyway where Jack Tucker's body had been discovered. Of course, they turned up nothing. Kate hadn't been expecting anything anyway—just hoping that maybe revisiting the scene would help her to view the murder through the eyes of the killer, to find some link between the alley and Ashton, the alley and Jack Tucker himself.

Following that, they huddled up back at the hotel, looking over the Jack Tucker case files. Kate made a meticulous list of things that they could potentially do to find some break in the case, prepared to pull an all-nighter if she had to. The list included: *examine shell casing from Ruger, speak to Detective Pritchard about how police handled scene from the start, check guest-logs of hotel Jack Tucker was staying in,* and *research client Jack was working for, RE: Adler and Johnson.*

Looking over the list, Kate knew that all of it was reaching. She could only hope that some useful nugget was buried in there somewhere.

She and DeMarco went their separate ways at 6:30. They agreed to split the list and reach out to bureau resources to get started on compiling the information. The first request Kate made was to find out recent clients and big-name jobs that Adler and Johnson had worked with. She was well aware that such a request could take several days and that she'd likely end up speaking with Daiju Hiroto tomorrow. She figured she could do some basic research online to get news-worthy details that were probably not relevant to their case but might lead them in the right direction. She planned to order dinner, shower, and do just that but was stopped before she could get into any of it when her cell phone rang.

She was rather confused and a bit hopeful when she saw that it was Duran. Maybe they'd had a break in DC. Maybe she could get out of New York and never have to step foot in Ashton again.

"Hello, Director Duran," she answered.

"Kate ... I just got notified of a request you made for the last two years of clients working with Adler and Johnson. Can you tell me what that's about?"

"Well, I know for a fact that they are currently working for a client that works in the nuclear decommissioning industry. The world *nuclear* makes it easy to believe that maybe not everyone is a fan of such a company, no matter what their motives are. I thought it might be worth looking into the business practices and recent contract Adler and Johnson have drawn up. Maybe there was someone Jack Tucker worked with that had it in for him."

"You know how miserable that task is going to be. An accounting firm as big as Adler and Johnson is going to throw roadblocks at us every step of the way. It would be months—hell, even maybe years—before we got what we wanted. If we got it at all."

"I'm aware of that, sir. But we're running out of places to look."

"I'm starting to see that," Duran said. "And look, Kate, you understand that with your lack of results on the Nobilini case, it makes me wonder if I made a mistake sending you out there. I think I'm going to call you in. DeMarco, too."

"Sir, it's only been two days."

"You're right. but word is starting to spread around here that Jack Tucker was at one time working independently with a senator up there in New York, as a private accountant of sorts. He's worried about his own ass, but won't tell us why. Use your imagination there. Fraud, maybe. Something else unsavory ... who knows? But he's getting antsy that this hasn't been wrapped yet and because of that, the bureau is under a spotlight."

"I'm hoping you're not going where it *sounds like* you're going with this," Kate said.

"You failed to close the Nobilini case eight years ago. If this story becomes a news item and your name pops up, people are going to make that connection. Yes, it would look bad for the FBI, sending an agent that already failed a similar—probably a *linked*—case. But it would not reflect well on you, either."

"So you're wanting to pull me to protect me?" Kate asked, her voice laced with sarcasm.

"View it how you want," Duran said. And the hell of it was, she did think she could hear some sorrow or disappointment in his voice. "But I want you back in DC by tomorrow morning. I'm going to line up some-one else for this—someone that can view the case with fresh eyes."

"Someone younger?"

The question was out of her mouth before she could stop it, and she instantly regretted it.

Duran was silent for a while—for such a lengthy moment that Kate thought he had hung up on her. "View it how you'd like, Agent Wise. But I'm more concerned about your failure to wrap the case eight years ago and how another potential failure could look. Perhaps this is my fault. I should have thought about all of this before assuming you'd be the best fit."

"Well, you know what they say about assuming, sir."

"Agent Wise, I understand that the working relationship between you and I—and the bureau, as well, for that matter—is a special and strange one at this juncture. But I'd advise you to keep a civil tongue with me from now on."

This time, he *did* end the call. Kate could hear the audible click when he hung up. She tossed her phone on the bed and looked around the room, not sure if she wanted to be angry or saddened.

When she realized that she had to break this sudden news to DeMarco, she was able to finally decide on an emotion. As she slowly made her way out of the room and across the hall to her partner's room, frustration sank in like a lead weight. And by the time she knocked on DeMarco's door, it was closer to devastation.

CHAPTER TEN

When she walked through the front door of her house in Richmond eleven hours later, Kate could still feel the weight of the case—of the unsolved murders of both Frank Nobilini and Jack Tucker—as if it had been bolted to her shoulders. She carelessly dropped her single packed bag to the floor outside of the kitchen and went to the couch where she collapsed in a heap. She was pissed off but there was also a logical part of her that understood Duran's decision—and that he also had no damned business assigning her to the case in the first place if he was going to be worried about covering the bureau's ass.

To get her mind off of it, she stretched out on the couch and texted Melissa. **Back home. Dead-end case. How are you and the little one?**

She then pulled her personal laptop off of the coffee table and opened up her email. She sent a short and sweet email to Duran, copying in DeMarco, just to let him know that she was back home and officially off of the case. It took a lot of effort not to throw in a little jab of some sort, but she managed.

She wondered if maybe Melissa would be able to come over with Michelle later, maybe for dinner. Or if Melissa was busy (she did, after all, have a family and a life of her own), maybe Allen would want to come over.

She'd be happy with either one, so long as she didn't have to spend the afternoon alone. If she did that, she knew her mind would stay stuck on the Jack Tucker case, trying to figure it out and dig for any sort of clues until her eyes slapped shut on her later in the night. As she managed to pull herself from the couch to see what she had in the fridge for lunch, her cell phone dinged at her as Melissa responded.

Sorry for the dead end. Michelle and I are good.

She responded with: **Want to join me for dinner later?**

The response came back quickly, making Kate assume that Melissa was on a break at work. **Sorry. No can do. Family dinner tonight. It's a big deal to the hubs.**

She was disappointed, sure. But she understood. Frankly, she was happy and relieved that Melissa had managed to become part of a happy and well-managed family. With a sad smile, she sent her daughter: **Maybe tomorrow we can do breakfast?**

She received a **Probably not** within seconds. **I have work. And then we're leaving town for a few days to go see Terry's parents. Sorry, mom. But I'm glad you're back home and safe.**

She completely understood it all but still, it hurt. She wondered if this was how Melissa had felt all those times she'd needed her mother but her mother was occupied with work. She thought of little Michelle and although she had seen her less than two weeks ago, she couldn't help but feel as if she were being an absentee grandmother. Even when she *was* home and not being occupied with her job with bureau, her mind was always there. Wanting to get better, wanting to stay sharp, wanting to make sure her age did not define her.

She set her phone down and then set about making lunch. She did her best to tuck the text conversation with Melissa into the back of her head.

She stood there, staring into the refrigerator, feeling lost. *On the hunt for a killer one day and realizing that I badly need to clean out my fridge the next,* Kate thought. *What the hell kind of a life is this?*

As she settled down at the kitchen table with a tuna sandwich, she couldn't help but wonder if Duran had a point yesterday in his thinly veiled little barbs. After all, she had retired a year and a half ago because she felt that she deserved it—that she had given all she could and that she had left her best years in the bureau behind her. Maybe she should have left it that way. If she had, she wouldn't currently be eating a cold tuna sandwich by herself, wondering if Duran, DeMarco, Michelle, Allen, and God only knew who else saw her as nothing more than a sad aging lady who just couldn't let go of her glory years.

Maybe this was her sign. Maybe this was the final indicator she needed to show once and for all that it was over. She should have stayed retired. She *should* retire. For good. Duran would probably see it as a godsend—an easy way out of a situation he likely wished he had never created.

She looked to her phone. All it would take was a single call. She didn't think Duran would put up too much of a fight. If he put one up at all.

She grabbed the phone and thought about it. She saw the body of Jack Tucker in the alley and then the body of Frank Nobilini in a very similar alley. Both shot in the back of the head as if it were nothing.

The shell casings from the Ruger.

Execution style.

Two relatively plain and boring men, discarded as if they were nothing.

Boring ...

She had no idea why that word seemed so important to her. It continued to nag at her, seeming to itch along the back of her head.

She pulled up her contacts and instead of calling up Duran to bail out of their little arrangement, she called Allen. He answered right away but he seemed to be lacking his usual good cheer.

"Hey there, Katie."

She smiled. She'd hated that name as a kid but she loved it when Allen used it. It made her feel young. She assumed it made *him* feel young as well.

"You got plans tonight?" she asked.

"I thought you were in New York."

"Yeah, that was fleeting. A dead-end case that, quite frankly, has me feeling a little down. I thought you might like to come over and change that."

"Yeah ... I don't know, Kate."

There was caution in his voice, as if he were choosing his words very carefully.

"Everything okay?" she asked.

"I'd like to think so, but I don't know. Kate … I know I mentioned this once before and we just sort of shrugged it off but I'm not a fan of only being called on or needed when it's convenient for you. When the job comes calling, it's Kate on Duty. You're in this whole other world. But then when things are in a lull, you rely on me. Honestly, I don't really care and if we were twenty-five years younger, I wouldn't care at all. But … I don't know."

"That feels a little unfair."

"Oh, I know. And I hate to even mention it. But it's unfair to me, too. You have to see that, right?"

She figured he had a point. She felt a little self-involved not to have realized it before. "So what do we do?"

"For starters, I'm going to stay here tonight. I think it might do me some good to not come running at your beck and call."

"Allen, I never meant for it to sound like that."

"I know that, too. And that's why I think maybe we cool it for a while. Take some time, Kate. Figure out what it is you really want. When you think you have an actual answer, please do call me. Because I'll be honest with you … I think I was starting to fall pretty hard."

"Yeah, me too." A flush of heat raced through her as she admitted this to him.

"Let's check back in later. As selfish as it might sound, I don't think I'm emotionally prepared to be second to work … especially in a new relationship. Especially at this age."

"Allen … I can't …"

He gave her a moment and then asked: "You can't what?"

But she wasn't sure how to respond. How should she explain the sense of failure and worthlessness she was feeling? How could she explain the feeling of being haunted by a case—by two men who had been killed in the same way, their killer eluding her completely?

"I can't make that decision right now," she said. She hated the feeling of the words in her mouth but knew that they were absolutely true.

"It's okay. I'm serious. Let's check back in later. You reach out to me when you're ready. I'll be here, though I can't promise for how long." He paused, cleared his throat to shove aside the emotion that was trying to climb into his voice, and then ended the conversation with a simple "Bye."

He ended the call, leaving Kate with a dead line in her hand. The feeling that swept through her was far too similar to what she had felt when Duran had ended their call yesterday. Disappointment. Sadness. The feeling of not being good enough.

As much as she loathed doing it, she felt herself starting to cry. First, realizing that she was slowly starting to drift away from Melissa, and now Allen had apparently had enough. Jesus, was she really *that* divided when it came to her personal life and her new situation within the bureau? Rogue tears cascaded down her cheeks. In that moment, her world felt entirely empty and void. Just her and a stupid tuna sandwich.

And somewhere out there, a killer who had shot two men in the back of the head, execution style.

When her phone rang just after six that afternoon, she was hoping it would be Melissa. She was almost equally as pleased to find that it was not her daughter, but DeMarco.

"You feeling like a total fuck-up today, too?" DeMarco asked her.

"A bit. But you shouldn't. I think you were removed just because you were paired with me. If anything, I think I need to offer you an apology."

"Don't you dare," DeMarco said with a laugh. "You probably can't tell because of my cool and icy demeanor, but I've learned a lot from you. I was excited when they paired me with you seven months ago and I'm still excited. I'm just as frustrated as you about being pulled from the case, though."

Kate thought about venting to her about the call she'd had with Allen earlier in the day but decided against it. Yes, they needed to become closer to one another, but that didn't necessarily mean they needed to fill any down time or silence with relationship grievances.

"Any idea what Duran is going to assign you to now that you're off of the Jack Tucker case?"

"I don't know yet. I'm going to make a push to dig into the Adler and Johnson stuff you were requesting. I'm sure it'll be better than whatever surveillance detail he'll stick me on until something better comes along."

"You don't have to do that."

"I want to. A well-to-do man working with people who are *that* filthy rich and connected to nuclear decommissioning ... I don't know. It sounds rife with possible scenarios."

Kate thought so, too. But she also knew that Duran had been right yesterday. Pulling those kinds of details would take months, and they'd be bogged down in paperwork and legalities the entire time.

"Well, let me know when you have a free weekend. I'd love to have you down here for a day out on the town."

"Include that cute grandbaby of yours in the deal, and I'll see what I can do. Later, Kate."

Kate ended the call, warmed by the gesture DeMarco had made by calling. It was a little unlike her and, Kate thought, was probably an attempt at putting the final touches on their attempt at patching up the tension that had been between them for most of their visit to New York.

It was even more depressing to realize that she had somehow managed to grow more attached to DeMarco, a representation of work, than she had with her family and personal life over the last half a year or so.

Then just quit, she thought. *The FBI will be just fine without you. Do you really think that highly of yourself?*

Again, she knew it would be easy. Just one phone call. But she knew she couldn't. Especially right now. If it had come on the heels of a successfully closed case, that would be one thing. But to quit now, right after yet another case in Ashton had managed to slip through her hands, it would be too much like admitting defeat—too much like giving up.

Feeling somewhere between melancholy and defeated, Kate changed into pajamas and sat idly in front of the television with a cup of decaf coffee. She stared at the television screen, tuned to one of those generic HTV home and garden shows, but she was not truly watching it. Her mind was elsewhere, as was usually the case.

Her mind wandered, running around the mental maze that was the Jack Tucker case as if she were stuck in some weird hedge maze.

And before she could allow herself to get trapped in it, she cut the TV off and went upstairs into the guest bedroom. There, she walked into the closet and opened the door in the back, the only entryway into the house's attic. She climbed the wooden stairs and entered the attic, a space that was always at least ten to fifteen degrees cooler than the rest of the house.

She turned on the light—a simple overhead bulb without a casing or shield. She and Michael had always planned on finishing the space off but had kept delaying it, waiting until they had more than enough money so they could make it really nice space. But after Michael died, she forgot all about it, not even thinking about finishing it until the random and rare moments she found herself walking into the space. The floor was solid, though it was nothing more than overlapped sheets of plywood that had been nailed into the underlying beams. She walked across this thin excuse for a floor toward an old beaten and worn miniature filing cabinet that she had shoved in the far corner many years ago.

There was also an old lawn chair propped against it, for use on the few times she had come up here. She unfolded it and sat down in it as she opened up the top of the three drawers of the cabinet. Inside, there were a few old folders and albums—all related to work. There were newspaper clippings of cases she had knocked out of the park, old awards and certificates for her successes, copies of closed cases she had used for reference materials, and on and on.

She skipped to the section she knew she was looking for: her handwritten and printed out personal notes on the Frank Nobilini case. They were paperclipped to Xeroxed copies of the actual case files, along with the handful of police reports she had accumulated regarding people in Ashton.

She had poured over these notes for more nights than she cared to admit. As she took the notes out and started to read them, a vibrant memory of Michael coming into the attic just after midnight popped into her head.

"We have a king-sized bed," he had said. *"It gets awful big when you're not in it."*

"Sorry," she had said, putting the folders back.

"It's okay," he said. *"I know that I'm but a second fiddle to your work."* He'd smiled here and then kissed her lightly on the back of the neck. *"But if you come to bed with me right now, I promise to make it worth your while."*

He had taken her hand and pulled her up out of the seat...

She grew a little teary-eyed at that. That memory was a fresh one—maybe three years before he had died. It was so fresh that she could nearly feel his breath on her neck.

"I'm sorry, Michael," she said.

And with that, she turned her full attention to the files in her hands. And this time, without anyone to come pull her away, she fell completely into them.

CHAPTER ELEVEN

She had the dream again.

Frank Nobilini had been walking toward her, stepping in the blood that had seeped out of the bathroom. Only this time, instead of his wife following after him, he was accompanied by Jack Tucker. They both held handguns, offering them to her.

"Here," Frank said. "Do it. Shoot us. Kill us. It's just the same as not finding who put these holes in the back of our heads."

He turned to show her the hole he was referencing. Jack did the same. As they turned their backs to her, the holes in the backs of their heads started to grow in size, eating away the rest of the heads like some strange fungus.

Kate sat up with a start, her heart surging in her chest. She felt her stomach lurching at that last image from the dream and for a moment, she thought she might need to rush to the bathroom to throw up. But she took a moment to steady her breathing and managed to fight the urge away.

She felt a little out of sorts as she readied herself for the day. By seven, she had the coffee brewing and some soft '70s rock playing on Spotify. She dressed for the day and ate breakfast at the kitchen bar. If not for the music playing, the house would have felt very much like a crypt or tomb. She'd been alone in this house a considerable amount of time ever since Michael died and Melissa had moved out but now, knowing that Allen wanted a break and that Melissa seemed too busy to spend time with her, it made it feel like some remote, ancient land where she was stranded and alone.

She needed to get out. She needed to get away from this unhealthy tension. She needed to work off her frustration, nerves, and feeling of loss. She wondered if she could call someone at the gym to have someone to spar with later today. A few rounds in the ring would certainly do her a world of good.

And while that was indeed a promising thought, another thought came to mind right behind it. Even the mere thought if it made her heart lighten a bit. She thought of a place that had felt like home ever since her first year with the bureau, a place that, whether it was sacrilegious or not, had nearly felt like a church experience to her when her career and life had seemed out of sorts.

Kate finished up her breakfast, went to the closet to grab her sidearm, and headed for the firing range.

While she would much prefer the more aesthetically pleasing shooting range at the bureau in Washington, there was something to be said for a locally owned shooting range. The people who owned and operated it—as well as the people who paid money to use the range—were not there because of training or necessity. No, they visited the range for the love of the sport, for their appreciation of firearms. Nearly every time she had been to her range of choice in Richmond—a place called Scope Skills, she had seen at least one person taking training courses for a conceal and carry permit.

As she walked through the entrance that morning, though, she was not at all surprised to see that she was the only one there. It was, after all, a little shy of ten o'clock on a Monday morning. She carried a bag in over her shoulder, containing her bureau-issued Glock 19M. She had no magazines on her, but she knew that Scope Skills carried the kind she needed.

She checked in at the front desk, where the owner, Jerry—a butch and well-rounded guy who could have been a stand-in for a WWE wrestler—greeted her with a smile.

"Agent Wise," he said. It was a running joke among them, as she had teased him before about how having a retired agent frequent your range meant that your range had better be following every law known to man with a scrupulous eye. He also thought it was awesome that a fifty-six-year-old woman rocked the gun range the way she did. "How's the morning treating you?"

"Not as well as I'd like," she said.

"Practicing for some big case or something?"

"Nah," Kate said. "Just letting off some steam."

"I hear that."

Kate booked a kiosk, purchased two magazines of ammo for her Glock, and then headed to the back. The smell of the place instantly calmed her. It was not necessarily the smell of expelled rounds that had somehow sunk into every corner and crack of the place. It was the smell of guns finely polished, of a slight tinge in the air that she liked to think was the expelled excitement and concentration of a shooter with a keen eye.

She loaded up the Glock, sent the first target out—a basic black-and-white representation of a human figure placed against a black background—and assumed a shooter's stance. She breathed in deeply, as if resetting herself, and felt her muscles settle into a groove.

She opened her eyes and fired. And fired again.

The next ten minutes were almost Zen-like for her. She'd always found this odd because at no point in her training had she ever truly become enamored with firearms. She knew the basics, plus enough to be able to participate in a mid-tier conversation about them, but she was far from what someone might describe as a "gun nut." She just knew that firing them at targets in a safe and secure environment was calming to her in the same way some people enjoyed fishing or baking. She wasn't the type of agent that could name each and every gun by simply looking at it, nor did she know much military weaponry history. She had always kept it fairly simple, using whatever the bureau's current issue was, with the exception of the Sig Sauer she had received as a gift from Agent Greene, her first partner.

She stopped firing suddenly, a thought dawning on her out of nowhere.

I've always used whatever the bureau has issued because I've been comfortable with it. I love this 19M because I am familiar with it and know it well. Before this, I felt comfortable with the standard-issue 9mm they sent some of us into the field with. I've always been comfortable with these more compact and easy-to-carry weapons because it's what I know.

She thought of the gun that had been sued to kill Frank Nobilini and Jack Tucker. She thought of the shell casings, identified pretty quickly by law enforcement as having come from a Ruger Hunter Mark IV.

The same gun on both men, eight years apart. Apparently, that's a gun the killer was comfortable with ...

Kate cleaned up the little bit of mess at her station and left the kiosk. As she headed for the front of the building where Jerry was currently arranging his accessory counter, he gave her a strange look.

"You've got sixteen minutes left for what you paid," he said.

"I know. But I was wondering if you could maybe help me out with something. You're fairly knowledgeable on guns, right?"

"Sure. And by the way, I prefer fairly knowledgeable over some of the descriptors my wife chooses to use when it comes to me and guns."

"What do you know about the Ruger Hunter Mark IV?"

Jerry thought for a moment, his arms crossed over his massive chest. "Well, I know that I don't have one here. I've never fired one, actually. But I've seen some at gun shows and what-not. Some of them come with a threaded barrel for suppressors. I guess in your line of work, it would be a pretty good choice for someone wanting to stealthily take someone out. It's a rimfire pistol and I think the newer ones can be taken apart really quickly. It's because of a really cool takedown mechanism."

"Have you yourself ever had someone ask if you could get one in for them?"

"No. While it's not a specialty gun or particularly hard to find, it's also not very popular."

"So it's also not considered a standard enough gun to be used haphazardly by just about anyone wanting something to protect their homes, right?"

"No."

She thought about this for a minute, feeling a trail start to assemble itself in her head. "With the suppressor, it would make the shot a little cleaner, too, right?"

Jerry shrugged. "I'm not sure. Maybe, maybe not. It depends on the shooter and what they're shooting at. It's a sleek gun, though."

"It sounds like it would be a perfect choice for someone who might want to quietly kill someone and leave no trace, right?"

"Except for the shell casings, yes, I suppose. Why do you ask?"

"Because I'm starting to wonder what sort of person would be comfortable enough to use such a gun on a regular basis."

Jerry grinned uncomfortably here and leaned forward on the counter. "Yeah, I think it would be a pretty good choice for someone that needed to kill quickly and quietly. I'm pretty sure I remember reading something about it not too long ago, how there are some people rumored to be working with the mob that use weapons just like that. Or maybe it was one of my military-style documentaries that I'm always watching—which my wife *also* hates, by the way."

Kate knew exactly where she needed to go, what she needed to do. She started for the door quickly, the trail in her head now complete.

"Thanks, Jerry," she called on her way out. "This was a huge help!"

He said something to her, but she was already outside. Yes, she knew what the next step was, even though Duran would tar her a new one if he found out. Still, she had to … to keep herself sane and to feel like she had not given up.

There was a downside, though. Wasn't there always?

While she knew the step she needed to take, it was a backward one. Once again, she was going to have to take a big step back into her past. And while it was a step in the right direction, she couldn't help but feel that it seemed more like falling behind than moving forward.

Chapter Twelve

Every now and then a potential lead would come to her and there would be some extra bit of information or convenience that would make her feel as if it was simply meant to be. She'd experienced it more times than she could count during her career as an agent and she felt it now, as she drove out of Richmond and toward the much smaller town of Dilwyn, Virginia. She had put away plenty of criminals in the course of her career, one hundred two to be exact, and they were scattered all over the US, in different prisons according to where they had committed their crimes in most cases.

But of those one hundred two criminals, there were a handful who had ended up in Buckingham Correctional Center. It was located in the center of Buckingham County, hidden away in a little nothing of a town called Dilwyn. Kate had visited the prison about five or six times in her career, so when she made the trip that morning it was like a little exodus back in time.

One of the men that she had taken down who ended up in Buckingham was a man named Alvin Carpenter. He had once worked out of the northeast coast as a hitman for hire. He'd had ties with the mob and an unnamed syndicate in New York. But when Kate had finally brought him down after the attempted murder of a bio-fuels engineer in 2005, he had been at work just outside of Alexandria, Virginia.

He had been silent on the names of his clients, never offering them up even in a plea bargain attempt during the trial. When two hits had been chained to him while he'd been in prison, his twenty-five years had been upgraded to a life sentence. Kate had not spoken to him since his initial arrest so she had no idea how he might react to seeing her. But she figured there was only one way to find out, and since she was no longer actively on the Jack Tucker case, she had plenty of time to spare.

She arrived at the Buckingham Correction Center just shy of 11:30, the drive vacant of traffic and taking less than an hour and a half. As she walked in, she tried to remember the last time she'd had to visit the place. She figured it had been at least ten years. She also wondered if she'd see any familiar faces and, if so, if they would recognize her own. The feeling of venturing back into her past had her looking for just about anything to latch on to, anything that might make her feel a little closer linked to that time in her career.

But as she walked into the lobby and to the visitors desk, she saw no familiar faces. In fact, she barely recognized the building at all. It had that stale yet almost astringent smell that had, weirdly enough, always reminded her of the way a post office smelled.

She checked in at the visitors desk, introduced herself, and made a request to speak with Alvin Carpenter. Because of her retirement and new agreement with the bureau, there were several hold-ups. As the woman at the check-in desk made a few calls, the weight of the situation fell on Kate. If they had to call the bureau, she'd be screwed. She had no idea how Duran would react to her still snooping into the case when he had, in so uncertain terms, removed her from it less than two days ago.

It took a while, but this worry was erased when, twenty-five minutes after making the request, she was given permission. Apparently, her name on the original arrest records of an inmate by the name of Alvin Carpenter had ended up being enough to grant her access to the prisoner.

Kate was escorted out of the lobby and down a connecting hallway that led to the prison itself. She was scanned by a walk-through metal detector and was finally assigned a guard to walk her to one of the visitation rooms.

"How has the inmate's behavior been these last few years?" Kate asked the guard as he led her to the visitation room.

"Not much out of him, really. He's quiet, stays to himself. He reads a lot. Lots of biographies and things like that. Not someone that really sticks out, you know?"

Kate remembered Carpenter being rather reserved. When he'd gotten his sentence, there had been no crying or wailing. He'd nodded in the courtroom and taken it like a man. She assumed that any hitman who would be willing to take the names of his clients to the grave even when several years of freedom were offered in exchange would be a resilient and almost resigned man once he was behind bars. He accepted life as it was, expecting nothing special. He'd killed people, now he was doing his time, and that was his life.

It made Kate feel like this might be a wasted trip. Would a man like that give her the kind of information she was looking for?

No use in trying to talk yourself out of it now, she thought as she was escorted into the visiting room. She took a seat at the small and battered conference table as the guard took position in the back of the room. He crossed his arms and stared at the door, apparently waiting for another guard to being in Alvin Carpenter. He then looked back at her, as if he was being extra protective. Maybe he felt uneasy with the idea of a woman her age meeting with a man like Alvin Carpenter.

The door opened a little over five minutes later. Carpenter came in first, his hands cuffed behind his back and a puzzled look on his face. He looked around the room for a moment, as if he didn't even see her. But when he finally realized what was happening, she saw the look of recognition and then the slight smile that crossed his face.

Alvin Carpenter was in his late fifties now. His head was shaved and he wore a mostly gray beard that was closely trimmed to his face. He had that same look of calm acceptance on his face that Kate remembered so clearly from the last time she had seen him at his final court hearing.

"Agent Wise," he said with something close to delight in his voice. "I'm not even lying when I say it's nice to see you. This is unexpected."

"Oh, it is for me, too," Kate said. "You look well."

He shrugged as he took the seat on the other side of the table. The guards both looked to Kate and she nodded. "We're good."

"We'll be outside the door if you need us," the guard that escorted her said. And with that, they exited the room.

"I do have to say," Alvin said, "I can't figure out why you'd visit me. You and your bureau friends found out everything—the other two jobs, all the details. I'd say I was pretty thoroughly buried."

"Well, I'm here for a different reason. And I hope you'll consider listening very closely and considering a request I have."

"I'm not giving up the names of my clients," he said.

"No, I know. I'm beyond that. This is different. Mr. Carpenter... if you had to take a guess, how many other people did you have in your network before you were arrested that were either hitmen or worked very closely with them?"

He thought about this for a moment before answering, waving his hand in a *so-so* motion. "Ten. Maybe a dozen. Of course, I have no way of knowing if they're all even still alive."

"Is there a weapon of choice among hitmen?" she asked. "Sure, you want to be quiet... that's a given. But was there a go-to gun that you ever preferred?"

"I toyed with sniper rifles for a while," Alvin said. "And I know it will make me sound like a monster, but I never cared for them because the target is so far away. For the job to be truly effective, I believe in being close and personal when that trigger is pulled." A slight grimace crossed his face, as if he were being unnerved by his own choice of words. "But I always went with a Beretta 70s."

"What about a Ruger? A Hunter Mark IV?"

He tilted his head and nodded. "A little heavy-handed for my tastes, but yes. That could go very well, so long as it was threaded for a silencer." He smiled again and sat forward, apparently very interested. "Are you chasing down another hitman, Agent Wise?"

"I don't know quite yet," she said. She also sat forward, letting him feel as if she were engaged—as if she was hanging on his every word. She hoped it might make him a little more willing to cough up some information.

"Ask what you need to," Carpenter said. "I must tell you, this is the most exciting thing that has happened to me in years. A break in the monotony. I greatly appreciate it."

"How would someone find you? I know many years have passed since I brought you in, so times have changed. But based on what you know, how might someone go about actually hiring a hitman today?"

"Many ways," he said. He then sat back, his posture relaxed. She knew that he was trying to figure out whether or not to go on with it. A man like Carpenter might fear that he was getting some colleagues from his past in trouble with this sort of information. "Can I ask why you're asking?" he said.

"I'm afraid not. And I know you're a man of integrity. That's why you never gave the names of the people that hired you. But I can give you my word that my current investigation has nothing to do with anyone you were ever involved with. Or, rather, if it is, it would only turn out to be a happy coincidence on the bureau's end."

That seemed to satisfy Carpenter. "Well," he said, "for someone that doesn't already have the contacts, the internet is going to be the place to start."

"The dark web, I assume?"

"Sure, there are plenty of guys for hire on there. Actually, guys in my profession just go where they need to go on the dark web and the jobs are there waiting for them. But even most people that want to hire hitmen aren't quite dumb enough to search around on the dark web. Instead, there are more public, more popular places. Craigslist, for example."

"How is that even possible?"

"The ads are worded very cleverly. Or, in some cases, if you go the personals, you'll find ads that are worded just oddly enough that it's clear that it's a hitman for hire or, in some cases, even people in search of a hitman. I see your look of disbelief, but it's more common than you think."

"I see…"

"Do you?" He paused here and sighed. "Tell me about the case and maybe I can point you in the right direction."

Now it was Kate's turn to be hesitant. She knew that even if Carpenter did decide to blab about it to his fellow inmates, the information would not leave these walls. But honestly, she didn't see him spreading it. Murderer or not, she did not think he was the sort of man who would use gossip or his knowledge of current FBI cases to his advantage while in jail—if such a thing was even possible.

So she told him about the Tucker case and how it appeared that it was directly related to the Frank Nobilini case. She told him about the weapon that had been used on both victims as well as the fact that both had appeared to have been execution-style shootings. Carpenter listened intently as she gave him the details. And before she was done, she could see a slight sense of understanding in his eyes.

"You say this is in New York?" he asked.

"Yes. Both bodies discovered in alleys in Midtown, but they were residents of Ashton. Why? Do you think you have something?"

"Probably not," he said with a shrug. "But the whole execution-style thing...that's a bit much. A power trip, really. You want to just get in there, get the job done, and split. Taking the time to get the jump on the guy and then making him get down on his knees...that's pure ego. Your killer is probably full of himself. Thinks a little too highly of himself. And I used to hear people talk about this one guy that worked up that way—in Queens and Manhattan, in particular. A real dick. Had a power trip for days. Clean work, good at what he did, but always taking one too many risks just to make himself stand out, you know?"

"You got a name?" she asked.

"I do, actually. But honestly, I doubt it's his real name. He was Zeus Beringer—I *think* that was his last name. The name Zeus seemed fitting because he went about his work like he thought he was a god, you know?"

"You think he lives in New York?"

"No clue. But I think that's where the bulk of his jobs were out of."

"Did you ever meet him?"

Carpenter gave her a wry smile and shrugged. "No clue. He wouldn't be much of a hitman if he told me his identity, now would he?"

Kate considered the information. It certainly seemed to line up with what she knew of both the Nobilini and the Tucker cases. It was the sort of information that, if she were still officially on the case, would certainly warrant the effort of locating this man known as Zeus Beringer.

"Thank you, Mr. Carpenter," she said, getting up from her seat.

"That's it?" he asked, disappointed. "Nothing else you need?"

She frowned, nearly feeling bad for him. This break in his monotony had been something out of the ordinary—something exciting, even. And now, less that twenty minutes after it had started, it was coming to an end.

"I'm afraid so," she said. "But I genuinely do thank you for your time."

He started to look irritated, but Kate turned away and headed for the door. The guard was already opening it for her when Carpenter called out from behind her.

"Agent Wise?"

"Yes?" she said, turning back around.

"While the man you're looking for is certainly a low-life asshole, you have to consider ... there was someone out there that saw it fit to hire such a man. And in the end, isn't that person you need to be concerned about?"

Kate let the comment sink in as she walked through the doorway. By the time she returned to her car, it sat there like a heavy rock poised to fall off a cliff.

CHAPTER THIRTEEN

Kate didn't travel very far after leaving the prison. She drove ten miles down the road, stopped by a McDonald's for lunch, and then pulled over in the parking lot. While she ate a very dry and flavorless salad, she called up DeMarco. As the phone rang in her ear, it occurred to her that what she was about to ask could potentially get DeMarco in trouble. And as that reality sank in, she decided to hang up.

But before she could, DeMarco's voice was in her ear. "Agent Wise. How are you?"

"I'm … good."

A brief silence filled the line, broken by DeMarco's musical chuckle. "You're still working the case, aren't you?"

"Maybe."

"Find anything?"

"I think so. Not sure yet. I was hoping you could get me some information without tipping off Duran."

"Kate … are you sure?"

She called me Kate rather than Agent Wise, Kate thought. *It feels like I'm being scolded. And maybe she has a point.*

"You're right. I can't ask you to—"

"I don't mind," DeMarco interrupted. "I can get you whatever you want without Duran finding out. I'm just worried about the repercussions on your end if it comes to anything."

"I'll be fine," Kate said. "After all, it may be nothing."

DeMarco hesitated, considering the options. Finally, she said: "What do you need?"

It took DeMarco less than forty-five minutes to come up with a list of addresses for males with the last name Beringer in New York City. There were thirty-seven in all—with an additional one hundred eighteen when alternate spellings were included—but Kate narrowed them down to the areas of Queens and Manhattan. And while there was no listing for a *Zeus* Beringer, there was only one listing in them all where the middle initial was listed as a Z. This was Malcolm Z. Beringer, a resident of Queens.

Had she actively been on the case, this would have been fantastic news indeed. Even if the lead turned out to be nothing at all, it was at least a solid indicator that the work she had put in today had been effective.

She plugged the address into Google Maps and winced at what she saw. From her current spot in the McDonald's parking lot, it would take her nearly six and a half hours to drive to Queens. She'd made far longer drives in the past, but never one that would be driving directly against the orders of her director.

"What's he going to do?" she asked herself. "Fire me?"

Hearing those words out loud helped her a great deal. So what if he *did* fire her? It would at least make her decision of whether or not to continue pursuing this part-time position much easier. She also knew that the alternative was that she might actually help break the case. And while Duran would no doubt reprimand her in some way for going against his orders, it would be worth it.

Not just to find the killer, but to finally close a case that had been haunting her for nearly a decade.

That made the decision easy. The long drive really wasn't even that much of an inconvenience. Besides... she had nothing but time to spare.

What else was retirement for, if not long spontaneous drives across the country?

She was fortunate enough to get into the city just behind the afternoon rush of post-work traffic, the gridlocked hell that occurred between 5:00

and 6:30. Still, by the time she pulled up in front of Malcolm Z. Beringer's address, it was 7:02 and the drive had taken its toll. She was cramped and tired and a little cranky. She nearly got out of the car and headed straight for the door but thought better of it.

If that was indeed the address of a hitman or some other unsavory man, she had to cover her ass—particularly because she did not have the bureau's backing. She idly wondered if there were already other agents in the area to cover the case. She made a mental note to ask DeMarco about it the next time they spoke.

Thinking of DeMarco, she pulled out her cell phone and sent her a text. **I'm here. Wish me luck.**

She then got out of the car and walked to the building. She saw a control panel along the front of the door. It was the sort of apartment building where you had to be rung in by the person you were visiting. Again, though, she got lucky. There was a delivery driver for Vinny's Pizzeria walking up the stairs, carrying two pizzas toward the door. Kate bided her time, waited for him to announce himself over the intercom, and then hurried up behind him.

"Let me get that for you," she said, taking the door as it was buzzed. She opened it, allowing the delivery guy inside, and then fell in behind him.

"Thanks," he said.

"Thank *you,*" she replied.

She then took the stairs to the third floor, the address telling her that Malcolm Z. Beringer—whom she could not stop thinking of as Zeus thanks to Alvin Carpenter—lived in apartment 306. She walked to the apartment as if she belonged in the building, like she made the journey through the halls and stairways every day.

This act came to a stop as she reached apartment 306. She had a rough idea of how she wanted to initiate the conversation. But she also knew that a man with a history of any sort of murder—especially murder for hire—was always going to be on the lookout for bait-filled conversations ... especially from strangers.

She knocked on the door and stepped back, making sure that anyone on the other side would clearly be able to see her through the peephole in the door. When there was no answer, she knocked again, louder this time. She even pressed her head to the door, curious to see if she could hear any movement from inside.

After thirty seconds, she was confident that no one was home. Or, if they were, they were dead asleep at 7:15 in the afternoon. She took a quick look up and down the hallway, found herself alone, and pulled the lock pick out of her coat pocket. She worked quickly, relishing the feel of something she had once done many times before. Now, years removed, it felt almost like a superpower. She felt and heard the lock turn all at once. Instinctually falling back on her training, she knew to enter at once. If there *was* anyone inside, they'd expect a bit of a pause between having their lock picked and the actual entrance. By going in right away, it created the element of surprise.

She entered at once, her hand instantly going for her Glock. She knew that any use of it would get her into serious trouble, as she was not actually on the case. Still, her need to survive was a bit stronger than anything else in that moment.

The door entered into a small kitchen. There were a few dirty dishes in the sink, and an empty pizza box sitting on the counter. The kitchen led directly into the living area. A lamp was on in the corner, dimly lighting the place. There was a single armchair in the center of the space with a TV and a bookshelf along the far wall. It wasn't a wreck of a place by any means, but it was clear that Zeus did not care much about interior decorating.

She stood in the center of the living area, now confident that no one was home. She ventured into the apartment's only bedroom and had a look around. There was nothing out of the ordinary at first glance. A small desk in the corner contained a newer model MacBook and a few magazines which, when she leafed through them, she found was a mixture of pornography and weapons-related titles—*Guns and Ammo, Tactical Weapons,* and so on.

She opened the laptop and powered it up, unsurprised to find that it was password protected. There was a notepad by the laptop, the top page blank, but clearly missing some pages. She picked it up and looked to the first empty page. There were clear indentations in the paper, indicating that something had been written on the page above it before it had been torn off. It was hard to make out all of it, but she was pretty sure it read: *Mon. 5:45. CI—Bronx. Rm 202*

It read almost like a puzzle as far as Kate was concerned. It actually made her pretty sure she had read it wrong. But she checked it one more time and found that she had read it right.

She studied it a while longer. Today was Monday. If the *Mon* on that note meant today, then Zeus had left this very apartment at some point today with an appointment somewhere in the Bronx at 5:45. Somewhere with a Room 202. It sounded like a motel room somewhere.

A stirring of excitement started to take over, making her feel certain that whatever had been written was important—that she might be holding something incredibly helpful. *CI, CI, what the hell is CI?*

CI. Room 202. 5:45. Where would a man like Zeus—a man who was presumably a hitman or something similar—be meeting that had the letters CI? Or the initials.

Okay, maybe an apartment complex with the initials CI...

No, the note says room *202, not* apartment *202.*

The answer came barreling at her like a train. She tossed the pad back on the desk and bolted out of the bedroom, directly toward the front door. On the way down the stairs back out to the street, she pulled up Google and typed in two words under a search within the Bronx: *Comfort Inn.*

She sped along the way, fully prepared to show her badge and ID if she was pulled over by local law enforcement. She'd been enough similar situations in the past to know that most cops wouldn't think twice about it when they saw a woman flashing FBI credentials. She was speeding not only in the hopes of getting to the Comfort Inn before whatever meeting Zeus was having was over, but because the day was wearing her out. Her drives, first out to the firing range and then to Buckingham Correction Center, felt like they had occurred three or four days ago, a sign that this very long day was catching up to her.

She pulled her car into the lot of the Comfort Inn seventeen minutes later, once again feeling quite fortunate that she did not live in New York and have to put up with the miserable traffic and busyness. Her nerves were starting to fire on all cylinders as she strode up the exterior stairs and to the open-air corridor that contained the majority of the second floor.

She took a deep breath, steadying herself as she came to Room 202. The fact that she had followed him here, based on his own personal notes, would be all the evidence Zeus would need to know that he was being investigated. There was a very good chance that this confrontation would get heated—maybe even violent.

Shit, she thought, hesitating at the door.

She then strolled by the window of the room, hoping to be able to peer inside. But the curtains were drawn and she could see nothing. With no other course of action to take, she steeled her nerves and knocked.

Just like the apartment, there was no answer. She knocked again, this time giving up on any sort of subtlety. "Mr. Beringer, it's very important that you open the door."

When there was still no answer, she looked back down to the parking lot and the neon Office sign. She went back down the stairs and into the office. A man dressed in a hooded sweatshirt sat behind the desk, typing something into an old laptop. Beside him, a woman was speaking to someone on a landline phone.

"Can I help you?" the man in the hoodie asked.

Kate showed her ID right away, not wanting to beat around the bush with formalities. "I'm Special Agent Kate Wise with the FBI," she said. "I need to know who is currently in Room 202."

The woman on the phone had taken an interest in the conversation. She was apparently the manager because she gave the man in the hoodie a shake of the head after looking closely at Kate's ID.

"That's private information, ma'am. I can't just give that out." He looked back to the manager, still on the phone. "Doesn't she need a warrant?"

The manager quickly ended her call and came to his aid. "Yes, you need a warrant," she said.

"Fine," Katye replied. "I'll get a warrant. And by that time, there will be enough police officers in the know. I'll have probably a dozen or so around here, in the parking lot—for everyone to see. Or, you can let me up there right now, just me, to keep it nice and quiet."

The manager sighed, looked to Kate's ID again, and nodded. "Go ahead."

The man typed something into the laptop, studied the screen for a moment, and said: "Adam Smith."

A fake name if I've ever heard one, she thought. "How did he pay?"

"Cash."

"Can you tell me when he checked in?"

Again, he studied the screen. "Five thirty-six."

"I've tried knocking on the door and there is no answer," Kate said. "I need a key to that room."

The woman strode over to the computer and looked over the information while the man in the hoodie retrieved a room key for Kate. "He called about the room yesterday afternoon. Reserved it for tonight."

The man handed Kate the key and she headed straight back out to the parking lot with a quick "Thank you," over her shoulder.

She wasn't quite as hesitant as she reached Room 202 this time. She went directly to the door. Before unlocking it though, she stood there for a moment, listening for any sounds from inside. After ten seconds of silence had passed, she inserted the key, turned it, and stepped inside.

She took one step in and froze.

She wasn't sure what she had been expecting, but it certainly had not been this.

With a trembling hand, she shut the door behind her. She then turned on the light and tried to make sense of what had happened to the dead body on the floor.

CHAPTER FOURTEEN

The man had been shot four times. One shot had gone perfectly through his throat and another had entered his face just below the right eye. The other two were almost directly beside one another, high up on his chest. Kate saw that the one under his eye had gone in at an angle—probably the one that had killed him before he'd had time to choke from the one through the neck.

She had plenty of time to access the scene; between the time she'd called the NYPD and the arrival of the first patrol car, she'd had a whole five minutes alone with the body. While she'd waited for the police to arrive, one of the things she'd done was check the man's wallet, which she found in his back right pocket.

The dead man on the floor was Malcom Z. Beringer.

The scene seemed pretty cut-and-dried at first—a dead body told the story pretty perfectly—but Kate quickly put a few other pieces together. First, the gunshot wounds looked identical to the one in the back of Jack Tucker's head. The only real difference was the amount of gore present at this scene; the shot that had torn through his neck had produced quite a bit of blood—blood that was still wet.

Apparently, someone had called and asked to meet him here. And he had been killed for his troubles. Killed by someone who apparently did not participate in whatever weird code most hitmen had. The four shots, all scattered around the body, indicated that whoever did this had not been a pro.

When she looked around the room, she saw the butt of a gun sticking out from under the bed. She pulled it out with the tip of her shoe, not wanting to contaminate it with her fingerprints. She was not a gun expert, but she was pretty sure the gun currently sitting on the floor was the one she had mentioned so often over the course of the last few days: A Ruger Hunter Mark IV. It was equipped with a silencer.

The police had arrived as she had been checking out the bathroom. There was a single damp washcloth hanging on the side of the tub but other than that, the place seemed unused.

"Agent Wise?" an officer called.

She joined the officer and two others that came in behind him. They were crowding the doorway as the third officer closed it.

"You know him?" the officer asked.

"Not personally. No. But he was a point of interest in a case concerning the murder of Jack Tucker right here in New York a few days ago. His name is Malcom Beringer—known to some unscrupulous characters as Zeus."

"You think he killed Tucker?" the officer asked.

"I don't know. But what I do know is that this Comfort Inn and this room number were written on a pad at his house. He was to meet someone here at five forty-five this afternoon. Whoever reserved the room checked in under the alias of Adam Smith."

"There was a local detective that was handling that Tucker case. Luke Pritchard. You want me to get him in on this?"

She thought it would be a smart idea but she was also very aware that she had discovered this body while not assigned to any particular case. Rather than dig her potential grave any deeper, she decided to play it safe.

"Run it however you'd like," she said. "I need to step out and call my director."

The officer nodded and the others parted to let her out of the room. She walked back out into the open-air corridor. She wasn't sure if it was her nerves or the approaching fall starting to make itself known in the air along the upper East Coast, but Kate felt a little chill. She knew what she had to do and although she hated to admit it to herself, she was a little afraid.

She pulled out her cell phone and dialed up Duran. She didn't bother with his office number, opting to go straight for his mobile.

"This is Duran," he said. The tone in his voice indicated that he was a little irritated. Perhaps he'd seen her name and number on the display before answering.

"It's Kate," she said. "I know I'm no longer on the case, but I feel I should let you know that I'm currently standing outside of a motel where a man has just been killed. A man that very likely owned and was killed by the same sort of gun that killed Jack Tucker and Frank Nobilini."

The three seconds of silence that followed this was heavy. When Duran finally spoke, there was a growl to his voice, the tone of a beast that had been nudged by a curious kid with a stick.

"Where are you?"

"New York. The Bronx."

"And what the hell are you doing there?" The rage in his voice was like a quiet lion, slinking through the grass on the hunt.

She did her best to walk him through the course of her day. From her revelation about speaking with Alvin Carpenter, to finding the information about Zeus's meeting at this Comfort Inn, from discovering the body and the gun to calling in the local cops. The only thing she left out was the bit of assistance she had gotten from DeMarco.

"That's all fascinating and promising," Duran said. "But you seem to be omitting the fact that you are there against my orders. You were here—present and accounted for and of a sound mind when I removed you from the case, correct?"

"Yes sir. And I apologize. But I think this murder and the gun involved...I think it points to something big in this case."

"You understand that had you done this while on active duty, you'd be suspended, right?"

"I do. And you can do whatever you feel you need to. I understand. But I'm here. Right now, I'm here in the middle of it. I just ask that you let me keep digging. Sir...the blood in that room is still fresh. He hasn't been dead for long. Whoever did it can't have gotten far."

"And what will you do when you find them? Have you considered that this man may have nothing to do with the Jack Tucker case?"

"I have. But the gun, sir. It's the exact same kind Jack Tucker and Frank Nobilini were killed with. The chances of that happening and me finding it … it feels related."

Duran let out a shaky sigh. She could nearly hear him gripping the phone tightly in frustration.

"What's the guy's full name?"

"Malcolm Zeus Beringer."

"Got an address?"

"Plugged into my GPS. I'll text it to you."

"Do that. I'll get someone on this … checking his cell phone records, criminal profile, the works. Give us until midnight. Kate … you do what you think needs to be done but you are walking on eggshells, you understand? And when this is over, you and I are going to have to have a serious fucking talk. Am I understood?"

"Yes sir."

"Good." And with that, he ended the call.

Kate relaxed a bit. While the conversation had gone much better than she had expected, her nerves were still chaotic. If nothing else, though, she now had a huge motivator going into the final stages of this case: based on Duran's reaction, it might very well be the last one she ever worked on.

CHAPTER FIFTEEN

The next several hours passed by in a flurry of activity. The police decided it would be more efficient to call in Detective Luke Pritchard and have him run the show, giving assistance where it was needed. A small base of sorts was set up in the parking lot of the Comfort Inn, where Pritchard tasked some of the officers were small jobs. He was taking charge within seconds of arriving on the scene. Kate was coming out of the main office as he started working things out, impressed with how well he worked with the cops.

She walked over, fully prepared to show her badge and ID. But before she could, Pritchard looked her way and gave a smile of acknowledgment. "Agent Wise," he said. "I hear you were the one that found the body?"

"That's correct."

"How did you manage that? The PD have told me a few details but that's about it."

She found herself again running through a quick breakdown of how she had come to Room 202 of the Bronx Comfort Inn. Pritchard took a few handwritten notes in a small ledger as she did so. When she was done, he scanned his notes, nodding here and there.

"I'll stop by his apartment and see what we can pull from that laptop. Any word on the gun you found?" "Almost certain it was the same kind used to murder Jack Tucker. It's been bagged and is on the way to the station."

"Great. And what are you up to right now?"

"I just finished speaking with the manager. They're rolling back through security camera footage from this afternoon to see if there's anything that might help to explain what happened. I've already got the bureau working on pulling up phone records and getting a criminal profile."

"Great. The blood in there … it's too fresh. I think if we work together on this, we can wrap it by morning."

"Let's hope so," Kate said.

"Agent?"

They both turned to the sound of the voice from behind them. It was the motel manager, standing by the front door of the office. She was waving Kate forward, a look of reserved anxiety on her face. Kate assumed it was not in the motel's best interests to have a murder investigation going on as it got later and later into the night.

"Let me check the footage," Kate said. "If there's anything worth noting, I'll let you know."

"Let me get your number then. I'll do the same if we can manage to get anything off of Beringer's laptop."

They exchanged numbers before Kate left him to his business. She headed inside the main office where the manager was waiting for her. She led Kate around the back of the check-in counter to where a small office was set up. The manager allowed Kate to sit in the chair behind the desk while she navigated around the security camera software. She showed Kate the ropes quickly—how to fast forward, freeze frame, zoom in, rewind, and so on.

Kate had used countless different security interfaces before so learning this one was rather simple. The set-up was only one screen, one view, but it was from the right edge of the property, taking in nearly the entire parking lot. The manager had brought her back to 5:30—six minutes before the so-called Adam Smith had checked into Room 202. Kate fast-forwarded through the next few minutes, stopping whenever she saw a car park in the lot. There were two that parked in front of the motel between 5:30 and 5:36. One was a man dressed in a button-down shirt and a pair of slacks. Another looked to be a mother and her young daughter, aged ten or so. Other than those two occurrences, there was nothing. She went back to the 5:30 mark and watched the entire thing again, this time at regular speed. She thought maybe someone had simply walked up. But after watching the footage, all she saw was a stray shadow that seemed to pass beneath the camera's angle. It could have been a person, she just wasn't sure.

Kate walked back out of the office, joining the manager back behind the desk. On the other side of the lobby, a policeman was interviewing the clerk in the hoodie—the man Kate had spoken to when she'd come in to get the key.

"Excuse me," Kate said as she walked toward the manager. "On the footage, I see a mother and daughter pair and then a single man that park, get out of their cars, and come into the office. I never see the man that I found upstairs. Can you check your logs and see how many people did indeed check in in those six minutes?"

"I've got it up right here," she said, pointing to her laptop. "I figured that would be the next thing you ask. There were three rooms that were checked into during that time. Two of those rooms were the mother and daughter and the single man. The third was Adam Smith."

"Did *you* check him in?"

"I did."

"Can you describe him for me?"

The manager took a moment to think back, shrugging. "Nothing special about him, really. Mid-fifties, I guess. Slight scruff on his face but not really a beard. Plain hair. Nothing special."

Kate nodded. She was describing Malcolm Z. Beringer to a tee. "Do you know if he was carrying anything?"

"I didn't take notice, honestly. I don't recall anything."

Kate stood there a moment, thinking. A man like Beringer would know to be aware of security cameras wherever he went. She wondered if he had parked somewhere nearby and walked to the motel, perhaps coming up along the side and walking very closely along the exterior walls. If he'd come in from the left side of the building, this would have just barely put him out of range of the security camera.

But the question still remained, even if he managed to get into the motel undetected by the cameras: who had he met with and how did they get in unseen as well? Did they go in *with* Beringer? If both parties were being careful, that was the most likely scenario.

She thanked the manager for her assistance and then headed back outside. The little makeshift base had mostly broken up. A few officers remained by a single car while another was upstairs along the breezeway, standing guard by the door. Kate assumed that Detective Pritchard had already left to take the laptop from Beringer's apartment. She made her way upstairs, the man by the door nodding to her and stepping aside.

"We're okay to the call the coroner now," she told him. "I think the body has told us just about everything it's going to tell us."

"Sure," the officer said and headed down to join the others.

Kate opened the door to Room 202 and stepped inside again. She retraced her steps from before, observing the room as slowly and as methodically as possible. The manager said she had not seen whether or not Beringer had been carrying a suitcase or bag and as far as Kate could tell, he had not. There was no luggage of any kind in the room.

She stood by the door, taking the size and dimensions of the room in. She looked to the TV and the small dresser it sat on. She looked to the bed and...

She paused there. She had noticed the sheets had been slightly unmade the first time she had looked the room over but now they seemed a little more relevant. The untidy nature of the sheets indicated that someone had done more than simply sit there. The bottom sheet was pulled tight and the top sheet—what passed for a comforter at the Comfort Inn, apparently—had been pushed hard to the left. It might seem flimsy to most but as far as she was concerned, that was evidence of a struggle. And that meant that Zeus Beringer had not simply walked blindly into the room and had someone unload on him. There had indeed been some sort of meeting before he was killed. Kate kept going back to the four shots, scattered almost randomly, and was certain the killer had been someone who was not a pro.

If we find out who killed him, that's going to lead to all the right answers, she thought. And even though there were no hard solid links, her gut told her that at the bottom of it all would be the answers she was looking for in the Jack Tucker case.

Now, as Pritchard was looking into the laptop and the gun was being run for prints, there was nothing for her to do but wait.

Once the coroner arrived, Kate drove to the local precinct to see what she could do to help expedite the process. As she made her way to the front desk, her phone went off in her pocket. As she answered it, she snuck a glance at the time and was surprised to see that it was already nearing eleven o'clock. She wasn't tired at all now, sensing that there were answers on the horizon.

She was delighted to see that it was DeMarco. "Hey, DeMarco. You didn't get caught assisting me, did you?"

"No. And I'm actually calling to let you know that I'm about to get on yet another plane and head to New York. It seems Duran doesn't quite trust you and wants me to watch after you."

"So you'll be my babysitter?"

"I know you mean that as a joke, but he's really pissed, Kate."

"I gathered that."

"Anyway, I also wanted to let you know that we've still got a team working on the cell phone records. However, we did manage to already get a criminal record on one Malcolm Zeus Beringer. He's a bad dude, that's for sure—or, *was,* I guess. A few B and E's from a young age, two stints in minimum security for basic brawls. Busted about fifteen years ago for carrying an unregistered weapon. He was the suspect in a murder that took place in Albany five years ago but there was never enough evidence to convict."

"Any word on what the unregistered weapon was?"

"A plain everyday nine millimeter. Nothing special. Anything moving there?"

"Detective Pritchard is looking into the laptop I found in Beringer's apartment. I think that and the cell phone records are going to be our best bet." She then took a moment to fill DeMarco in on the state of the body and the room—as well as the discovery of the Ruger just beneath the edge of the bed.

"Yeah, it sounds like a match," DeMarco said. "Just know this: if you've solved this thing by the time I get there, I'll consider this a wasted trip."

"I'll take that into consideration." Her phone dinged at her while it was held to her ear. She took it away from her ear, glanced at it, and saw that it was a text from Duran. **Cellphone records complete,** it read. **Check your e-mail.**

"Gotta go, DeMarco. Duran just texted. Beringer's cell phone records are on the way."

"Good luck with that. See you soon."

They ended the call and Kate walked quickly to the primary front desk in the lobby. Behind the woman at the desk, the precinct was buzzing lightly with pre-midnight activity.

"Can I help you?" the woman at the dispatch desk asked.

"Yes," she said, showing her ID. "I'm Special Agent Wise, working homicide with Detective Pritchard. I have some documents I need to print out from my phone and need access to a printer."

"One moment."

The woman picked up her landline and buzzed someone elsewhere in the precinct. While she waited, Kate did as Duran had instructed. She pulled up her email on her phone and found a new mail with an attachment, straight for Duran's account. She opened the mail, then the PDF attachment, and waited as it loaded.

"Agent Wise?" the woman at the dispatch desk said. "Right this way."

And with that, Kate was led down the hall and toward a small private office. The dispatch worker handed her over to a tech operator in charge of the dispatch network and had her up and running within five minutes, right down to a loaner laptop.

She smiled for just a moment, as a memory of Michael surfaced in her head. He'd always teased her about how when she got really down to the grit and nails of a case, she seemed to have the demeanor and hard-set attitude of all of those New York detectives that were all over primetime TV. And now here she was, working out of an office in a New York City precinct. If there was a heaven, and Kate was of the opinion that there just might be, she hoped he was getting a good glimpse of this.

It was just the bit of motivation she needed as she pulled the cell phone records up on the precinct's borrowed laptop and dove further into whatever secrets Zeus had been hiding.

Secrets she hoped would help her to close not only the Tucker case, but the Nobilini case, thus finally closing a very open scar on her career.

CHAPTER SIXTEEN

It took her less than fifteen minutes to understand that the phone records may prove to be worthless and yet another ten to feel all but *confident* that they had been a waste of time. As she finished looking over them, fully prepared to pull at least a handful of very weak leads from it, there was a knock at the door. She looked up and saw Pritchard standing there.

"You got a sec?" he asked.

"Yeah."

He entered the room and, without another seat to take, simply stood against the wall and showed her the laptop under his arm—the same laptop she had seen when she had been looking through Beringer's apartment.

"All the laptop tells us is that Beringer had a soft spot for Asian pornography. While his history does show recent visits to Craigslist, his email history shows that it was to partake in the NYC singles ads. But here's another thing. He's got the Tor browser downloaded on his computer. He went to some fairly decent lengths to hide it, but it's there."

"Tor … that's dark web stuff, right?"

"Yeah. Tor is the most popular darknet software out there. And naturally, because of the way it works, we're going to have a really hard time figuring out what sort of sites he was visiting." He chuckled and pointed at her. "That's usually where you and your bureau friends come in handy."

"Is having the software enough to safely say that Beringer was a hitman?"

"In a perfect world, sure. But you have to realize that the dark web is very accessible these days. Any curious thirteen-year-old can get on just to look around. There's a whole movement of YouTube people going on just to snoop around and film it. So no … having a darknet browser isn't enough for us to make that assumption. But between the evidence we have, including the exact same gun used to kill Jack Tucker, *plus* the fact that he visited the darknet with some regularity … I'd say it's enough to continue looking into him."

"So is that it?"

"Yes. How about you? Any luck with the cell phone data?"

She shrugged and showed him the printouts. "He only made two calls today. One was to his brother in Florida. And you can see on the records that it's a call he made at least once a week. The other call I had to actually call myself to see who it was. Turns out it's just a garage in the Bronx. They were obviously closed when I called, so I may go by tomorrow just to make sure it's legit."

Pritchard nodded, folding his arms over his chest. "How close did you come to wrapping the Nobilini case when you were originally on it?" he asked.

"Not close at all," she said. "There were no leads, not even a single clue at all outside of knowing the make and model of gun used."

"With this Beringer break, do you feel any closer to solving this one?"

"I just don't know," she said. "I feel like it's moving forward but every single lead I get only takes me to another hopeful moment that, in the end, becomes nothing more than a number to a garage or your darknet software."

"It's tricky," he said. "Knowing that there has to be some answer at the end of it all but having everything presented to you be so basic and boring."

"Yes, it's certainly no—"

She stopped here, struck by that word once again. *Boring.*

Only this time, when the word sped across her brain, she was able to snag it. Before, whenever she'd heard it and thought it meant something, it would get away from here, nothing more than a fuzzy idea with no real edges or substance. But this time she not only snagged it, but she focused on it.

"Agent Wise?"

She ignored Pritchard's voice, slowly sitting up in her chair and putting all of her attention on the memory that came to her. She gave a small smile of frustration as she fully understood the memory and what it would mean.

Another case. Yet *another* case in her past... only this was much farther back than Frank Nobilini or Alvin Carpenter. How long ago had it been, anyway? It felt like another life.

"Twenty years or more," she said out loud, answering her own question.

"Excuse me?" Pritchard said.

"Sorry. Talking to myself. Detective Pritchard, I'm so sorry, but could you give me some privacy? I have an idea I want to run with and if I don't get to it now..."

"Say no more," he said, opening the door. "I know how it feels. I'll be just down the hall if you need me."

With that, he closed the door as he left, leaving Kate alone with her thoughts. She turned toward the laptop and used her cell phone to place a call to the bureau resource desk for the second time in the last few days. She was pretty sure the voice that answered on the other end was the woman that had assisted her the first time.

She gave her badge number and location and then, knowing that she'd be in for a long night, requested assistance to remotely and securely access the bureau's database.

The case had occurred twenty-four years ago, when Kate had only been three years deep into her career as an agent with the FBI. She could remember the case well enough, a triple homicide in Georgia, but the names were still muddied by both time and the unreliability of human memory. Therefore, it took her a while to find the case she was looking for. When she opened up the first file, it was like being slapped in the face by her past. The case was old enough to where the only digital files on it were scanned documents and notes, many of which had been written in her own, much younger, hand.

The first victim had been a man named Jimmy Keenan and then, shortly after, his brother and best friend. The investigation had lasted about three days and in the end, the murderer had turned out to be Keenan's wife. When asked why she found it necessary to kill her husband, the answer had been simple enough, albeit a little sad and depressing.

Kate read through it all as she sat at the desk, looking at a scanned picture of the wife's testimony, typed up almost twenty-five years ago.

"Married for sixteen years, and you know what the most exciting moment has been for me over the last five of them? The nights when he goes out and plays poker with his friends. That lets me stay at home and do whatever the hell I want, watch whatever I want. He used to be fun and exciting and he couldn't keep his hands off of me. But lately ... he just got very routine. Very boring. Just boring, boring, boring. And when he accused me of not ever wanting to do anything fun ... I snapped.

Then, later on further down the testimony, she went on:

"Do you know what it's like to hope day after day that the person you married might resurface? He'd complain sometimes that this wasn't the life he wanted—not the life he'd envisioned for himself. But he never did anything about it. He just sat in it. But I couldn't do that. Could not live that fucking boring life. God, what a fucking bore he was there at the end. You know what? I take back what I said earlier. The most exciting part of the last five years was slamming those hedge clippers into the side of his head."

She had then gone on to kill his brother, mainly because he was visiting and out in their garage when she had killed her husband. The best friend, she'd said later, was because he'd attempted to rape her during a Christmas party early in her marriage and when she'd told her husband, he hadn't believed her.

Kate read her testimony twice. *Boring. Boring.*

How many people had she spoken to who had described Jack Tucker in that same way?

It might be a stretch, but it felt right ... in the same way it had felt right to look into Malcolm Zeus Beringer.

The mere idea of Missy Tucker killing her husband seemed absolutely ridiculous. Sure, she did not know the woman on a personal level, but she had seen all kinds of grief during her career—both genuine and staged. And Missy had been an absolute wreck.

Ah, but maybe there are things about her husband she was blind to in her grief, she thought. *A few days removed, maybe she'll be able to offer something more ...*

It was worth a shot. Besides ... the Zeus Beringer link was looking to come up at a dead end. What other options did she have?

She sighed, sat back in her chair, and read through the old testimony one more time.

CHAPTER SEVENTEEN

Kate met DeMarco at the airport at 5:45 after catching a few hours of sleep at a hotel near the precinct. She filled DeMarco in on everything she had learned since they last spoke, ending it all with the speculations she'd had after revisiting the files from the case in Georgia twenty-four years ago. She did it while fighting off grogginess. Yes, she could spar in a boxing ring and work as a well-rounded agent, but one thing age was not being kind to her about was in regards to sleep. After fifty-five, she apparently needed at least a solid six hours.

"I see why you might go there," DeMarco said. "But then that means you also need to apply that same filter to the Nobilini murders. We've been working to prove that they're linked but I think this, if anything, might work *against* that."

Kate had considered this but figured it was a bridge they could cross only if some new information was found. "That's true," she conceded. "But if I'm being honest, I'm a little hesitant to ask a grieving widow under what circumstances she *would* have killed her husband."

"Do we know what date the funeral is scheduled for?" DeMarco asked.

"No." She was glad to have DeMarco with her. While she still fully intended to speak with Missy again as soon as possible, DeMarco was grounding her a bit. Perhaps it was because of their little bit of tension following the first visit to the Tucker household wherein they had broken the news of Jack's death and DeMarco's reaction to it. Whatever the reason, Kate could feel more of a balance between them.

As Kate parked in front of the precinct she had spent several hours in the night before, DeMarco was looking over her own notes from the

Tucker case. "You know," she said, "I can't help but wonder if there is someone else we can speak to before Missy. I'm not too keen on talking to her right now. Not to take several steps back and get all pissy about it again, but I'd prefer to let her handle the storm of shit that's on her way: the funeral, her kids at the funeral, sleeping alone in that house for the first time after watching her husband's coffin lowered into the ground."

"Jesus, DeMarco, that's grim."

She shrugged. "I know we spoke to Alice Delgado and she gave us the names of Missy's best friends. She mentioned a woman named Jasmine Brooks that we never managed to get in touch with. I say we try her one more time before going straight to Missy."

Kate nodded her agreement as they got out of the car and headed inside. She felt rushed and even a little off her game in that DeMarco had recalled the name Jasmine Brooks while she, Kate, had let it fall by the wayside. Sure, she'd had a lot to deal with since then—being pulled off of the case, visiting Alvin Carpenter, and then discovering Zeus Beringer's body—but she should not have simply overlooked a potential lead, no matter now sure she was that it would pan out to nothing.

Kate led DeMarco back to her little private office. DeMarco took a quick look around at some of the work Kate had done the night before. The printouts from the old Georgia case, a borrowed whiteboard with checklists and a link-chart, most of which has been marked through, and the little desk, complete with the laptop and an empty coffee cup.

"I see you made yourself at home here," DeMarco said.

"I'd hate to see what your home looks like," Kate quipped.

"So all we're waiting on are forensics reports from the gun, right?"

"For right now, yes."

"And you've been working closely with Pritchard?"

"Not closely. He ran the laptop check while we were waiting on the phone records."

"I see," DeMarco said.

Her hint of teasing was clear in her voice, making it known that she rather liked the idea of Kate working with Pritchard. Kate nearly commented on it, but let it go. It would only lead to a good-natured conversation about her love life and right now, given the nature of the last conversation she'd had with Allen, that was not something she wanted to get into.

"So, Jasmine Brooks," Kate said, before DeMarco had the opportunity to venture any further into that territory. "Let's get an address and pay her a visit. But if nothing comes of that, I think we *have* to speak with Missy."

"I can live with that," DeMarco said. "You start digging for the address. As for me, with that red-eye flight and very little sleep under my belt, I'll take charge of coffee duty."

Jasmine Brooks lived in a two-story house on a secluded plot of open land in one of the nicer parts of Ashton. When Kate and DeMarco pulled their car into the Brooks' driveway, Jasmine was standing on the porch, watching her child—a girl of about twelve or so—as she stood at the end of the driveway. Given that Kate had gotten behind two different school buses on her way out to Ashton, she assumed the child was waiting for the bus.

Jasmine Brooks gave them a peculiar look as they got out of the car and started walking toward the porch. She almost looked afraid, Kate thought. She was inching toward forty with a headful of gorgeous blonde hair and a figure that most healthy twenty-one-year-old women would covet.

"Can I help you ladies?" Jasmine asked before they even reached the porch.

Kate revealed her ID as subtly as she could, not wanting the child at the end of the driveway to see. "Agents Wise and DeMarco, with the FBI." She looked back out to the kid along the end of the driveway and asked: "Waiting for the bus?"

"Yeah. She does that and I drink my cup of coffee on the porch. It's our little morning ritual. Until the weather gets cold, anyway."

As she said this, a county school bus came around the bend, slowing to a stop. Kate extended the courtesy of allowing Jasmine to watch her daughter get on the bus before getting into her questions. Her daughter turned and waved before getting on the bus. As it started accelerating down the road to the next stop, Kate nodded up the porch stairs.

"Can we come up? We'd like to ask you some questions about Jack and Missy Tucker."

Jasmine's frown was immediate, but she nodded. "They still don't know who did it?"

"Not yet, no," Kate asked. "And we're trying to learn more about Missy and Jack as we get further along. We keep hearing the same things—how they were a perfect couple, how they were great together, how Jack was this impossibly kind man. So kind and straight down the middle that some have gone go far as to refer to him as *boring*."

Jasmine chuckled, but stopped it before it could sound anything close to happy. "That's a little unfair, though I suppose I can understand that."

"We understand you are very close with Missy," DeMarco said.

"Yeah," Jasmine said, though there wasn't much enthusiasm in her voice. "We've known each other since high school. Some would say we were best friends."

"Were?" Kate asked.

Jasmine sighed and sat down in a white wicker rocker. She rocked slightly as she held her cup of coffee. "Yeah. Missy and I haven't really been very friendly as of late."

"Any reason?"

Jasmine was quiet for a while. It was clear that she was struggling not to weep. In the end, about ten seconds after the battle started, she lost. A few stray tears went rolling down her cheeks. She didn't bother wiping them away.

"I don't want to spread her business," she finally said.

"We can respect that," Kate said. "But at the risk of sounding cold, hearing that they were perfect and that Jack was an incredible man isn't helping us. He was killed for a reason. And any secrets they might have been keeping—or secrets about them individually that their family and friends might know—are huge stepping stones towards finding out what happened . . . and why."

Jasmine gripped the edges of the armrests on the rocker and whispered a curse.

"It's okay," DeMarco said. "You can remain anonymous."

Jasmine shook her head. "No I can't. I'm the only one that knows."

Kate and DeMarco remained quiet, giving Jasmine the time and space she needed. Kate could tell by the look of guilt on Jasmine's face that she was going to tell them what she knew; it was just a case of getting beyond the guilt to share it.

"It was about six months ago," Jasmine finally said. "Maybe a little less. We would usually meet for lunch when she was free on Wednesdays. We'd always meet at the same place—Emmanuel Bakery and Kitchenette—at the same time. Twelve thirty, Wednesday afternoon. But she called me one Wednesday morning and asked if we could meet here, at my house, instead. I told her sure, and that's what we did. We had lunch right at my kitchen table. She told me she had to tell me some-thing—something that was going to kill her to get out. I gave her some time and she started crying before it came. She told me that she had done something awful, something she couldn't forgive herself for."

Jasmine stopped here, struggling with more tears. Kate already knew where it was going; she'd heard it countless times in her career. But she needed to hear it from Jasmine Brooks for it to mean anything.

"She said she'd been having an affair. Not just a one-time thing, either. She never gave me a number, but she said it was several times. She was wrecked about it."

"Was she actively involved in it when she told you?" Kate asked.

"She said she'd ended it the week before and that he was in agreement."

"Do you know why they ended the affair?" DeMarco asked.

"I think that's what hurt her the most . . . why it was so hard on her," Jasmine said. "She said it was purely physical at first. The kind of sex women assume is long gone after thirty. But she said over time, there was an emotional connection. Not just on her part. It was mutual. They were falling in love."

"Who was the affair with?" Kate asked.

Again, it was clear that Jasmine did not want to reveal this informa-tion. She had finally started to wipe away some of the tears that were falling, giving in to the fact that she was losing the mental wrestling match within her heart.

"Garret Blake." She said the name as if it were a curse word, slowly and softly, looking away from them as if ashamed.

"And are you sure you're the only person she told?"

"At the time she told me, I know I was. She made it a very clear point to let me know that. But in the time that passed between then and now, I can't say for certain."

"So we've gathered that you *used* to be friends with Missy Tucker," DeMarco said. "What happened to the friendship?"

Jasmine shrugged. "She became distant after she told me. And it got worse week after week. I think the guilt or shame or whatever kept her away. I tried reaching out, but she ignored me. When we'd pass by each other at school functions for the kids, she'd basically just ignore me."

"Do you know Garret Blake?"

"Not well. I see him at school functions from time to time as well."

"So he lives in Ashton?"

"He does. But he works in the city. Co-owner of a trendy little marketing firm. Look ... I know you have to do your job and all, but if you could somehow *not* let it be known that I gave you this information ..."

"We'll be very discreet if it does come up," Kate said. "Ms. Brooks, thank you for your time. And thank you for sharing. I know it wasn't easy."

She nodded and then, as the agents were headed down their stairs, called out with one last detail to share. "I can sort of see where you're trying to go with this," she said. "But from what I know of Missy Tucker and Garret Blake, I can pretty much guarantee you that neither of them would be capable of killing."

"We'll keep that under consideration," Kate said.

But even she could hear the doubt in her tone. Because if nearly three decades in the bureau had taught her anything, it was that just about anyone was capable of *anything* if they were trying to hide a damning secret.

CHAPTER EIGHTEEN

The marketing firm that Garret Blake worked for was called One-Up. It was located in Manhattan, in one of the trendier little nooks where everything seemed to be bookended by coffee shops, music stores that were stocked full with vinyl, and expensive juice bars. They found the place easy enough and by 9:45, Kate was parking in a small garage across the street from the building One-Up was located in.

The interior was cute and welcoming, decorated mostly with glass walls and bright blasts of color with encouraging phrases. The woman at the welcome desk was in her mid-twenties with a nose ring, an eyebrow ring, and a shock of bright purple in her black hair.

"Can I help you?" the secretary asked.

"We need to speak with Garret Blake," DeMarco said.

"Do you have an appointment?"

"No," Kate said. "But he's going to want to talk with us."

"Can I ask what this is in regards to?"

"No."

The girl looked at them awkwardly, apparently never having caught any sort of attitude from women older than her before.

"One moment, please," she said. She got up, walking behind one of the glass doors and into an office on the far side of the workspace.

"You ever have hair like that when you were younger?" Kate asked DeMarco.

"I did, actually. Red tips. But that was also around the time I was wearing blood red lipstick and wearing chokers with little spikes on them, so..."

"I'd like a picture of that someday, please."

"I don't think so."

The camaraderie was brought to an end when they saw the secretary coming out of the office with a man trailing behind her. He was a younger man, maybe thirty-five or so. He was the sort of guy who managed to look ruggedly handsome thanks to the scruff on his face and the broadness of his neck and shoulders, yet also looked modern and sophisticated because of his sleek yet semi-casual attire.

He greeted them with a smile as he came to the front desk. He looked them over for a moment, trying to place their faces. "What can I do for you ladies?" Garret asked.

"We were hoping to speak with you," DeMarco said. "For just a moment."

"And preferably in private," Kate said. She pushed some edginess into her tone, hoping he'd feel the urgency in it. She really didn't want to have to show her ID in front of the secretary; she wanted to be able to keep this as quiet as possible. But if she had to pull her ID, she most certainly would.

"Yes, that's fine. We can meet in my office. But I do have a conference call I need to be a part of in fifteen minutes."

"I don't think it will quite that long," Kate said.

He turned away quickly, something Kate could not help but take notice of. He led them around the first glass partition and through the tidy industrial-looking workspace. His office was just as tidy—perfectly smooth edges and a complete lack of clutter anywhere. He closed the door behind him and walked to his desk while they took two of the three guest chairs in front of his desk.

"You detectives?" he asked without waiting a single moment.

"No," Kate said, finally pulling her ID. "FBI. I'm Agent Wise and this is Agent DeMarco. What made you instantly assume we were detectives?"

"The way you're dressed," he said. But he then leaned back nervously in his chair and started to look antsy. "And if I'm being honest, I've been expecting the police or a detective or someone to show these last few days."

"Why is that?" Kate asked. She wanted him to offer as much information as possible without having to guide or bully him into doing so.

"Well, I know that Jack Tucker was murdered. I didn't know him well but if you are here in regards to that, I'm assuming that you somehow found out that I know his wife quite well."

"That's all correct," Kate said. "And it took us a while to find that out. In fact, we were told that Jack and Missy Tucker had a perfect marriage."

"They did, from the outside. Great house, great kids, great people. What I knew of Jack, he really was a stand-up guy. But I think under the surface, the marriage had gone sort of stale. Missy never gave me any details. She just said there was no excitement. No passion or fun. She said things had gotten predictable and boring."

"How did the affair start?" Kate asked.

Garret sighed and looked away. So far, he had not spoken with any sign of true regret, nor did he particularly seem proud of what he had done. But now he seemed to be wrestling with something. Perhaps whether or not to share the details of his affair with Missy Tucker.

"Look...I've made mistakes. I look back on them now and am ashamed. I was married when the affair happened. Still am...to the same woman. She doesn't have to find out about this, does she?"

"Not unless you turn out to be a likely suspect," Kate said.

Relief flashed across his face instantly. It was nearly enough to make Kate feel as if he wasn't a suspect at all. He was just lucky to have dodged another bullet that could have ended his marriage.

Poor woman, Kate thought, thinking of his wife.

"She came here, looking for pricing on brochures for the middle school band," Blake said. "An errand for the PTA. Usually a woman named Melissa Carter handles it, but she was on the verge of having a baby and I think Missy was sort of just filling in. She hated it. She was very uncomfortable with the responsibility of it all. Now, she and I have never truly known one another—just in passing at school and there were two times where Jack and I both helped work on the elementary school Christmas float for the Ashton Christmas parade. When we were wrapping up the meeting, I offhandedly asked how Jack was. And I don't know...it sort of devolved into this spiel about how he seemed like a different person. I myself was divorced ten years ago, so I knew what she was talking about. My first wife sort of just drifted off. We ended things amicably after just two years. No hard feelings. We knew we were growing apart and that was that. So I gave her some advice ... advice, I might add, that was intended to help her heal whatever was wrong with her marriage.

"Anyway, she came back in the following week to place the order and to go over color schemes and all of that. She thanked me for talking to her the week before and asked that I please not tell anyone about it. I assured her I wouldn't. And ... hell, I don't know. Honestly can't even recall how it happened. One minute I'm standing right there beside her, showing her a sample of another brochure on my computer and the next, I'm turning around and we're sort of pressing into each other. It was heated and quick ... right here, in the office."

"How long ago was this?" Kate asked.

"Maybe a little over a year ago."

"We understand it wasn't a one-time thing," DeMarco said. "What happened after that first encounter?"

"It was two weeks later. Someone knocked on my door at home, at six or seven in the afternoon. It was Missy. She'd only come because she knew my wife was out of town on business. She said she'd been thinking about what we had done, but not in a shameful way. She said it made her excited when she thought about it. I agreed. And that was the second time it happened. When it was over, we decided to try to make a run of it ... an affair, in secret of course."

This infuriated Kate but she had to remind herself that not everyone held the same set of morals she did. So she tried to keep things as civil as possible by asking: "Did you have no qualms about sleeping with a married woman?"

"Oh no, I did. We nearly ended it several times. Guilt finally caught up with both of us. It almost ended several times but ... I think after several months we both started to understand that it was becoming something more than just a physical relationship. And *that's* when she truly got scared."

"Did she ever talk about leaving Jack for you?" Kate asked.

"A few times." He paused here, clearly uncomfortable, and then added: "You have to understand, I don't enjoy sharing this ... especially in light of what happened. But I was ready to leave my wife for her. To answer your question ... yes, I think if she didn't have kids with him, she would have left him."

"And would you have taken her?" Kate asked.

'I believe I would have. I have no problem admitting to myself that I was starting to fall in love with her."

"Was there any conflict when it came to an end?"

"No. She said she knew if we kept doing it, she'd let her feelings override her logic and she'd get caught. And she did not want to put her kids through that."

"And you just let it end?" DeMarco asked. "Just like that?"

"Yes. Look ... I'm not proud of the affair. And while I still have strong feelings for her and I enjoyed our time together ... I'm not a big enough asshole to be the man that causes a family to deteriorate."

Kate believed him but was still not confident in the fact that he was innocent. If he did indeed still have feelings for Missy, that alone would give him motivation to kill her husband.

"Mr. Blake, do you own any guns?" she asked.

"No. I used to. Actually, it was my first wife's. She hated to have it, but she claimed it made her feel safe. She took it with her when she left."

"Have you ever fired one?" DeMarco asked.

"Sure. My father was into hunting. We spent one week each summer for about three years or so in a cabin in Maine, hunting deer. But that was when I was like thirteen or so. I don't think I've even touched a gun since then." He seemed to understand where the line of questioning was leading; a look of sour disgust came over his face. "Are you seriously considering the fact that I killed Jack?"

"Given your recent history with his wife, you understand how we would have to at least consider the option," Kate said.

He nodded, though the look on his face indicated that he felt offended. "So long as you can keep the news of the affair away from his family and those closest to them, you're welcome to look into whatever you need. My home, my phone, whatever. I'll cooperate within reason."

"We appreciate that," Kate said. Before getting up, one last thing came to her. She was thinking of small towns like Ashton and the process of gossip being spread. "I can't tell you how we found out about the affair," she said. "But is there anyone you know of that would have known about it?"

"Well, I think Patricia, the secretary you encountered out front, was suspicious. But she never actually *knew*. And I certainly never told anyone. I can't say for certain who Missy told."

With that, Kate finally allowed herself to stand. DeMarco, apparently having no further questions either, did the same.

"We appreciate your time and honesty," Kate said. She then handed him her business card and added: "But if you *are* keeping anything from us that you just can't bring yourself to admit, please call me if you decided to come clean. Any potential sources of new information for this case would be extremely helpful."

"I give you my word that I've told you everything."

Kate only nodded as she took her leave. As she and DeMarco walked through the workspace and to the doors beyond, the secretary eyed them suspiciously. She gave them a hesitant wave goodbye as they headed through the doors.

Back out on the street, DeMarco's entire mood seemed to change instantly. Her shoulders slumped and she was looking down to the ground.

"DeMarco? You okay?" Kate asked.

"No. I think he was telling the truth. So if we want to know if there was anyone else that might have known about the affair, I know who we have to ask next. And it sucks."

"I know," Kate said, and left it that.

They got into the car and headed out of the city in silence. And the closer they got back toward Ashton, the heavier that silence became.

CHAPTER NNETEEN

As they drew closer to the Tucker residence, Kate noticed that DeMarco seemed to be growing more and more anxious. As they turned onto the street Missy Tucker lived on, DeMarco pulled out her cell phone. Kate listened with a heavy heart as DeMarco spoke to the director of Ashton's only funeral home.

It hurt Kate to hear the conversation—almost as much as the fact that she knew that DeMarco would soon grow out of this uneasiness. Soon, she'd learn to roll with these sorts of punches ... to be able to put common decency and kindness on the back burner for the sake of the case. It was something most agents simply grew desensitized to. For Kate, it had happened after the first three or four years, case after case that required her to question grieving family members with some very hard questions. She admired the spark of decency in DeMarco and wondered how much longer she'd be able to hang on to it.

"Tomorrow," DeMarco said. "Jack's body was released to the funeral home today and the service is scheduled for tomorrow afternoon. And we're about to go throw an affair in his wife's face."

"I'm not looking forward to it either," Kate said.

"I know. It just ... God, it sucks."

That was the last thing said on the topic. Kate pulled her car up alongside the curb in front of the Tucker house. They got out of the car and walked up to the house slowly. Kate knocked on the door, DeMarco keeping a step or two of distance between them.

The door was answered by the daughter. Kate could not recall the girl's name but knew that she was thirteen and a dead ringer for her mother. Without so much as waiting for Kate or DeMarco to say anything, the girl turned and called for her mother, walking back into the house.

Within a few seconds, Missy Tucker was walking toward the door. She looked much better that she had three nights ago. She looked better rested but still quite forlorn. She looked surprised to see the agents, though Kate could not tell if it was a hopeful sort of surprise or an aggravated one.

"Agents ..." she said, clearly at a loss.

"Mrs. Tucker, I do apologize for bothering you again," Kate said. "But we were hoping we could speak to you for just a few moments."

"Did you find ... someone? Did you find out who killed him?"

"I'm afraid not," Kate said. "But we have come across new information we were hoping to discuss with you."

Missy nodded and invited them in. Inside, the house still felt cold and lonely. Kate had always thought there was an almost supernatural sort of sensation in a house that had just suffered the loss of a major inhabitant—something dreary and detached that crawled on the skin like dew.

Missy led them into the living room and headed straight for the couch. Kate and DeMarco sat down—DeMarco on the couch with Missy, and Kate in an armchair to the right of it.

"Mrs. Tucker," Kate said, "did you ever hear about the Frank Nobilini case from several years back?"

"You know ... I did, but I didn't even make the connection," she said. "I recall you telling me that Jack's murder was very similar to another one that had occurred, but I was in such a state of shock that I didn't even stop to consider that you were referencing Frank Nobilini's murder."

"Do you know Jennifer Nobilini very well?" DeMarco asked.

"Pretty well. We're about ten years apart in age, so we never knew one another in school. But some of our social circles interact from time to time. We've never really had much in common but we're decent friends, I suppose. Well, now I suppose the thing we have in common is what happened to our husbands. She called to check in with me after she'd heard what happened. She can sympathize, obviously."

"That was kind of her," Kate said.

"It was. Now ... what new information have you come across?"

Kate took a moment before she started. She listened out for the children. She could hear footsteps upstairs somewhere, and a light murmur of conversation somewhere in the downstairs. She leaned forward and tried to keep her voice as quiet as she could without being reduced to a whisper.

"We just came from the city," she said. "From a meeting with Garret Blake."

Even if Missy would have played dumb on the topic, the immediate reaction to the mention of that name gave her away. She reeled back, her lips began to tremble, and her eyes grew wide for a moment before returning to their normal size. To say the name had shocked her would have been an understatement.

"Why?" was all she managed to say, the word coming out in a gasp. She continued to tremble, now clenching her fists in an attempt to steady herself.

"It's where our trail led us," Kate said. "And please understand that we aren't bringing this up to cause you any more pain but we *do* need to know a few things about what occurred between the two of you."

"What good would that do?" Missy asked. She was crying now and the expression on her face made Kate think that she was doing her absolute best to decide if she wanted to be pissed off or devastated.

"It would help us rule out certain people as suspects and—"

"He didn't do anything to Jack. He wanted to me to stay with him— to keep my kids happy and my family together." She was nearly spitting the words now, becoming more and more aggressive.

"Mrs. Tucker," DeMarco said, her tone just as soft as Kate's. "Can you at the very least tell us who might have known about the affair?"

"Well, I think you know at least one," Missy said with biting sarcasm and bitterness. "It was Jasmine, wasn't it? I'm sure she couldn't wait to tell someone."

"She was actually very upset to tell us," Kate countered. "And the only reason she did is because she is concerned about you."

"Garret Blake did not kill my husband," she said. "I highly doubt the man has ever touched a gun." She seemed to realize that she was speaking rather loudly, so she quieted her voice and leaded forward on the couch. She took a deep breath and the anger seemed to fade as she exhaled. "It was a mistake and I regret the hell out of it," she said. "Jack did not deserve it and now I have to live with it. But I can assure you that nothing about my relationship with Garret had anything to do with Jack's murder."

Kate knew better than to believe such a blanket statement but still leaned toward Blake being innocent. If it came down to it, basic inter-rogation and cross-checking of alibis would likely prove it.

"Who else other than Jasmine Brooks might have known?"

"I honestly don't know," she said. "Jasmine was the only person I told. And I don't think Garret told anyone. I asked him not to and he swore that he hadn't. Please ... does this have to come out?"

There was something there—maybe a flicker in her eyes or the way she looked away quickly. Something was there ... something that made Kate wonder if Missy was being completely truthful.

"No," Kate said. "There's no reason for that. But I hope you can understand that given how everyone—including yourself—told us how great and perfect your marriage was, a hidden affair suddenly has to become our main focus until it's been properly investigated."

Missy nodded but without any real enthusiasm. "With all due respect," she finally said, "I hope you've got the information you need, but I'd really like for you leave now. True ... I did this to myself. But I don't need you picking at that one scab ..."

Kate stood up, feeling as if she were moving underwater. The tension and angst coming off of Missy was strong—stronger than the thick feeling of loss Kate had felt upon entering the house. As they saw themselves out, a voice called out from the end of the hallway. It startled Kate enough to make her jump slightly.

"Agents?"

Missy was calling out to them. As Kate watched her come back down the hallway toward them, she felt like she was on some weird loop, stuck in a *Groundhog Day* type of scenario.

"I was wondering if you had spoken with Jennifer Nobilini since you'd gotten back into town."

"No. I had considered it, but I didn't see the need in bringing all of that pain back up for her."

"That's considerate."

"Any reason you ask?" DeMarco asked.

"For that very reason. It's a very touchy topic. She fears that's how the town sees her now. The widow with the husband that got shot in the back of the head. I think she gets depressed whenever it comes out in conversation. We may not be best friends by any means, but I do care for her. Just looking out…"

Kate understood that, but she also wondered if Jennifer might still be holding something of a grudge against the FBI not finding her husband's killer eight years ago.

"Do you think you *will* speak with her?"

"I don't know," Kate said. "And if I were, I can't exactly tell you about the details of our investigation when it concerns other people."

Missy nodded, but looked a little put off.

Kate could feel herself growing aggravated. Rather than responding in any way, she simply gave a quick nod and turned away. "Thanks again for your time, Mrs. Tucker," she said. "I know it can't be easy."

When she was outside and headed down the porch steps, she didn't realize that her entire body had gone tense until DeMarco closed the door behind them and caught up with her on the sidewalk.

"You okay?" DeMarco asked.

"Yeah. I just…I still feel like she's hiding something. I think more people might know about the affair. And as of right now, I really do wonder if we should speak to Jennifer Nobilini after all. Damn, I hate this town. I know that's an immature thing to say, but it is what it is."

"She never got answers," DeMarco said. "She probably still needs someone to blame. And without a killer tucked securely behind bars somewhere…"

"I know, I know."

But as they got into the car, DeMarco taking the driving duties this time, Kate's anxiousness slowly faded away and became something else.

She thought about Frank Nobilini's murder and how she had come across some of the same obstacles while dealing with that case: a lack of clues, a perfect life with no scratches or rough edges anywhere. Everything about that case had been exactly similar to Jack Tucker's, right down to the way in which they were murdered.

So why would it stop now? If everything had been the same so far, maybe this new development would be the same, too. What if there was some secret affair buried in Jennifer Nobilini's past, too?

Stop painting everyone in this town as an adulterous demon, she told herself. *Just because the seemingly perfect Tucker family had a provocative skeleton in their closet doesn't mean everyone does.*

Still, the discovery of Missy Tucker's affair had thrown her for a loop. And then, when they had gotten here to question her, Missy had specifically asked about Jennifer Nobilini. Given the situation, it did make sense; Jennifer had apparently called her, just checking in on a recent widow who was enduring the same pains and sorrows Jennifer had faced.

True, Kate thought, looking back to the Tucker house as DeMarco pulled away from the curb. *But what if? ...*

CHAPTER TWENTY

Kate grabbed the most recent printouts from the printer as DeMarco looked through the handful of sheets that had already been sent through. She looked unconvinced but the tiniest bit excited.

"Okay," DeMarco said. "Explain to me one more time how this isn't a huge assumption."

"I never said it *was* anything other than a huge assumption. But it hit me as we were leaving the Tucker house. Everything about the Nobilini case and the Tucker case have been exactly the same. *Everything.* The way they were murdered, the location the bodies were found, the perfect marriage, a great job, perfect life, same town, and on and on. And now, today, we get this bombshell that Missy Tucker was actively involved in an affair up until not very long prior to her husband's murder. No one expected it or would have thought it could happen. So rather than assume it's the one thing that makes the cases different and being content with that, maybe we need to consider the fact that it might just be yet another similarity in the cases."

"Yes, but you already said that there was no adultery with the Nobilini case."

"I did. And before we spoke with Jasmine Brooks, we didn't think there was any adultery in the Tucker case, either."

"Okay, so what am I looking at?" DeMarco asked. "I see men's names and a few handwritten notes."

"This is a list of the people I spoke to regarding the Nobilini case. The conversations took place over a span of about three months. I think it came down to about twenty-two people."

"So what are we looking for?"

"I think we'd be better served to try to find friends of Frank Nobilini rather than Jennifer. You've seen it yourself so far—people are very hesitant to share dirt on a widow. But if we go after this sort of information under the task of trying to solve a man's murder rather than digging up dirt on his widowed wife, I think we have a better chance of getting information. What we need to do is find a few men on this list that still live around here and that seemed willing to talk openly when the case was still open."

"So we're cold-calling friends of Frank Nobilini's?"

"Pretty much."

DeMarco had no arguments or further questions. Kate felt like she was scrutinizing DeMarco's every move. After her reaction to delivering news of Jack's death to Missy when the case started, she was afraid something similar might happen after the most recent visit. But DeMarco seemed to be taking it all in stride, making no snide comments or acting rude or defensive in any way. She was, though, asking more questions than usual. And Kate was pretty sure she knew why.

"We joked about it before on the phone," Kate said, "but Duran asked you to babysit me, didn't he?"

"More or less. I'm supposed to keep track of your methodology and how you approach the case."

"He thinks I'm slipping in my old age, I take it?"

"No, not at all. He thinks you're as sharp as ever, actually. But—and if you ever tell him I told you this, I'll deny it to the grave and never talk to you again—he thinks that coming

off of retirement and being in this sort of part-time limbo, you're being a little lackluster in adhering to bureau protocol. He didn't use the term *loose cannon,* but that's basically what he was getting at."

"Loose cannon," Kate said with a little laugh. "Hey, I've been called worse."

"And if this case keeps going the way it has," DeMarco said with her own laugh, "I'm sure you'll continue to hear worse."

Kate knew that it was a joke, but it still hurt a bit. Whatever babysitting tasks Duran had tasked DeMarco with, she was taking them seriously. And that was fine with Kate. She had no problem proving to two different people that she still had enough gas in the tank—maybe even enough to not only wrap Jack Tucker's case, but Frank Nobilini's as well.

The best man to speak with—who had been the most helpful and insightful when Kate had been in Ashton eight years ago for Frank's murder—was no longer a local. He had taken a job in Iceland and moved his entire family to Reykjavik. That left a handful of other men to visit, none of whom Kate remembered clearly from the Nobilini case.

The first was a man named Robert Jansen. He lived on the same block as the Nobilinis and had a job as an executive banker in Manhattan. That's how they ended up going back into Manhattan, scrambling for a parking space in the hurried post-lunch congestion of Midtown. After grabbing a quick lunch of their own, they paid a visit to one of the largest banks in New York City. The first-floor ceilings were cavernous, all glass and black décor, like some legendary castle with a modern industrial twist.

They checked in at the front lobby desk, greeted by a woman who, as cruel as the judgment seemed, looked like she was *meant* to work at a high-scale bank.

"We need to speak with Robert Jensen," Kate said.

"Of course," the woman said in a rehearsed yet cheerful tone. "I assume you have an appointment."

"No."

"Well," DeMarco said, leaning forward and quickly showing her ID, "we do *now*. This is urgent, ma'am. We need to see him as soon as possible."

The woman was flustered as she got up from the desk and nodded to them. "Oh, yes, of course. Have a seat, ladies. It may take five or ten minutes, but I'll get him for you."

They took a seat and it took Kate less than ten seconds to see that DeMarco was still very antsy. "What is it?" Kate asked.

"I don't want you to think I'm doubting your instincts, but it seems almost like a waste of time to be venturing back to this case. If there were hard evidence, sure, I'd understand. But we're talking to people that you talked to eight years ago—people that even by your description, weren't able to offer help."

"No, that's a legitimate concern. However, I also know that time heals all things. If these people were purposely not sharing dirt on the Nobilinis, the chances are such loyalty might have waned over time. Plus, the fact that we're still asking about it eight years later might clue them in to just how important it is."

DeMarco nodded her head but still did not seem convinced. Kate did not take offense. After all, in the end, it might turn out that DeMarco was right.

It took another six minutes before the woman from the desk reappeared. She was escorting a short plump man down an expansive corridor that led between the check-in desk and the remainder of the bank that sat beyond. The man spotted Kate and DeMarco and came walking over with the kind of caution a man might show as he walked through an active minefield.

There seemed to be a flicker of recognition as he looked to Kate but it was fleeting. He took a seat next to them, leaning in and speaking quietly. "I'm told you're from the FBI?"

"Yes," Kate said.

He looked worried, making Kate wonder if there might be something he was doing here at work that he was afraid might potentially attract the FBI. But she tucked this feeling to the side. She could not allow herself to be distracted by such rabbit trails.

"I don't know if you remember me," Kate said. "I spoke with you about eight years ago after—"

"That's it. I thought you looked familiar! You were the agent looking into Frank Nobilini's murder, right?"

"That's correct. I'm Agent Kate Wise, and this is my partner, Agent DeMarco. We're actually looking back into that case to try to solve a recent murder—another person from Ashton, the body discovered here in the city."

"Oh my God," Jensen said. Clearly, he had not yet heard about Jack Tucker. "Well, what can I do? I'm not sure how I can help."

"In the case notes from the Nobilini murder, I have you down as being rather helpful. You were a friend of Frank's correct?"

"I was, yes. Not *best* friends by any stretch of the imagination, but I knew him well."

"And did you or your wife know Jennifer well?" DeMarco asked.

"Not as well as Frank. Jennifer was the type that was quiet at parties. Always sitting by herself. Not in a rude or isolated way, but she just wasn't as outgoing as Frank."

"But in your opinion, she was good to Frank?" Kate asked.

"God yes. Those two were inseparable. The type that was always holding hands or exchanging little kisses out of nowhere. Really sweet."

"So if I asked you if you thought there was any way she might have been involved in an affair, your reaction would be what?"

"No way. You know, I don't even know if she's dated a single time since Frank died. They were maddeningly in love. Sickeningly so, if I'm being honest." He smiled, as if remembering the two of them together. "They just … they had it together, you know? A lot of other couples in Ashton wanted what they had."

"Given that Ashton is such a small town, I find it hard to believe that not a single negative word was never breathed about either of them," Kate said.

Jensen seemed to be thinking about something, as if his brain and snagged on a particular memory. "If I'm being honest, I don't remember *anything* negative about them while they were alive. But pretty recently— maybe within the last two years, actually—I do remember one thing."

"What was it?"

"I got a promotion here at the bank two years ago. It meant more pay, but also more work. A lot of weekend trips away to Chicago and Dallas in particular. My wife is a stay-at-home mom but she does have a small business that she operates from home so she attends the occasional conference on the weekends here and there. So we looked into hiring someone to help around the house. Not a nanny per se, but more like a housekeeper. We have four kids, so we thought it was necessary. We asked around for good reputable housekeepers and got the names of a few women. We interview three and one of them used to work for the

Nobilinis—right around the time they had their first kid, I believe. We asked about her experience and even told her that we had known Frank and Jennifer quite well. She told us about her time there and one of the things she honed in on for highlighting her experience was how she had handled everything in stride and grace in the midst of Frank and Jennifer arguing all the time. This, of course, shocked my wife and I."

"Did she say what the arguments were about?" Kate asked.

"No. She didn't go into detail. But she said it was almost a weekly thing. Sometimes, she said, it would be pretty bad. Honestly, though, that's about as detailed as she got."

"Did you end up hiring her?" DeMarco asked.

"No, we ended up going with someone else and it's worked out well."

"What's the name of the woman that worked for the Nobilinis?" Kate asked.

"Lizzy Trabisky."

"Do you know if she is currently working as a housekeeper in Ashton?"

"Yeah, actually, I think she is. For the Nolan family."

Kate felt a little out of sorts; here she was, elated that they finally found someone who had something negative to say about a murder victim from eight years ago. It was an odd thing to feel triumphant about for sure.

"Thank you, Mr. Jensen," Kate said as she got to her feet.

"Forgive me for asking," Jensen said. "But two murders so similar, eight years apart. Is this something we should worry about? We—as in anyone living in Ashton."

"It's far too early to make such a statement, but based on the span of time between the murders, I would highly doubt it." But even as she gave this answer, she dwelled on the idea for the first time. She started to wonder if there had been other murders in Ashton that might be linked to the Tuckers and Nobilinis but, because they had seemed so common in nature, had not been highlighted.

Stop overcomplicating things, she told herself. *You're already having to reach back into a nearly decade-old case. How much harder do you want to make it on yourself?*

Robert Jensen seemed to take comfort in her answer, though. He gave them a quick and awkward wave goodbye as he headed back to work. Kate and DeMarco headed straight for the door, finally with a promising lead to explore.

As they got into the car, Kate tried to recall how many times they had made the jaunt back and forth between New York City and Ashton, but she had lost count.

Hopefully, she thought as she wound her way through traffic, *this will be the last time.*

CHAPTER TWENTY ONE

It was hard to consider it ironic because Ashton was so small, but the Nolan family lived on the same street as Cass Nobilini, right on the outskirts of Ashton's main hub. It was a very quaint cottage-style house. An honest-to-God tire swing hung from one of the several trees in the side yard, which was separated from the neighboring yard with a beautiful yet cliché white picket fence.

As it turned out, Lizzy Trabisky was much the same as the house: beautiful, but cliché. She looked to be roughly thirty with gorgeous auburn hair and just enough makeup on to highlight her sultry eyes but not be overbearing. She wore a thin spaghetti-strapped tank top that was cut just above the belly button and a pair of yoga pants that were so tight, they may as well have been painted on.

She answered the door with a confused smile. Kate hated herself a bit for her initial reaction of Lizzy. She had never truly believed that people this pretty could be legitimate. She did her best to shove that feeling aside as she and DeMarco introduced themselves.

"Yeah," Lizzy said with feigned sorrow. "I heard about Mr. Tucker a few days ago. It's so terrible. But I don't see how it's the same as what happened to Mr. Nobilini."

"Well, that's what we're working on," DeMarco said. "And in speaking with Robert Jensen, we discovered that you once worked for the Nobilinis. Is that correct?"

"Yes. It was right before he was killed. I think they let me go about four months or so before his body was found."

"Can we come inside and talk it over?" DeMarco asked.

"I'd rather do it on the porch," she said. "One of my duties as the Nolans' housekeeper is to serve as a part-time nanny for their youngest kids. Darcy is three, and she's down for a nap right now."

"That's fine," Kate said.

"Want me to grab some tea or lemonade or something?"

"No thanks. This shouldn't take very long."

Seeming a little disappointed, Lizzy stepped out onto the porch. There were five wicker chairs situated around the porch and each of them took one, right beside one another.

"We wanted to speak to you," Kate said, "because Mr. Jensen said he had interviewed you about a housekeeping job in the past."

"He did. About two years ago, I think it's been."

"During that interview, you spoke a bit about your time working with the Nobilinis. Particularly about some arguments they'd had. Do you remember any of those arguments?"

"Not well, but I *do* remember them arguing quite a bit. I also remember, though, how the Jensens seemed very shocked by that. I think they had this picture-perfect image of the Nobilinis in their mind."

"Was there ever physical abuse?" DeMarco asked.

"No, not that I knew of. Some of the arguments got a little heated, but I'm fairly certain neither of them had the sort of mean streak to actually attack one another."

Kate didn't quite know why, but she was fairly certain Lizzy was lying to them. It was all over her body language and the way she refused to keep her eyes in one place. She had a shitty poker face and, as far as Kate was concerned, it was telling her just about everything she needed to know.

"With all due respect," Kate said, leaning forward in her seat, "I'm going to ask you to please stop lying. I don't know what you're lying about, but I need the truth here. Frank died all those years ago and we never found the killer. And now there's a good chance that he's back, and has killed Jack Tucker. There's a connection somewhere in there and we can't find it because for some reason, no one in this town cares to shed some light on the dark places. I don't know what you're afraid of, Lizzy ... but I need you to tell us the truth."

With each few words Kate spoke, she could see a sheen of tears gathering in the corners of Lizzy's eyes. She went tense and there was a single moment when Kate thought she was going to get up from her chair and escape inside.

"Bear in mind," Kate added, "anything you tell us stays with us and, at most, our superiors and local PD. No one in this town has to know anything you tell us."

"I just... God, I just wish I'd never worked for them."

Kate gave her a moment to get a rein on her feelings and then pressed forward. "What was it, Lizzy? What happened?"

She started right away, as if afraid she might lose the nerve. "Well, they were always bickering about something. Money, how to raise the kids, what church to go to on Sundays, things like that. But when they were in public or had people over at the house, it was totally different. They were like this dream couple. But there was one argument that was the worst. I nearly missed it because I was scheduled to leave at six... that was when my job was over for the day. But I was behind on something—I honestly forget what—and was still there around six thirty or so when they started yelling at each other.

"I think what happened was that Frank had found some sort of message on Jennifer's phone... a message from another man. I don't know what it said, but it was enough to make him accuse her of cheating. She blew up on him, asking him how he could dare accuse her of such a thing. I saw that it was getting bad, so I took the kids out into the front yard and drew on the sidewalk with some sidewalk chalk. I caught bits and pieces of the argument from outside. He threatened to take the kids and leave. She dared him to. There was a lot of shouting and then it was just over."

"Did anything at all happen after that?" Kate asked.

"Not with them, no. But Jennifer came outside a few minutes later and told me everything was good and that I could go home. I worked for them for three more days and then they let me go. I don't know for sure if it was because they knew what I'd heard or what... but it's what I have always assumed."

"Did you have any kind of interactions from them after that?"

"No. But it seemed weird to me. They never gave me a straight answer as to why they fired me, but they told me that I could use them as a recommendation for future jobs. And as far as I know, they've done that at least twice."

"What about the kids? Do you see them around anymore?"

"Here and there, just in passing. I don't think they really know anything that happened before their dad died. That's sort of become their world, you know?" She wiped a tear away and looked surprised that she had been crying at all.

"Thank you, Lizzy," Kate said. "I know this was hard for you. But if you don't mind me asking, why were you trying to lie about it?"

She shrugged and looked down to the boards of the porch floor. "I don't know. It seems wrong to remember the dead like that, you know? And I know how this town feels about Jennifer. She's treated with this weird sort of reverence. Everyone loved her before Frank died but then after he was murdered...I don't know. People see her like a saint or something."

Well, that makes the next step in this case a very awkward one, Kate thought. She looked over to DeMarco and the slow expression of despair creeping across her features indicated that she knew where they needed to go next as well.

They had to pay a visit to Jennifer Nobilini.

And they were going to have to ask her—apparently the patron saint of Ashton, New York—about the potential affair she'd had just a few weeks before her husband had been killed.

CHAPTER TWENTY TWO

Jennifer Nobilini looked like she had aged almost twenty years in the past eight. She looked worn down. She still had a slender frame and a well-chiseled face, but she looked perpetually tired and, despite the beaming smile she offered, a little rundown when she answered the door. While she did look surprised to see Kate, it was clear that she recognized her.

"Agent Wise," she said.

"Mrs. Nobilini," Kate said. "I'm flattered that you remembered me."

Jennifer smiled thinly. "Of course I remember. And even if I managed to forget, my mother-in-law was a little taken by your hard work when you were working Frank's case."

Was she? Kate wondered. *Seems to me, she thought for a while that she could do my job better than I could.*

"Would you have a few minutes to spare for us?" Kate asked. "This is my partner, Agent DeMarco."

"Oh, of course. Come on in."

Jennifer seemed almost excited to have them in as she stepped aside and opened the door wider. As Kate walked in, she felt a wave of déjà vu tingling across her skin and through her heart. She'd been somewhat taken off guard by the way she'd felt walking into Cass Nobilini's house a few days ago, but this was something altogether different. This was like literally carving open her memory banks and physically stepping inside.

Jennifer led them into the living room which was exactly the way Kate remembered it. A couch and a loveseat, a television perched over the fireplace. Pictures of their family on the walls. In a few of them, Frank Nobilini peered out at Kate, as if asking her what in the hell was taking so long to find his killer. Afternoon sunlight was coming in through the two living room skylights, making the place feel warm and almost ethereal. Honestly, the entire thing was creeping Kate out. It was far too surreal to be back here, back in this house with this same woman that she had failed all those years ago.

And now she was about to turn this poor woman's life upside down.

Or maybe she's not some "poor woman," Kate thought. *She didn't tell me about any of the arguments Lizzy Trabisky told me about. What else was she hiding from me when I was here eight years ago?*

"Jennifer, forgive the abruptness of the question, but could you maybe tell us why you called Missy Tucker?"

"I heard what happened to Jack. Honestly, I've never really been too close with the Tuckers, but I know them well enough. And when I heard how Jack was killed ... it brought it all back to me. And I remembered how I had people that were there for me when Frank died, but no one could fully understand what I was going through—what it was like to know that he had been murdered like that. And I thought I could maybe help ease her through it ... as much as I could."

"She did seem appreciative," Kate said.

"I imagine this has to be very strange for you," Jennifer said. "Back in this town again with the same sort of murder. Is it going any better this time around?"

"Well, we *are* finding some clues. And quite frankly, a lot of the leads we're getting are all coming back to your husband. And to you as well."

"Really? How's that?"

Kate knew there was no way to ease the woman into the conversation. She also knew that by simply trying to shock people with information, it was a great way to gauge whether they were lying or not.

"As we were looking into Jack Tucker's case, we found that there were many similarities between the Tuckers and you and Frank. A seemingly perfect couple, very much in love. No one could imagine why *anyone* would want to murder either of these men. Yet it happened. And, to be honest, the more we dug, the more skeletons we uncovered."

"Skeletons?"

Kate had really been hoping that Jennifer would willingly admit to the information. But it seemed she was not going to be so lucky.

"Well, for one, it seems that you and Missy Tucker have more in common than husbands that were murdered in a very particular way."

"Liken what?" Jennifer asked. Her tone and posture made it clear that she was shifting into defensive mode.

"Alleged affairs, for starters."

Jennifer sat up straight, her eyes going wide. She looked not particularly shocked, but *scared*. It was like she'd seen a monster and her brain wasn't sure how to handle the sight.

"And these would be affairs that occurred not too long before the deaths of your husbands. In your case, it's looking like about a month or two. In Missy's it was—"

"Would you care to tell me how in God's name you have come to this insulting conclusion?" Jennifer demanded. She was crying, the tears pushed by both sorrow and anger from the looks of it.

"I can't reveal my sources," Kate said. "But Missy has admitted to hers. She did it almost right away, when we confronted her with it. And with a little more digging, we know that you and Frank had—"

"Don't you *dare* speak his name in that context!"

"Fine," DeMarco said, seemingly happy to take over. "Here are the facts as we know them. In both cases, you and Missy Tucker were cheating on your husbands. Both marriages were seen as these perfect storybook marriages in Ashton. And both of your husbands are dead."

"This is sick," Jennifer said. "How can you even think of accusing me of something like this?"

"We have a pretty good reason," Kate said. "A good witness."

"Fucking Lizzy! It was her, wasn't it?"

"Think what you want," Kate said. "But you've now had about two minutes to refute my claims and you haven't."

Jennifer got to her feet and started pacing. She walked the length of the living room and with each step, Kate felt her feet ready to pounce and give chase if Jennifer tried to make a run for it.

"So what if I did?" Jennifer asked, wiping a tear away. She now stood still, her arms crossed over her chest. "Everyone cheats in these towns.

Hell, some of the spouses know about it and don't care. If you were going to accuse people of affairs in this town, everyone would be linked. You'd stay busy for *days*."

"Maybe that's true," Kate said. "But as it stands, you and Missy Tucker are the only ones that have husbands that were killed execution style and discarded in an alleyway in Midtown."

Jennifer took a single step forward and pointed an accusing finger at Kate. "You were a lousy agent back then and you're still terrible at your job. You're here to solve a man's murder and all you can do is prove that two women were involved in affairs. Hey ... wow, great work there, Agent Wise."

"Jennifer, I only bring it up to show you that there are connections here that go beyond the murder of your husbands. The affairs ... if there are any links within those as well, we might be able to find out who the killer is. And if not *who*, then almost certainly *why*. We just need your cooperation and—"

"We all have ghosts and demons, Agent Wise," Jennifer said. "I am not proud of mine and the timing of my transgressions is unfortunate. But that's something I have to live with every day. I certainly don't need an FBI agent who is apparently terrible at her job throwing it in my face!"

DeMarco got to her feet but remained as calm as she could. "Mrs. Nobilini, your truthfulness can help us find a killer. You could—"

"I want you both out of my house right now," Jennifer said. "And just be warned that I fully intend to file a complaint to the FBI for having two of their agents trying their best to tarnish the reputation of a widow—a widow who has never had full closure over her husband's death due to the negligence of one of their agents. Now *get out*!"

Kate took a few moments to consider her options. She could continue pressing and perhaps hope that Jennifer would crack under the pressure. She had just admitted to an affair, though had given no details. Perhaps the admission of an affair was enough. Because if they now knew the affair had legitimately occurred, there had to be *someone* else who knew about it. Particularly the man that Jennifer Nobilini had been sleeping with.

She finally got to her feet. She did not bother with a thank-you or an apology of any kind. She simply took her leave, with DeMarco trailing behind her. The closer Kate got to the door, the more she realized how much the Nobilini house was making her feel suffocated—as if the past had grown a pair of hands and had them wrapped around her neck.

When they were outside and back in the car, Kate wasted no time in cranking the car and pulling away from the curb.

"You think she was bluffing about the call?" DeMarco asked.

"Hard to tell. That woman had so many emotions riding through her..."

"So how in the hell are we supposed to figure out who she was having the affair with?"

"I don't know yet. But think about how we found out about this affair in the first place. We spoke to Lizzy Trabisky. A housekeeper who worked for the Nobilinis. Everyone else had this picture of perfection of them. But it was the housekeeper that knew about the potential affair. Because they work on the inside, if you will."

"And?"

"Well, anytime there's a crime in a suburban neighborhood where there are housekeepers and nannies, they almost always have the best insights. They hear and see a lot that others in the community aren't aware of."

"Lizzy Trabisky already said she didn't know much."

"True. But she's not the only housekeeper in Ashton. And I'm sure there are countless nannies and regular babysitters."

Before DeMarco could respond, a thought occurred to Kate. "Do me a favor, would you? Call Robert Jensen's bank and get him on the phone. He said they interviewed three potential housekeepers, passing on Lizzy Trabisky. Find out who he *did* hire and get her information from him. We'll start with her and work our way down the Ashton grapevine."

Nodding with enthusiasm, DeMarco did as Kate asked. Kate listened as DeMarco spoke with a receptionist, waited patiently for a bit, and then started speaking with Jensen. The conversation was brief and went well. DeMarco seemed pleased when she ended the call.

"He says his housekeeper's name is Tonya Gallahan. She's at their house right now—works Monday through Thursday from eight in the morning until four in the afternoon. If she's not there, Jensen says to wait around a bit; it means she's just not back from picking his older son up from school yet. He said he's going to call ahead and let her know we're on the way."

"Great. Look, I know this might seem like a shot in the dark..."

"No, not at all. I trust you. You've got far more experience than I do." She paused for a moment and added: "Look ... yes, Duran has me sort of watching over you. But unless it's something completely reckless, I'm never going to question your approach. This whole case seemed dead and hopeless two days ago. And now I finally feel like it might all be leading somewhere. So please know I see myself more as a partner than ... well, a *spy*."

"I appreciate that," Kate said. "Now, can you pull up directions to Jensen's address?"

"He gave it to me on the phone," she said with a smile. "It's only about a mile away."

"God bless a small town," Kate said with a nervous smile.

CHAPTER TWENTY THREE

The timing was perfect. Kate parked her car in front of the Jensen residence just as two kids and a driver climbed out of a black Audi that had just parked in the paved driveway. As Kate and DeMarco got out, the kids looked their way. The youngest—a little boy of about four or so—waved excitedly at them. Kate waved back with a smile. She honestly didn't miss these younger years with children, but she did miss the joy kids seemed to have over everything at that age.

The driver, a young woman with her hair in a ponytail and wearing a New York Giants T-shirt, waved at them as well. This, presumably, was Tonya. "Mr. Jensen said you were coming," she said across the lawn. "Come on in and join the chaos."

Kate and DeMarco accepted the invitation, walking across the perfectly green lawn and to the porch. The little boy held the door open for them. Kate's heart warmed a bit when she watched DeMarco give the boy a fist bump and a smile. The kid smiled right back and then went rushing into the house. The older kid—another boy, around the age of ten or eleven, if Kate had to venture a guess—gave them both a lazy wave as he scrolled through his phone while walking through the door.

Tonya Gallahan came next, nodding into the doorway. "Go on, go on," she said. "I'm always lagging behind. These kids are fast."

They entered the house to the sounds of the youngest boy rummaging in the kitchen for a snack. Tonya led Kate and DeMarco into the kitchen as well. Tonya gave them both a quick *one second* gesture and turned to the kids.

"All right, guys, I need you to be really quiet and do something together for a little while, okay? These are some friends of your dad's and they're here to ask me some important questions."

"Can we play Fortnite?" the young one asked.

"It's too violent for you," the older brother said with great satisfaction. He then sighed and took his brother gently by the arm. "Come on. We can play that dumb game you like."

"Yay! Candyland!"

And with that, both of the boys exited the spacious kitchen, snacks in hand. Tonya looked back to Kate and DeMarco with her eyes wide and a tired smile on her face. "Sorry about that."

"Are you kidding?" DeMarco asked. "They're incredibly well behaved. And you're very good with them."

"Thanks. Yeah, they can be pretty stinking sweet when they want to be."

"Tonya," Kate said, "how long have you worked for the Jensens?"

"Nearly two years now. I started out just as a two-day sort of thing, but when Mrs. Jensen's small business from home picked up, they asked me to come on four days a week."

"Do you enjoy it?"

"Most of the time. I'm twenty-seven and not through with college yet. So it's sort of a means to an end right now."

"Mr. Jensen said he'd call ahead and let you know we were coming," DeMarco said. "Did he tell you why we needed to speak with you?"

Tonya looked out of the kitchen and down the hall to make sure the boys were indeed out of earshot. "Something about Jack Tucker's murder is all I know. He said it was just innocent questions and that I had nothing to worry about."

"And that's exactly correct," Kate said. "However, I have been at this job long enough to know that in small towns like Ashton, babysitters and housekeepers are typically the best source of information when it comes to gossip and dirt. Please forgive the stereotype."

"Oh, no offense taken. Besides ... I'd say that's pretty accurate."

"Did you know Jack Tucker at all?"

"No. But I know Missy. I see her from time to time at the school when there are programs and fundraisers."

"And how about Jennifer Nobilini? Do you know her?"

"Only by name. From what I hear, her husband died eight years ago in pretty much the same way Jack Tucker was killed. Is that right?"

"It is," Kate said. "Though we can't provide you with any details. Tonya… the reason we're here is because we do feel that the two murders are connected. And again, while I can't give details, we *have* come to discover that there might be more links to the two murders than we thought. But, as you can imagine, not everyone in Ashton is particularly being honest or forthright with us."

"Yeah, I can believe that."

"I want to know your feelings about Missy Tucker first," Kate said. "Do you know her well enough to give an informed opinion?"

"Not really. All I can say is that she's been nothing but nice to me in the past. And her kids are very polite. They don't really hang out with the Jensen boys, so I don't really know them all that well, either."

"And what about Jennifer Nobilini?"

"Like I said, I don't know her. So any opinion I have wouldn't be based on much."

"What about rumors?" DeMarco asked. "Have you heard anything about her or her lifestyle either before are after her husband was murdered eight years ago?"

Tonya shook her head. "No. I think she's sort of untouchable around here. After her husband's murder and everything, people kind of really respect her."

"So you've heard nothing about her?" Kate asked. "Maybe about her and a romantic relationship with someone?"

"No. Sorry."

"Have you heard her name mentioned at all in the last few months?"

"No. I can't… wait. Yes, actually. Oh my God. Okay, so last Wednesday when I went to pick Owen up at school … there was this sort of commotion at the top of the car rider line. I was about a dozen cars deep, so I didn't see it all. But the whispers and gossip spread down the line quick. There was someone there to get the Nobilini kids, but it wasn't

Jennifer. And that was strange because Jennifer *always* picks her kids up from school. She's usually among the last of the parents to swing through the car rider line, but she's always there."

"Who was trying to pick them up?" Kate asked.

"I don't know. I never heard a name. Just some man. The woman in the car in front of me said he looked creepy and was getting sort of verbal with one of the teachers manning the car rider line."

"Did the police get involved?" DeMarco asked.

"I don't think so. Before things got too heated, the guy just left. From what I understand, nothing was ever done about it. But really, that's all I know."

Some guy shows up and tries to pick up the Nobilini kids sometime very soon before Jack Tucker was killed, Kate thought. *What the hell is going on?*

"I'm sorry I can't be more help," Tonya said.

"Oh, this is a huge help," Kate said. "Tonya, thank you so much for your time. And if you can keep these questions between just the three of us, that would be greatly appreciated."

"Sure, of course."

Tonya walked them back to the front door. Kate could hear the boys giggling, playing Candyland somewhere down the house's main hallway. Outside, the day was cooling a bit as the afternoon wound down. Kate knew they had received a lot of information today and had constantly been on the move, but she didn't realize so much of the day had escaped them.

As they got back into the car for what felt like the hundredth time, Kate looked over to DeMarco and asked: "Feel like going back to the elementary school?"

"You thinking maybe they caught the guy on the security cameras?"

"That's the hope."

As Kate sped away from the Jensen residence and back out into Ashton, DeMarco got on the phone and called the school, ensuring someone would be there after hours. Kate meanwhile was still stuck on the puzzle that had come to her while speaking with Tonya.

Jack Tucker is murdered in the same way as Frank Nobilini; it's discovered that Jennifer Nobilini and Missy Tucker were both having affairs that took place within a few months of their husbands' murders; while the Tucker case is active, a strange man tries to pick the Nobilini kids up from school.

Just what in the hell is going on?

Kate wasn't sure yet, but as they neared the school and she kept going through that chain of information in her head, she certainly felt like they were finally headed toward some definitive answers.

CHAPTER TWENTY FOUR

Most of the faculty and staff had left for the day by the time Kate and DeMarco arrived at Ashton Elementary at 5:04 that afternoon. The only staff remaining in the office was the vice principal and the school nurse. The art teacher was also running around in and out of the office, preparing for an art show the next day. She was making copies in the office copy room while Kate and DeMarco waited for the vice principal to come up front.

"That's some impressive work," DeMarco said, pointing to a photocopy of a black and white sketch.

"Oh, thank you," the art teacher said. "There's going to be a lot of fantastic work at our show tomorrow. Are you parents of students here?"

"No," DeMarco said. "Just visiting."

"That's a shame. It's going to be a great show. The pieces are even going to be auctioned off. Nothing huge, of course. Fun little bids that will go to local charities. Something the PTA set up. It was a nice touch, I thought."

"That sounds wonderful," Kate said.

"Well, if you can't make it tomorrow, feel free to swing by the gymnasium and look at some of the work I've already put up. The kids here are quite talented."

"I doubt we'll have time, but thanks all the same," DeMarco said. "And good luck with the show tomorrow."

The art teacher grabbed up the last of her copies and dashed back out the door. As she did, the vice principal finally made her way to the front desk. She was a tall older woman who introduced herself as Mrs. Talley. She showed the agents the monitor that sat behind the check-in desk, showing three different angles around the school: the front parking lot, the rear parking lot, and the central playground sitting on the western edge of the property.

"Of course, this is all live feed," Mrs. Talley said. "Anything we need to do to enhance or review the footage needs to be done from the central console. I'm not the best with it, but I can probably do enough to get you what you need."

She then led them from the front part of the office toward the back. They passed a few staff offices, the nurse's office, and then came to a small filing room. Sitting against the front wall was a small table with a relatively new security hub on it.

"When I got your call, I took the liberty of pulling up the afternoon in question, but I haven't had a chance to scroll through it yet."

"Do you mind?" DeMarco asked, sitting down behind the monitors.

Kate wasn't sure if DeMarco was asking her permission or Mrs. Talley's. Kate nodded just in case, while Mrs. Talley said, "Of course."

While DeMarco started to look through the footage, Kate did her best to get a better understanding of what happened.

"Mrs. Talley, were you outside when this all occurred?"

"No, I was in the office. But I got a very detailed report from the teachers that were there. You see, over time, we start to notice trends in the arrival of the parents. There are a few that are always first in line to get their kids at the end of the day, and there are a handful that are almost guaranteed to be last. Jennifer Nobilini is nearly always in the last ten cars or so."

"How long does the dismissal process go on for car-riders?"

"Usually about twenty minutes or so. We have a crossing guard up on the main road, and that helps a lot. It's very thorough and efficient."

"And how are the kids let out?"

"Well, that's one of the nice things about living in a smaller town. Many of our teachers know the child by the car that is waiting on them. The children remain on the sidewalk or breezeway, a good distance from the parking lot, while the cars cycle through."

As she explained it, Kate could also see it on the screens. There were roughly twenty kids lined up, waiting for their rides. Many others were behind them, back closer toward the school. She watched as three kids were motioned forward by a teacher standing at the edge of the sidewalk and then watching them as they entered the cars of their parents.

"Right there," Mrs. Talley said, pointing to a red car at the start of the car rider line. "That's the man."

"How long into the dismissal process is this?" Kate asked.

"About four minutes," DeMarco said, pointing to the elapsed time in the bottom corner of the screen.

The three women watched as one of the teachers started to engage with the man in the car. The teacher spoke to him and then looked back behind her—for the Nobilini kids or for more support, it was impossible to tell.

They watched the scene in real time. About fifteen seconds later, the man actually opened the door and started to get out.

"That right there," Mrs. Talley said, "proves that he's not accustomed to the car rider line. At the beginning of the year, we send out a notice for all parents to please remain in their car unless there is some sort of emergency or, in the mornings, if their child needs help getting out of the car. So this was the second red flag ... the first, of course, being that the two teachers that saw him did not recognize him."

They watched as the man got out and pointed at one of the teachers. When he realized that he was making a scene and that there were impatient parents behind him, he gave up, got in his car, and sped off. The license plate was in view for only a moment; it was blocked by either other cars or out of the screen at almost every moment the car was visible.

"DeMarco, can you back the footage up and zoom in on the man?" Kate asked.

"Yeah, one sec."

DeMarco worked quick, making it evident that she was very well trained on newer systems. The footage reeled backward and when the man was back to standing outside of his car, tuned toward the teachers on the sidewalk, DeMarco froze the footage. She zoomed in slowly and by the time the man became more than just a vague shape on the screen, a hard lump formed in Kate's throat.

"Oh my God," she said.

"What?" DeMarco asked. "Who is it?"

She looked closer, making sure it was not simply her eyes playing tricks on her. It took a second or two for her to be absolutely certain.

"That's Zeus Beringer."

"How in the hell is that even possible?" DeMarco asked as they exited the school. "If this guy had plans to kill Jack Tucker within the next day or so, why would he be here trying to pick up the Nobilini kids?"

"I don't know," Kate said. "It doesn't make sense."

But even as she said that, she thought she felt a connection being formed in the back of her mind. She'd been looking for a connection and here it was, practically slapping her in the face. But what did it actually *mean*?

They had gotten back into the car, Kate thinking it might be a good idea to go to the precinct to dig up everything they could on Zeus Beringer outside of his basic criminal record, when her cell phone rang. When she saw Duran's name on the display, she winced. Nine times out of ten, when his name popped up on her cell display, it was bad news.

She answered it, determined not to let whatever bad news he had derail the progress they were making on this case.

"This is Wise."

"Agent Wise, I just got off of the phone with a very irate Jennifer Nobilini. Would you care to tell me how accusing her of an affair has *anything* to do with Jack Tucker's case?"

"Sir, it's where the trail led us. More than that, her affair—"

"*Alleged* affair," Duran interrupted.

"—it adds yet another link between Tucker and Nobilini. It turns out that Missy Tucker was also having an affair during the time leading up to Jack's murder."

"That seems very coincidental. Besides … I still don't see what affairs have to do with these murders. On the surface, it looks like you're doing nothing but digging up dirt on these widows and I shouldn't have to tell you how damning that is for the bureau!"

"I know it all seems like a stretch, but these bits of unfortunate information have given us perhaps the strongest lead in the case." She went on to tell him about the security footage they had just watched—how the man she'd found dead in a Bronx Comfort Inn had showed up at Ashton Elementary in an attempt to pick up Jennifer Nobilini's kids.

The moments of silence after her explanation told her right away that she had Duran hooked. He, too, knew there was something there.

"You may be right, Wise. But if I'm being honest with you, this ... well, this case has been eye-opening for me and shows me that we might have made a mistake. I want you back in DC tomorrow. And when you get here, be prepared to hand in your badge. Have DeMarco keep working on the case. But I can't have you on it."

"What? But you—"

But Duran had already ended the call. Kate stared at her phone for a moment and then set it down slowly.

"He's pissed, huh?" DeMarco said.

"Yeah."

"What did he say?"

She thought about not telling her any of it—of telling her it was just a slap on the wrist and that they could carry on as usual. But she could not put DeMarco in that position. God only knew how much trouble she could get in. Besides, she was sure Duran would inform DeMarco soon enough, just to make sure Kate didn't interfere.

"He said the case is yours now. He wants me back in DC by tomorrow. Jennifer Nobilini wasn't bluffing. She called and filed a complaint." She decided to leave out the part where Duran had told her that she would be handing in her badge when she reported back to DC. There was no sense in placing that thought in DeMarco's mind while they worked to finally wrap this damned case.

She thought of Zeus Beringer as they headed back to the precinct. She thought of his sparse apartment and the lack of any real results that had been pulled from his laptop. Sure, Pritchard had found the dark web software, but, as he had said, that really didn't prove much of anything.

But the Ruger found in the motel room seemed to tie it all together.

It was, quite literally, the smoking gun.

And Kate thought that if they could find who had pulled the trigger on Zeus, it would wrap the entire case. And it would be all the better if she could find out before she headed back to DC.

CHAPTER TWENTY FIVE

It was a special sort of hell for Kate to be sitting in her hotel room at 7 o'clock that afternoon, knowing that DeMarco was hard at work down at the precinct. They had parted ways rather awkwardly; it had been clear DeMarco wanted Kate to remain by her side but Kate also knew what was going through the younger agent's head. This was her opportunity to show Duran that she respected him and his orders—and a chance to prove that she could close a case like this one on her own.

She sat on the bed, eating a takeout pizza and staring at the TV, though not watching it. Her mind was still wrapped tightly around the case. She felt a little bit like a villain, but she was trying to figure out a way to wrap the case even without her official FBI capacity. In the end, if she was successful, she'd have to blow her own cover—would have to rely on her position as an agent. Besides—Duran had said she'd have to hand her badge in when she got back to DC. That *technically* meant she was still an active agent. She would not be considered inactive until that badge and ID went across Duran's desk.

She didn't know how rigid Duran was going to be on this, so that meant she could not risk accessing the bureau's network remotely. If he wanted, he could check in on her to see if she had accessed it. That left her with only the scant notes she had on the case that had been printed out. She laid the information she had on Zeus Beringer and Jennifer Nobilini side by side, trying to figure out how the two were connected.

At first glance, it made no real sense. And because of that, Kate let her mind go where it wanted to naturally go. It meant making some assumptions, but she was fine with that for now.

Based on the little bit of evidence at her disposal, she was fine making the assumption that Zeus Beringer had killed at least one of the men she was looking into—probably both of them. The gun in his motel room as well as his reputation among a small group of hitmen seemed to point in that direction. And now that he was dead, that made the *who* question just about obsolete.

There were, of course, a few questions that remained. Why did he kill them? And why was he trying to pick up Jennifer Nobilini's children from school?

She stated to put a theory together—one that made little sense at first but grew more and more appealing the more she thought about it. There was one piece that didn't quite fit, though. And even if she *did* feel comfortable using the bureau network, she wouldn't be able to find the information she needed there anyway.

Her mind kept going back to Jennifer Nobilini and how she had managed to keep her affair mostly quiet. And even after she had more or less admitted to it in front of Kate and DeMarco, there still seemed like she had been hiding something. The fact that she had called Missy Tucker when she barely knew her, even if they did share a similar tragedy, was quite strange, too.

She's hiding something, but what?

Kate considered calling DeMarco to share her theory but thought better of it. DeMarco deserved to be holding the reins of a case. And the last thing she wanted was for DeMarco to feel as if Kate was trying to steal it from her—especially after Duran had removed her from the case.

She had driven to the city this last time so she didn't have to bother with booking a flight. This probably meant that Duran would expect her to drive to DC tonight or, at the very latest, early tomorrow morning. She started to wonder just how late she could leave tomorrow without attracting attention to herself.

While she was thinking, a thought suddenly occurred to her. She recalled their visit to Ashton Elementary that afternoon. She remembered the art teacher, working frantically to get a little fundraising exhibit set up for tomorrow. Hadn't she said something about how the PTA had set the event up?

With a new idea hatching in the back of her head, Kate pulled out her laptop and Googled Ashton Elementary. She went to the website, clicked on the events link, and started to read. The first event, as they were listed in order of scheduled dates, was the art show tomorrow. It was being called The Art Auction Extraordinaire and boasted *"more than fifty art pieces from our very talented fourth and fifth graders."* It was scheduled to start at 8:45 a.m., in the Ashton Elementary gymnasium.

Then, at the bottom of the event information, Kate came across something that all but verified that she was on the right track—that she might be destined to wrap these two cases after all. The last thing listed on the event listing was: *For more information and details about this exciting event, contact Jennifer Nobilini or Alice Delgado.*

Their numbers and email addresses were then given, but Kate had no interest in either of them. She read over the information again with a nervous smile crossing her face.

She already had a plan in mind. Duran had stripped her away from the case. That meant she could get in some very big trouble if she visited a private residence—for instance, paying another visit to Jennifer Nobilini. Besides ... she wasn't sure what a visit would really accomplish at this point.

But this art show ... well that was open to the public. It was a loophole that would benefit her in the long run, albeit one that Duran could potentially use as a noose to hang her from.

But it was a chance she was willing to take. Because if Duran was already planning on taking her badge, what else did she have to lose? This was yet another thing she thought age was making easier for her—not giving too much of a damn what people, particularly Duran, thought about her.

She'd set her alarm for 6:30 the following morning, but she was jerked awake by her cellphone at 6:16 instead. She saw that it was DeMarco and answered it right away, hoping there had been a break in the case. For a moment, she even dared to hope that at some point in the night, DeMarco had managed to find the one missing piece and blown the case wide open.

"Hey, DeMarco."

"Good morning. How are you doing?"

"Jaded. Bummed. Not wanting to drive back to DC today. How about you?"

"Good. Look, we dug up everything on Zeus Beringer last night and there's nothing new. We did see where his name came up in a few other cases—guys that were hired to kill. We're going to revisit some of those cases today—maybe even visit a few in jail to see if we can get more information."

"Good idea," Kate said. She meant it. But she also wasn't going to tell DeMarco about the potentially reckless thing she had planned for the morning. She wasn't going to tell her how she was planning to visit the school and corner Jennifer Nobilini during the art auction—in a place where there would be multiple witnesses if Jennifer tried to get away from her. A place where she would have to remain civil.

DeMarco would almost *have* to report it to Duran and if she did, that would be the end of it. She hated to keep such a secret from DeMarco. When all was said and done, DeMarco would probably be pissed at her for sneaking around behind her back.

But she was willing to risk that.

"I just wanted to wish you well," DeMarco said. "I hate that you were taken off of this. I really do. If it makes you feel any better, Duran chewed me out later on last night. Said I had no backbone and that you apparently swayed me."

"Well, I can sway with the best of them."

"Seriously, Kate. You okay?"

"Yeah, I'm good. It's not the first time I've irritated my superiors."

"You need anything from me before you head back?"

This question hurt a bit. It made Kate all but certain that DeMarco had only made this call to check in on her—to see when she planned on following Duran's orders and heading back.

Makes us even, I guess, she thought. *Given what I plan to do in the next few hours, her little ruse is barely an offense.*

"No, I'm good. I'm going to get dressed, grab some breakfast, and then I'm out of here. How about you? You good?"

"Yeah, I think so. Thanks for getting me this far."

"Sure thing."

They ended the call, Kate riddled with an odd sort of guilt. She nearly called DeMarco back to tell her what she had planned. But that would go one of two ways; either DeMarco would turn her in or she'd go along with it and then she, too, would be reprimanded. So she left the phone where it was as she climbed out of bed and got ready for the morning—a morning that was already starting to feel tense and filled with a sense of finality.

When Kate pulled into an empty parking spot at Ashton Elementary school, the last of the school buses had parked in the rear lot, having delivered the last round of students. She headed for the entrance and saw several parents and other adults stepping into the double doors where they were then asked to sign in and have their driver's licenses scanned.

As Kate neared the station to scan her license, she knew this could come back to bite her But then again, if Duran was going to take her badge, effectively ending this little second career she was compiling, she figured it didn't really matter.

The woman at the scanning station asked her to sign in while she scanned Kate's license. She then looked to Kate with a smile and said: "Are you a parent of a child here?"

"No," she said. "Just visiting. I was here yesterday on business and heard about the auction. I thought it might be a fun way to spend the morning."

"Ah, I see. Well, you certainly aren't the only non-parent here. We've got quite the turnout today. It should be quite the special event! Now, the artwork is already up, but the students won't be in the gym until nine."

The woman then handed her a stick-like name tag that came out of a small mobile printer at the back of the little station.

"Thanks." Kate picked up a nearby flyer for the show and, with an adhesive name tag on her chest, walked into the school for the second time in about fourteen hours.

She followed the small group of adults through the central area of the school and into the gymnasium. However, before she walked into the gym, Kate stepped to the side of the doors and pretended to be looking over the flyer. She peered quickly over it and checked out the inside of the gym. There were many well-designed wooden boards, boasting ten to twelve pieces of art. There were simple sketches and rather elaborate paintings as well. Some of them did indeed look quite nice.

But she wasn't concerned with the artwork. Instead, she glanced around the edges, against the gym's walls. And there, stationed in a corner with a fold-out desk and a steel folding chair, was Jennifer Nobilini. She was speaking to someone standing nearby while also typing something into a laptop. Seeing the laptop, Kate realized that her morning had gotten significantly better.

If that's her laptop, this is going to be much easier than I had thought, Kate thought.

She checked her watch for the time and saw that it was 8:41. The events page on the school website had the auction schedule for 8:45, and the woman at the check-in station said students would be arriving in the gym at 9:00. That was a lot of moving parts and would mean lots of people in and out of the gym, plenty of witnesses to see her if she approached Jennifer and things got heated—which she was certain they would.

She kept the flyer in her hand, making sure she blended in and didn't look suspicious. She eyed the surrounding area, getting a grip on the scene. Adults were still filing in for the art exhibit. The women in the main office, visible through the large picture window that allowed them to see out into the hallway, were chatting and getting ready for another school day. A lone janitor was pushing a large trash can along on wheels, smiling at a passing parent.

And that's when she saw her opening. Right there, between the gymnasium doors and the space where the janitor was standing. She walked slowly in that direction, cautious as she was now out of the throng of adults. She kept the flyer in her hands, pretending to read it as she positioned herself directly in front of the fire alarm on the wall.

She checked quickly to make sure the janitor was not looking at her and there were no teachers or staff looking out of the large office window.

When she was certain there were no eyes on her, she reached up and pulled the handle down.

There was a very brief silence between the time she pulled it and the moment the alarm started to blare. She took a single large stride away from it and started to look around in confusion, relying on her rather weak acting skills. Fortunately, she didn't have to rely on them for very long. Within seconds, the adults who had filed into the gym came out in a quick yet organized line. Those that were in the process of coming into the school and headed into the gym were rerouted back the way they had come. Over the din of human movement and a few teachers in the hallways directing people where to go, the alarm blared on.

About ten seconds later, the classrooms started to empty out. Some children were laughing while others were clearly a little frightened. Their teachers led them out of the exits calmly and without much fuss.

Through it all, Kate kept her eyes on the gymnasium doors. She watched the people file out until she caught sight of Jennifer. She was speaking hurriedly to someone in the throng of people, her eyes set dead ahead toward the exit. When Jennifer had passed by within several feet, Kate darted through the crowd of people, the only person heading *toward* the gym rather than away from it.

There were only a handful of people still working their way out of the gym when Kate entered. She figured her best bet was to appear as if she had been there the entire time. She ran toward the back of the gym to where Jennifer Nobilini's little station had been set up. She saw that in her haste, Jennifer had not done anything to protect her computer. Her screen was just it was when she had left it. Currently, there was a document up with a listings of children's names and their artwork, next to empty slots with the headings AUCTIONED FOR and PURCHASED BY.

Kate minimized the document and found that the internet browser was already opened. Kate wasn't at all sure what she was looking for, but she figured she'd know it when she saw it. She hoped maybe her email would be up and already logged into, but there was no such luck there. The browser's window was blank, opened up to the basic Google home page. Thinking quickly, Kate pulled up Jennifer's browsing history. She could tell right away that she was not the type who cleaned it out often;

there appeared to be several weeks of online activity still listed under her basic history log.

Shew scrolled through it all, scanning each entry. There were lots of email log-ins and Pinterest pages but nothing of any real substance. That was, until she came to a Craigslist listing. She recalled Alvin Carpenter mentioning that some hitmen would use Craigslist for their business, either posting clever and subtle ads or waiting for clients to post ads.

She opened up the page and found a very brief listing. Only, it was not an ad that she had responded to, but one she had posted. The ad had been posted thirteen days ago and was posted under Relationships. The listing title was **Tired of My Husband.** All the ad said was: *Tired of my husband. Seeking a man with a keen eye for detail and can get the job done.*

It was an alarming ad for sure, but Kate was more confused than anything else. Frank had been killed eight years ago. Why would she post something like this last week? It was a clever ad, especially if it was meant for someone in particular. There was a certain provocative tone to the wording but someone who was looking for something non-sexual could certainly see something else as well.

A keen eye ...

... can get the job done.

And it had been posted last week.

The theory she had been stitching together in her head since last night suddenly all fell into place. It was like being overcome with an epiphany or a moment of clarity. She knew that anything she did from this point on would be scrutinized by Duran and would likely result in the end of any hope she had of reconciliation with the bureau. But she also could not let this go. She could call DeMarco, sure, but there was no guarantee that DeMarco would go with her hunch—especially not if Duran had already instructed her to cut Kate out of the case.

"Shit," Kate breathed, and ran back out of the gymnasium. She fell in at the back of the line that was even still meandering out of the school and out toward the rear parking lot.

From what she could tell, this exit had only been for those in the gym and the front office. It appeared that the kids and the teachers had taken an exit on the opposite side of the school. Kate could hear some excited chatter from the other side of the building, mixed with the still-blaring alarm. There was no real sense of panic among the adults. It was as if everyone knew that there was no real threat here. Still, there was just enough commotion for Kate to blend in with everyone else. She used that advantage to scan the crowd for Jennifer Nobilini.

It took her about twenty seconds to locate Jennifer in the crowd of seventy-five or so people. She slowly made her way over, coming in at an angle so that Jennifer wouldn't see her and try to make an escape. She made her way through the crowd with a few simple *excuse me* statements and managed to come up directly behind Jennifer.

"Mrs. Nobilini..."

Jennifer turned around. When she saw Kate, she recoiled a bit, as if she had been slapped. "What the hell are you doing here?"

"I know what you did," Kate said. This wasn't one hundred percent true, but she felt that she knew enough to do what she was about to do.

"You made that perfectly clear yesterday," Jennifer spat. "What the hell are you doing here? Trying to publicly embarrass me?"

"I'd prefer not to do that. It would be much easier if you came peacefully with me. Mrs. Nobilini, I'm placing you under arrest."

"Are you fucking kidding me?" She said this loud enough for a few people around them to take notice.

Kate leaned closer and said, "I know about the Craigslist ad."

Again, Jennifer looked like someone had reached out and slapped her. It was more than enough of a reaction to tell Kate that was indeed some kind of guilt there.

"I'm placing you under arrest. You can come with me peacefully or I can handcuff you right here in front of everyone. Your choice."

"I complained about you yesterday," Jennifer said. "And I was told explicitly that it would be handled. I have a feeling you arresting me without hard proof is going to be bad for you."

"I'm willing to take that chance. Again, it's your choice, Mrs. Nobilini."

Kate could have never expected what happened next. Jennifer Nobilini tried to slap her. It came fast but with great inexperience. Kate caught the slap easily, then twisted the arm so sharply that it caused

Jennifer to twist her body around. She yelled out in pain—whether out of actual pain or just attract attention in the hopes of generating some bullshit brutality charge, Kate wasn't sure. Whatever the reason, it made it that much easier for Kate to slap the set of handcuffs that she had been hiding under her jacket onto Jennifer's wrists.

There were a few gasps but the crowd had fallen mostly silent. The fire alarm continued to blare behind Kate as she pushed Jennifer Nobilini along toward her car. She roughly placed Jennifer in the back of the car and locked the door. Before she got behind the wheel, though, Kate knew there was one other thing she had to do ... something she was not looking forward to.

She took out her cell phone and placed a call to DeMarco.

When DeMarco answered, Kate took a breath and said: "I did something you aren't going to like very much. Can you meet me at the precinct in half an hour?"

CHAPTER TWENTY SIX

One thing Kate had not been prepared for was for the NYPD to also know that she had been removed from the Jack Tucker case. When she arrived at the precinct and tried to take Jennifer Nobilini inside, she was met with resistance from several of the officers. She made it no farther than the lobby before she was stopped.

"Agent Wise, we can't let you process this woman," one of the officers said. "And we won't do it for you. We know that you've been removed and—"

"Jesus, Kate!"

This was DeMarco's voice, coming from the hallway beyond the bullpen. She was glaring at her from across the bullpen, her eyes filled with fire.

"DeMarco, you need to hear me out."

DeMarco walked up to her, standing face to face. She was acutely aware of the staring officers, but was trying to save face for both of them.

"You should be on the way to DC."

"I should. But something didn't feel right. And I couldn't send you on to seek out my theories out of fear of Duran getting upset."

"You'll be fired for this," DeMarco said sadly.

"Probably."

"You have a good reason for having a handcuffed Jennifer Nobilini?"

Jennifer answered first, bucking against Kate and shouting, "No, she doesn't."

"Yes," Kate said. "DeMarco, give me five minutes to tell you everything I learned this morning ... my theory and how I think this all played out."

She could tell DeMarco was at war—part of her wanting to show Duran that she could handle this by herself and was a good babysitter when it came to Kate, and another part knowing that Kate tended to do her best thinking when under pressure.

"Five minutes," she said. "Officer Stephens, can you please take Mrs. Nobilini to a private room for five minutes."

"Sure. Should I uncuff her?"

"Yes. But don't let her leave. Not yet."

DeMarco led Kate back down the hallway, to the small office that had been given to Kate four days ago. As they reached the room, Kate's cell phone started to ring. She knew it would be Duran before she even saw his name on the display.

"You told him what I did?" Kate asked.

"I had to," DeMarco said, closing the door behind them. "You may not give a shit about losing *your* job, but I need mine."

It was a good point and honestly, Kate didn't blame her. She answered the call, fully prepared to catch an absolute nuking from Duran.

"This is Agent Wise," she answered.

"You can drop the *agent* part from your name as of this very second," Duran said. "Kate, listen to me. I respect you and I would be an idiot if I was blind to the amazing career you've had. And for that reason, I am not going to publicly fire you. Rather, I don't want to. But if you so much as look at Jennifer Nobilini in a harsh way, I'll fire you. I'll make a fucking *proclamation* of it if I have to. You blatantly disobeyed me and then you arrested a woman that was never given the relief of having her husband's killer found. What in God's name were you thinking?"

"That's just it," Kate said. "I think I do know who the killer is. For both Frank Nobilini *and* Jack Tucker. Sir, can I put you on speaker to explain this to you and Agent DeMarco at the same time?"

"Make it quick. And let me make this abundantly clear one more time: your reputation is very likely on the line here."

She placed the call on speaker and set it down on the table that DeMarco had claimed as her own over the last twelve hours or so. DeMarco was looking at her with a sense of distrust—and honestly, Kate didn't blame her. She probably felt hurt or even stabbed in the back. If there was to be any future between them, Kate knew an apology would be in order very soon.

Kate did her best to explain her theory … and all of the interlocking pieces that supported it. "A nanny that once worked for the Nobilinis is the only person I have spoken to that claims to have witnessed a less that perfect version of them. Arguing all the time, to the point that one night, Frank threatened to take the kids and leave. He'd found suspicious texts and confronted her about it. I went back to Jennifer and confronted her about it—asking why she lied to us. And she never denied—she basically admitted that yes, she was involved in an affair right around the time of Frank's death. Now this morning, I was able to look at her computer."

"How did you manage to do that?" Duran asked.

She was not at all proud of herself as she walked them through the morning's events. Duran let loose a few expletives from his end of the phone. But he went quiet when she explained the link she had found to the Craigslist ad.

"That's one of the methods your friend Alvin Carpenter said he's known other hitmen to use, right?"

"Right. It's almost like speaking in code."

"Well then how would she know how to reach out to him?" DeMarco asked. "And why?"

"I think she hired Zeus Beringer eight years ago to kill her husband. Frank was threatening to leave her and take the kids—making for an ugly scene. Something that Jennifer Nobilini wasn't willing to risk."

"Okay," Duran said. "Even if I was willing to buy that—and I'm not saying that I am just yet, what about Jack Tucker?"

"I'm not absolutely sure yet, but I have a theory. Director … all I ask is one more chance to speak with her."

"Absolutely not. You're already in enough trouble because of her as it is."

"You're right. But you know how interrogations work. Who is she going to get more defensive with? Who is she most likely to accidentally let something slip with? A woman she loathes or a brand new agent that she's barely spoken to?"

There was a moment of silence—a moment in which DeMarco gave her a pained look. She could sense where this was headed. She could sense that this case, in a few moments, would no longer be hers to run.

"You're right," he said. "But for right now, let DeMarco and this Detective Pritchard fellow tackle it. You can stay there for now as support *only*. But I'm not sending you in there unless it's an absolute last resort."

"Okay," she said. She was surprised and a little deflated; she had been certain Duran would allow her to speak with Jennifer. *Or maybe you're just thinking a little too highly of yourself,* she thought.

She ended the call and looked to DeMarco. "I'm sorry," she said. "But I couldn't let this go. It wasn't because I didn't think you could handle it ... I just—"

"I know. It still isn't the best feeling." She sighed and nodded toward the door. "Detective Pritchard is in the conference room with some of the cops. I'm sure they'd appreciate the help."

It was a blow to her ego but she said nothing about it. She simply nodded and took her leave, locating the conference room. Before she could step inside, though, Pritchard was heading out.

"Agent Wise," he said, "I'll skip the pleasantries and just say that I'm sorry to hear about the hot water you're in."

"Yeah, me too. Is there anything I can do to help while Jennifer Nobilini is being interrogated?"

"I'm on the way out to the school to get her computer right now. You're welcome to ride along. Things here are going to get a little heated. Nobilini has already reached out to her lawyer—and she's got a good one. So honestly, unless we can prove something in the next day or so, she's not only going to walk, but she's also talking about suing you and the bureau as well. And if we can't find anything on the computer, she may be able to walk as soon as this afternoon."

"Yeah, then let's go get that computer."

CHAPTER TWENTY SEVEN

It was obvious that Pritchard felt a little awkward to have her riding along with him. They both tried to break the ice with both small talk and pertinent details about the case, but it all fell flat. It then occurred to her that because of her inability to let things go, she had placed herself and the bureau in a fairly bad situation. And now she was left with about a day—if that—to clean up her mess.

When they arrived at the school to pick the laptop up, things had resumed as normal. The art exhibit was finishing up. Parents were leaving the school with art pieces proudly tucked under their arms. Kids had all gone back to their classes and the office was business as usual.

When they got back out to the car, Pritchard walked toward the passenger side. "You mind driving? There's not much I can pull off of this thing without certain software, but I might be able to find a few things."

"No, that's fine."

She got behind the wheel and, for the second time that morning, exited the Ashton Elementary parking lot. As she got onto the main road, she kept track of what Pritchard was doing. She watched from the corner of her eye as he went into his phone's settings, cut on the feature to use it as a Wi-Fi hotspot, and then used it to get Jennifer's laptop online.

He did the same thing Kate had done, going to the internet history and looking around. "Well, if she *was* up to something, she's not very stealthy about it. There's at least three weeks of internet history right here."

He located the ad she had found and read it out loud. "Yeah, that doesn't sound good. But what I don't get . . . well, her husband died eight years ago. Why is she talking about her husband in this ad?"

Kate almost said *I don't know*. But she was starting to have a good idea. Not one that she was quite willing to share just yet, though.

A few minutes later, Pritchard let out a small *hmmm* sound. "She went to a banking website a day later. And there's no other occurrence within this three-week span that she visited the site. So she's not big on online banking apparently. Just this one occurrence, right after the ad."

"Could we call the bank and get her information?" Kate asked. "I could but, as you know, I don't really have those privileges right now."

"I'll call Agent DeMarco. I'd let the PD handle it but when it comes to banking and getting people's personal info, us lowly detectives and cops don't have the same pull as FBI agents. Depending on who you speak with, they may ask for a warrant."

"Then let's get it. As quickly as possible."

He did it right there and then, calling up DeMarco while Kate drove. It made her feel useless but she also knew that she should really just be glad that Duran hadn't completely yanked her off of the case this morning. He'd had every right to do so—a fact that made her wonder if she was taking advantage of his good graces.

He ended the call less than a minute later. "She's on it. She's calling the bank and is going to start the warrant process right away. I think it might be a good idea if we just swing by the local branch on the way back to the precinct. What do you say? I know your privileges have been somewhat revoked, but you still know how to flash that ID, right?"

"I do." And it wasn't like it would be the first time she'd used it when she wasn't supposed to. She'd done it a handful of times since picking her career back up post-retirement.

He continued to search around her browsing history but the only other comment he made between their and the local banking branch Jennifer used was: "Damn, this woman loves Pinterest."

"You know the NYPD better than I do," Kate said. "How long on that warrant?"

"With the FBI pushing for it, I'd guess two or three hours."

"Not bad. I wonder if there's anything we can do at the station until it comes through."

"There's always digging through research," Pritchard joked.

But that was perfectly fine with Kate. In fact, *anything* she could do to help in that moment would be welcome.

When Kate parked in the bank lot, she felt the pressure of the day on her. She could almost hear the ticking of a clock, counting down not only the moments until Jennifer Nobilini would be released, but the moments until her likely removal from the bureau and any legal damages that might come about as a result of Jennifer's hasty and public arrest.

When they walked into the bank, Kate carried the warrant with her. It had taken two hours and twenty minutes to get it in her hands—nothing short of a miracle based on some of the experiences Kate had seen in the past.

They discreetly share their business with a woman at the front cashier's window and were then asked to wait one moment. It was a quick moment, no more than twenty seconds, before they were greeted by an older man who came from somewhere in the back of the bank.

"Are you the agents asking about a client's accounts?" the man asked. His name tag identified him as Ray Kirby.

"Yes," Kate said, showing her ID and cringing internally as she did so. "I'm Agent Kate Wise and this is my local assist, Detective Pritchard. We were told Agent DeMarco called ahead for us."

"She did. Come on into my office and let me see what I can do to help you."

He walked quickly, whether out of the excitement of a break in his daily monotony or out of the desire to get a federal agent out of his bank right away, Kate wasn't sure. He led them down a small hallway behind the primary cashier windows and into a large office. He invited them to have a seat in the chairs on the front end of his desk while he sat down behind it.

"I already took the liberty of pulling up Mrs. Nobilini's account information based on what Agent DeMarco told me," he said.

He turned his desktop monitor at an angle where all three of them could see it. "As you can see, most of her transactions are rather large, though there aren't many. But we've tracked this one transaction you see over and over again, and it is to pay off her credit card every month. It seems she puts all expenditures on the cards and pays it off regularly. What I have here on the screen goes back eighteen months and the largest is for a little over three thousand dollars. However, there *is* one large transaction right here," he said, pointing to a transaction from two days before Jack Tucker's death. "And I can't make heads nor tails of where this money was sent. A private account, perhaps."

Kate looked at the transaction. It was a transfer of twenty thousand dollars. Then, below that, there was another transaction, a transfer to the same sender, this one for two thousand dollars.

"What would we need to find out where those transfers were sent?" Kate asked.

"We can try it from here, but it might take a while," Kirby said.

Kate had known this would be the answer; she hated the fact that she knew it would take only a single call to the bureau to get someone started on figuring this out. It might take a day or two to get it cracked, but it would get done. It was just another task she'd have to ask DeMarco to handle, in light of her new designation.

She then looked to Pritchard as one of the strands of her theory started to thrum. "Do you still have Beringer's laptop in your possession?"

"It's stored away in Evidence at the precinct."

And as he said it, he seemed to pick up on her train of thought. He stood up quickly, thanked Ray Kirby for his time, and then hurried out. Kate did the same, loving the thrill of the hunt but wishing she had more time.

Within an hour, Kate was back at the precinct, in a conference room with Pritchard, DeMarco, and a few cops who had been assigned to help as needed. Pritchard was working closely with the precinct's top tech guy to figure out where the twenty-thousand-dollar transfer was sent while Kate looked over a printout of all of Jennifer Nobilini's transactions dating all the way back to the year Frank had been killed. It had been waiting for them when they arrived at the station, sent on behalf of Ray Kirby from the bank.

Meanwhile, Jennifer Nobilini's lawyer had showed up. She was practically demanding to speak with Kate, but Kate ignored her. She even had DeMarco threaten to press charges against her if she continued to be so domineering and trying to interrupt the investigation. Kate could actually hear them speaking loudly outside the conference room door as Pritchard knocked on the table's surface in celebration of a discovery.

"We did find something else," he said. "Not where all of that money went, but a Wikihow page. She was looking into how to purchase a large amount of Bitcoin between the time she posted that ad and Jack Tucker was killed. It looks like it might have actually been the same day that Zeus Beringer showed up at Ashton Elementary."

"I know what Bitcoin is but I'm not as cool as I look," Kate said. "Can you explain the relevance?"

"Bitcoin is the basic preferred currency on the dark web. Drugs, prostitution, child pornography, weapons, all of it. About eighty percent of all transactions on the dark web are conducted in Bitcoin."

"Is that what she spent the twenty thousand on?"

"I don't think so. Not unless she was buying them from someone that really went all out on being private. But based on the fact that she wasn't even smart enough to erase her browsing history, I highly doubt it. No ... if this money was sent to someone, I think it was a wire transfer and nothing more. But whoever she sent it to directed it to an account that is incredibly difficult to trace. Maybe on offshore account or some sort of encrypted cash-related site on the dark web."

It wasn't the information they were looking for, but it spurred Kate on. They were defiantly on to something ... now it just came down to making all of the pieces fit and finding that one last piece that would make it all make sense.

A few moments later, Kate heard a little murmur of excitement from Pritchard and the tech guy as they apparently figured out how to access her history beyond the point of the last time she had cleaned it out.

"Here's something else," Pritchard said. "A little over a month ago, she visited a site that offers dark web software. It spends most of the time describing Tor. But we've already checked her computer for things like that and there's nothing. Maybe she read up on it and got scared."

"Which begs the question why someone like Jennifer Nobilini would even want to access the dark web," Kate said. "Or want any sort of anonymous browsing."

She turned back to the printouts of Jennifer's bank history. She had made her way down to the year of Frank's death. It was the last page of fifteen and it was there that a large number jumped up, springing out of nowhere.

"This might be it," Kate said, pointing to the entry. "Pritchard, look at this. March, eight years ago—a month before Frank was killed. There are three transfers, to an undisclosed recipient."

They all looked to the entries in question: three transfers of twelve thousand dollars, all within a span of four days.

"How did her husband not figure this out?" the tech guy said.

"Because it's a personal account," Kate said. "They might have seemed like a perfect couple to everyone else, but they apparently didn't trust one another with their money."

"So," Pritchard said, "a few days before Frank Nobilini is killed, there are these three transfers from her bank account. Fast forward eight years and there's a twenty-thousand-dollar one and a smaller one to go along with it, just a few days before Jack Tucker is killed. That's not just coincidence."

A knock on the door interrupted them as DeMarco stepped in. "Kate, this lawyer is going to end up pissing me off. Can you just talk to her? Just to shut her up, if nothing else."

"Not yet," Kate said. "DeMarco ... look at this. I think we've got her."

DeMarco stepped inside and took a seat at the table. Kate and Pritchard filled her in on the discoveries they'd made since confiscating Jennifer's laptop from the school. A look of something close to fascination came over DeMarco's face as she leaned back in her chair and let out a deep breath.

"That's one hundred percent better than anything I've gotten out of her all morning. She *has* admitted to the affair. But she won't give a name. But with all of this," she said, indicating the laptop and the bank printouts, "the affair seems like small potatoes."

"I want to speak to her," Kate said. "Would you risk calling Duran for me?"

DeMarco hesitated for a moment and then nodded. "Sure," she finally said. "It's not like *my* head is on the line." She then looked to Pritchard and the officer apologetically. "Can we have the room, guys?"

The men nodded and got up without any argument. Pritchard gave Kate a little smile as he walked through the doorway and closed the door behind him.

"This makes no sense to me," DeMarco said. "Sure, I can see where all of these revelations lead, but it makes no sense."

"Not at first," Kate said. "But there's something there, buried under it all." She then took a few seconds to explain her theory to DeMarco—how they had all of the answers and, more importantly, the right person in custody.

DeMarco rubbed at her head in frustration and then pulled out her cell phone. She called Duran, looking back and forth between Kate and the bank printouts. Kate listened as DeMarco filled him in on these new discoveries. She also detected the waver in DeMarco's voice as the conversation reached its end.

"All of this came from Agent Wise," DeMarco said. "And with all due respect, sir, I think she was right earlier. I think the heat between her and Jennifer can work in our favor—especially in light of these new discoveries."

There were a few seconds where Kate could only hear the murmurs of Duran's voice. DeMarco then slowly handed the phone to Kate with a mock look of fright. "He wants to speak to you," she said.

Kate took the phone. She knew that if there was any chance of redeeming herself and potentially salvaging her reputation with the bureau, it rested on this call and anything that came after it.

"Yes, sir?"

"I'll give you fifteen minutes to speak with her," Duran said, short and straight to the point. "If noting comes of it, I want you out of New York right away. If I have to, I'll immediately fire you and have you escorted out of the city by the police. Please don't make me do that, Kate."

"I won't. Thank you, sir."

She ended the call and handed the phone back to DeMarco. An uncomfortable silence hung between them for a moment before DeMarco broke it. "Be careful," she said. "I honestly hate you a little bit for stealing the show from me, but that doesn't mean I want you to go in there and totally ruin your second career run."

Kate smiled. *Second career run. Is that what this is?*

"Thanks, DeMarco. You want to come in with me?"

"No. I'm good watching from the observation room." She opened the door for Kate and said: "Good work. I... well, I never get tired of being surprised by you."

"I could say the same for you."

DeMarco smiled and headed out. "Let me make it easier for you. Give me two minutes and I'll have a few of the policemen take the lawyer in another room, pretending to care about what Jennifer is claiming as her side of the story."

"Duran would not approve of that," Kate pointed out with her own smile.

DeMarco only shrugged as she started down the hall.

And with that, Kate left the conference room and headed down the hall to speak with Jennifer Nobilini one last time.

CHAPTER TWENTY EIGHT

When Kate was sure that DeMarco had occupied the lawyer with a few poor policemen, she entered the interrogation room. Jennifer sat up straight in her chair behind the basic interrogation table. She looked like a tiger had entered the room, not a fifty-six-year-old woman. She looked beyond Kate, to the door as it closed, as if hoping someone else would be entering as well.

"What the hell are *you* doing here?" Jennifer asked.

"I don't like leaving loose ends untied. Also, I thought I'd give you a proper thank-you for filing that complaint to my boss. That made my day a lot more pleasant."

"Did you think I was bluffing?" Jennifer asked.

Kate sat down in the other chair across the table from Jennifer. "Oh, no. I'm beginning to understand that you aren't the sort of woman that bluffs. You pretty much shoot straight from the hip, don't you?"

"So why are you here, Agent Wise? Trying to dig up more dirt? Want to try to pin something else on me in addition to adultery?"

Kate smiled, a little amused at how easily this evil woman was falling right into her hands. "As a matter of fact, yes. You see... I know you think that you're very smart and very clever. And for all I know, that is true for certain things. But not when it comes to covering your ass." She gave Jennifer a moment to respond but when it was clear that she was going to remain quiet, she added: "When the fire alarm sounded this morning, you left your computer in the gym. It was unlocked and I got to it before the password screen could come up. For a woman trying to hide things from people, you should know to delete your browsing history more often."

True fear shone in Jennifer's eyes for the first time but she did her best to hide it. She sat up as rigid as a slab of stone and said, "I won't say another word without my lawyer."

Kate smiled again and leaned in close. "Are you sure about that? Because your browsing history is not the worst of your problems. If you really want your lawyer here, that's fine. But it might serve your pretty little reputation a bit better if she *doesn't* hear what I'm about to say over the next few minutes. Your call."

Jennifer sneered at her with such force that Kate would not have been surprised if the woman were to spit in her face. "Say what you need to say then."

"I'll say this: I find it very odd indeed that there are significant bank transfers from your account to some undisclosed and secretive recipient within several days of not only your own husband's death, but Jack Tucker's as well. I also find it a little peculiar that you took the time to look into how to make sure you didn't get caught—looking into dark web software and using bitcoins for your transactions—but decided against it. Why was that, Jennifer? Would doing such things make you feel as if you were actually *guilty*?"

"This is ridiculous," she said. "I did not kill my husband! And I didn't even know Jack Tucker!"

"Oh, I'm not accusing you of killing your husband. I don't think you have it in you."

"Then why are you bringing it up?"

"Well...it all comes down to a man named Zeus Beringer. Did you know him?"

She hesitated, clearly acting—and doing a decent job of it. "No. Should I?"

"Well, we're fairly certain he killed Jack Tucker. It's hard to tell, though. We can't question him because he's dead. Recently dead."

"What does he have to do with this?"

"You know him," Kate said. "Maybe very well."

"No. I told you ... I don't know that name."

Ignoring her, Kate went on with her interrogation technique. "Well, maybe you didn't know him all that well. You don't have to know someone very well to kill them, do you?"

"You're insane!"

"Four times. With his own gun. The same gun that killed Jack Tucker ... and Frank all those years ago."

That's what did it. She tried to hide the reaction of hearing the connection, of hearing her sins so blatantly in her face. The question roaring through her head might as well have been written on her forehead in bright red marker: *How do you know that?*

"Here are the facts of the case, Mrs. Nobilini," Kate said, knowing she had her now. "Stop me when you hear something that isn't correct. Your husband and Jack Tucker were both killed by the same type of weapon within just a few days of large transactions being made in your bank account. This time around, the transactions did not total quite as much—and perhaps *because* of that, the man you hired was not pleased. Maybe he wanted more money. Maybe you were going outside of whatever terms you two had agreed to. So to make sure you paid what he wanted, he put a scare in you by showing up at your kids' school. Does that sound about right?"

Jennifer said nothing but her tears and trembling gave the answer.

"I suppose this motivated you to do what you could, to maybe call him off. So you met with him. Maybe then you—"

"It was my children," Jennifer said, softly.

"I'm sorry, can you repeat that?"

"My children! He was after my children and ... and I knew that I was over my head. He had come for my children."

"Do you want to tell me why he was a piece of this at all? Eight years after you hired him to kill your husband? Why again?"

"Because ..."

It was a word that was just as good as an admission. She *had* hired Zeus to kill her husband eight years ago. She was not doing anything to argue against it.

"Jennifer?"

"Because I saw it in Missy, too! On two different occasions, I heard her gripe about her husband, how he was boring her to death, how she wanted out of her life. She'd had an affair and felt guilt-ridden over it. And I … I felt sorry for her! I had been there! But I knew how to fix it and …"

"Did she ever ask you to?" Kate asked.

"No. But she said she was going to tell her husband. She said she had to. Said the guilt was too much. To love another man while her boring, useless husband was not paying her the attention she deserved …"

"So you spent at least twenty thousand dollars to release another woman from her marriage? Is that about right?"

Jennifer slammed her fists down on the table and when she looked at Kate, Kate saw something in her eyes that was more than fury or sadness. There was something there that seemed unhinged—something she had seen sparks of in the eyes of men and women who had worked toward an insanity plea and, more often than not, got it. It wasn't a complete surprise to Kate; she'd glimpsed the slightest bit of it when she had confronted her about her affair the first time.

"Yes!" She then let out a roar of a scream that turned into an obscenity. "She was so fucking weak! She would have told her husband and he would have left her and taken the kids. Her life would have been over! She would have never gotten to see her kids and she'd have a reputation … would probably never find anyone else. She would been ruined. So I freed her of it …"

"So you were friends? Close friends?"

"Of course, you moron! Why the hell else would I do it? I told her about two mornings ago. I told her what I had done, to free her. She … she snapped on me. But she also wanted to protect me. So we pretended we didn't know each other well. Great FBI work on your part there, I have to say."

Kate let the comment slide off her back, recalling how she'd thought Missy had been lying about whether she had told anyone other than Jasmine Brooks about her affair. *She'd told Jennifer, too,* Kate thought. *Maybe more than she told Jasmine.*

"You hired him for the murder of Jack Tucker," Kate said. "There was a discrepancy of some kind, he went after your kids, and you killed him. You arranged a meeting with him at the Comfort Inn in the Bronx and you killed him."

"With his own gun, too," she said, rather proudly. "He thought I was going to sleep with him to buy me some time for the rest of the payment. And just as things got heated, I kicked him in the balls, grabbed his gun—I guess he never goes anywhere without it or he was thinking I was going to turn him in or something. And then I k...I killed him."

The last three words caused her to weep. Saying it out loud apparently brought it home for her. With her money, she had killed two men. But she had killed Zeus Beringer with her own hands, by her own plans and action.

Kate slowly got up and headed for the door. She damn near felt sorry for Jennifer Nobilini. The woman was clearly unhinged but the question that remained was whether she had always been this way or if it had happened after she had arranged for her husband to be killed eight years ago.

"You understand, right?" Jennifer screamed as Kate reached for the door. "Missy Tucker was weak and was going to waste her life with a man that did not deserve her. I was helping. I was freeing her."

"Why don't you ask her how being a widow feels right now?" Kate asked, a tremor in her own voice "Why don't you ask her children how they feel to not have a father?"

"And what about mine?" Jennifer hissed. "I'll go to prison for this. They'll not have a mother...no one to look after them."

"That's right," Kate said. "It's a damn shame you also made sure they don't have a father."

Kate opened the door and closes it quickly to shut out Jennifer's wails of sorrow and anger. Kate realized that she was also weeping and quickly wiped a tear away before anyone could see it.

DeMarco came out of the observation room, a look of respect and shock in her eyes. "Jesus, Kate...that was brutal. And it took less than ten minutes." She tapped her pocket, making a knocking noise against her phone. "Also, Duran called me back immediately after you went in there. Said he wanted to see it. So I FaceTimed him. He saw the whole thing. I think it's safe to say your job is safe. That was...that was impressive."

"I don't know about the job part of it," she said. "But thanks for the compliment. I feel sort of like a bitch for how I just wrecked that poor woman. But hiring someone to kill a husband ... it ..."

She had to stop here as visions of Michael and his smiling face came flooding into her head.

"Kate?"

"Sorry ... I just need a minute."

She rushed away from DeMarco, in search of the nearest restroom. And as she went looking, she could still hear Jennifer Nobilini's cries as her lawyer finally entered the room.

CHAPTER TWENTY NINE

Kate woke up three days later to someone knocking on her front door. She sat up in bed and looked at the clock. When she saw that it was eight in the morning and realized that she had slept for almost nine hours, she felt instantly energized even though her eyes were still heavy with sleep. She got out of bed, shoved her feet into her slippers, and walked through her house to the front door.

When she opened it and saw Allen on the other side, she was shocked. She had no idea what to say, no idea how to react. They had not spoken since he had told her on the phone that he wasn't sure he was a good fit for her chaotic life. But now here he was standing on her front porch carrying a box of bagels and a drink coaster with two coffees from her favorite coffee shop just down the street.

"I figured if I showed up with coffee, you might let me come in," he said.

"You were right," Kate said, plucking one of the coffees out of the carrier. She let him inside and then closed the door behind her. They walked into the kitchen without talking and settled down at the table.

"I usually don't question handsome men that bring me coffee," Kate said, "but what are you doing here?"

He sighed and picked a bagel from the box. As he opened up a carry-out container of hazelnut cream cheese, she could tell that he was nervous.

"I hope you don't mind, but I texted Melissa yesterday. I wanted to know if you were done with this latest case you were on and if you were back home yet. And based on the last conversation we had, I didn't think you'd want me calling or texting you."

"It would have been okay."

"Well, I wasn't sure. Anyway, Melissa didn't text me back. She called me. And she and I had a very good conversation."

"Dare I ask what about?"

He had layered his bagel with cream cheese and now took a bite. He answered as he chewed—a pet peeve of Kate's but he somehow managed to make it cute.

"She called me to ask if I thought she was being selfish because she doesn't like you going back to work. She told me her worries and about the conversations you two have had about it. I told her I thought it was a perfectly normal reaction but that I wasn't the best person to ask about it. I told her about our phone conversation—about me trying to break things off—and she proceeded to tell me I was an idiot."

"Yeah, that sounds like Melissa."

"Your daughter... she's very much like you. She let me know that you were always like this with your job and that it's not because you don't care about family and friends but because you're so passionate about your job—about helping other people."

"She didn't see it that way when she was younger."

"I know. She told me all about that."

"Is there anything you *didn't* talk about?"

"No. We covered everything. We're, like, besties now."

"Please, Allen. Never say *besties* again. Ever."

He nodded and sipped from his coffee. "But you know, I think she's right. I've seen it in you all over the place—the way you care about people. The way you love your job, your daughter and your granddaughter. In the way you tip *way* too much at restaurants. And I started to think about how someone with that kind of a heart must be affected by a job like yours. A job you returned to after retirement because you cared so much about it."

"Allen, but you were right. I did put my job above others sometimes. I don't mean to, but it does happen from time to time. Melissa suffered from it when she was younger. And Michael... there are so many things I wished we could have done differently. Spent more time together... but I can't now. And my job is to blame for that."

"I won't presume to know how your late husband felt about such things," Allen said. "But if he passed on any of his traits to Melissa, I can pretty much guarantee you that he understood it."

"I don't know how much longer I can do it anyway," Kate said. "If at all. This last case … it just proved that at my age, I tend to get to personally connected. To the case, to the people I meet, to DeMarco …"

"And that's a bad thing?" Allen asked.

"My director thinks so. And with good cause."

She thought about the last conversation she'd had with DeMarco, during the debrief on the afternoon of Jennifer Nobilini's arrest. She'd commended her for her work but they had left the meeting with her future very much up in the air. And the only thing that had eased that awkwardness was a visit to Cass Nobilini to let her know that her son's killer had been found and brought to justice. She had left the finer details out, stating that it had been the work of Zeus Beringer. It was not the entire truth, but it had been enough for a mother who could finally find that sense of closure that had eluded her for so long.

"Well, I'd like to ask that you forget everything I said on the phone," Allen said, bringing her back into the present. "I was irritated and lonely and … worried about you. Just like your daughter. We both love you and—"

He realized what he had said and stopped himself with another mouthful of bagel.

"Don't dodge it," Kate said with a smile. "I heard it. You said it."

"Shit. I guess I did. But it's true. I worry about you because I love you. I have for a few weeks now, I think. And I think that's where my pushing came from. So please … can we pretend it never happened?"

"Only if you tell me everything you and Melissa talked about."

"Sorry," he said. "Can't. Besties don't share each other's secrets."

Kate laughed and tossed her bagel at him. He dodged it, reached out and took her hand, and pulled her forward. When he kissed her, Kate thought that it felt right—more right than it ever had before.

She supposed she loved him, too. And that was a hard thing for her to admit. Not just because of Michael and her job but because she knew that when she loved, she loved hard. She wasn't sure if she would be capable of such a thing this late in her life.

Are you really going to deny yourself the chance, though? she asked herself.

It was a good question, especially coming off of a case where she had spent most of the time dwelling in the past. When she looked beyond that case, beyond the Nobilinis and the Tuckers, there was more past there—a past where she had cheated her family of memories and affection because of her job.

If she had learned anything from solving those two murders, it was that the past was always there, always offering memories and lessons that she could use to learn from and to fix present-day hurts.

And as their kiss deepened, she thought it would certainly be worth trying with Allen. And with Melissa and Michelle, and on and on until she could truly leave her past behind her.

Now Available!

IF SHE HID
(A Kate Wise Mystery—Book 4)

"A masterpiece of thriller and mystery. Blake Pierce did a magnificent job developing characters with a psychological side so well described that we feel inside their minds, follow their fears and cheer for their success. Full of twists, this book will keep you awake until the turn of the last page."

—Books and Movie Reviews, Roberto Mattos (re Once Gone)

IF SHE HID (A Kate Wise Mystery) is book #4 in a new psychological thriller series by bestselling author Blake Pierce, whose #1 bestseller Once Gone (Book #1) (a free download) has received over 1,000 five star reviews.

Two parents are found dead, and their twin 16 year old daughters are missing. With the case quickly growing cold, the FBI, stumped, must summon their most brilliant agent: retired 55 year old FBI agent Kate Wise.

Was this a random murder? The work of a serial killer?

Can they find the girls in time?

And does Kate, haunted by her past, still have the ability to solve cases as she used to?

An action-packed thriller with heart-pounding suspense, IF SHE HID is book #4 in a riveting new series that will leave you turning pages late into the night.

Book #5 in the KATE WISE MYSTERY SERIES will be available soon.

IF SHE HID
(A Kate Wise Mystery—Book 4)

Did you know that I've written multiple novels in the mystery genre? If you haven't read all my series, click the image below to download a series starter!

Made in the USA
Monee, IL
29 June 2021